STARS
AND
SMOKE

ALSO BY MARIE LU

The Legend Series
Legend
Prodigy
Champion
Rebel

The Young Elites Series
The Young Elites
The Rose Society
The Midnight Star

The Warcross Series
Warcross
Wildcard

Batman: Nightwalker

The Kingdom of Back

The Skyhunter Duology
Skyhunter
Steelstriker

STARS

and

SMOKE

MARIE LU

PENGUIN BOOKS

PENGUIN BOOKS

UK | USA | Canada | Ireland | Australia
India | New Zealand | South Africa

Penguin Books is part of the Penguin Random House group of companies
whose addresses can be found at global.penguinrandomhouse.com

www.penguin.co.uk
www.puffin.co.uk
www.ladybird.co.uk

First published in the USA by Roaring Brook Press 2023
This edition published in Great Britain by Penguin Books 2023

001

Text copyright © Marie Lu, 2023
Jacket illustration © Jessica Cruickshank, 2023
Jacket design by Aurora Parlagreco, 2023

The moral right of the author and illustrator has been asserted

Printed and bound in Great Britain by Clays Ltd, Elcograf S.p.A.

The authorized representative in the EEA is Penguin Random House Ireland,
Morrison Chambers, 32 Nassau Street, Dublin D02 YH68

A CIP catalogue record for this book is available from the British Library

HARDBACK ISBN: 978–0–241–64653–3
TRADE PAPERBACK ISBN: 978–0–241–64654–0

All correspondence to:
Penguin Books
Penguin Random House Children's
One Embassy Gardens, 8 Viaduct Gardens, London SW11 7BW

To you, my reader.
Thank you for the love and comfort you've given me over all these
years. I hope this book keeps you company in the way you have kept
me company, and that we get to share many more stories together.

CLAREMONT

MISSION LOG

AGENT A: "Winter Young?"

AGENT B: "I said what I said."

AGENT A: "Tell me you're kidding."

AGENT B: "You don't think he can do it?"

AGENT A: "He's a pop star, ███████."

AGENT B: "Correction: He's the biggest superstar in the world."

AGENT A: "I only accept semantics on Fridays, please."

AGENT B: "Oh, cheer up, ████. Name a better cover than a superstar. The boy's exactly what this mission needs."

AGENT A: "Why? Because he can do a backflip?"

AGENT B: "Because he's the only one who can get us in."

AGENT A: "He doesn't know the first thing about what we do!"

AGENT B: "Isn't that the point? Our agents are unconventional."

AGENT A: "I meant that I doubt he's capable of doing our kind of job."

AGENT B: "Well, it's not as if we have a better option."

AGENT A: "The CIA's not going to like this pitch."

AGENT B: "We're the ████ Group. They never like our pitches, and yet they always seem to hand us a contract. Isn't that funny?"

AGENT A: "Hilarious."

AGENT B: "Is that your blessing I hear?"

AGENT A: "Fine. But you owe me."

AGENT B: "How much this time?"

AGENT A: "The nicest dinner in the city."

AGENT B: "Orleana?"

AGENT A: "Naka."

AGENT B: "Listen, if I can get a reservation at Naka, I'll quit my job."

AGENT A: "If Winter Young can actually pull this off, I'll quit mine."

Those That Birth Obsession

There was nothing particularly distinct about the car that wound its way across the parking lot, streetlights striping across its sleek surface in a hypnotic rhythm.

The only thing that made it stand out was the two black SUVs following it, both full of security personnel. The mini caravan made little sound as it approached the back of the stadium, avoiding the barricades near the front where ninety thousand fans had already congregated in a shifting mass.

Behind the first car's tinted windows sat a lean figure with one leg crossed idly over the other, his chin resting thoughtfully on his hand as he watched the throngs of people milling around in the distance.

At first glance, it was hard to tell that the boy was dressed in luxury. His clothes—black sweats with no logos in sight—looked simple enough. But closer inspection would reveal his careful choices, the hand-sewn details along the seams, the fine quality of the bespoke fabric, then the thin rings on his fingers, one studded with tiny black diamonds, the other platinum and engraved with his logo, a stylized rabbit head with ears shaped like two halves of a broken heart. He wore his favorite custom Gucci sneakers, a birthday gift from the fashion house, along with a pair of pink-tinted aviators that, an hour after being photographed in public, would be sold out worldwide.

Even if his clothes didn't grab your attention right away, the rest of him did.

Winter Young—the most famous superstar in the world, the boy everyone talked about—was so beautiful it was hard to believe he was real. His was a luminous sort of presence that could turn every head on the street: messy hair so lushly black it gleamed blue in the light, geometric ink running along his forearms that ended in a snake coiled around his left wrist, slender dark eyes rimmed with long black lashes, a mysterious grace in his movements, an expression that could somehow switch between shy and mischievous in the space of a second. But it was more than that. Many people were objectively gorgeous, but then there were those few, the stars with some undefinable quality so searingly bright that they birthed obsession. Once the world got a glimpse of them, it would move heaven and earth just to see them again.

Now Winter was staring at the window, studying the beads of rain on the glass and the million different colors refracted within them, humming an experimental bridge of music under his breath as his mind worked away on a new tune. Beside him, his manager tapped on her phone.

"If Alice reschedules you for a quick photoshoot tomorrow morning at six thirty A.M.," she said, "can you make do with a fifteen-minute breakfast around five? No answer means yes. Don't forget to return that call for Elevate's CEO—Miss Acombe wants to pitch you on endorsing their upcoming sneaker redesign. Oh, and if you want to shorten your New York dates, you'd better tell me now." The stadium's lights through the car's tinted windows cast the woman's dark skin and glasses in a green tint, and her voice, dampened against the backdrop of the rain, had the tone of someone who was used to winning arguments with him. "Ricky Boulet's tour schedule will coincide with yours, and I'd really rather not spend an hour of my life fighting with his manager about why we're"—her voice took on an exaggerated inflection as she rolled her eyes—"*stealing his weekend.*"

"Let's do all the dates," Winter said to the window.

Claire peered skeptically over her phone at him. "No one does four consecutive days in New York."

Without looking, he held a hand up to her. "You know we'll sell them all out."

She swatted away his high five with little slaps. "I'm talking about your health, obviously, not your star power. Please don't make me deal with you collapsing onstage again."

Winter finally turned his head to give her a sidelong smile. "Five years and still no faith in me at all."

"None whatsoever. Did you even eat lunch today?"

"Do three churros count?"

Her expression turned stern, and she nudged his leg with her boot. "Winter Young. I got you sandwiches specifically so you wouldn't just eat empty calories."

He rested his head against the seat and closed his eyes. "How dare you. Churros are a perfect food, and I won't hear blasphemy against them."

She sighed in long-suffering patience. "I wish you'd stop working so much and take care of yourself, for once. Go hiking. Go on a date. Have a fling, at least. You want me to reach out to anyone's agent for you?"

The thought made him weary. They'd had this conversation before, and he wasn't interested in explaining himself all over again. After too many empty nights, he'd come to hate flings. And the thought of dragging someone through all the mud that came with dating him made Winter cringe. During his last breakup, his then-girlfriend had told him that the media circus made him *undatable*.

But to Claire, he just shrugged and said aloud, "There's no one interesting."

"Are you saying you're the most interesting person in the world?"

"True until proven otherwise."

"I think it's already been proven otherwise in this car."

Winter put a hand on his heart in mocking pain.

"Besides," she went on, "it's not about interest. It's about free publicity and a little fun for you both."

"Really? I thought it was about love."

"Ah, Winter." Claire shook her head. "Nineteen years old and already given up on romance."

"Learned it from the best. Have you seen anyone since you broke up with that magazine editor?"

Claire sniffed. "Susan and I technically haven't broken up."

Winter gave her a pointed look. "Right. You just haven't talked in two years."

"Stop changing the subject. We're trying to fix *your* love life."

He gave her a sly smile. "But I already love *you*."

She waved a flippant hand at him. "See that charm coming out right there? Why don't you make it useful?"

Winter couldn't help laughing a little. Once upon a time, he was just an awkward-looking, unpopular high school freshman with lanky limbs and a bad haircut who spent his lunch hours alone, rehearsing dance routines in the empty gym after class, scribbling down melodies and nurturing a big dream. Then he'd booked a gig as a rookie backup dancer for Ricky Boulet—at the time, the hottest star in the world. Winter's performance at Ricky's opening concert had been so extraordinary that a video of him went viral overnight.

Claire, then an ambitious young associate at a management company, had seen the potential behind that video and called him the next morning to nab him before anyone else could. He was the get of the decade; she was the compass for his success. The two of them had risen together as life catapulted him from backup dancer to record deal to one of the biggest pop careers in history.

You're going to be famous someday, his older brother, Artie, had once teased him, back when Winter was only twelve and had first started writing songs.

Winter had only laughed. *You're so optimistic.*

Optimism is my hidden power, Artie had said with a smile. Then his brother had looked at him squarely. *There's a restlessness in you. A conviction that something bigger and better must be waiting further down the road.*

Winter's fingers played mindlessly with his phone. It took him a minute to realize that he was swiping it locked and unlocked, then pulling up his brother's name before swiping it away again.

Artemis Young.

As Winter stared down at his phone, the memory returned of their final day together. Just a pair of brothers, twelve years apart in age, sitting on the edge of a pier watching the sun sink into the ocean. The salt and wind frizzed their hair. The Ferris wheel in the distance was alight with bands of blue and yellow, the colors reflecting off their faces. He could still smell the sea, could recall staring at his brother's profile and wishing with his whole heart that Artie wasn't leaving again the next morning.

Don't spend your entire life searching, okay? Artie had said to him. His brother had round dark eyes where Winter's were narrow, and wavy black hair that hung thickly over his brows, and looked so unlike Winter that no one ever guessed they were related.

What do you mean? Winter had asked.

I mean, sometimes you already have what you want. You just don't know it yet.

Winter had nodded along without really agreeing. It was an easy thing for his brother to say. Artie was the meticulously planned son, the favorite, the one from Mom's first marriage. Winter was the accident, the afterthought, the mistake from her second one. Maybe that was what made Artie think Winter would be famous someday. He knew that Winter craved attention, that he hungered for love every minute of every day, would seek it out to the ends of the earth. Artie had understood, even then, and pitied him for it.

Winter had shrugged at the time. *All I want is to be like you,* he told Artie.

Artie laughed, a rich, throaty sound that Winter was always trying to copy. *Be like* you, *Winter. Be good.*

Artie had worked for the Peace Corps and died. Winter had become a shallow superstar and lived. Good never won in the end.

The memory faded, along with the bits of music he was working on in his head. Winter put the phone down and shook his hand out. Still, his fingers twitched. He didn't know why he kept his brother's number. Artie was gone. Only a stranger would be on the other end.

Finally, their car came to a halt at the stadium's back entrance. A team of security guards were already in place in front of barricades, but that hadn't deterred the massive wave of admirers pressed in on either side of the path from the car to the stadium door. There had to be hundreds of people here. He recognized a few of the signs they held up, some of the same fans who'd attended his soundcheck earlier in the day.

"Chin up," Claire told Winter as they both straightened. "You're about to wow this audience."

Winter tucked his thoughts away like a loose hem, reminded himself of where he was and who people expected him to be. He took a deep breath and winked at Claire. "Always do," he replied.

The two of them tapped fists. A bodyguard outside opened the door, and Claire turned away from him to step out of the car.

The crowd cheered at the familiar sight of her, knowing what her arrival meant. Then the cheers turned into an explosion of screams as Winter emerged.

Cold rain blew against his face. As the blinding flash of lights hit him, he cast the crowd a casual glance and saw a sea of phones turned in his direction. Frantic shouts peppered the chaos.

"Winter! Oh my god, oh my god—WINTER!"

"WINTER!!!"

"OVER HERE, WINTER!!"

"I LOVE YOU, WINTER!!"

Everyone here had clearly been waiting for hours, their hair soaked from the rain. They waved frantically at him as his bodyguards ushered him down the path, then shrieked as he touched his fingers to his lips in a quick kiss.

Posters and markers, along with desperately reaching hands, were shoved out at him as he passed. The dozen security guards tried to push them back, but Winter still made a point to pass near the edge of the barricades, forcing his entourage to stop so he could scrawl a few hurried signatures on some of the posters. He was about to autograph a sign for a little girl when one of his guards pulled him away.

"Let's keep moving, Mr. Young," he said, shaking his head.

Winter shot the girl an apologetic look as he was ushered toward the rear entrance. The rain and screams cut off abruptly as the door closed behind them.

Up ahead, Claire slowed down and gave him a disapproving look. "We talked about not doing that," she said. "I know you think it's just a couple of posters, but it's not safe."

Winter frowned. "Come on. They've been standing in the rain for hours. Can't we at least pitch a tent for them or something?"

"I'll take care of it," Claire called at him over her shoulder as she led them down the stadium's corridor.

Winter pulled out a thin notebook from the pocket of his sweats. It went everywhere with him, this collection of scribbled lyrics and half-finished song bridges, words he found beautiful and choruses he wanted to run by his producers. Now he hurriedly scribbled his signature on a blank sheet and ripped it from its binding, then handed it to his nearest bodyguard.

"For that little girl in the blue raincoat who was waiting out there," he said. "Please."

The bodyguard gave him a small smile, then nodded and took the paper.

Winter watched him go, his throat hollow. There was a time not long ago when he could afford to spend hours talking to fans, one by one, and would leave them feeling rejuvenated by all their love. He couldn't remember exactly when it switched to this rushed, soulless routine. He looked on until his bodyguard disappeared around the corner, then followed Claire down the hall.

They made it to the greenroom, a space crammed with makeup chairs and a table sprawled with snacks, where Claire finally left him. Winter did a few quick stretches until his muscles felt warm and loose. Then he poked halfheartedly around the snack table. His stomach rumbled. Claire was right—he should've eaten something more than just churros, but it was too late now, and he didn't want to cramp up.

He'd just managed to tear his eyes away from the plate of croissant sandwiches when someone shoved him roughly in the ribs. He grunted and looked to one side. There stood a handsome brown-skinned boy with a headband holding back his crown of lush dark curls, his eyes fixated on the cookie plate. Leo.

"If you're not gonna have anything," he said, "can you at least move aside so I can?"

Winter rolled his eyes as he took a step backward. "Don't you think you should eat a little earlier? We're an hour from showtime."

Leo scooted toward the plate, grabbed a cookie, and shoved half of it in his mouth before replying. "You're one to lecture me about food," he answered. He looked ready to wipe his hands on his shirt, then seemed to remember that he was already in his stage clothes and makeup. He idled there for a moment, then wiped his hands on a tall Black boy passing them by. Dameon.

Dameon frowned at Leo. "Seriously?"

Leo shrugged. "You're not dressed yet."

"Doesn't mean I don't like this shirt." Dameon shook his head, dread-locks swinging, at the grease stain Leo had left on his sleeve. Then he looked at Winter. Even right before a concert, there was a serenity about him that Winter found soothing. "I'm heading to the practice room. You want to do one more run before we go out?"

Winter turned his eyes away from the snack table with a sigh and shook his head. "No, they need me dressed soon," he replied. "You guys go ahead."

Leo put a hand on Dameon's shoulder as they walked. "How many run-throughs until you're happy?"

Dameon shrugged. "As soon as you stop being half a beat late on everything." He glanced back at Winter and gave him a smile. "See you out there."

Winter waved, eyes lingering on them for a moment. Then the real chaos began. Makeup artists and designers fluttered around him, trans-forming his casual getup to the first of his shimmering stage ensembles. Meanwhile, the arena had begun filling with fans. Even down the hall and far from the center of the stadium, Winter could feel the shudder of their claps and chants, could hear the sporadic waves of their cheers.

The call finally came. Winter's bodyguards scattered to the front and back of his path as he walked down the hall, adjusting his earpiece and the small mic curving around to his mouth. Already he could feel the electric pulse of his fans in the arena fueling the fire within him, bringing forward the strength he didn't think he had even an hour ago. His steps turned more confident, and the young, unsure version of himself—the one that had sat on the pier all those years ago, laughing with Artie—retreated behind the carefully crafted version that the rest of the world saw: the curve of a seductive smile, a trained narrowing of his dark eyes, the swagger of his walk, the lines of his body moving with hypnotic grace.

The music swelled in the arena, the bass of the beat so strong that it shook the floors. The screams of fans rose and fell. Winter ducked under the latticework beneath the stage, moving silently until he reached his designated spot. There, he bent into a crouch as workers hurriedly strapped him into a series of harnesses. He followed their instructions obediently, moving his limbs as they asked and checking his devices to ensure they were working. Every step the same as it'd always been for years. He worked mechanically, unthinking.

At last, his team cleared away, leaving him alone. He bowed his head, bracing himself.

The beat announcing his cue came.

The platform he crouched on rose, vaulting him up onto the main stage.

The audience exploded with cheers. The harnesses around Winter's arms and legs suddenly pulled up, and Winter launched high into the air in a spin. As the beat dropped, the harnesses dropped with it. He landed lightly on his feet in front of his backup dancers, who had materialized on the main stage behind an enormous, neon-lit sculpture of his rabbit logo.

The crowd shrieked their enthusiasm. Winter closed his eyes and breathed deeply, soaking in the tide of love that enveloped him. *This* was what he really craved, the only time he ever felt a true, fiery connection to the world, and it was never satiated.

He raised a hand to the sky.

"Are you ready?" he shouted at the top of his lungs.

The world roared back at him. He tilted his head up, his figure ghostly in the midst of the stage's smoke and fog, and hurtled into his first routine.

As always, everything afterward felt like a blur.

A dozen people swarmed around him the instant he stepped back down beneath the stage. He smiled numbly as hands patted his shoulder in congratulations and he thanked the crewmen unhooking the harnesses from his body. The post-concert haze draped over him, covering him in its weight. He could feel the tremors in the ground as the arena continued to cheer long after his disappearance, clusters of fans still breaking into spontaneous song.

He'd done well. He was flush with the knowledge of it, even as he could already feel that rush seeping out of his limbs and giving way to bone-deep exhaustion. As he followed the crew through the same corridor from hours earlier, the roar of the stadium began to recede, until it sounded only like background noise against the echo of his shoes.

Claire was at his side now. He couldn't remember when she'd popped up. She was smiling at him, but in her eyes, he could see her concern. She knew how he got right after concerts.

"That was legendary," she said to him. Her cool fingers curled around one of his arms as she guided him down the hall.

"Did she come?" he asked.

Claire looked at him, then shook her head. She didn't have to ask to know he meant his mother.

Winter nodded, his expression blank. "Can you send someone to make sure her car's in her driveway, that she's home safe and isn't stuck at the airport?"

"I'll take care of it," Claire reassured him.

The dance crew streamed by around them, whooping at Winter when they saw him. He looked over as Dameon and Leo passed by, clapping their hands in the air.

"Dinner in your room!" Leo shouted. "We're gonna buy out the hotel's champagne!"

Dameon's grin was more subdued. His eyes followed Winter, studying him in his quiet manner. He seemed to notice Winter's expression, in the way that he always noticed everything about Winter, but didn't comment on it.

"Take your time!" he called to Winter.

Winter's eyes locked gratefully with his for an instant. Then Dameon and Leo were gone, moving with the tide of people down the hall toward the rear exit. Winter followed Claire to the greenroom.

"Take some time for yourself," she told him. "But I want to get you out of here way before we open up the lots. Ten minutes, tops. Okay?"

He flashed her a grin as he wiped his forehead. He didn't even know who'd put a towel in his hand. "Got it."

She grasped his chin firmly and gave him a gentle shake. "And for chrissakes, eat something."

"I promise," he answered.

Then she released him and left him alone.

The greenroom was empty now. Winter found himself wandering around the space, past the tables and empty makeup chairs. The silence seemed overwhelming after the screams of tens of thousands of people.

In about an hour, the headlines would start all over again. How his new concert had been. How he'd looked and who he was wearing. Alongside news about war and protests would be how many thousands of dollars his upcoming tour's tickets could fetch for resale. New rumors and gossip. He'd linger over a late dinner with Dameon and Leo, recounting the best parts of the night. Then he'd lie awake, alone and listless, and feel his soul beating weakly in time with his pulse.

He leaned against one of the tables and bowed his head. Sweaty strands of his hair hung across his vision. For some reason, he found his thoughts returning to the sight of the soaked fans who'd been standing outside the side entrance, waiting for him to emerge from the car. He thought of the little girl shivering in the rain just for the chance to get a piece of paper with his scrawl on it.

The last lyrics he'd written in his notebook echoed in his mind.

'Cause what am I doing here? What are we all doing here?

They all came to see him, gave him their hard-earned money, handed him this magical life of his. What did he give them in return? Once, it felt like he offered them something substantial—his music, his performances, his heart. Something to help them forget about whatever worries might plague their lives. But now it felt less like that and more like . . . well, he didn't know. Repetitive interviews and thick barricades. Meetings and attorneys. Fans who thought they loved him but didn't get to know him at all. A never-ending cycle of rote actions: wake up, makeup, show up. Pose. Recite answers to the same questions. Rehearse smiles for the same photos. Eat and sleep in a hotel room.

And the love he needed to thrive, to *survive*, felt more and more distant every day. Were his creations still creations, an expression of love? Or had it all just become business? Was he worth the world's adoration? Was he deserving of their love that he so desperately craved?

He was never sure. Just as he was never sure whether his mother would remember he existed, or when she might fail to take her medications, or if she was proud of his successes, or whether she loved him.

Just as he was never sure why his brother had to be the one who died.

Ah, Winter, Artie had once told him gently after a failed audition. *You don't have to be famous to matter.*

But Winter didn't know how to matter without being famous.

Artie had given his life for something that made the world better. What was Winter giving?

Suddenly he couldn't stand it anymore. The high from the concert had dissipated, leaving only exhaustion. The restlessness that always roamed inside him ached now, pulling forever toward some unattainable version of himself that was a better person than who he currently was.

If he could just reach it, he would be worthwhile. He would be happy.

But he couldn't. So all he wanted to do was flee to a hotel room. Maybe he'd bail on dinner with the boys, too. Claire had said ten minutes, but he looked at the clock on the wall.

"Five minutes," he muttered.

Long enough. Knowing her, the cars were probably early and ready for him anyway. He straightened and ran a hand through his messy hair. Then he headed out into the hall and away from the arena stage.

His bodyguards hadn't come for him yet; maybe it was too early, and they were all waiting somewhere near the back entrance. He walked alone down the corridor until he reached the small, nondescript side door leading to the back.

Winter stepped out into the cool, wet night. His sight settled immediately on a sleek black SUV waiting right at the entrance. As he walked toward it, the car's door opened automatically for him, revealing a plush interior.

Winter let out a small sigh of gratitude as he slid inside. Claire must have upgraded the cars during the concert. This one had tinted windows that were currently playing some soothing video of an ocean scene, a feature that his other car definitely didn't have, and new leather seats that were already heated to a cozy temperature.

The door closed automatically behind him, sealing him in. Then the car pulled away.

That was when he realized something wasn't right. The woman sitting in the shadows beside him wasn't Claire. And the driver wasn't someone he recognized, either.

Winter blinked. "Is this the wrong car?" he asked.

"It's exactly the right car," the woman answered.

And in that moment, Winter realized he was being kidnapped.

Those That Walk in the World's Shadows

I t took another second for Winter to convince himself that he wasn't jumping to conclusions. He'd rushed into plenty of black SUVs before where he didn't recognize the driver or had to speed off for some reason or other. Claire didn't always have time to tell him everything, and over the years, he'd simply learned to get in first and ask questions later.

Maybe there was an explanation here, too.

But something about this driver and woman dressed in impeccable suits seemed different. Winter felt his sixth sense prickling the hairs on the back of his neck.

"Are we heading back to the hotel?" he asked them.

They didn't answer. The serene ocean videos continued to play on the windows, giving him the illusion of driving along a Mediterranean coast. Only the front window stayed clear. They were driving toward the wrong exit.

"Stop the car, please," Winter said instead.

No answer.

Now he knew he was in trouble. No driver of his had ever, in his entire life, not done what he asked. But the driver kept going, his gaze fixated on the gates at the far end of the stadium lot. The man's brows were so dark and intense that they looked like they might smother his eyes entirely.

"Stop the car," Winter said again, sterner this time. "And let me out immediately."

"I'm afraid we can't do that, Mr. Young," he said over his shoulder. Streetlight outlined the scruff of his short beard.

I'm being kidnapped. It's finally happening. The thought rushed through Winter like a river of ice. It'd always been a possibility—and the real reason Claire seemed perpetually paranoid about his safety. He could hear the blood pounding in his ears. Was this why none of his bodyguards had been around? Had these people done something to them?

"And why not?" Winter asked as calmly as he could. As he did, one of his hands ran along the edge of the door, seeking the lock.

"They're all auto-locked from the driver's side," said the woman sitting beside him. She ran a light hand across the side of her blue hijab, then regarded him with a pair of calm, deep-set eyes.

Winter's hand stopped, and he reached instead for his phone, ready to trigger its emergency call feature. "If it's a ransom you want," he said quietly, "contact my manager. But I'm warning you. Claire won't be happy to hear this, and you really, really don't want to piss her off."

"No ransom needed. It's not money we're after, Mr. Young." The woman nodded at his hand. "Keep your phone where it is. It won't work in here, anyway. This is just a CPU."

Winter's hand stopped short of the phone. "A what?" he asked.

She waved a flippant hand. "A car pick up. A meeting. We'll only take a few minutes of your time."

Now they sounded less like kidnappers and more like . . . solicitors? Winter frowned at her, his temper rising. "A few minutes? What the hell is going on? Who are you?"

They had exited the stadium gates now and were heading up the street. The woman reached into her pocket to pull something out. Winter tensed, wondering for a split second if he was going to have to wrestle a gun out of her hand—but then the woman held up a badge and flipped it open to an ID.

"Sauda Nazari, Panacea Group," she said.

Winter shook his head. His heart was still pounding in his ears, and he blinked, trying to make sense of the situation. "What?"

"The Panacea Group. Panacea means a solution—"

"I know what panacea means," Winter snapped. "What's this? Who are *you*, some kind of CIA agent?"

The man up front snorted. "Close. But good guess."

Winter shook his head. This was getting more and more confusing.

"The CIA hires us for the jobs they don't want to do," Sauda explained.

"I really don't need your jokes right now."

She looked at him. "These are not the eyes of a joker, Mr. Young."

He stared at her before she finally broke her gaze and glanced ahead at the windshield. Up in the front, the man sighed.

"What did I tell you?" he grumbled. "There's still time to return him to the stadium. Should we just drop him off and pick someone else?"

"Give him some time, Niall." She looked at the man through the rear-view mirror and gave him a small, winsome smile. "Please, for me."

He muttered something unintelligible again, but settled back into silence.

She turned to eye Winter. "We're who the CIA calls when they're looking to . . . outsource some work," she said. "The Panacea Group is a private company, and we look for unconventional agents. We have a certain amount of leeway that our government-run cousin doesn't. Less red tape, more funding, if you will. The ability to move faster. So we take on anything that slips through the CIA's political cracks."

"You really are serious," Winter muttered.

"That's what I said," Sauda replied.

"The CIA."

"The Panacea Group."

"Panacea. Okay." Winter rubbed his forehead. "Is this standard procedure, kidnapping people without telling them what you want? Is that legal? Because I hope you know that in about half an hour, my missing status will be the top headline on every newscast in the world."

Sauda leaned forward on her knees. "Rest assured, Mr. Young, that as soon as we finish this conversation, we will drop you off wherever you want to be."

"And the conversation is?"

"We need your help."

At that, a bubble of laughter rose in Winter and emerged like a bark. "Okay. That's great." He shook his head. "If this is one of Claire's pranks, I'm firing her the instant I get out of this car."

The woman didn't laugh. Somehow, something in her expression made Winter's smile fade. There was an authenticity to her that he couldn't quite shake.

"You're Winter Young," she said.

"Yes. Impressive espionage work."

"As you're well aware, you're one of the most famous superstars in the world, with quite a wide range of fans." She crossed her arms. "And we are interested in one of those fans."

Winter crossed his arms. "Is that so?"

"For the last few years, we've been tracking the activities of Eli Morrison. Do you know who that is?"

The name sounded vaguely familiar. "Not quite," Winter said.

"Eli Morrison is one of the world's richest men," Sauda explained. "Thanks to his shipping empire, he's worth thirty-seven billion. The CIA has attempted to arrest him in the past, with little success."

"I didn't know shipping things was illegal."

"Shipping some things is. Like drugs. And people. And weapons." Her smile looked grimmer. "We prefer to call that trafficking."

"What the hell does that have to do with me?"

Sauda looked unfazed. "Morrison's daughter, his only child and the apple of his eye, is turning nineteen soon. Her father is planning a multiday celebration that will—pardon the accuracy of my quote—'beat the shit out of any birthday party that anyone has ever had.'" She nodded at him. "And she's your biggest fan."

Winter felt a weight drop in his chest. "I get that a lot," he muttered.

"I think this one might actually mean it," she said. "In about eight hours, Morrison's people are going to be reaching out to you and your manager. They are going to offer to hire you to put on a private concert for the celebration."

Performing for the daughter of a criminal tycoon. Well, this was new. "Where?" he asked. His throat felt dry. "When?"

"In a month," she explained, "in London. He is having ten thousand guests flown in, all on a fleet of private planes."

"Holy shit."

"I told you it was a big party." She shrugged. "Security for the week, as you can imagine, will be extremely tight."

He looked back and forth between her and Niall. "You want me as your in?"

"We want you as our in," she confirmed. "You would attend this week of exclusive events."

"In order to do what?"

"To help us get a crucial piece of evidence that we need to arrest Eli Morrison."

Winter raised an eyebrow at her. "Is that all?"

She smiled a little. "You won't just be any guest, Winter—you'll be the personal invite of Eli Morrison's daughter, the most precious person in the world to him. You'll likely be seated beside her and her father at dinner every night and invited to every private party after the main events. That kind of opportunity doesn't come around every day."

Winter leaned back against the seat. "No, thanks," he said.

The woman narrowed her eyes at him. "Mr. Young, I am asking you to think this through."

"I *am* thinking it through, and now I have finished thinking it through. The answer is still no."

"Mr. Young—"

Winter looked at the window. "Stop the car and let me out."

Sauda stared calmly at him, as if she knew this would be his response. "A butterfly flaps its wings and changes the world." Her voice softened. "Your brother. Artemis Young. Peace Corps, right?"

Winter froze, all sarcasm leaking out of him. "Careful there," he said quietly. "Now you're treading on some dangerous ground."

"He talked a lot about you to his colleagues," she told him. "That he was proud of you, but that you were always searching for something bigger than what you had, some purpose, some reason to be worthy. I suspect that even now, as renowned as you are, you feel like you haven't found it."

Winter could hear the words as if they had been said by Artie himself. And suddenly, he could see a ghost of his brother sitting in the car, too, leaning back against the seat and regarding him with an easy smile. To his frustration, he could feel moisture welling at the corners of his eyes, his throat tightening against his will.

"Why are you digging up info on my brother?" Winter said, his voice hoarse.

"Because I assume there's a lot you don't know about him," Sauda answered, "or how he died. And that you'd probably like to know."

The world seemed to tilt. The night outside the car looked hazy.

"Artie died during a Peace Corps assignment in Bolivia," he said slowly.

"Did he?" Sauda replied.

His heart started to pound. "Am I wrong?" he asked.

Sauda's expression looked gentler now. "This isn't the time or place to tell you everything. And maybe you don't want to know. If that's truly the case, then just say the word, and I will have you dropped at your hotel, no more questions asked." She nodded. "But if you want to know, you'll need to sign some paperwork with us. And to do that, you may want to consider my offer to you."

Nothing made sense anymore. Winter's hands tingled; his limbs felt numb. Artie, who had always fought for something bigger than himself, who had never talked about what he did. Winter felt like he was in some sort of waking nightmare, hearing about a version of his brother distorted through a circus mirror.

What if Sauda was telling the truth? What had really happened to Artie? How much did he not know? Why did *Sauda* know? Winter wanted to scream the questions at her, demand that she tell him what she was purposely withholding. His hands shook with restraint—his breath came out shallow and uneven, and his tears threatened to spill over.

Embarrassed, Winter wiped his eyes impatiently and scowled at Sauda. "Using my brother against me is a pretty low blow."

Sauda looked unfazed. "I'm only doing my job. Nothing personal."

"It's always personal."

"It's for a greater good." Sauda tilted her head. "Something I know you think about constantly."

Winter scoffed and looked away, heart stretched tight. "I'm just an entertainer," he muttered.

"You're our perfect spy."

Winter's frustration spiked. "I am the literal opposite of a spy," he snapped. "You understand that, right?" He waved a hand at her. "Isn't the entire point of your work to stay in the shadows, to never be recognized for what you do?"

"It's the most thankless job," Sauda agreed.

"Well, my entire career revolves around being recognized."

Sauda leaned toward him. An intense light illuminated her gaze. "What is a mission but a performance? You know how to make a scene, how to get people to look where you want them to look. You know how to work a crowd, to pivot in the moment when something goes wrong, and to transform your entire personality depending on your audience. You know how to lie on a whim. Best of all, no one will suspect you. That's the beauty of being an unconventional spy." She tapped her temple with one finger, the nail spring green. "Let yourself think bravely, Winter Young. You may presume that you belong in the spotlight and I operate in a secret world, but perhaps we exist in the same place."

Winter swallowed hard. "I can't do this," he whispered.

"You've been staring at all the success in your life and wondering why any of it matters. You spend your nights awake, feeling grateful and guilty for your fans, wondering if you're worthy." Sauda leaned toward him. "I know you want to do good. To *be* good."

"I'm not my brother," he muttered.

"You have his heart." She tapped her chest with a finger. "You're searching for something. Validation, maybe."

"And you think I'm going to find that by working for you," he said coldly.

"I think you might find satisfaction in knowing that you can use your considerable stardom for justice, yes." Sauda smiled a little, and behind that smile was something tragic. "Maybe doing a thankless good deed for a change is exactly what you're looking for."

Winter didn't answer for a moment. He stared at the rhythm of light and shadow moving through the car.

"I hope you're not expecting me to kill anyone," he finally muttered.

A hint of amusement touched her lips. She sat back. "No murders required, I promise. Now, Morrison will undoubtedly require that you use his own technicians to set up the stage for you. You will be restricted from bringing most of your own backup dancers and crew. But we can install one of our own agents with you to masquerade as your bodyguard. I already have the perfect person in mind."

"That so?"

"We call her the Jackal."

Winter lifted an eyebrow. "She sounds nice."

"She's not," Sauda replied, just as dryly. "But she's very good at her job."

A Panacea agent for a bodyguard. A limited number of his own people with him. This had to be a dream. He would jolt awake in his hotel bed, drenched in sweat, the images of this woman and this car already fading from his mind. It was all madness—why did he need to do any of this? He had a wildly successful life on paper. He could simply go back to it without agreeing to these agents' demands. Could just force himself to forget what this stranger just told him about Artie. Nothing would bring him back, anyway.

"You don't have to agree to the mission right now," Sauda said quietly, studying his expression. "You just need to be interested in hearing more."

Just interested in hearing more.

Winter felt himself dangling over a precipice with a blindfold on, struggling to see beyond it. He felt that eternal restlessness in him awakening, insatiable and ravenous.

A thankless good deed.

"I want my mother protected," Winter finally said.

"Done."

"And if any of my staff and crew are coming with me, they better be guarded."

"They will be."

"And I want a nice car."

"We can start you off with a Mazda."

Well, it was worth a try. Winter stared at her calm, collected face. How did these people do this job? How could you stay in the shadows of the world, day in and day out, doing things that others would never see?

"I'm going to regret this, aren't I?" Winter said.

"It's possible."

Winter sighed. "How do I hear more?"

"Sign a contract, of course," Sauda replied. "Obviously this entire conversation is strictly confidential. You will be bound to that until such time as we feel otherwise."

Winter pursed his lips. "Contracts. Finally, something I understand."

"Then you'll do great with us." She smiled. "Welcome to the Panacea Group, Mr. Young."

3

The Jackal

Sydney Cossette got the call shortly after she stepped away from the bus stop across from her apartment complex, backpack bouncing, her messy blond bob blowing haphazardly in the breeze. The street was wet with drizzle and clogged with parked cars, and she made her way through them, squeezing between a van and a black sedan to reach the curb on the other side. Her lungs still hurt from her kickboxing session. She'd pushed them a little harder than she should have.

The news ticker along the top of the bus stop was running frantically. All week, it had been broadcasting the same headlines as the billboard screens near her home.

WINTER YOUNG TANTALIZES AGAIN ON STAGE

**INTERNATIONAL SENSATION WINTER YOUNG'S NEW ALBUM
DEBUTS AT #1 IN STAGGERING 70 COUNTRIES**

**WINTER YOUNG SURPRISES WITH AN UNCONVENTIONAL SHOW,
SETTING BAR HIGH FOR UPCOMING WORLD TOUR**

Sydney squinted in the rain and muttered a swear in Portuguese under her breath. She wasn't Portuguese, but she absorbed languages like

Winter Young collected Grammys and found herself picking out certain ones to use on certain days based on her mood.

Today was a Portuguese day.

Puta que pariu, she thought now. Millions of people were suffering all around the world from one catastrophe or another, but *this* had been the top headline on every news service for the past week? As she looked on, the billboards near her complex played videos of Winter Young—some of him from the middle of his last performance, others of him scribbling his autograph on posters for fans. Still another played a clip from a recent interview.

Are you aware of just how famous you've become in the last few years? said the subtitles for the interviewer.

Winter smiled coyly. *I don't know,* he replied. *Am I?*

Sydney rolled her eyes.

He was cute, sure. Stunningly beautiful, if she cared to admit it. Sydney appreciated thick lashes and a pretty mouth just like anyone else. And sure, his music *was* unconventional—the use of Chinese drums with hip-hop, for instance. A unique sound that had allowed him to sweep last year's Grammys and inspired a hundred imitators and even a subgenre of music that people affectionately called Winterpunk. She and the rest of the world had seen him in some of the most breathtaking outfits ever to grace a stage—sometimes he danced in black leather draped in silver, sometimes in silks like a goddamn fairy prince, and one time in a gold business suit that was quite literally on fire.

The boy loved to put on a show. He was born for the stage, that was for sure.

But as Sydney stepped into the warmth of her complex's lobby, she let herself take some halfhearted guesses at what Winter must be like: gorgeous and fully aware of it, maybe a shameless flirt, probably an asshole. She could see it in the smirk on his lips and the way he tilted his head, like he knew a secret about you. He was the kind of boy who probably barked demands and expected them done, and probably didn't care by who. The kind of boy who could point to anyone in a crowd of his screaming fans and have himself a new fling.

It wasn't that she begrudged him his lifestyle. But musicians were the worst kind of celebrity. She'd had to shadow one once on a mission, and it'd been the longest forty-eight hours of her life. The spontaneous tantrums. The inability to function without an assistant. Treating *her* like an assistant. The incessant humming. She'd given Panacea an earful about it afterward. All that energy musicians fed off while onstage went straight to their heads and clogged the arteries. They loved excusing their behavior in the name of *art*.

Her lungs trembled in another small spasm of pain, and she winced, annoyed. "Enough already," she muttered at the billboards in the distance. The sooner the media stopped reporting every last detail about him, the sooner the world could get on with something more important.

Today the front desk had put out a new display—an assortment of glass décor and a cup of pens, a bouquet for the picking. Her eyes caught on the figurines dotting the counter as Sydney flexed her hands, both of them still wrapped in white cloth from her kickboxing training session.

The young man at the desk smiled when he noticed her. "Good afternoon, Miss Madden." Not her real name.

She gave him a flirtatious smile, eyes twinkling. "Hey there, George."

He blushed, his gaze following her. She fought the itch to walk up to the desk and toy with him, then when he wasn't looking, slide one of those glass figurines into her pocket. It'd be so easy. She wouldn't keep the figurine, of course—she tended to either toss or sell what she stole—but the thrill was in the taking, not the hoarding.

Even after years of training and therapy, the urge to shoplift was always there in the corner of her mind. At least she'd gotten much better at resisting it, though, and today, she turned her eyes away from the figurines and toward the elevators.

"See you around," she called to George in a singsong voice.

"See you," came his answer, always a tiny note of hope in it that she'd ask him out or invite him upstairs.

At the elevators, she punched in her code by the doors and headed up. Minutes later, she arrived on her floor, headed to her apartment, and stepped inside.

For a nineteen-year-old, she was paid well: upper five figures, with more promised once she got promoted to full agent. The apartment was nice, too, as a result—a tidy, one-bedroom place with a little balcony that led out to a view of Seattle's gorgeous skyline. A thousand times better than the dump she grew up in.

But the inside was sparsely decorated, with the look of a place that could belong to anyone. No portraits on the walls, no personal items on display, no photo albums on the shelves. If someone broke in and ransacked the place, they would find nothing revealing about Sydney in the generic books on her coffee table or the menus from chain restaurants on her fridge. They would find no discernible personality in her closet full of clothes that could be in any girl's wardrobe. They would find no valuable jewelry, no evidence of hobbies outside of a subscription to the *New York Times* (all put in a neat stack on the kitchen counter, unread), no knick-knacks from vacations, no family heirlooms or keepsakes. No part of her heart left exposed anywhere.

It made her feel safe. She was the kind of person that every intelligence agency wanted: devastatingly smart, good at keeping secrets, and with no family or personal attachments to speak of—at least, no one that wasn't estranged. Sydney Cossette walked alone through the world, and she liked it that way.

She headed to the fridge and started pulling ingredients out for a sandwich. Deli ham, American cheese, white bread. That was generic, too, but there was a piece of her heart hidden in there. She used to hate sandwiches because she'd eaten so many of them at the hospital's cafeteria whenever she used to visit her mother. Afterward, though, Sydney had gotten into the habit of making herself sandwiches whenever she needed some comfort. At the very least, it made her feel like she had some control over her life.

As she went into the kitchen and pulled sandwich ingredients out from her fridge, a notification popped up on her phone.

Incoming Call

Unknown

Sydney knew, of course, that the call must be from Niall O'Sullivan. She stared at it for a moment. Panacea had given her a week off after a particularly exasperating assignment looking after a whiny criminal turned informant—and yet here they were, pinging her three days in.

She stepped out of the apartment and onto the balcony overlooking the harbor. There, she leaned against the railing and stared out at the empty bus stop she'd come from earlier. At least her lungs felt a little better now, and she could breathe again without wincing.

"Nani?" she said in Japanese.

"Stop it, Syd."

She switched to English. "And here I thought you were going to give me a real holiday, boss."

"Like you were doing anything fun with your downtime."

"You don't know that. I could be lying on a beach in Cabo."

"And are you lying on a beach in Cabo?"

For a second, Sydney considered pulling up a random video with the sounds of ocean waves. "I'm sure you know exactly where I am and what I'm doing," she muttered, glancing up briefly at the sky, half expecting to see a tiny drone watching her. "Isn't that our specialty?"

"For someone only two years in the field, you're particularly mouthy."

"Forgive me. I'm a child. What's up?"

"A mission, of course."

"Don't tell me I'm going to spend another week babysitting a minor suspect."

"Oh, believe me, it's much worse than that."

"Is that so?" she said. "Sounds worthy of my time."

"But if you succeed at this mission, not only will you be promoted, but you'll receive a healthy bonus."

Promotion. That caught her attention. "Full undercover operative? You're sending me overseas again? I still need a new passport after Moscow last year."

"Don't get too excited. I still question whether I should've hired you at all."

Sydney couldn't help smiling. She'd never heard Niall sound happy about any of Panacea's missions—the analyst seemed to believe everything was always a terrible idea. She'd started to think of his grumpy rumble on the phone as good luck.

"You know you're thankful every day for hiring me," she replied sweetly.

He just grunted. It was by sheer chance that Niall had visited her high school campus while reluctantly accompanying a CIA recruiter and seen her pick her way through a set of locked gym doors to steal some of the school's boxing equipment. When he'd confronted her, she'd tried to convince him that she couldn't speak English well, blurting out a paragraph in Russian so smoothly that he'd almost believed it was her native language.

Your consonants, she could still remember him lecturing at her.

She'd just shaken her head innocently at him.

Don't aspirate so much, he said. *It gives you away. Very well done, though.*

To her surprise, she'd felt a rush of pride at his compliment. After agreeing to not tattle on her, he'd asked her some questions, sussing out the dozen other languages she had picked up on her own, and then whether or not she'd be interested in joining a training program to work for the Panacea Group.

Is it in tourism or something? she remembered asking.

Something like that, Niall had replied.

I don't care what it is. I'll do it.

Excellent.

But I have one condition.

Niall had raised an eyebrow, probably amused by a sullen teenager's demands. *Money?* he'd asked. *We pay our interns well.*

No, she'd answered. *A ticket out of this town.*

He'd looked questioningly at her. *One way?*

She'd nodded. *Tomorrow. Today, if you can.*

She was still grateful that Niall had never once asked about her home situation. Maybe it was because he worked for a spy group and already knew everything there was to know about her. Or maybe it was because he'd recruited before from the kind of run-down town she came from, because he knew those towns were full of people yearning to escape.

Whatever the reason, he'd said, *We can arrange anything.*

She hadn't believed him. Nor she did understand who *we* were. But there had indeed been a black car waiting for her outside her driveway by the time she arrived home an hour later. She hadn't even bothered stepping back inside the house.

"You sound especially unhappy today," Sydney now told him. "It must be a very good mission."

"Don't get me started," Niall replied. "You're headed to London. We need you to play at being a bodyguard for some parties."

"Sounds like babysitting to me. Who's celebrating?"

"One Eli Morrison."

A tremor of excitement and fear jolted through Sydney at the name. "You're putting me on a Morrison operation?" she hissed through her teeth.

"If we do it right, it'll be the last Morrison operation."

Sydney could recall the CIA targeting Eli Morrison at least four times in the past, each a fresh attempt to put the man behind bars, each failing because they couldn't get close enough or gather enough evidence or were defeated by some high-ranking official secretly in the tycoon's pocket. Sydney had seen news footage of the man at a ribbon-cutting ceremony for a new children's hospital in Hamburg at the same time his operations delivered thirty tons of cocaine through the city's port; of him shaking hands with France's president for a photo and then, hours later, hearing intel reports that he'd beaten a hostage to death with a hammer; of him resting in a chair, sipping wine, while his men massacred an entire family at an undisclosed location. He was the kind of man that haunted Sydney's dreams, the type who understood how to hide his monstrosities behind a good suit and posh accent and powerful friends. The kind who knew how to slip through the cracks.

"Mission details?" she asked.

"We have the rare opportunity to get two operatives into his inner circle—and you're going to be one of them. Morrison needs to see someone he will underestimate, someone he'll relax around. You're one of our brightest, kid, and with all due respect, there's not much on you interesting enough to dig up."

"And who am I bodyguarding? Who's the second operative?"

Niall hesitated. "He's a bit famous," he finally said.

Her excitement shifted to skepticism. "That so? Anyone I've heard of?"

"Does the name Winter Young ring any bells?"

Sydney stared blankly, then squeezed her eyes shut. She must not have heard that correctly. The billboards outside her house were still playing videos of his face.

"Hello? Still there?"

"You're sending a pop star as our in?" she said incredulously.

"Air your grievances to Sauda, not me," he said with a sigh. "But we've never been successful at getting an agent this close to Morrison. Winter Young has been personally invited to put on a private concert for the birthday of Morrison's daughter, and it's the best opportunity we're ever going to get."

"No."

"I know you hate musicians, but hear me out."

"You *are* putting me on a babysitting mission, aren't you?"

"If it helps, we had a chat with him in the car and he seemed pleasant enough, if a little sarcastic."

"I can't wait," she said.

"It's like you two are the same person, really."

"And what are we after?"

"A single piece of evidence. If you succeed in getting it, we can take Morrison down the morning after his daughter's birthday celebration."

Sydney's gaze settled on the billboards in the distance. A few had gone dark as they prepared to rotate onto other news, but she could still see a faint burn in the screen of the boy's profile.

She couldn't shake the feeling that sending in a pop star for a mission like this was a huge mistake. Eli Morrison wasn't just a criminal tycoon. Once, he had ordered a hit job on a businessman and left behind nothing but a neat row of limbs for investigators to find. Another time, he'd figured out that one of his crew was a mole solely because of the flowers the man had chosen for a banquet's centerpieces; the man—and his entire family—had vanished that night. Eli had eyes and ears everywhere. He was the kind of job that required infallible precision. He missed nothing. He had no qualms about killing someone with his own hands. And he always got away with it.

So the thought of recruiting Winter Young seemed laughable. What had he ever done to qualify himself to face a target like that? Did they even have time to train him? Would he break their cover within five minutes of landing in London? Would he be the reason why Morrison ordered them beheaded? Sydney grimaced at the thought, annoyed that her death might come down to a pop star's idiocy.

"Well?" Niall asked. "You want the mission or not?"

She almost laughed. Niall knew the answer would be yes. Sydney said yes to every mission. She'd fallen into the work like a fish was born able to swallow the ocean. Everything about it—the secrecy, the meticulous planning, the danger, the satisfaction of handing bad people what they deserved—took her one step away from her past and one step forward into her future, where she got to choose her path and what she risked herself for, where she got to be damn good at what she did.

Her lips tightened. What would this mission mean to Winter? Just some fun and the future perk of being able to brag about working as a spy? If he turned Panacea's offer down, wouldn't he just go home to his millions and his careless life of wealth? What if he decided halfway through that he didn't want to do it anymore, that he wanted out?

She felt herself bristle again. Sydney said yes to every mission, but that didn't mean she had to like them.

"Any day now, Syd," came Niall's grumble.

Sydney turned her eyes away from the billboards.

"I'm in," she said.

"Figured you would be," Niall replied without a change in his tone. "There's already a car waiting for you downstairs. Get yourself to head-quarters. We've got a lot of work to do."

The Panacea Group

Winter didn't know what he expected to see at Panacea's headquarters.

He'd been picked up at his home inside a gated Los Angeles neighborhood, in a nondescript black car equipped with automated drive, its windows tinted with a false landscape so that no one from the outside could see him in it. He'd been shuttled quietly to a private plane at the airport's VIP terminal, then touched down in Saint Paul, Minnesota, three hours later.

None of his usual entourage was with him—no bodyguards, no Claire, no Leo or Dameon, no assistants. Two paparazzi that had decided to camp near the edge of his neighborhood only saw an unrecognizable car leave with no driver inside.

He hadn't mentioned a word to Claire about his incident two nights ago. As promised, the agents Sauda and Niall had dropped him off at his hotel after their conversation, and Winter had gotten a minor earful from Claire about leaving the stadium on his own without telling her. He'd eaten dinner with the boys and gone to bed around three A.M. Had woken up two fitful hours later for an early photoshoot, then flown home. Not a mention anywhere.

Then, at the airport, Claire had texted him to share the news.

Billionaire Eli Morrison wants you for a private concert, she had exclaimed. *Big money! Let's talk.*

The text confirmed that Winter's strange meeting in the back of that car hadn't been a fever dream. The Panacea Group was real. Sauda had really offered to make him a secret agent.

Winter felt a little bad about keeping a secret from Claire. In all the years they'd been together, he'd told her everything, from the bad to the worst. This time, though, he'd just texted back, *Sure*.

The details that Claire gave him afterward matched up with everything Sauda had told him. A daughter who was his biggest fan. A private concert in London. Ten thousand guests flown in on a fleet of planes.

Afterward, Winter had hung up and then vomited all his nerves out in his bathroom.

The little sleep he'd gotten since then had been plagued with nightmares about Artie. He sat alone overlooking a black ocean, the lights on the pier all turned off, and sensed a dark silhouette sitting next to him. It felt like Artie, but no matter how hard he tried to make out the person's features, he couldn't see anything. And even though he couldn't remember trying to talk to the silhouette in his dreams, he woke up with a hoarse throat, as if he'd been shouting all night.

Now he sighed, rubbing his temple, and stared out at the cityscape. Usually he found himself idly composing during the moments of travel in his life, but today, fragments of music flitted in and out of his mind, unable to congeal. None of this felt real. Maybe he hadn't really woken up at all.

Finally, an hour later, the car pulled inside a gated entrance and stopped at the back of a building.

It was the Claremont in downtown, one of the newer luxury hotels in Saint Paul. He stared at the Grecian columns that framed the building's entrance as he stepped out, then back at the main street beyond the gated entrance he'd passed through, to where other cars were dropping off and picking up passengers from the front of the hotel.

A young associate was holding the door open for him. A gold pin bearing the hotel's elaborate crest gleamed on the lapel of her jacket.

"Hit some traffic, Mr. Young?" she said to him politely as he stepped in.

"I guess so," he answered, looking quizzically at her. "How did you . . ."

She tapped the watch on her wrist. "The car was sending me updates about your location and road conditions. Follow me, Mr. Young. We don't want to keep your team waiting."

His team. Just not the one he was used to.

They walked down a serene corridor that opened into the domed atrium of a high-end dining room. Winter noted the restaurant's name carved into the nearest pillar.

FOOD FOR THE GODS

Beyond it was another corridor that led out to the hotel's main lobby, where he could hear the muffled din of the hotel's unsuspecting guests.

This atrium, though, was a place in the hotel set slightly apart from the rest by a gold rope, as if for private events. A massive chandelier hung from its overhead, illuminated by shafts of light coming in from the dome's curved slivers of glass. Marble pillars lined the walls, and between them, the panels were covered with panoramas of pastoral European scenes. Dining tables and chairs dotted the space, filled with a smattering of well-dressed guests speaking in low voices. The faint scent of sugar and jasmine lingered in the air.

Winter blinked at the scene. The occasional guest looked up at him, as if gauging who he was—a few even smiled—then returned to their conversations. Winter couldn't remember the last time he hadn't caused a stir, not even when he went to the grocery store. He had the uncomfortable sensation of being unmoored, of having entered another dimension with no one to lean on but himself. His hand fiddled unconsciously with a leather bracelet around his wrist.

"This way, Mr. Young," the associate said, ushering him down another hall branching from the atrium. "You have a private room."

At the end of the hall was a metal detector and a security officer. The officer ran them both through the checkpoint—scanning of his bracelets and jewelry, identification checks, a series of basic questions—and then the associate guided him down a branch of the hall until they reached a small elevator. The panel beside it seemed to scan their faces. The elevator's door slid open with a pleasant ding.

The associate held a hand out again to Winter. "After you," she said.

"Panacea's located inside a hotel restaurant?" he asked her as the doors closed.

"A Michelin-starred restaurant," she corrected, as if slightly offended. She folded her hands behind her back. "Sometimes the best secrets are kept out in the open, Mr. Young. By the way, your phone won't work in here. Agency equipment only. No location trackers allowed. Sorry."

When the elevator opened again, they stepped out into an identical hall—except this time, the associate took an abrupt turn and pushed through a set of double doors. "This way," she said.

They headed into a kitchen operating at full capacity. The aroma of butter and roasted garlic filled Winter's senses. Workers in white aprons and tall hats bustled past him—occasionally they would make eye contact and he would hear his name ripple through the air.

They turned a corner in the kitchen and came upon a wall lined with massive refrigerators. The associate opened the door to the second fridge.

Then she stepped inside it.

Winter froze. Through the refrigerator door was a long hallway, where the associate had now paused to wait for him.

"Follow me, please," she said politely, as if this were perfectly normal.

Maybe it wouldn't have mattered if Winter had told Claire where he was going—she wouldn't have believed him anyway. He stepped hesitantly inside. The fridge closed behind him.

At the end of the hall was another door, where the associate tapped in a code to reveal a long, luxurious corridor similar to the first one they'd entered, populated with what looked like doors of polished oak, each of them bearing a brass knocker in the shape of the hotel's crest.

At last, the associate stopped before one of the doors. She rapped once with the knocker, the sound strangely metallic. Only now did Winter realize the door wasn't made of wood at all, but of solid steel. The door unlocked with a click, and she ushered them both inside.

"He's here," she said, then ducked out of the room, closing the door behind her.

It looked like a fine restaurant's private dining suite, with its own chandelier hanging from a high ceiling and similar marble columns lining the walls.

No windows.

Winter saw three people seated inside before elegantly plated meals. Two of them were Niall and Sauda, the agents that had picked him up in the car outside the stadium. Today Niall wore a stylish suit of deep blue that struggled to contain his big, burly frame, his intense eyebrows and beard trimmed to perfection, while Sauda was dressed from hijab to shoes in a pretty pale green. Their colors stood out against the room's muted grays. Both of them wore the same gold crest pin on their clothes as the attendant did.

"Hello," Niall rumbled, as grumpy as ever.

"The hotel's logo is Panacea's?" Winter asked, his eyes still on the pins.

"What do you mean?" Sauda said with a smile. "We're just hotel staff."

Winter snorted. As he took note of the room again, he now realized that behind the dining façade was some unusual technology. The walls were fitted, floor to ceiling, with screens. As he stood there, bits of text drifted into existence on the screen nearest to him, spelling out his name and profile.

Winter Young
19 Years Old
Birthplace: Los Angeles, CA, USA
Ethnicity: Chinese American

The text went on, displaying everything from his home address to his social security number, from the restaurant he most frequented to the last phone number he'd dialed. His hackles rose.

Sauda nodded at the screens. "Avalon, our headquarters' friendly neighborhood AI, just likes to run through the data of all newcomers to the building. But don't worry. None of this information is new to us."

As Winter was debating whether this made him feel better or worse, the text on the screens disappeared, replaced with a single line.

Good morning, Winter Young! Welcome to Panacea.

"What if Avalon goes rogue?" Winter said before looking back at the agents.

"You've watched too many movies. Sit down," Sauda said, waving him toward the table's empty chair.

Winter's stomach rumbled in response. He took a hesitant seat in front of a bamboo steamer of bao, a little dish of gleaming tea eggs, and a bowl of hot porridge, its surface still bubbling gently as if it'd just come from the kitchen.

"My favorite brunch?" he said, glancing back up at Sauda. Just how much did they know about him?

"What a coincidence." Sauda smiled, then glanced at the third, unspeaking person sitting beside her. "I'd like to introduce you to Sydney Cossette. She will be your bodyguard."

He turned his attention to her.

So this was the Jackal, the Panacea agent that they were sending in with him. She was a pale girl with a wavy, blond bob who looked like she must be around his own age, dressed in black jeans and a black bomber jacket with the crest pin on it, her arms folded across her chest.

At first glance, she seemed like someone who was probably older than their appearance. In fact, if they hadn't all been sitting in Panacea's headquarters, he would've thought she was one of his former classmates. He would've done a double take because she had that kind of face: small and heart-shaped, almost innocently pretty if not for her eyes. Those eyes were what made him hesitate: dark blue and stone cold, brooding underneath a pair of full, furrowed brows that gave Niall's a run for their money. There was an entire world in there—secrets and knowledge and opinions he didn't know and was a little afraid to ask about. Five years he'd spent in front of crowds all over the world, and yet somehow her stare unnerved him. She noticed him in a way he wasn't used to, as if she was methodically memorizing everything about him, as if he were less a person and more a pile of data.

"You look different in person," she said to him in greeting, her voice slightly raspy and deeper than he expected.

"Nice to meet you, too," he replied dryly. "How long have you been with the Panacea Group?"

"Long enough to be on time," she replied.

"Sorry," Winter muttered sarcastically, annoyed that her words stung. "I got lost going through the fridge tunnel."

Sydney turned to look at Niall. "You're right," she said with a completely blank face. "He is funny."

"Be polite, Sydney, and eat your risotto," Niall admonished, his brows scrunching lower. He glanced at his partner. "Go ahead, Sauda."

"You're currently inside a secured information room," Sauda told him. "We call it a SIR. What that means is no information revealed in here enters or leaves this room without special clearance. The walls are designed to prevent the transmittance of any signals outside of those approved on our agency equipment. Even your brunch today is classified information. So don't go raving about our porridge to your manager."

Winter studied her face. "What if I'd said no?" he asked.

"To telling your manager about our porridge?"

"To your request in the car." He frowned. "You told me an awful lot in there without any guarantee that I'd work with you."

She smiled a little. "We've been studying you for a bit longer than that night. Months, actually. We've been gathering intel on you, your team, your music, and your beliefs. What matters to you. We take risks, Mr. Young, but calculated ones—and when we drove you off in that car, we knew we were coming into your life during a time when you were questioning it. Makes you an ideal potential asset. Avalon calculated the chance of your successful recruitment at ninety-three percent."

Winter opened his mouth a little, then closed it. His head buzzed with the number. They had been psychoanalyzing him for months.

"And how accurate are Avalon's calculations?" he finally said. On a whim, he glanced over his shoulder at the walls. "Avalon, am I cute?"

A second later, text drifted onto the wall.

Based on available data of online mentions, cuteness attribute is 89%.

Winter gave Sauda an offended squint. "It's broken."

Sauda put down her fork and said, "Avalon, dim the lights and load up the mission."

The room dimmed. As it did, Niall tapped on the table and made a swiping motion upward. Two photographs materialized over their plates, sliding up with his movement to hover in the air above the table.

One photo showed a girl around Winter's age, her hair pinned high on her head, her eyes wide and doe-like, her expression earnest and a little lost. The second depicted a man in his late sixties, someone who was clearly her father, wearing a pair of round glasses and an expression with none of his daughter's innocence—he looked polished and shrewd, a businessman with the kind of charisma that warned he was not to be messed with.

"Eli Morrison has been on our list for years," Niall explained. "On the surface, he's the magnate of a legitimate shipping empire that has made him a billionaire many times over. In reality, his legal businesses are in debt and he's made the majority of his fortune by being a major shipper for drug lords, dealers in illegal weapons, poachers, human traffickers . . . You name it, he's shipped it. He has a complex network of ties in politics and police enforcement that's granted him safe passage through major ports. It's made him difficult for us to pin down."

Niall swiped the two photos away, then flung up a few new holograms of past court convictions. "A few years ago, the CIA did manage to arrest him on fraud charges, but he succeeded in getting a plea deal that only gave him a year of probation and no jail time. So the CIA tapped us. We need stronger evidence against him in order to make a better conviction, the kind of evidence that involves too much red tape for the CIA."

Sauda grimaced. "In other words, the kind of evidence the CIA doesn't have the scruples for. Too many layers of approval needed."

As Sauda spoke, Sydney shifted. Winter's eyes darted to her as she took a quiet, subtle breath in through her nose and then breathed out slowly and evenly through her lips.

"So," Sydney said. "What do we need to find?"

"Just one thing." Niall folded his arms against the table. "Evidence from Eli Morrison's latest shipping ledger."

Winter could feel the knot in his stomach tighten. "And what's that ledger for?" he asked.

"Shipping a massive supply of illegal chemical material from a corporate supplier in Corcasia to Cape Town, South Africa." Sauda tapped the air, and the court convictions disappeared to make way for a map of Eastern Europe, highlighting the country sandwiched between Estonia and Russia.

Niall sighed. "Not just any illegal weapons material," he said. "Have you ever seen footage of what the atomic bomb drops on Hiroshima and Nagasaki actually looked like?"

Winter had not. He recalled a documentary he'd once watched in school that showed the blasts of a nuclear bomb at a US test site, the way the trees bent sideways as the explosion engulfed the world around it. Some of his classmates had even laughed at the sight, it seemed so overwhelming.

"There's a new lab-grown chemical called Paramecium," Niall explained, "that we call chemical warfare's answer to the atomic bomb. Corcasia's terrorist cell has been working with a sister cell in Switzerland to manufacture it, and they're relying on Morrison's shipping empire to send kilos of it for human experimentation. Detonating a Paramecium bomb in a city center can kill hundreds of thousands of people, anyone who breathes in a trace of it."

His words met the silence of a tense room.

"In other words," he said softly, "we're about to prevent a new world war."

Winter had the strange sensation that he was no longer inside his body but watching himself on the outside of it, that this wasn't a briefing for some upcoming performance but a warning of what, exactly, he was about to get into. Like he had dipped his foot into water cold enough to kill.

Across from him, Sydney breathed calmly in again and exhaled slowly through her lips, a subtle enough gesture that no one else seemed to note.

"We know Morrison has already begun shipment of these materials hidden on board one of his biggest cargo ships," Sauda went on. "He has allies at the Kiel Canal who have apparently allowed the shipment to pass on to London." She paused to tap on the map, first on a canal in Germany connecting the North and Baltic Seas, and then the narrow strait between Spain and Morocco. "We need to intercept it before it reaches the Port of Gibraltar, where it will be transferred onto a different ship in order to help erase his tracks. But we need warrants, and we can't get those warrants without evidence of this contract."

"So all we need to do is get some kind of ledger?" Sydney asked. "Does he even keep track of his shipments and contracts?"

Niall nodded. "As you can imagine, many are handshake deals. Verbal agreements. But like anyone running a billion-dollar corporation, Morrison needs proper accounting. We believe any information related to his illegal business transactions is kept strictly offline and on a series of drives he stores at a location in London."

"So we need those drives," Sydney said.

"We need those drives," Sauda echoed with a nod.

Sydney raised an eyebrow. "What a coincidence that his daughter's birthday party is happening at the same time."

Sauda pointed briefly at her. "A gold star for you," she said. "Morrison is hosting his clients in London soon, when the shipment goes out, and to disguise these meetings, he's having the biggest bash in the world for his daughter at the same time. There will be heads of state in attendance, along with other celebrities and wealthy elite. No reason to suspect that any of those people showing up in London that week aren't there for his daughter. It's a big cover for an important deal."

"Good thing my schedule was open," Winter muttered.

"Lucky him," Sydney replied.

Winter scowled at her. "For you, I'd charge more."

"You presume I'd hire you."

"If you could afford it."

"Enough," Niall grumbled, and both of them halted. "Save your bickering for the job."

"How are we supposed to get to these ledgers?" Winter asked. "I'm guessing they're not going to waltz us to them."

"Eli's daughter," Niall answered. He swiped away the map and replaced it with a new photo of the same girl from earlier, a telescope-lens shot of her standing outside a shop in Paris, giggling with a few friends. "Penelope Morrison," he said.

"Despite his unsavory reputation," Sauda explained, "Penelope checks out from our analyses. She is uninvolved in his business and has as normal a life as a billionaire heiress can have. Eli seems to genuinely dote on her, perhaps partly out of grief over the death of his wife from a terminal illness some time ago."

At that, Sydney looked away. "Monster has a heart?" she said coldly.

"So small you'll miss it if you blink," Sauda replied with a nod. "But he *is* genuinely protective of his daughter, reluctant to get her mixed up with his dirty politics, and keeps her clean."

"Penelope Morrison is the only person in the world that Eli trusts," Niall added. "That means that if anyone can get us close enough to her father's world to incriminate him, it'll be her."

"What good is she if she's uninvolved in his businesses?" Sydney asked.

Sauda smiled. "Not entirely uninvolved."

She brought up a third photo, this time of a young man with a narrow face and a scruff of beard, his eyes sharp and wary behind a pair of tinted glasses. "This is Connor Doherty, who reports directly to Eli Morrison. On the surface, he's a young financial advisor who helps manage Penelope's trust fund. In truth, he's in charge of tracking Eli's dirty money and cleaning it up. He ensures payments come on time and in the correct amounts, and then are moved into banks as legitimate money, without leaving a trail."

"Penelope has had some tension with her father lately," Niall added. "We think it has to do with how suffocatingly close Eli guards her. So, part of her quiet rebellion against her father is a secret affair she's been carrying on with Connor, someone whom she seems to have had a crush on for some time."

Sydney let out a low whistle. "Scandalous romance in the House of Morrison. I like this girl."

"Connor is a mysterious figure for us, and almost impossible to get near. We rarely see him photographed at any of Eli's business meetings or events. Even Eli's other associates don't know him well, and he's quite intentional about keeping them at arm's length. But because of his management of Penelope's funds—and their affair—he can occasionally be found with her. He'll definitely be in attendance at her party."

"What's she like?" Sydney asked.

"We don't know much." Sauda nodded at Winter. "But we do know one interest she has."

"Painting?" Winter suggested wryly.

"Bad taste in music?" Sydney answered.

Winter felt heat creeping up his face and opened his mouth to argue.

Sauda frowned at Sydney, who just held her hands up in mock innocence. Then the woman turned her attention back to Winter. "Winter, Penelope has attended over half of the concerts you've put on in the last two years. She has been in the audience during some of your interviews, has bought two of your old stage outfits from charity auctions—each of them at price points over two hundred thousand dollars, and she even met you once at a VIP backstage event for a handful of your fans. You probably don't remember her—she's quite shy and keeps a low profile."

He swallowed, his mind automatically flipping back through the hundreds of meet and greets he'd done before, trying to remember her face. "True fan," he murmured.

Sauda nodded. "I suspect that you're a bit of an escape for her, and the oppressive world her father has built around her. Now, like Eli, Connor Doherty is a possessive man. He cherishes the beautiful things he owns, and one of those beautiful things at the moment is Penelope. He's quite aware of her overwhelming fondness for you, though, and I imagine it won't be hard for him to be lured out if Penelope is hanging on your arm throughout her party."

The danger of this setup sent a shiver down Winter's spine. "You want me to seduce her?"

Sauda shrugged. "Doesn't matter to us. Be a flirt, be a confidant, be whatever you need to be. Walk the line of making Connor just jealous enough to want to get to know you, and not so much that he shuts you out."

Winter's attention shifted back to the photo of Connor Doherty hovering beside Penelope's. If there was anything he was good at outside of music and performance, it was knowing just how much charm he needed to dial up in order to get the specific results he wanted. He'd just never expected to use it for espionage.

"Yeah, sure," he muttered. "Piece of cake."

Sauda nodded. "Excellent. If we can get close enough to plant something on Connor, I believe Sydney can steal the evidence we need."

"Not to criticize any part of this," Sydney interjected, "but I have serious doubts about whether or not Winter can maintain our cover."

"This sounds a lot like a critique to me," Winter said.

She eyed him. "You didn't even know what a CPU was."

Winter held a hand out at Sauda. "You told her I didn't know?"

"Well, he knows now," Sauda said, casting a stern look toward Sydney before turning back to Winter. "We'll prepare you. But the best part of your cover, Mr. Young, is that it isn't really a cover at all. Your cover is *you*. So just be yourself."

His gaze went back to Sydney. Her eyes stayed away from his, and everything about her body language told him that she would do everything in her power to avoid him unless it was necessary for them to cooperate.

There would be no small talk with her.

Fine. Winter tightened his lips and kept his focus on Sauda, too. He wasn't joining the Panacea Group for this mission to make new friends, anyway. By the end of it, when they made it out, they would never need to see each other again.

"Are we all on the same page?" Niall asked, his eyes settling on each of them. When no one added anything, he nodded and turned off the hologram. The photo of Penelope vanished, leaving the middle of the table bare. "Excellent." He tucked his hands in his pockets and gave Winter and Sydney a tight smile. "And get to know each other. We'd like you to give off the impression that you both get along, or are at least polite."

"This is the most optimistic I've ever heard you, Niall," Sauda said.

"I'm only doing it for you," Niall replied.

Sauda put a hand against her heart. "Flattered as always."

Niall just grunted. "Optimism is my hidden power."

Optimism is my hidden power.

The familiar phrase jolted through Winter like a lightning bolt. Suddenly, he saw a flashback before him of Artie leaning back on the couch in their old home, teasing Winter as he scribbled bits of lyrics in a notebook.

The flashback vanished, and Winter found himself staring again at Niall. His head swam. "Wait," he said, holding a hand up. "Why did you say that?"

"Say what?" Niall asked.

"Optimism is my hidden power." He looked at Sauda, then back at Niall. "My brother used to say that all the time. Why are *you* saying it?"

Niall and Sauda exchanged a knowing glance.

Winter's eyes had turned solemn and cold. "I've signed your paperwork and heard you out," he whispered. "So I think it's time you told me the truth."

Sauda laced her fingers together on the table and gave him a steady look. "We recruited your brother a month after he joined the Peace Corps," she said. "He worked for us. He was a Panacea agent."

All the World's a Secret Stage

Winter should have known.

Should have guessed it during his first conversation with Sauda and Niall.

But who the hell would automatically assume that his late brother was a secret agent?

All those missions. All those times his brother had left for weeks, then come back and told him elaborately detailed stories about what he did. Lies.

No, not lies. He *had* worked for the Peace Corps. It just wasn't the whole truth.

Had Artie once sat in the back of a car and listened in disbelief to Sauda making him an offer? Had he refused, then agreed? How had he really died?

"Are you okay?"

Winter looked up through his swimming thoughts to meet Sydney's frown.

"If you need some time to process this," Sauda said, "we can reschedule the remainder of today's meeting."

"No." Winter squeezed his eyes shut. "Yes. I mean—I don't know."

"Quite a remarkable family," Niall said.

"Your mother doesn't know," Sauda went on, her voice gentler now. "She still doesn't. I am going to order you to keep it that way."

"I don't have much of a choice, do I?" Winter snapped. There was no use being angry at Sauda, but he couldn't help the fury roiling in his veins. How could he even fathom telling his mother something like this?

Sauda just looked coolly away and stood up. "Are you ready for the rest of the meeting, Mr. Young, or shall we postpone?"

"Sauda," Niall said quietly.

"What?" She lifted her chin at the man. "Delay the inevitable?"

"The boy's going to take a while to digest this." Niall glanced at Winter. "Maybe we should give him some space."

"No," Winter blurted out, and all of them turned to look at him.

"No," he repeated more firmly. "I don't need time to myself, and I don't need you to *give me space* to process anything. I need information. I need you to tell me everything. What did he do for you? Where did you send him?" His voice turned quiet, the weight on his heart buffeted by a current of anger. "How did he die?"

The smile that Sauda now gave him was sad, as if she had always known that his link to Artie would be their in, that somehow he was destined to be here. She sighed and stood up. "You want to know the truth?" She nodded toward the door.

"Yes," Winter replied.

She opened the door and gave him a sidelong look. "Then follow us."

Winter felt like he was walking through a dream. His body swayed slightly as he trailed after the others down the corridor until they reached a second elevator. Unlike the first, this one had doors made of clear glass. When they stepped inside, the doors hissed shut and text materialized over them like the screens in the office room.

Where to?

"Experimental Design," Niall said.

The text vanished, and the elevator began moving down.

"Underground?" Winter asked.

"Just a little bit," Sauda replied.

They traveled in silence for a minute before he finally said, "How little?"

"About two thousand feet." Sauda nodded at him. "Ready for an official introduction to your new side hustle?"

Winter was still trying to figure out how to answer her when the dark shaft outside the elevator gave way to a floor that stretched as far as the eye could see.

Winter stared through the glass doors at a place that seemed impossible.

"Holy shit," he whispered.

The room was circular and at least several stories high, designed in a similar style to the luxurious, neoclassical hotel aboveground. Pillars decorated the space, and between them were massive stone archways, each of them leading down halls.

One of the arched halls was filled with parked commercial airliners, another with fighter jets. Yet another had rows of cars. Other archways had clear glass across them, the doorways occasionally sliding open and shut to allow workers dressed in cobalt blue jumpsuits and helmets to pass through. Each of the halls had its arched ceiling painted a distinct color.

Winter swallowed, and when he spoke again, his voice sounded hoarse. "Artie worked here?"

Niall nodded. "Stood almost exactly where you are right now, the first time he took this elevator down."

It was as if Winter could feel the ghost of his brother here, taller and older and wiser, hands in his pockets and eyes fixed on the scene before him. Did he gape like Winter did now? Did he take it all in stride? Did he make a joke?

How could this be real?

Winter glanced over at Sydney. She was leaning against the back of the elevator, unconsciously cracking her knuckles, her expression almost bored. As he looked on, she took a subtle, calm breath again before exhaling slowly through her mouth.

This was the third time he'd seen her do it. Winter noted it quietly, then looked away.

"The Panacea Group has been active since the United States' Revolutionary War," Sauda explained. "After the signing of the Declaration of Independence, our founder, Charlotte May Hughes, widow and heiress to the Hughes family fortune, thought it necessary to create a secret agency not beholden to the government, one wealthy and independent enough to operate on its own terms. Over the centuries, our agents have been involved in everything from protecting the Underground Railroad to spying on the Confederacy during the Civil War, to fighting the American mafia during Prohibition, to carrying out missions against the Nazis during World War II. Sometimes we partner with the CIA and other agencies around the world, but not always." She folded her arms. "Mrs. Hughes wanted us to always have the power to choose what is right over what is diplomatic. That's the creed we strive to honor here."

She turned to nod at the enormous chamber. "Our current location had originally been intended for a series of iron mines that were abandoned back in the nineteenth century. Then there were plans to convert it into a particle collider laboratory. The lab ultimately decided to move their location deeper into the desert, and the Claremont Hotel went up over this space. So we bought the hotel and outfitted this subterranean space for our needs. Underground, shielded from prying eyes, good to experiment with small-scale versions of new weapons, good for keeping secrets locked away. Good for keeping people off our property, too, and also good for not being in the news for excavating a mysterious new place."

"And what, exactly, is this?" Winter asked.

"Where we keep and test all the equipment you and the rest of our agents use," Niall answered as the elevator finally came to a stop. "Weapons, disguises, customized phones and listening devices. You name it, we'll have it. Many of the floors above this space are dedicated to research. You'll spend your time here, and the floor below it."

"There's more?"

Sydney nodded and spoke for the first time since entering the elevator. "Training floor's under us," she told him. "We all have to practice somewhere."

Artie had been here. He had worked here, had wandered this secret world.

His gaze finally settled back on Niall. "What was Artie's job?"

"He began as a junior analyst," the man answered as the doors opened and Sauda guided them out. "Interned for me for six months, breaking codes and intercepting messages. But his Peace Corps work—which became his cover—made him more ideal for placement as a field operative."

"So, an actual spy."

He nodded gravely. "A good one."

There was unspoken grief in his voice. Winter felt a lump suddenly lodge in his throat. All those times he had rushed out of the house to wave goodbye to Artie as he drove off to the airport on some Peace Corps mission or other, he'd really been saying farewell to a secret agent heading into some of the most dangerous situations in the world. And yet, every time Artie came back, he brought presents for Mom and souvenirs for Winter, would tell animated stories during dinner about his supposed adventures, as if everything were normal. Sometimes Winter would catch him acting uncharacteristically quiet, but he always assumed it was because Peace Corps work could be heavy on the heart.

What had Artie really endured on his own?

He followed the others numbly as they turned into one of the arched halls, this one filled with rows of cars. He could make out a few of their brands—Mercedes, Porsches, McLarens, Bugattis. Sandwiched between them were cars in every make and model, from supercars to tiny smart cars to cars that could be in an average family's driveway.

"They may look like vehicles you recognize," Sauda said to him, "but they're not. None of those models exist in the world above." She paused in front of a titanium-colored Mazda, then clapped her hands twice.

Instead of opening as Winter expected, the Mazda's doors slid sideways, and the sedan's interior transformed into a flat space with the chairs folded back, with a secret compartment under the floor.

"For transporting injured people," she said, "and tending to their wounds on the go without the attention and publicity of an ambulance. Or for smuggling informants and high-risk refugees." She clapped three times, and four sharp-edged triangles of metal extended out from the vehicle's underbelly. "For slicing the wheels of any car that might be harassing you."

Then she clapped again—and the car's entire body shifted, its wheels sucking up underneath its frame and new plates of steel coming down to seal the entire bottom of it in metal. "For if you need to change gears, quite literally, to aquatic travel."

Winter had seen his share of unusual cars before, but he found himself staring speechless at the transformed sedan.

Beside him, Sydney let out a low whistle. "Do we get one of these for our mission?" she asked.

Sauda clapped a final time, and the car reset itself until it once more looked like a family car. "Not this time. Maybe someday."

They exited the car hall and moved on, stepping onto a transporter that lifted them up to a higher level of archways. Here, she ushered them toward another hall, this one with an entrance sealed by a glass wall. She laid her palm flat against the glass, and it slid open without a sound, opening up to a series of adjoined cubicles. The door sealed behind them with a hush, and suddenly the bustle of the main floor cut off. Winter shivered as he looked up at the vaulted archway's ceiling. It both felt comforting to be in this sealed space—and a little like he'd just stepped into a catacomb.

They stopped before a row of podiums, each of them supporting glass display cases. His gaze settled on the first case. It took him a moment to realize what he was staring at.

"Those are my earrings," he said.

"They're not," Niall replied gruffly. "They just look like them."

Winter looked back down at the case in disbelief. The earrings were an exact replica of a pair that Claire had gifted him years ago—right down to a slight scratch on the left's silver frame.

He looked sharply at Sauda. "Why?"

Sauda tapped the side of the glass case, careful to press her finger-print flat against its surface. The glass panels folded back like a blooming flower to reveal the jewelry within.

"Go ahead," she said, nodding at him. "They're for you."

Winter gingerly picked up one of the earrings. It felt similar to his pair, although he could tell that it was very slightly heavier than his own.

"Your jewelry is, of course, some of the most extraordinary in the world," Sauda continued, "but I think our version is just a bit . . . fancier."

Winter scowled down at the earrings. "If I wanted fancier jewelry, I would've just called my stylist."

Sauda pulled out her phone and tapped on the screen. Immediately, it replayed Winter's words, his voice clear and unmistakable on it. *"If I wanted fancier jewelry, I would've just called my stylist."*

Sydney grinned at Winter's expression, and for a moment, her hostile, sarcastic demeanor gave way to something that looked like delight. He noticed her hands were still restless, her thumbs pressing against the joints of her fingers as if she didn't know what to do with them otherwise. "Nice sound quality, isn't it?" she said.

Winter found himself staring at her deep blue eyes with a mix of wariness and awe. He hadn't quite believed she was a secret agent until now. She stared knowingly back at him, head slightly tilted, so that her blond hair curtained softly in front of one cheek. Somehow, he couldn't imagine her looking as shocked as he did when she first began working for Panacea.

Sauda nodded. "Embedded within the silver of these earrings are the tiniest voice recorders in the world. They can pick up most conversations around them in crystal clear definition."

Winter tore his gaze away from Sydney's dark blue eyes and back to Sauda. "You're telling me you have eavesdropping tools like this," he said, "but you've still never been able to gather the incriminating evidence that you need to nab Eli Morrison?"

"Talking yourself out of the job already?" Sauda replied.

"It's one thing to have an elaborate listening device," Niall said. "Quite another to get close enough to make it useful. Eli is careful with whom he hangs around and what he says. We're always trying to get one step ahead."

"And with that," Sauda said, walking to the second case in the cubicle, "here is your new ring."

Winter found himself staring down at one of the most beautiful rings he'd ever seen in his life. It was a coil of what looked like black diamonds ending in a length of beautiful black rock, all studded with crystals to look like a snake.

He let out a breath. It was exactly the kind of thing that he liked to wear, something that would match his collection of jewelry. "I don't have a ring like this," he said.

"Of course not," Sauda replied. "We designed this ourselves."

Winter looked up skeptically at her, then pulled his sleeve up to reveal the snake tattoo that coiled around his left wrist. "You've been custom-making stuff for me months ahead of time?" he asked.

"Do you think we're amateurs?" Sauda replied. "Of course we have."

She looked at Niall, and a tone of admiration entered her voice. "You and the design team went all out. It even matches the angle of his tattoo."

At Sauda's praise, Niall's cheeks turned slightly pink. The big man coughed, thick eyebrows furrowing lower. "Didn't take long to make," he rumbled.

"A symbol of some significance to you, I presume?" Sauda asked Winter.

"Just my zodiac," Winter replied, turning his arm this way and that. "On the Chinese calendar, snakes are loyal, crafty, and good luck."

Sauda seemed to sense there was more to his reason than that, but she just nodded. "Well," she said with a shrug. "Hopefully that good luck extends to all of us." Beside her, Sydney's gaze flitted curiously across his face.

Winter rubbed the tattoo out of instinct. He didn't mention that when he was six, months after Artie had first left for college, he'd drawn a snake around his arm with a Sharpie after overhearing his parents screaming at each other during one of his father's rare visits, his mother saying that everything they'd done together had been a mistake: *the engagement, the marriage, the baby.* His father had snorted and replied coldly, *I never asked for a son.* Winter had drawn the snake on himself after his father stormed out of the house, adding intricate details onto the scales, as if covering himself with a symbol of good luck could fix everything. He'd shown his mother his work, and she'd smiled sadly at him with those vacant, baggy eyes she always got after his father's visits. Then she'd left the house without warning for two days and Winter had spent them alone, as he usually did, watching old concerts online and foraging in the freezer for nuggets.

The memory vanished. He tugged his sleeve back down before returning Sydney's gaze. "Guess I got pretty lucky," he decided to say. She just gave him a flat smile and looked away, and he wondered how much Panacea might know about his past.

"This snake ring is a recording device and infrared camera," Niall said as he nodded down at it. "And that rock you see studding the top of the ring is a genuine chunk from the four-point-five-billion-year-old Hierapolis pallasite meteorite, one of the most expensive meteorites in the world."

"So don't lose it," Sauda said.

Winter stared closer at the stone. Scattered throughout the dark rock were shimmering bits of a green-gold mineral that caught the light.

"Olivine," Niall said, noting Winter's interest. "Beautiful, isn't it?"

"Absolutely stunning," he said honestly.

"We've tracked Connor's buying habits and noticed how he bids at auctions," Niall went on. "A man with exquisite taste in fashion. A big fan of rare jewels. An especially big fan of rare meteorites. He's a collector and a patron of many museums. He'll recognize this stone immediately—that is, if you're given access to him. That's where your work with Penelope will open doors for you."

"If she introduces you to Connor at a party," Sauda said, "we want you to gift this to him. He'll be delighted to wear it, and we'll have planted a device on him."

Winter picked up the ring and slid it onto his middle finger. It felt cool and heavy.

"What makes you think Connor will accept a gift from Winter?" Sydney asked.

"With anyone else, I'd agree," Sauda replied. "Everyone suspects those they don't know. But from him?" She nodded at Winter. "Would you think a spontaneous gift from the biggest celebrity in the world would be bugged to report back to a spy agency? Especially if you were the one who invited him in the first place?"

Sydney grunted, but she didn't argue the point.

"This is where Winter's identity will come in handy for us," Niall said. "You're not exactly what people expect to come out of here."

"I'm not sure whether that's a compliment or an insult," Winter said.

Niall shrugged. "Neither. It's just a fact."

They continued. Each of the pedestals held something that made

Winter's head swim. There was a credit card identical to his own, except equipped with a listening device. There were poisons disguised as colorful mints in plastic containers. There were pens that could shoot bullets, hairspray that could paralyze, and phones that could hack into a city's traffic signals, equipped with trackers. There was also the hotel crest pin that Sauda, Niall, and Sydney wore, except that when pressed twice rapidly with its owner's hand, it would both shoot out a needle-like blade and send an alert and location back to headquarters.

Sauda pointed at the tiny tracker chip inside one of the displays. "We'll be switching out your SIM card for this," she said. "Slides in and out fairly easily."

All Winter could think about as they went on was what Artie must have had for his own missions, what he might have used. What might have failed him during his final moments.

At the end, Sauda reached for something small in her coat pocket.

"Finally," she said, "there are these."

Sydney made a disinterested sound in her throat, as if she knew what was coming, but Winter frowned at the two tiny vials in Sauda's palm, each filled with an amber liquid that reminded him of whiskey.

"Toxins," Niall said.

"We always give these to our operatives on every mission," Sauda said, "and you are no different." Her voice shifted, turned graver. "In the event that something goes catastrophically wrong, in the event you find yourself in a situation from which you cannot escape, take this."

Winter's blood ran cold at her words. He stared at the vial. It was a suicide drink.

"They act quickly and painlessly," Sydney told him.

"I'm not killing myself," Winter said automatically.

"Everyone thinks that," she went on in a quiet voice. "Until you're put in the position and you realize you weren't so different all along."

We always give these to our operatives, Sauda had said. That meant Artie, too. Winter stared at the vials and felt his throat close up.

"The chances of you needing this are slim," Sauda went on at his silence. "Still. Agency protocol."

Sydney was staring closely at Winter now. "What's wrong?" she asked.

"Is that how my brother died?" he whispered, turning to face them. "Was he forced to commit suicide?"

There was a heavy pause. Niall sighed, looking to Sauda as if for her approval to speak. When Sauda nodded, his furrowed gaze returned to Winter.

"No," he replied. "Your brother died because he went back for a hostage during an exchange gone wrong, against Panacea's orders. He died saving a life."

Winter closed his eyes. Once, when he'd eaten too little after a hectic week of touring and a rushed visit home to check on his mother, he'd fainted during rehearsals and had to cancel several concerts in order to let his body recover. He felt like that now—the same blurring of the world around him, the same rush in his head, the same loosening of his body.

Of course Artie had died saving a life.

When he opened his eyes, he saw Sydney take an instinctive step toward him, as if preparing to catch him if he fell. He shook his head at her and stepped away. He didn't know what to say. He didn't know what to do. Words sat on his tongue and melted.

"You've witnessed many things, Winter," Sauda said softly to him now. "Have you ever witnessed war? I've been sent on assignment into one. Do you know what it's like to be trapped in something you can't escape?" Sauda looked at him with an expression of pity, and he felt his insides recoil from it. "The only reason we are putting you in danger's path is because an entire population is depending on us. And when I say that, I want you to picture what that really means. Mothers walking their kids to the bus. Construction workers eating lunch together. Fathers waiting at the train station for their families. Children on their first day of kindergarten. People in love, people with friends, people with full lives. Good people." She nodded at Winter. "Your brother fully understood the dangers of this job when he accepted it. I want you to, as well. I'm not going to lie to you about how dangerous this will be, but I promise that you won't go in unprepared. Okay?"

He swallowed hard. Sauda's voice seemed far away. "Okay," he heard himself answer.

As they stepped out of the cubicle and back into the rest of the Experimental Design space, he could feel his heart hammering against his ribs. The enormous room felt like it might swallow him whole. There was a cry bottling in his throat, the edges of his eyes threatening to tear up, grief seeking the relief of spilling out. He imagined Artie wandering this place, taking assignments from his superiors, pocketing the tiny vials of toxins without question. Accepting that he might need to use them someday.

"We don't have much time," Niall said as he stopped in the hall and turned to face Winter. "So, we're going to be training you hard in the coming weeks." He cast a steely gaze between Winter and Sydney, who gave him a sullen look. "I suggest you two become acquainted quickly. You'll need it. Understood?"

"Yes, sir," Sydney replied, and Winter nodded in silence.

As Niall and Sauda walked ahead, Sydney leaned closer to him.

"Just don't push me," she said in a low voice. "And don't get in my way. Do what I tell you, and we'll get along fine."

Like hell he was going to cry in front of this girl. He pushed down his tears. "I always appreciate a partnership where I get no say at all," he replied irritably.

She rolled her eyes at him. "With all due respect, I've got a promotion on the line because of you. So come talk to me again when you get some experience."

Winter stopped in his tracks, and Sydney stopped with him. "You know," he said, "ever since I set foot inside that meeting room upstairs, I've felt like you wanted to cut my head off. I'd love a clue as to why you're giving me a hard time."

She stared up at him with such a level look that he felt like she was burning a hole through his head. When she did speak, her voice sounded chipped with ice. "Here's your clue. I've seen plenty of people like you."

"Like what?" he snapped.

"You cultivated that swagger of yours to hide all your insecurities. But you actually wanted to become famous because you were afraid not to be. Ah, I'm right, aren't I? The more swagger, the more insecurities. And I've learned over time that insecure men are the worst, prone to falling apart at the most inconvenient times."

He narrowed his eyes at her. "And what about you?" he said. "It seems to me like you're hiding a few things of your own. Bad family life? Mean parents? You must have gotten your shitty attitude from somewhere. But I guess we all have our issues, don't we?"

He knew he shouldn't go after her seeking to hurt. The words that came out of his mouth now didn't sound like him at all. But his heart felt like it had been shredded today, and he couldn't bring himself to care.

Sydney's stare went flat, the blue darkening like a storm.

"I wish your brother was still alive," she said, her voice cool and steady. "Maybe we wouldn't need you."

"Don't bring my brother into this," he said quietly.

"Then don't make me," she called over her shoulder, then waved a leather bracelet in the air. "Also, you need to keep a better eye on your things. I'll drop it at reception for you."

She'd somehow managed to slip one of his bracelets right off his wrist, and he hadn't felt a thing. He glanced down at his arm, then stared at her retreating figure, his mouth open in shock, unable to find the right words. All he could do was watch her walk blithely away without looking back.

The New Job

The first assumption about Winter Young that Sydney admitted she'd gotten wrong was that he was foolish.

Stubborn, yes. Dense . . . yes. But definitely not foolish. The Winter Young that she'd met at the Panacea headquarters had been a boy with a careful eye. She had noticed it about him the instant he stepped inside, the way he'd taken in the room around him and assessed her and the other agents with a single, sweeping gaze, the gestures in his hands and the tilt of his head, the way his gaze jumped from person to person. The anger in his eyes that had sparked when she'd mentioned his brother's name.

In those moments, she saw right away why Sauda had chosen him.

Now she was lying on her bed in the thickening dark of evening, listening to the faint sound of sirens on the streets far below her apartment, methodically memorizing the contents of a black folder Niall had delivered to her apartment.

The folder contained all the documentation for her new cover as Winter Young's bodyguard. Fake name (Ashley Coving Miller), fake driver's license and passport, fake high school diploma, fake passwords and account numbers for Ashley's supposed direct deposits into a fake personal bank account. An acceptance letter to a real bodyguard company, Elite Securities, that occasionally worked with Panacea, which Sauda had secured for Sydney. There were fake business cards for her in case she needed to hand them out, fake photos of fake family members, fake email accounts filled with fake emails dating back to over a year ago, fake phone contacts for fake best friends. A custom-made phone with a bunch of instructions on how to unlock its encryption and secure call lines back to Panacea. There were even fake credit cards that her fictional persona hadn't paid off, fake expired gym memberships, fake achievement certificates for martial arts, fake gun licenses, and fake rants on fake social media accounts, complete with fake replies posted by fake acquaintances.

Details littering a fake life that made it look real.

Sydney read and reread the papers until she could feel her true identity blurring into this imaginary one. Then she closed her eyes, thoughts of Winter swirling in her mind.

Winter was smart, smarter than she cared for—even if he'd made it too easy for her to slip his bracelet off his wrist. Simpler subjects were less work; they did what they were told and didn't stray from the plan. Sydney would have to make sure Winter didn't get any wild ideas of his own during this mission and lead them off on some tangent.

Her second mistaken assumption was that his fame was a gimmick. No, this boy was destined for it. He was a unique kind of beautiful that made her nervous, the kind that didn't belong at all with the rest of society. Everything about him—dark eyes and thick lashes, the rich black hair that looked effortlessly perfect, the pillow-soft lips, the tattoos that decorated his forearms down to his left hand, the grace in his stride, the lines of his figure—drew the eye. He'd stepped into the meeting room, and it'd felt like his presence had lit the air itself on fire. Those at Panacea who'd seen him that day had been trained to stay calm in all circumstances—but even so, everyone at headquarters was abuzz with news of Winter's visit.

It made her want to laugh. It made her want to tell Sauda to fire him. Spies didn't look like him. As far as she knew, his brother certainly didn't—although she'd never crossed paths with Artie Young. Spies were meant to have looks that blended in, to be able to melt into the shadows.

Winter Young couldn't disappear if he had the superpower of

invisibility. Frankly, she was surprised he wasn't covered in moths all drawn to his light.

How the hell was she supposed to complete a mission—let alone get promoted—while saddled with a boy like this?

Sydney opened her eyes in the dark and ran her hand idly across the silken sheets of her bed. She didn't know why she disliked him so much, why she wanted to give him such a hard time. He'd stepped into the meeting room yesterday, and she'd felt a lurch of irritation deep in her gut, an emotion that made her want to memorize every bit of him so she could figure out how to bring him down to size, to force him to take a step back and feel unmoored in a new place.

The feeling had left her with a pounding heart and an ache in her stomach. No wonder she hadn't been able to resist swiping his bracelet.

She pitied him in regards to his brother's death, she really did. The pain on his face had been real and deep. But Winter Young got to *choose* to be here. He hadn't come to Panacea because he was forced to, because life had left him no other options and steered him down a path of no return. Winter chose this, just as he'd chosen to become an entertainer, chosen what kind of star he wanted to be, who he could surround himself with, what he wanted to do.

Sydney was here because this was her only way out of her childhood. She had to run from the ghost of her mother, from the memory of the incessant beeping sound in the hospital room and the wheeze of her breathing. She had to escape the leaf-strewn curb in front of her childhood home, the angry rumble of her father's drunken voice. She had to learn how to stop stealing, had to break the temptation to shoplift from shelves and desks, the obsessive need to control *something* in her life.

Her fingers twitched, aching always to take. She looked to her side and out the floor-to-ceiling window of her apartment at the vast city below. Told herself that she no longer lived in North Carolina but in Seattle, far from the other coast. That she was no longer a child.

Her phone buzzed with an incoming call from an unknown source. Sydney rolled over to grab her earbuds.

"Ich schlafe," she said in German.

"No you weren't," Niall muttered on the phone. "And stop it, Syd."

"What is it?"

"Sounds like bodyguards at the birthday functions will also need to be in costume. Something about good aesthetics for the official photos."

"Good aesthetics?"

"They don't want a bunch of penguin suits in every shot. So you'll get to wear something fancy and we'll be busy implanting a listening chip in it."

She sighed, even as a part of her mind perked up at the thought. Eli Morrison was going all out. "Please give me functional shoes."

"And we're officially starting you with Winter next week. Tuesday. Be here early, so we can get your current measurements for a fitting. And cut him some slack, all right?"

"Sauda told you to say that, didn't she?"

"Well, Sauda's not wrong."

"Do you think she's right about hiring Winter?"

"I think it's a bit too late for that question, kid, and I also think it's not your place to question Sauda's decisions."

"Sauda would tell me to speak my mind," she replied. "And I think we're making a mistake."

"And is that because you think he can't do the mission, or because you just don't like him?"

"Can't it be both?"

"Honestly, I didn't think you'd be a good Panacea agent, either. And yet here you are."

Sydney laughed. The sound choked for a second in her throat, and her weak lungs gave a little spasm.

"You okay?"

"I'm fine, Dad," she replied. "Just a tickle in my throat."

She could almost see him rolling his eyes in exasperation at her nickname for him. She didn't tell him, though, that in moments like this, she didn't use it as a nickname at all. She'd said it because she liked imagining that he was the father she could have had.

But that was a silly thought. Niall wasn't a father to her. She was just an employee, under contract. If Niall knew about her lung condition, he'd terminate her immediately from Panacea's program. So she'd never told anyone about it, and she'd managed well enough for this long. Someday, when it worsened, she'd have to disclose it, but until then, well, this worked fine.

"Okay," came Niall's low rumble. "Tuesday, then. I don't expect us to turn Winter Young into a spy in a single week, but I expect him to at least be reliable enough for one mission. Sound doable?"

"We'll see, won't we?" Sydney stared out at the city outside her window, dreading the start of training Winter. "And what about you?"

"What about me?"

"When are you going to ask Sauda out on a real date?"

Niall made an annoyed sound in his throat, and Sydney had to stifle a smile. "Against regulations, Syd. You know that."

"Oh, come on. I won't tell headquarters."

"Good night, Sydney," he muttered, then hung up.

She put on a looping track of rain on her phone, then tossed it aside and closed her eyes. The sound of water filled her thoughts, and she felt the rising tension in her muscles relax a bit, her neck loosening, the tightness in her jaw fading. She closed her eyes again, then tried to concentrate on nothing but the sheets on her bed.

Instead, the image of Winter arriving at their meeting remained vividly in her mind, the details still intact from when she'd taken in everything about him. He hovered there in the darkness, refusing to disappear.

Sydney frowned. She envisioned herself taking up a shovel and literally heaving him out of her thoughts.

Maybe Winter would turn out to be a pleasant surprise. Maybe he could learn the ropes faster than she expected. Maybe she could prepare him enough to at least survive this mission and get her promotion to full agent. Then he could go back to his life and she could go back to hers, and she wouldn't have to deal with him again.

She let herself stew in that resolution until she finally fell asleep, Winter's face still burned into her mind.

The Afterthought

When Winter knocked on the door to his mother's apartment, he knew immediately that his visit would be a bad one. He always knew.

If he could hear hurried shuffling inside, followed by the opening of the door and Mom standing on the other side, it would be fine. It meant she was doing okay, that she was happy to see him, and they could even have a normal conversation. But today she didn't answer right away, and the door stayed closed. A second later, Winter heard the soft click of the lock on the other side, followed by his mother's singsong voice coming from somewhere far away in the apartment.

"Come in," she called to him. "Door's unlocked."

His heart sank a little. He'd done this a thousand times over the years, and nothing about it was ever a surprise. But today he was leaving to begin his Panacea training, so his nerves were already frayed. The thought of being under Sydney Cossette's tutelage for a week had him on edge. And having to endure this painfully awkward visit right now made him feel like turning back around and heading down the elevator to the street below.

But he didn't. Even though his life had become a never-ending current of plane rides and hotel stays, he had never once failed to check on his mother before leaving on a trip. So instead, he fixed one of the rolled-up sleeves of his collar shirt, rested the bouquet of flowers in his hand against his shoulder, and opened the door.

Five years and hundreds of concerts in front of millions of fans—yet he still felt his heart flutter with anxiety as he stepped inside.

The apartment looked like it always did—a state of pleasant clutter that was somehow both chaotic and organized, the kind that would appear artistic if drawn by a skilled hand, as if everything had paused in the middle of being done. The side table near the entryway was filled up underneath and on top with piles of books organized by their interior color, all with their dust jackets removed. A buttery yellow blanket lay half-folded and strewn over the couch, and every inch of the coffee table was hidden under an assortment of books, magazines, and potted plants that trailed haphazard vines down to the rug. A fishbowl with two goldfish sat next to a milky pink ceramic figurine of Buddha and a lucky cat sculpture on the dining table. Stacks of blue-and-white Chinese porcelain dishes sat unsorted on the marble kitchen counter, pulled out from the dishwasher but not yet put away.

Down the hall leading to the bedrooms, Winter could hear her humming the refrain of an old song over and over. She had a beautiful voice—he'd inherited his own from her, if nothing else—and now he found himself stopping to admire it, listening to the sweet notes repeat themselves.

"Hi, Mom," he called out to her. The singing paused. He held out the bouquet of flowers before him, as if she could see it. "Got a spare vase?"

"Zài shuǐ cáo xià," she called back in Mandarin. *Under the kitchen sink.*

He could hear the tension in her voice now, the slight disappointment tainting her musical voice that always seemed to pop up whenever he visited.

As he went to the kitchen to pull out an old glass vase from under the sink, his mother emerged from her bedroom in a quiet flurry. Today, she was dressed in a chunky white sweater and a pleated green dress that swished as she walked, and her wavy black hair was tied back with a bandana, the locks draping over one of her shoulders. A large tote hung from her arm. Like the apartment, everything about her appeared hastily thrown together, but in a way that looked like perfection. His mother, always stylish even without trying.

But he knew she did try, of course. She'd probably been up for several hours already, pulling on and taking off outfit after outfit, unable to stop until she finally managed to settle on something that ended the cycle.

"Thank you for the flowers, baby bear," she said breathlessly, this time in English, as she put her earrings in without a mirror. "They're beautiful."

Winter nodded, even though she wasn't looking directly at him and hadn't even seen the flowers. "I got you tulips."

"I love tulips."

He knew that, of course. Knew that tulips were her favorite flower and that yellow and blue were her favorite colors, had personally gone to the best flower shop in the city that had closed just for him, had hand-picked each tulip so that they looked the freshest.

He had put his heart into the bouquet, even though he knew his mother wouldn't notice.

"I'm leaving for a retreat tomorrow," he added as he looked for a pair of scissors. "And then a concert overseas. I'll be back in a few weeks."

She fumbled in the side table's drawers for her wallet, then cast him her first direct look and a brief smile. "That's great, Winter!" she exclaimed. "You're going to be amazing."

No questions about what the retreat was for or where he'd be. No questions about his concert. No *Be safe!* or *Bring a jacket!* At least keeping Panacea a secret from her would be easy. He kept a straight face as he cut the stems of the flowers and arranged them in the way he knew she preferred. "You know that billionaire guy from the UK? Eli Morrison?"

"Mm-hmm?"

"I'll be performing for his daughter for her birthday," he said.

"Oh?" Mom turned slightly to look at him with a raised eyebrow, her wallet now in hand. She switched back to Mandarin. "Nǐ gēn tā hǎo le?" *You're dating her?*

He laughed. "No. I'm just the entertainment."

"Ah, xióng bǎobǎo." *Ah, baby bear.* She dropped her wallet into her purse. "Zǒng huì yǒu yì tiān, nǐ zhǎo dào shì hé de nü péng yǒu." *Someday you'll find the right girl.*

There she was, half listening to him as always, assuming that he just dated girls, answering him but not really taking in what he was telling her. Winter bit his tongue as he turned on the kitchen's faucet and filled up the vase. "No, I'm not trying to date her," he explained again. "It's just a really great opportunity, and I think I'll meet some important people at the parties during the week. It's a big celebration."

Back to English. "Sounds like it!"

He sighed as he walked over to the living room and carefully cleared a space on the coffee table for the flower vase. "Nín haí hǎo ba, Mom?" *You're doing well, Mom?* It was his way of asking if she was taking her medication regularly.

"Haí hǎo," she said. "I'm taking a trip later today to New York for the week, with some friends."

Of course she was. He hadn't even seen Mom wheel out her suitcase. Knowing her, she'd probably made the decision to go just this morning.

"Sounds fun," he replied, pushing aside a small stack of magazines on the couch to sit down.

She smiled at him again as she took out her phone. "What have you been up to?"

His latest album had just come out a month ago, and he'd done a national tour for it. He'd broken records with it. He'd been on every talk show, day and night, had graced the covers of *Rolling Stone* and *Vogue* and *GQ* and a dozen other magazines.

Mom hadn't asked about any of it, hadn't even sent him a congratulatory message.

Artie used to endure long interrogations from her about where he was going and for how long. Knowing now what Artie really did for a living, Winter felt even more impressed that his brother had managed to keep his secret from their mother.

Winter wouldn't have any such trouble.

As a kid, he had sometimes screamed in her face about it. *I'm right here! Why can't you see me?* But he was nineteen now and just didn't have the heart for it anymore. He knew this was her way around him, that she willfully ignored what was happening in his life in an attempt to protect herself.

He knew it was because he looked exactly like his father, her second husband, the man she had fallen wildly in love with and divorced in the span of a year. Whom she hated now with every fiber of her heart. He knew that every time she looked at Winter, she saw *him*, that she was reminded not of her son but of a man who used to pick apart everything from her face to her clothes to her words until she became a shell of herself. Winter knew that she'd left him home alone so often because she couldn't bear to be in the same room as him for long. To watch Winter succeed felt a little to her like watching *that man* succeed.

Winter leaned his elbows against his knees and said, "Just the usual. I've been fine."

"Fine's good," Mom said as she came over to sit across from him. "How's Claire?"

"Haí hǎo." *Fine.*

"Still as busy as ever?"

"She's been looking after me well, if that's what you mean."

"Good, good."

Winter stole a glance at her, aching to ask her about Artie. To probe for clues about how his brother had managed to keep everything so under wraps. To see if his mother really hadn't known, when she'd always been so fixated on Artie's life.

But the questions died on his tongue. Even bringing up Artie's name would open a Pandora's Box, and he had no intention of ruining this entire visit.

Instead, Winter dug into his back pocket and pulled out a red envelope, perfectly crisp. He handed it to his mother.

"Oh, baby bear," she said, tilting her head at him and shaking her head. She smiled. "I'm supposed to be giving *you* hóng bāo."

"Nah. I'm an adult, Mom," he said, dipping his head to her once. It was his habit, the flowers and the red envelope, every time he was about to leave town for a while. After her divorce and Artie's death, after the lengthy trauma had triggered in her endless sleepless nights and an inability to settle for longer than an hour, a therapist had suggested flowers for her as a calming ritual. So Winter brought them whenever he could. The red envelope was carefully stuffed with a couple thousand dollars in crisp new bills because he knew his mother's aversion to cash with any wrinkles on it. Once, she had gotten stranded in France after being unable to find a bank that could give her new bills. Winter had flown there himself to deliver her the money and help her get sorted.

Besides, it was an excuse for Winter to see her. This was the only way he knew how to visit. If he didn't, she would never ask for him, never come over, never call. Never miss him. At least their frequent farewells gave him an excuse to bring gifts over.

Mom looked at him for a moment with that wistful, searching expression, then took the envelope. "Duì nǐ mā zhēn hǎo," she said, patting his cheek. *You're good to your mother.* He felt himself lean into the coolness of her touch.

"What are you doing in New York?" he asked.

"Having some fun, letting off some steam. I'm going to see this amazing new Broadway show, *Highland Street Hustle*, that everyone's been talking about, and then head to a rental house upstate." She made a *tsk* sound. "My friends all ask about you. Katie wants to know if her daughter Emma can get a signed album from you, and I told her yes."

"Of course."

"Thank you, baby bear. I think you'd like Emma. She's a nice girl, and get this—she also interned for a summer in Baltimore, just like you did in senior year. I should tell her, she'd love—"

"No, don't."

"Why not?"

"Because I didn't."

"Yes, you did."

Winter cleared his throat gently. "I didn't go to Baltimore. That was Artie."

His mother's frenetic movements by the side table suddenly paused, and when he looked over at her, she had her eyes fixed on him for the first time since he'd arrived, her entire body rigid like she was an insect trapped in amber. Her eyes widened as she realized her mistake.

"Oh," she murmured. "Duì, Artie did."

Winter shuffled uncomfortably, hating that he had to bring his brother up. There was nothing new about Mom mixing up his past with his late brother's—she frequently confused Winter's birthday with Artie's, substituted Artie's favorite foods and clothes and haunts in place of Winter's. It had worsened considerably after Artie's death. But Winter still hated that even the mere mention of Artie's name could get his mother to halt in her tracks and forget everything else, when nothing he said or did could make her stop and pay attention to him.

Then he felt like an asshole for being jealous of his dead brother. His Peace-Corps-turned-secret-agent brother. His emotions roiled in a familiar storm.

"I'm sorry," Mom said now, and this time she genuinely meant it. He could see the grief flood into her eyes, shrouding the restless energy that had danced in them just moments earlier. "I knew, I just—"

"Méi shì, Mom," he interjected, giving her as carefree a smile as he could muster. *It's okay.* "Emma sounds nice. Send me your rental house's address. I'll ask Claire to post the album to you."

"Thank you." His mother hesitated, her expression suddenly lost, and he felt his heart lurch in sadness. He could still remember that fateful phone call Mom had gotten at exactly six in the morning, could recall the time on his clock as he rushed out of his bedroom to the balcony at the sound of her scream. He had pressed his face against the banisters as he listened to her broken, trembling questions drift up from below. *How? When? What happened? Are you sure it was him?*

Since that day, Winter had never been able to sleep past six.

As much as he missed Artie, he knew his grief couldn't compare to his mother's, to how she had crumpled to the floor at the news of Artie's death, to the smallness of her figure curled alone in her bed in the months that followed, the bottles of antidepressants and methylphenidate sitting open on her dresser. How she had been so lost in her sorrow that she never even noticed when Winter would sneak some of her pills to suppress his own pain. Sometimes he imagined her as a young woman cradling a newborn Artie in her arms, marveling over every tiny feature of her firstborn son. Kissing his eyelids, his nose, his little mouth, his perfect fingers. Of her delicate voice singing him lullabies, promising him the whole world. He pictured her in what must have been those heady first days of love and tried to remind himself to be gentle to her, this woman who had to endure losing that baby boy decades later. Who would never know who he'd really been or why he had really died.

Winter tried not to wonder whether she remembered she had a second baby.

Now his mother's gaze broke away from him. A small shiver seemed to course through her body, and then her hands were moving again. She grabbed the keys from the side table and adjusted the tote on her arm. As she did, Winter stood up to leave. Neither one of them said a word.

Winter reminded her too much of everything. Of her awful, short-lived second marriage. Of the second husband she loathed. But worst of all, of the fact that her beloved firstborn son was forever gone, and that only Winter, her afterthought, remained.

As they stepped out of the apartment together and his mother locked the door behind them, she stretched up to plant a quick kiss on his forehead. Even now, she didn't look directly at him.

"Lù shàng xiǎo xīn, xióng bǎobǎo," she said. *Take care of yourself, baby bear.* Her eyes were already turning away, her body angled toward the elevator as if she had finally reached the limit for the amount of time she could spend around him.

He could command the attention of ninety thousand people in an arena, could attract screaming throngs whenever he stepped out any door, could be on the covers of every magazine in the world. And yet he could never convince his mother to stay.

"You too, Mom," he said, his hands in his pockets. "Love you."

She gave him a smile over her shoulder and waved at him. He didn't hear her say it back. Then she was gone, hurrying toward the elevator, leaving nothing but the faint scent of jasmine perfume on the air.

Winter stood there for a long moment, his heart still struggling in his throat, feeling the crush of loneliness curl its cold fingers around him. He pictured the vase of tulips back inside his mother's apartment, beautifully fresh blooms that no one would appreciate, ready to spend the week alone, dying. By the time his mother came back from New York, they would be dead.

He shivered, suddenly missing the company of his entourage. Of the roar of the crowd. Of anyone.

As if on cue, his phone buzzed in his pocket. When he pulled it out, he saw an incoming call from Claire.

"What's up?" he said, his voice hoarse.

"This new girl you hired," Claire said, sounding slightly irritated. "Did you tell her to meet up with us for lunch today? Because she's at my door and asking where you are. She's cute, and she looks like she could kill someone."

Sydney. Winter felt the shards of his grief retreat a bit, and the bubble of a laugh rising in his throat. Sydney really wasted no time getting on the nerves of others in his circle.

"I did," he sighed into the phone. "And I'm on my way."

"I'll order your usual," Claire said. "Don't take too long picking your outfit. Love you."

She hung up before he could say anything back. Winter stared at his phone, the weight of being alone momentarily lifted by the relentless cheer in Claire's voice. The ease with which she showed him affection.

He could never understand how she always knew when he needed her.

He slid the phone back in his pocket and headed for the stairs, leaving his mother's empty apartment behind.

Rules of the Game

One floor below the Panacea Group's Experimental Design level was a massive, underground training area. Running around the circular space was a fifty-foot-wide tunnel with a track on the ground and on its walls, designed for agents to practice driving and riding techniques. The main floor was split into quadrants, and those quadrants then equally split into various habitats, spaces that simulated extreme heat or cold or humidity or dryness, complete darkness or baking sunlight, every environment they could think of in order to push their agents to their limits. There were physical therapy training areas and gyms, matted spaces for learning martial arts and self-defense.

There was everything.

The first time Sydney had ever visited this space was when she was fifteen, two months after she officially joined Panacea, determined to become the best agent they'd ever had. Sauda had shown her around the area herself, watching Sydney's stunned expression as a young teen, the hungry way her eyes took in everything around her. She had trained relentlessly down here, earning her entry into specific quadrants and environments, graduating into levels of weaponry and vehicles and combat. She had survived an immersive course where they'd transformed the entire space into a realistically functioning city of spies and assassins, had spent six months living in that simulation and come out of it so entrenched that sometimes she still felt like she was living in that fictional world.

Sydney had studied for two years down here.

Winter would spend a week. And she was in charge of getting him up to speed.

Maybe that was also why she felt a little resentment toward him, she realized as she watched him step out of the elevator to meet her on the main training floor, his hair casually swept up and his hands in the pockets of his black sweats, his gaze skipping sharply around the vast space. Life seemed to have handed him shortcuts for everything.

His eyes locked on her. A smile twitched at the edge of his lips before he forced it away and held up his phone.

"What does *huyl* mean?" he asked, glancing at the text message Sydney had sent him minutes earlier.

"Hurry up, you're late," she replied.

He nodded. "Very intuitive," he said.

She ignored his sarcasm and stared at the neon yellow words emblazoned in a stylishly bold font across his black sweatshirt.

I'M A SPY

She raised a withering eyebrow at him. "Really?" she muttered.

He looked down at his sweatshirt, then back up at her. "What?" he said innocently. "It's from Balmain's new Fall collection."

Sydney pushed down an urge to deck him.

As with his first meeting, his presence seemed to draw the attention of everyone in the space. She could see a few workers walking the floor shift slightly in his direction, their conversations hitching for a moment to take notice of him. Two agents currently gearing up for a test drive paused to turn toward him. Then they all continued about their business, but not without full awareness that Winter Young was down here.

Not that he seemed to notice or care.

"Come with me," Sydney replied as she turned away from him and walked off toward the east quadrant. "And don't touch anything."

He gave her a teasing nod and followed obediently.

Secretly, she was grateful to look away. She'd felt his magnetic pull in her gut just like everyone else had, and it irked her.

"So, you're training me," he added. "Who trained you?"

"He's dead now."

Beside her, Winter stopped in his tracks.

"I'm kidding," she said. "Sauda taught me."

There was something so satisfying about the way his pretty lips tightened in exasperation.

"Oh good," he muttered. "I'm excited about an entire week of this from you."

Instead of following in her wake, he came up to walk alongside her, and for a moment, their shoulders brushed. Even with the simple motion of his stride, she could tell that he was a performer. Every part of him screamed grace. Details about him from her research flitted through her head. Received formal ballet and street dance training after he was discovered. Studied dance in Russia for six months. Handpicked each of his backup dancers by working individually with them for a day.

"You'll find this week a bit overwhelming," she said. "They don't ease anyone into this, and you'll be getting no ease at all. But I figure you're probably used to that sort of intensity."

At that, he snorted, still seemingly annoyed with her. "And what, exactly, are we doing today?"

"Basics." Sydney led him through an automatic sliding glass door and into a large room, then turned to press her palm against one of the room's walls. Like the office where they'd first met, the wall responded to her touch, a series of buttons popping up on the wall around her hand.

KELLY STREET

KING'S CROSS ST. PANCRAS

WATERLOO

She tapped the first one. The buttons scrolled away. The temperature changed slightly, the air cold and crisp and damp, and the sound of the rest of the training floor cut abruptly off. The walls around them shifted, replaced with a London street—red phone booths on the sidewalks, hanging pots of flowers draping from lampposts, cars and double-decker buses driving by. Even the sounds changed, speakers installed in the ceiling and floor and walls playing all the cacophony of a city street, so that for a moment, it truly seemed like they had stepped into London.

Winter froze for a moment. Sydney watched as he turned in a circle, then let his gaze settle back onto hers, his easy swagger from just seconds ago giving way to an unsettled awe.

Sydney couldn't help softening at his expression. She remembered feeling that way once, the realization that here was a world she could never have dreamed of.

"Basics for you is going to be a bit accelerated," she said. "So, I'm going to start with some universal rules you should always keep in mind as an agent." She folded her arms. "Do you know what your ultimate goal is?"

"To succeed at our mission?" he guessed.

"No." She shook her head. "To come out of it alive. There will always be another mission. But losing an agent is a harder hit than any failed job. You aren't just a life. You're an investment. So everything you'll learn here will be geared toward keeping you unharmed."

Winter's attitude turned sober at that. Sydney watched the light change on his face, the spark of grief that came and went in his eyes, and felt a twinge of pity for him. No doubt his thoughts had gone to his brother.

She nodded to the space around them and shifted the topic. "This is one of our many simulation rooms. I've created some presets for us in various London locales as we go through some situations for you."

He nodded once, turning his back to her again to study the setting. "And what are these universal rules I should start with?"

"First," she replied, "don't ever look behind you. You don't need to. Simply assume that someone is always watching you. Look back, and you clue them in to you being conscious of their presence—and up to something."

At her words, Winter turned back around to face her and tilted his head. "Nothing new to me."

There was something about that head tilt of his that made her want to linger on him. She looked away. "Second," she went on, "be prepared. Always. If something goes wrong, be ready to pivot. If something unusual happens, you'll need to adapt in a split second. Harder than it sounds. Think of it as one of your performances. You must have had all sorts of things go awry onstage and been forced to shift midsong."

He nodded stiffly. "What kind of things?"

"Here's an example." She took a few steps away from him, as if walking to the end of the simulated street, and then turned back around.

"Ready?" she asked him.

He didn't seem like it, but to his credit, he lifted his head and gave her a steady nod. "Sure," he replied. "Hit me."

She wanted to smile a little at that, but held it in. Then she headed in his direction like she was a passerby.

As they drew near to each other, Winter started to say, "I hope you know it's been a long time since I was able to walk down a street alone like this—"

Before he could finish his sentence, she pretended to trip and fight for balance, stumbling into him hard enough to make him step back. One of her closed fists came out of her pocket to strike him in the side.

He flinched away from her with a startled gasp. As he did, she widened her eyes and held up her hands at him. "God, I'm sorry!" she exclaimed, then continued hurrying down the path. Then she stopped and turned back around.

She unclenched her other fist to reveal a pen-like weapon in her hand. When she tapped the end of it, a long, needle-thin blade shot out.

"What I just did was exactly how an anarchist assassinated the Empress of Austria in 1898." She compressed the blade back into its holder again. "It only takes the blink of an eye."

She half expected him to pale at her words, but instead, his eyes just fell to the blade in her hand before going back to her face. There was a glimmer of grave awe toward her in his expression, and she wondered when the last time was that he'd been taken completely off guard like this.

"And how should I be constantly prepared for a knife attack?" he asked.

"Your instincts are more valuable than you know. The only difference between a normal person's instincts and an agent's is that an agent is trained to react in more ways. Now, in this scenario, what would your current instincts tell you to do?"

"Run?"

"That's honestly not a bad plan," Sydney answered. "If you can, dodge and run. You're fast, I'll give you that—I've seen your onstage footage enough times."

He gave her an amused smile. "Have you, now?"

Sydney scowled, forcing down a rising flush at his words. "Yes. It's called research for work. Anyway, use your speed to your advantage. Escaping might be your best choice."

He frowned. "And if not?"

"I'll show you." Without warning, she tossed the knife at him.

To her surprise, Winter darted quickly back and caught the knife in one hand.

"Nice reflexes," she said. "Left-handed?"

"Ambidextrous." He glared at her. "Now what?"

"Try to get me."

Winter took a deep breath, then retreated a few steps. He walked toward her in the same nonchalant fashion. Again, Sydney found herself feeling impressed. He had memorized her previous movements, even the way she had blinked and looked around, and replicated it so well that it was as if he had already been trained in this exercise.

As he passed her, he stumbled and fell against her. His right hand flashed as if to attack her with the pen-knife. So he was ambidextrous, after all.

Sydney moved faster than she could think. Her body curved instantly away—in the same move, her arm shot out and seized his wrist in a vise-like grip. She twisted it hard, hearing him grunt, then yanked him toward her while angling backward and pulled his arm into an uncomfortable right angle. Her leg came out to trip him. In the blink of an eye, she had her knee on his chest and the knife at his throat, their faces barely a few inches from each other.

He blinked, stunned momentarily into silence, and she found herself studying his pupils out of habit. They were constricted in pain, revealing all the golden-brown slashes in his irises. His shallow breaths were warm against her skin, and she noted the hard panels of his body as his chest rose and fell beneath her knee. He was staring at her now, truly taking her in—and although she didn't know what he saw, she felt her heart lurch unexpectedly at his attention.

Then he winced, his arm still locked painfully down by her other hand. "Okay," he said hoarsely. "Let go."

She released him, then offered a hand to pull him up. "You practice that for two straight years," she said, "and it becomes a new part of your instincts. Like another immune system."

"Good to know."

"Now you try it."

When Sydney had struggled early on to pick up combat moves, Sauda had reassured her, telling her most people took time to train their reactions into instinct.

But when she lunged at Winter this time, he reacted instantly. Each of his moves mimed her earlier ones perfectly, right down to the specific angle of his body and the turn of his arm. He performed it so accurately that she didn't have time to get out of his lock. His leg swept her off her feet.

She fell—and a blink later, she found herself on her back, Winter's knee pressed lightly against her chest, the knife held to her throat.

For a moment, she just stared at him, heart pounding, all sarcasm forgotten. Her lungs squeezed in a painful spasm, and she sucked her breath in sharply. It'd taken her weeks to master those moves. Two years to make them part of her instinct. And this boy had just absorbed them like it was nothing.

Trained dancer, indeed.

"That was almost too good," she muttered.

He winked, then got up, holding a hand out to her. "It's just like learning choreography," he answered.

She narrowed her eyes, studying the brief emotions flitting across his face. He wasn't telling her something.

"You've been attacked by a knife before," she said carefully.

He hesitated, then nodded. "Once," he replied. "Outside an after-party, when a crowd swarmed me and I got separated from my bodyguards. Claire made me take a self-defense course after that."

She frowned. "There was no article about it."

"Because I didn't know I'd been stabbed until Claire got me into our car," he explained. "And I insisted on my private doctor treating me instead of going to a hospital. No word got out."

"You told no one?"

"No one except Claire."

Somehow, she'd thought that a guy like Winter would have wanted to talk to the press about an incident like that to drum up publicity. She wouldn't even have blamed him for it.

Maybe Winter really was private. She analyzed his face, wondering how else to pry him open. Trying not to think about her own encounters with a knife.

"Nice of you not to worry your mom," she finally said, gentler this time.

"She wouldn't have been worried," he answered.

She looked back up at him to see that his smile had taken on a faded quality. "I'm sorry," she decided to reply.

"We're fine."

She studied his expression and filed it routinely away, annoyed by the flicker of sympathy that rose in her chest. These were the kinds of things someone would tell a person they'd consider a friend, and even now, she could sense him letting a little of his wall down to her, confiding something to her that he seemed to hold close to his chest.

But she wasn't his friend. She was an agent training him. So she sighed, then confessed, "Do you see how I asked you those questions?" she asked.

He looked at her, confused by her pivot. "What do you mean?"

"While you were busy practicing my second piece of advice," she said, waving the knife once, "we were also going over my third."

Winter hesitated for a moment before realization dawned in his eyes. "You were interrogating me?"

Sydney nodded. "Being a secret agent is really about building another's trust in you. Every moment is an opportunity for you to get details out of someone about their life, and for them to do the same thing back to you. I made you concentrate on learning how to defend yourself with a knife. Your focus was somewhere else, and I took advantage of that, asked you questions about your past while you were distracted and had let your walls down. So here's my third universal rule. Always make the people around you trust you, and never trust anyone else."

For the first time, there was hurt in his eyes. She had genuinely wounded him. She could see the way something in his gaze shuttered, the slight recoil of his body away from her, the sting of betrayal sharp on his face before he smoothed it over, let his walls come back up again.

She always hated this part of the training, even with someone she disliked. But deception was one of those instincts that had been trained into her, and it kept her cold.

"It's a lonely job," she said, "but you won't realize just *how* lonely it is until you start. You'll learn to cope with it, eventually."

His gaze seared through her now. "Is that why you do your secret breathing exercises?" he asked. "To cope? Or do you have bad lungs?"

Now it was his turn to surprise her. She blinked at him. "What do you mean?"

She could tell from his face that he knew he'd hit on something. When he spoke again, his voice was lower, as if he wanted to make sure no one heard them. "Your breathing exercises. I noticed it from our first meeting—how you take a measured breath through your nose and then exhale twice as slowly through your mouth." He nodded, looking side-long at her. "I was taught the same exercise to strengthen my lungs for my performances. But why do *you* need breathing therapy?"

Well. Sydney reminded herself yet again that Winter wasn't stupid. He had turned the interrogation back around on her, had snapped back at her just as she was pitying him. For a second, she just stared at him.

The memories rushed through her—

—the sound of her mother's labored breathing at the hospital—

—Sydney's persistent chest pains that began in adolescence, worsening whenever she was under extreme stress—

—her diagnosis coming back as her mother's same chronic condition—

—the way she'd struggled for air when her father had once threatened her with a kitchen knife—

The memory disappeared, leaving only an old fear sitting in her chest.

Winter tightened his lips. "Panacea doesn't know, do they?"

Three years, she'd hidden this successfully from everyone at an intelligence agency. How did *he* figure it out? How could he have noticed so quickly?

"Are you suggesting I'm a liar?" she said, her voice low, a thread of anger in it.

He stared straight at her. "I'm suggesting that two can play at your game."

"Creative of you," she replied tersely. "But my lungs are doing just fine."

He studied her. "I won't tell them, you know," he said quietly.

The boy standing before her had the power to end her career right now. To dissolve everything that mattered to her.

Her training kicked in. Her eyes narrowed. Instead of answering, Sydney tossed the knife back at him. "There's nothing to tell," she said.

Winter caught the knife smoothly in one hand and twirled it, as if this was just another dance move he'd been practicing all his life. Then he tossed the knife back. She caught it.

"You learn fast," she said.

"Yes, ma'am," he replied, his gaze still locked on her. "As fast as you can spin a story."

He was poking holes in her shield, hunting for clues about her past as ruthlessly as she had for him. She could feel her heart racing, suddenly that trapped girl again, desperate to escape.

She didn't know if he noticed discomfort in her expression—she doubted it, as she had trained well to keep her emotions off her face. But his words rang in her head as she continued their lesson. She had no idea if he would keep her secret, or if he would run straight to Sauda and Niall after this—and she couldn't bear the idea of asking him to keep it to himself. Admitting it was true.

But whatever the reason, he backed off, then picked up the knife and turned it around in his hand.

"Glad we're in sync," he said.

She understood what he meant. *If I can trust you, you can trust me.*

"Let's keep it that way," she answered.

He smiled a little at her. And when they moved on to the next exercise, he sounded like he always had around her, with no indication that he knew anything about her secret.

She had to be better about keeping her distance. She had to be more careful around this boy.

The Calm Before the Storm

Y ou're seeing someone."

Winter turned an exasperated look toward Dameon as they sat together around the cooker on their table. "No, I'm not," he replied. The Korean barbeque restaurant was bustling with activity, but their corner was quiet, the tables around them taken by security staff while eager onlookers lingered out on the streets. A couple of the fans were wearing sweatshirts emblazoned with the words *I'M A SPY*, a nod to his recent outfit that had quickly become the latest fashion trend.

"Then you're at least thinking about someone," Leo went on. "I can tell."

It was true that he was thinking about someone—specifically, Sydney Cossette—although it certainly wasn't because he wanted to date her. After a week of grueling training, his mind swam with nothing but techniques and strategies and the image of Sydney's cool, steely face. He couldn't stop puzzling over the mystery of her, the way she could pull details from his life just by noting the hesitations in his answers, the scowl she'd given him when he'd confronted her about her breathing techniques. At night, when he had time to work on his music, he found hints of her creeping into the bars and the words, fragments of melodies that reminded him of her.

Not that he could tell any of this to Leo or Dameon. One of Sydney's lessons sprang unbidden into his mind.

Sometimes people just want validation. Give a little to them, and you'll be surprised how much of a conversation you can steer.

So he said, "Fine. It's a girl. But not because I like her."

Leo leaned closer and grinned. "Yes you do."

"I do *not*. She's annoying as hell."

"Like my mama always says—don't lie to me about the truth."

"Wait." Dameon paused as he was flipping their strips of steak on the grill. He pointed the tongs at Winter. "Didn't you just hire a few new security folks? One of them is a girl our age."

"I saw her the other day, having a lunch meeting with Claire." Leo's eyes went wide, then back to Winter. "It's her, isn't it? She's cute."

Dameon whistled, his eyes lingering thoughtfully on Winter. "Body-guard romances are rough."

Winter threw his hands up. "It's not, because there's no romance. I just hate having her around."

"Why?"

"She's . . ." Winter struggled for a descriptor. "Too observant."

Dameon lifted an eyebrow. "She stares at you too much?"

"She makes me feel like I always have something stuck in my teeth."

"So . . . she's just good at her job?"

Leo smiled sidelong at Dameon. "I think it's because she didn't take one look at him and melt. Threw him off his game."

"No one *melts* when I look at them," Winter scoffed, annoyed at the rising flush in his cheeks as he grabbed the tongs and dropped finished strips of steak onto his friends' plates.

"It's like Mexico City all over again," Leo went on. "You remember last year, when we were there? Winter woke up late after our concert."

"I never wake up late," Winter replied. He wrapped a small piece of steak in a thin slice of pickled radish and popped it in his mouth, savoring the burst of flavors.

"You *were* late, though," Leo insisted. "That's why I remember that morning. *Because* you were late to practice, and because I found that weird."

"I wasn't *that* late. Our set just ran over the night before," Winter answered. "You don't remember?"

"Four encores," Leo said. "I remember."

"We were up till five at the hotel. Max ran tlacoyos upstairs for us from that stand at the corner down the road." He snapped his fingers twice, as if trying to remember the street names.

"Tonalá and Campeche," Dameon recalled serenely from Winter's other side as he doled out more cooked meat onto each of their plates.

"And then you didn't go back to your room," Leo added with a sly grin.

"I did," Winter said.

"No you didn't," Leo pressed. He peered at him through his mess of thick curls. "Because they dropped off a sleep mask for you to my room by accident and I walked it over to your room, and you weren't there."

"I was probably passed out," he said.

"Not the way I was pounding on your door, you weren't." Leo pointed a finger at Winter. "You went off to that girl's place," he said. "Mercedes. Our opening act. Five in the morning, and you left the hotel on your own, came back in a cab. I *knew* you were still seeing her back then. Every time you're in Mexico City, isn't that right?"

"I didn't go to her place," Winter said with a glare. A pause. Then he muttered, "I didn't want people finding out where she lived."

Leo clapped his hands in delight, like a little brother who'd just solved a mystery. "Rented a private estate somewhere with her, then."

"How is any of this like what happened in Mexico City?" Winter protested.

"Because you couldn't stand Mercedes either during practice. You two were practically screaming at each other. And then that turned into you both shoving your tongues down each other's throats."

Dameon laughed a little, but his eyes were still following Winter, studying him in that quiet way of his. Winter tried to ignore it, but he could feel the heat on the back of his neck. Dameon always had that way about him; it'd been part of the reason they'd gotten so close so quickly.

He could sense all the small disturbances in Winter's mood—when he'd had a bad conversation with his mother, when he didn't get enough rest on tour, when he wasn't up for a press junket day. It both unsettled and comforted him, made him want to confess his secrets.

Winter knew Dameon could sense something off about him now, too. But when he spoke, he just went along with Leo's train of thought.

"Damn, boy," Dameon said. "You had it bad for her. Can't blame you." He nudged Winter, making him spill a bit of the soju he was sipping. "Just like in New Orleans. Who was that girl you brought to my mama's barbecue?"

"Aleksa," Winter said, putting his glass down and wiping his shirt.

Dameon snapped his fingers. "Aleksa," he said. "Hottest human I've ever seen in my life."

"Really?" Winter nudged Dameon back, hard, in the ribs. "What about that guy who came with us to Italy?"

"Jinhai? I guess." Dameon lifted an eyebrow at him. "Almost as pretty as you."

Winter rolled his eyes at the way his friend skirted around their past in front of Leo. He could still remember the first night he visited Dameon in his hotel room. It was on their second tour together, when the pressure on Winter was keeping him up at all hours. Before Dameon opened his door on that sleepless night, Winter had only meant to have a heart-to-heart with him, had been looking for a kindred soul—or, at least, a sleeping pill. Instead, he'd taken one look at Dameon still dressed in a crumpled, half-buttoned collared shirt and ripped jeans, his dreads tied casually up, his expression unsurprised as if he'd been expecting Winter to show up all along . . . well, in the end, they had ended up in bed together. They'd carried on every night for several weeks before ending it, both too stressed out by the weight of a secret relationship interfering with their work. Since then, they'd settled into friendship, the kind you could only have with someone who knew you like no one else.

Now he could feel Dameon still studying him, trying to figure out his mood. "You keep in touch with him?" he asked, as if trying to change the subject. "It's been years."

"Nah." Dameon shook his head. "It's too bad. My mama liked him."

"You know why you two aren't in long-term relationships?" Leo said, unaware of the secrets being passed back and forth between them.

"Because we're never in the same city for longer than a month?" Dameon suggested.

"No, because you don't know how to cook."

"You're not in a long-term relationship, either," Winter said.

Leo ignored him blithely. "You can't even make toast."

Winter jabbed a defensive finger at Leo. "That was only because I didn't have a toaster and I was making it in a pan."

"You did set off the entire hotel's fire alarms," Dameon admitted.

Leo shook his head. "All my tías would be disappointed in you both."

Winter smiled winsomely at him. "Your aunts absolutely love that we don't know how to cook for ourselves."

"More than they love me, that's for sure," Leo retorted, although there was a small grin on his lips, too, knowing that wasn't true. Winter had seen for himself how Leo's family fussed over him, and the suitcases of gifts he'd bring home for them in turn.

"I'm going to teach you both how to cook a good stew on our next tour," Leo went on, eliciting groans from the other two as if this conversation had happened before. "No, listen—trust me. My mama always said, you learn how to make a good pozole, you'll get anyone to commit."

As Leo and Dameon fell into an argument about pozole, Winter allowed himself a slow breath. At least their brief interest in Sydney's relationship with him had been sidetracked; at least Dameon had finally spared him and turned his curious eyes away. And at least Sydney wasn't here tonight—she wouldn't start guarding Winter until tomorrow, when they left for London. But it bothered him how easily Leo had been able to read him, how Dameon had known immediately that something was different, even if he couldn't guess exactly why.

It didn't seem to matter that Sydney wasn't physically here. He couldn't get her out of his head, her piercing gaze or the frown that lingered on her lips, the sharpness of her tongue or the slight thrill of fear he felt every time he was near her.

How had a girl like her stumbled into an agency like Panacea, anyway?

Winter's eyes instinctively found Claire, who was already looking in his direction from the adjacent table. She tilted her head questioningly at him, then mouthed, *You can head out.*

He gave her a weary nod, grateful she could read his mind. Briefly, he recalled the incident when he'd been stabbed. He'd been so keen on getting out of the mob and into his waiting car that he didn't even feel the ache in his side. Claire had been the one to point out the blood soaking his shirt inside the car. He could still hear her horrified gasp, could remember collapsing weakly into her arms as he bled all over her hands.

No, he could remember pleading with her. *Not the hospital.* Not because he didn't want them to treat him—but because he was afraid of the possibility that it would be all over the news and yet his mother still wouldn't bother reading about it, that she wouldn't show up to visit him there.

His eyes turned to the windows, toward the streets shrouded in night. For a moment, the sounds around him felt muted, and the images of those he knew—Leo and Dameon arguing, Claire discussing strategy with her team—felt far away, a safe space he somehow couldn't reach.

By this time tomorrow, he would be in London. From then on, he would be out in the darkness of the field, unable to confide in anyone except a girl who seemed to want nothing to do with him. He wasn't even sure he would return.

Sydney's words from his training week echoed in his mind.

It's a lonely job, but you won't realize just how *lonely it is until you start.*

He could already feel it. And somehow, it was familiar.

MISSION LOG

AGENT B: "Just be happy they're cooperating with each other."

AGENT A: "I *am* happy."

AGENT B: "Oh. A scowl is a confusing way to signal that."

AGENT A: "I'm just concerned."

AGENT B: "About them getting along?"

AGENT A: "About the Orange Alert."

AGENT B: "We get an Orange Alert every year over something or other. The cafeteria staffer has already been arrested and interrogated. Nothing was taken from our servers."

AGENT A: "Look, I'm not saying to cancel every mission over an Orange Alert."

AGENT B: "You're worried about ███████."

AGENT A: "I know we've sent her into bad situations before. But it's one thing to tail ██ ██████████, and another to do it after a security breach at headquarters."

AGENT B: "Shall I pull them?"

AGENT A: "No. This is just me fretting to you."

AGENT B: "I was going to call ████████████ in London, tell them to keep a closer eye on our pair once they arrive. Don't worry. We'll get a full brief on the breach tonight."

AGENT A: "Good. Thank you."

AGENT B: "Are you all right?"

AGENT A: "Fine."

AGENT B: "I know that look, and I say this with love. She's not your daughter."

AGENT A: "Believe me, I've never been more relieved about anything in my life."

Monsters Look Like Gentlemen

t never ceased to surprise Sydney how wildly different her pickups went for various missions. A year ago, she'd climbed into a jeep at four in the morning, disguised as cleaning crew, at a military base overlooking the dark tropical seas surrounding the Kwajalein Atoll in the Marshall Islands. Seven months ago, she'd hopped into the back of a rickshaw while arguing in French with the driver as they left the bank of the Congo River in Kinshasa, while a protest rippled around them between a luxury development's security guards and the fishing village downstream.

Today she was dressed in a black suit more expensive than her monthly rent, disembarking from a private jet at London Heathrow with a superstar named Winter Young; his manager, Claire; two of his backup dancers; and four other security guards.

It was early evening, and the prelude to a storm was starting to drizzle across the tarmac. The edges of the sky were awash in tones of deep purple and blue. Attendants lined up at the bottom of the stairway, and as Winter emerged from the jet with his entourage, they took their items and shuttled them to a black sedan. Clean wet cloths were handed to them, along with refreshing spritzers and a set of luxury toiletries. There was even a shoe shiner at the sedan's door, giving each of them a quick polish on their boots before they headed into the car.

As they waited to enter, Sydney saw Winter tilt his head up to the sky and savor the feeling of rain sprinkling on his face. There was something endearing about the gesture that made her smile. A pair of aviators tinted the skin around his closed eyes a faint green. Under a draped peacoat, his collared shirt was rumpled as if he'd slept in it—the sleeves pushed haphazardly up to his elbows and exposing the geometric lines of his tattoos, his collar's top buttons still undone—and his hair was the perfect level of mess. His trousers were clearly designer, tailored perfectly to end just above his ankles. He both looked like he'd literally rolled out of bed, and somehow also better than at any point over the past week, which she found truly insufferable after a ten-hour flight.

He caught her expression. "What?"

Her smile wavered. She snapped back to herself. "Nothing," she said.

They all piled in. Leo whistled appreciatively as they slid into the plush leather seats. "My aunties want me to bring back some chocolate for them," he said to Claire. "Think we can make a detour?"

Claire lifted an eyebrow at him. "Noted. Any special requests?"

"Cadbury Twirls," Leo said.

"Anyone else?" Claire said as she tapped on her phone.

"Yorkies," Dameon answered.

"Galaxy bars," Winter added. "Kinder Buenos."

"Just Necco Wafers," Sydney said. "If you can find them here."

They all looked her way.

Dameon blinked at her. "Necco Wafers?"

"Yeah."

"You're the only person I know who eats those," Leo said. "Don't they taste like chalk?"

"I like them," she replied.

Winter shrugged. "Leave her alone," he said, returning to his scribbles.

She smiled a little at their reactions. As if to prove it, she pulled out a roll of Necco Wafer candies she usually kept in her pocket, then held it out.

Everyone shook their heads politely.

Sydney popped a wafer into her mouth, crunching idly. "More for me, I guess."

Leo and Dameon fell into a low conversation about something, while the other guards sat in silence and ignored her. Sydney ignored them in return as she fiddled with the waxy paper of the candy roll. Her eyes settled again on Winter, who was leaned back, left leg resting across his right knee, and lost in concentration as he scribbled on a well-worn notepad. Writing music, she assumed. She had to hand it to him, at least—the boy worked with an intensity that surprised her, had trained with her with the laser focus of someone used to throwing his entire being into his craft. Maybe he would even remember everything she'd taught him.

She felt the familiar itch to steal something, and her gaze lingered on his notebook.

His eyes flickered to her, as if he'd heard her thoughts. She looked quickly away, pushed down the urge, and bit down on another Necco Wafer.

"We land," Claire was saying now, looking at none of them as she scanned her phone, "we get picked up to head to the place Eli Morrison has set you up in, and then we head out for dinner at six."

Sydney analyzed Claire as the woman went on. As good as she was at talking, she could tell Claire wasn't a natural speaker. Not an extrovert, either. She noticed it in the way the woman didn't seem to know exactly what to do with her hands when talking to others, so instead she'd clutch her phone at all times as an unconscious comfort.

Her gaze darted to the two backup dancers sitting with Winter. It was jarring to see such attractive boys all in a row. She knew the one to Winter's left was named Leonardo Medina Santiago, handsome and cheery, the youngest of a family of four who—she'd learned while doing research on Winter's crew—had given up an offer to attend Stanford University in order to pursue his dream of being on a stage, much to the anguish of his parents. She studied how his body twitched with restless energy, how he leaned in toward Winter. His confidence was genuine, the kind that came out of a solid family.

The other was Dameon Carter, hazel-eyed, long and lean with dreadlocks, prettier than he was handsome, a Black boy from New Orleans who had five younger brothers—which might explain the endless amount of patience he seemed to have. Dameon lounged quietly on Winter's other side, his eyes closed, content to listen as Leo rambled on. Whenever Winter laughed or answered, his eyes would slit open, as if pulled by his presence. There was some kind of past there between him and Winter, and a serenity about the boy that intrigued Sydney, particularly because he also still seemed to notice everything.

Finally, Dameon looked at her and said, "I apologize on behalf of these knuckleheads, Ashley." He tilted his gaze in the others' direction. "And that you have to put up with Winter from now on."

Ashley, her cover name. Sydney smiled at Dameon. "Believe me, I've seen it all in this line of work."

Leo leaned forward conspiratorially toward her. "You've got to have some stories to share with us, right?" he murmured to her with a wink. "Adventures in guarding folks?"

"Oh," Sydney replied. "Do I ever."

Leo laughed. "I've never been more excited to be traveling with you all."

Dameon looked curiously at her. "How old *are* you, anyway? How many assignments could you have had?"

Sydney smiled a little at him. "You'd be surprised."

Claire raised an eyebrow at them from over her phone. "Ashley came recommended to us by Elite Securities," she said. "You boys behave yourselves around her. And I mean it." She glanced at Ashley, her own gaze wary. "I was told she's one of their best bodyguards. Winter convinced me to bring her on. Now leave her alone. She's here to make sure you all stay safe."

Leo whistled a little. "Elite Securities. Best in the business."

"That's no joke," Dameon added, looking impressed. "I heard you all trained in the marines."

Winter leaned on his knees. "So best be careful with what you reveal around her," he said. "She catches everything."

Sydney narrowed her eyes at him. He still hadn't entirely forgiven her for their training sessions. "I'd say it's my job to notice you, Mr. Young," she replied.

Winter smiled innocently at her. "And?"

And you look like the hottest damn person who's ever existed. The honest answer shot unbidden into her mind.

She loathed that she could feel a slight flush rising on her cheeks—especially since she knew he was trying to get a rise out of her.

So instead, she said coolly, "And you should update your cologne. It's awful."

It wasn't—it made him smell like a dream. But Dameon let out a low whistle and exchanged a knowing look with Leo, then glanced at Winter.

Winter just settled back into his seat and looked away with a scowl.

The rest of the ride passed uneventfully. The wet streets of London blurred by outside the windows, the cacophony of tall red buses and motorbikes, ambulances and crowds mixing into a steady ambience. Sydney's fingers toyed with the roll of wafers in her pocket as she reviewed their plan in her head.

An hour later, they pulled onto a rain-washed path in Kensington. The car dropped off Leo and Dameon at a complex reserved for them and several other crew. Then it stopped before an elegant, Georgian-style estate, the bare limbs of a wisteria plant climbing across its white stone façade.

Two men in black suits were already waiting for them here. As they stepped out, one of the men came over to hold a hand out at them.

"This way, please," the guard said.

They followed him through wrought-iron gates to the front entrance, a black rectangle twice as tall as she was. The man pushed the door open, and it revealed what looked like a dream.

No matter how many times Sydney ran missions for Panacea in rich neighborhoods, she would never get used to setting foot in houses as glamorous as this. Sydney had grown up in a two-bedroom shack of a place, the curtains all rotted away, the carpet dotted with black mold from the time their home's ground floor had flooded during a winter storm.

This place was bigger than any residence in London should be. The main foyer opened to a wide room with a back wall made entirely of glass that stretched all the way up to the third floor. From the inside, Sydney could look through it to a huge, elegantly manicured garden. A waterfall curtain ran down one section of the glass wall, trickling into an indoor infinity pool that ran the back width of the house. The pool was designed in such a way that someone could swim in the cozy warmth of the indoors while watching the rain outside. Before the glass wall and the pool, a dramatic staircase of smooth white stone coiled up, spiraling around a modern chandelier of dripping crystals.

Beside her, Claire made a sound of approval at the space. Winter studied the home with a careful eye. Sydney realized to her annoyance that a space like this must be second nature to him, that his own home probably contained similar luxuries.

A man's voice drifted to them from somewhere in the living room that they couldn't see, calling for them to step in. Sydney felt the hairs stand up on the back of her neck. As they made their way down the rest of the foyer and into the living room, she found herself staring straight at two figures seated on a curving couch on the right side of the fireplace.

Eli Morrison and Penelope were already here. Before them on the low table lay an elegant feast—dishes of fresh caviar, slices of iced fruit, carefully cut meats, artfully plated meals of filet mignon and lobster. Glasses of champagne that looked like they'd just been poured.

Claire leaned over to them. "Nix the dinner at six," she whispered. "I guess we're eating now."

Sydney felt a lurch in her chest. Eli Morrison waited for no one. He was a billionaire, and plenty of people greeted guests for him so that he didn't have to.

But here he was, in the flesh, ready and waiting with his daughter. The man looked tall and fit, with a deep tan and a head of silver hair and wrinkles in his smile. He wore a luxurious linen shirt underneath a perfectly tailored suit, and his hands sat easily in his pockets, giving him an easy sort of confidence. Behind his glasses was a glimmer in his eye and a warmth that, if Sydney had known nothing about him, she would have found genuine.

Now all she could do was imagine that glimmer in his gaze while he oversaw the torture of a hostage. While he snapped his fingers and ordered the execution of an entire family.

She noted an attendant standing in the corner, waiting to fulfill any request. Two more stood near a large sliding glass door that led to the gardens. She had no doubt there were guards stationed throughout the house.

Eli Morrison gave them a smile and stood up. Penelope did the same, her hands wringing nervously.

"Well!" he said. His voice was quiet and kind, not what Sydney was expecting. Chills ran down her spine. "I imagine the city's traffic must have you both in a mood. Hopefully your temporary home will soothe that."

Winter smiled at him. "I'll say."

Sydney let herself stand a little closer to Winter. Let Eli think that Sydney was playing the role of a good bodyguard. Beside her father, Penelope Morrison uncrossed her arms as they drew near. Now Sydney could see that the girl was shaking slightly, her smile oscillating between excited and terrified. Her hand repeatedly tucked her hair behind her ear even though there were no loose strands. Her eyes looked glossy with excited tears, her gaze hooked on Winter as if she was physically incapable of turning away.

His biggest fan, indeed.

When she glanced at Winter, he seemed at ease, completely unbothered. No doubt used to this kind of reaction.

Eli smiled at the superstar. "Winter Young," he said, offering a hand to him. "I'd like to extend to you and your team my deepest thanks for fitting us into your busy schedule. I like to make sure I know anyone in this world worth knowing—and I'd say you're at the top of that list for a lot of people."

To Sydney's relief, Winter didn't miss a beat. He took a step forward, returned the man's smile, and shook his outstretched hand. "The honor's mine, sir," he answered. "If I'd known you were going to greet us here yourself, I'd be much more anxiously dressed."

Eli laughed, waving Winter's deference away. "And what does that look like, Mr. Young?"

Winter glanced to Eli's side and met Penelope's gaze for the first time. She startled. "A guy trying to make a good first impression," he said, giving her his polite, secret smile.

She looked away from his gaze immediately, as if she couldn't bear it. Her eyes wandered instead to Sydney. Sydney offered her a courteous nod.

"This is my daughter, Penelope Morrison," Eli said, squeezing the girl's shoulder affectionately. Sydney noted that Penelope didn't respond to the gesture. "She's been talking my ear off about you for years."

Winter gave her a bow of his head. "What an honor, Miss Morrison," he said to her.

"Oh!" she breathed, and for a moment, she seemed at a loss for words. "The honor's mine," she managed. Her voice was trembling a little, but otherwise it sounded high and clear. "I've been a fan of yours since your first single." Her nervous smile returned. "I love everything you've ever put out."

Winter laughed a little in surprise, as if this was the first time he'd ever heard such a compliment. "That means a lot, coming from you," he replied, and she blushed so red that Sydney thought she might buckle.

Winter glanced at Sydney. "This is Ashley Miller, one of my best bodyguards." Then he nodded at Claire, who offered them both a polite smile. "And Claire Richardson, my manager."

"Of course," Eli Morrison said, giving Claire a respectful nod of his head. "Please, sit. Eat. Make yourself at home."

"It's the best celebration we'll attend all year," Claire replied, sweeping her hands in front of her in an elaborate gesture. She took a spoonful of caviar and heaped it onto a tiny toast. "Winter's excitement at your invitation was something to behold."

"We've attended several of your concerts, you know," Eli told Winter as they sat down. Beside him, Penelope nodded, her lips pressed together. "You put on an impressive show."

"Thank you." Winter said with a shy smile. "I do my best."

"I think I enjoyed your performances almost as much as she did," Eli said with a laugh. Penelope fiddled with the edge of her dress. "You're one of the only things we can agree on, Mr. Young."

"I'm flattered," Winter said.

"And when should we expect to see you next?" Claire said to Eli. "I want to make sure we're ready for our next encounter."

Sydney felt a rush of affection for the woman. Claire couldn't seem to care less that she was talking to a billionaire—she was cool and unbothered all the same.

"I'll look forward to your presence at the concert," Eli said.

Penelope took out a little yellow card and pen from her pocket. When she flipped the card over, Sydney saw that it was a portrait of Winter. "I was wondering if I could get your autograph?" she asked hesitantly. "Maybe a photo?"

As Winter got up to accept her card and take a picture with her, Sydney's eyes flickered to Eli. The man was staring at her. He offered her a kind smile. "You must be very good at your job," he said, "to be the only bodyguard that Winter Young chose to have with him."

Sydney studied the man's expression behind his glasses. He would expect her, a lowly security hire, to defer to him without cowering. So she lowered her eyes, then said, "I assure you I'll keep him safe, sir."

"And how old are you?" he asked.

"Nineteen, sir."

"Nineteen," he mused. "Just about the same as Penny, then." His eyes flickered briefly to his daughter, who was fixing her hair as she pressed against Winter for a photo. "American?"

"From Houston, Texas, born and raised."

"Ah, a Texan. Suburb?"

He was testing her for lies, Sydney realized, looking for holes in her answers. Behind his kind façade was the man she was looking for, the one who could ship tons of illegal chemical weapons across borders. But Sydney just replied obediently, following her cover, careful to look like she was pleased by his attention. "Pearland, sir. Attended Shadow Creek High School."

"Pearland." He nodded. "One of my directors grew up there. What brought you into the security world?"

Nearby, Winter said something to Penelope in her ear and she let out a tiny gasp behind her hand. They both laughed quietly. At least he was playing his part well so far.

"I'd actually hoped to join the navy," Sydney said to Eli, "but got kicked out of boot camp for, uh, poor behavior. I worked security in a parking lot for a while before getting accepted into a bodyguard training program."

"In Houston?"

He was mapping out her past and storing it away for future reference in case she ever said something that didn't match. "Out in San Diego, sir," she said.

The man raised an amused eyebrow at her. "Did the navy kick you out for picking fights?"

"Yes, sir." Sydney pretended to blush in shame.

"Claire told me you came from Elite Securities," Eli went on, his eyes still searching her. "Impressive, and so young."

"She did," Claire confirmed, sounding nearly defensive.

"And what brought you to them?"

Even for a trained agent, Sydney felt the pressure of his quiet interrogation. Winter looked over at her for the first time since he'd joined Penelope's side. Behind his cheery exterior, she could see him shoot Eli a wary glance. So, he sensed an underlying menace to the man's tone, too.

"They were aggressively recruiting people like me," Sydney replied.

"People like you?"

"Young women, sir," she said. "We are a very trendy security hire this year, as our presence tends to blend more seamlessly in at formal events."

"Yes, I know." Eli nodded. "I've hired a few like you as well, and they have all proven to be very effective at their work."

There was a slight lilt at the end of his sentence.

Realization jolted through Sydney. Eli was implying that she was here because Winter was sleeping with her. A convenient booty call.

Winter's eyes shot to her at the same time she looked at him.

That's a good thing for Eli to assume, she told herself forcefully, trying to convey it to Winter through her glance. It was in their best interest for the man to think that she'd been chosen to come on this trip because Winter wanted to bring his current fling with him. It would serve as the perfect red herring, would keep him from taking her seriously.

It still didn't stop the heat from rushing to her cheeks. That was good, too, her genuine reaction to his insinuation. So she let her expression turn bewildered, and opened her mouth to protest.

Beside her, Winter nodded as if he hadn't caught the subtle reference. That was also what a star would do in this scenario, she thought, if it really were true. Pretend he knew nothing. "Ashley's as professional as they come," he said.

"I have no doubt," Eli replied. His insinuation was gone now, as if he'd never made it. Sydney closed her mouth and let the moment ride itself out.

Her eyes darted briefly to Penelope. She didn't seem to catch her father's suggestion, either—her smile was still fixated on Winter as he took his place at his seat across from her.

To her gratitude, Claire jumped in and offered Penelope a winsome smile. "We're so delighted to be here to celebrate your birthday, Miss Morrison. And we're going to make it one for the history books."

"Or your money back," Winter quipped, winking at Penelope, and the girl laughed again, running a hand nervously through her hair.

The rest of their dinner passed smoothly, and at least there were no more interrogations. Eli seemed uninterested in doing the same to Winter. Another point for Sauda, Sydney reluctantly conceded, choosing someone like Winter for this job. Eli probably had no suspicions about Winter's very public history. What dangerous secrets could a pop star hold?

At last, they rose. Sydney looked on as Winter shook the man's hand a final time.

"If you have a need," Eli now said, "I will make sure to accommodate it. There's an entire staff at your beck and call on this property. And if you find something upsetting, just say the word." The man smiled. "I can make most things happen."

He said it in his quiet, considerate voice, but it didn't sound like reassurance to Sydney. It sounded like a threat. It felt as plain as if Eli had tied them both up and held a knife to their throats. He could make most things happen—he had the money and means to make sure they had a comfortable stay, or that they disappeared.

His smile widened and, satisfied, he turned away from her to escort his daughter down the stairs. Penelope looked over her shoulder at Winter, her smile giddy, and he gave her a conspiratorial nod in return.

At the entrance, two men greeted them and ushered them into their waiting sedans. Then the cars departed, and they were finally alone.

Only then did Winter cast Sydney a meaningful look. "So we're sleeping together, are we?" he mumbled.

Sydney winced, then dropped her face into one hand.

Claire let out her breath. "Well!" she said breezily. "What an absolutely monumental prick."

Someone Is Always Watching

The first thing Sydney did, as Claire left and Winter set about unpacking his dozen suitcases, was to run a scan on the house.

It was an even more impressive space than she'd suspected. On a subterranean floor directly underneath the main living and dining room, there was a private cinema and bowling alley. The second floor had a private salon and beauty parlor room, along with closets as big as her entire apartment back home. Out on the opposite end of the gardens was a separate two-story house meant for staff. Above the third floor bedrooms was a massive deck and rooftop garden, from where Sydney could see London's night cityscape sprawling before them, a twinkling wonderland under a curtain of rain and fog.

Sydney wandered around each floor, taking out a Necco Wafer from her pocket every now and then and popping it into her mouth. At each floor, she pressed a small button on her key ring. The scan ran silently. She could see a red grid layout appear on her phone as it went, mapping the home's rooms and searching for bugs built in beneath the drywall.

As she suspected, several dots lit up in the common living spaces.

Good to know, she thought grimly. Not that she would do anything about them. Disabling those bugs would just tip off Morrison's crew to the fact that Winter's bodyguard might be more capable than was normal. But at least she knew where they could whisper more freely in the house and where they needed to disguise their conversations behind noise or stay entirely silent.

She checked the mirrors in the bathrooms, pretending she was cleaning the glass while running a finger idly along the surface, making sure they weren't one-way or contained extra panels that might be recording anything. A gap between her finger and its reflection meant a safe mirror—no gap meant something was up.

The bathrooms cleared her tests.

As she stepped out of the final bedroom to head down the stairs, she saw Winter heading up in her direction, his dark eyes following her curiously. His dancer grace was perfect for their mission, but it bothered her that he could move so quietly that even she hadn't heard him approaching.

"Awed by this place, too, huh?" he said with a small smile.

She knew by the look in his eyes what he was really asking her. *Did you find anything unusual?*

She gave him a pointed shake of her head. "Nothing *too* surprising," she answered.

By that, she meant *Be careful how you act in here. We're being watched.*

He noted her gesture, but just waved a hand in agreement. "Well, I certainly don't have a heated indoor pool in my living room," he said, glancing down at the bottom floor.

Sydney knew this was an opportunity for her to turn their charm together up within earshot of the house's bugs, to lean into Eli's assumption about them. She walked down the stairs until she was just a single step higher than him.

"Then we'd better make good use of it," she said coyly.

Winter frowned. Then he leaned closer so that he could murmur in her ear. "What the hell are you doing?" he whispered.

She caught the scent of him—clean laundry, shampoo, and the delicate musk of a boy. He was very warm when he stood this near to her. She smiled a little to herself. Flirting was a course she'd aced during training.

"What do you mean?" she replied, resting a hand lightly on his arm, as if to steady herself. "You don't want to use the pool? Oh, come on."

He raised a skeptical eyebrow at her.

"Fine." She sniffed. "I'll use it by myself. But just so you know," she added, looking sidelong at him, "I didn't pack a swimsuit."

It gave her a thrilling jolt of satisfaction to see his breath hitch for a second, his pupils dilating. At least he wasn't immune to her flirtations.

Then realization seemed to dawn on him. A small smile appeared on his lips. He leaned against the side of the stairs, his hands in his pockets, and regarded her like a challenge.

"That sounded a little like a dare, Miss Miller," he said.

"Oh?" she answered. "And what do you think I'm daring you to do?"

He leaned forward so that his arm brushed against hers. "You tell me. Entertain you in the pool?"

Her skin tingled at his touch. "Something you're experienced at?"

"Well, it *is* my job to make people happy."

"And are your customers satisfied?"

He looked straight at her. "I'm very, very good at my job."

His voice was just soft enough to seem like it was meant for her alone to hear. And in spite of their little game, she found herself hesitating for a heartbeat.

The pause in her reply couldn't have been longer than a fraction of a second—but Winter caught it. He laughed, a small, bright sound at the base of his throat. There was a satisfied glimmer in his eye, as if he'd won, and annoyance flared in Sydney's chest.

Oh no, you don't.

Without warning, she leaned up to his ear so that her lips brushed his skin. She felt him shiver a little. "Speak up," she whispered. "We're putting on a show, remember?"

His smug look wavered, making way for a pout. He turned his head to whisper back, "You're no fun at all."

Insufferable. Sydney's heart was still beating rapidly. She hoped he couldn't sense it. "Believe me," she murmured coolly, with her cheek near his, "I'd rather be stuck flirting with a tree."

He lifted a taunting eyebrow at her. "Now, I *know* that's a lie."

It was. But the last thing Sydney wanted to do was let him win this flirting game, so she pulled all the way back and gave him a tight smile. "A tree wouldn't be so irritating," she retorted in a hushed voice.

His smile turned into a grin. "Too bad," he murmured, his breath tickling her ear. "I was having a good time."

He whispered it so casually that he could have just been commenting on the rain outside. *I was having a good time.*

He was doing well staying in character. No surprise there, of course. He was a star, after all, someone who probably flirted every single day of his life. Or was he mocking her ability to be an effective spy? Unless he really meant—

Then he pulled back, his eyes darting away from her in seeming disinterest.

Of course he was just mocking her, still under cover, and more successful at it than Sydney could have hoped. She wanted to hit herself for being pulled into their routine.

She composed herself in an instant and let her voice turn professional again. "Any errands you want me to run, Mr. Young?"

He stepped to the other side of the staircase, then walked past her. "Just the postcard for my mom," he said.

"Don't fall asleep until I'm back," she called over her shoulder. "You'll make your jetlag worse."

"And a latte, too, then," he called back. "Thanks."

It was a rehearsed question-and-answer between them upon arrival: a way for Winter to send Sydney out of the house to meet a local asset working with Panacea, who would then deliver her a parcel containing items they needed.

Winter headed up the stairs and toward his bedroom. Sydney turned around, refusing to look back to see if he would do the same. Then she went down the stairs and out the front door. A good stairway exchange right out in the open. If someone on Morrison's team really was watching them, it should have looked like just a genuine, supposedly secret moment between a star and his bodyguard flirting casually with each other, trying to keep up a hot, hidden affair. Frivolous celebrity behavior.

The night was cold, the drizzle still going. The chill in the air helped clear her head. It wasn't that she'd never flirted while undercover with an agent—Sydney had messed around on the job before. She just hadn't expected this particular agent to have an effect on her.

Too bad. I was having a good time.

She could still feel the sear of his dark eyes on her as he said it, see the intensity of that look. Just mocking her, she reminded herself. And why did she care anyway? Not that she did.

Scowling deeper, she wrenched her thoughts away from Winter and shoved a Necco Wafer in her mouth, sucking on the candy to distract herself.

She walked in the direction of the café several blocks down, strolling leisurely enough to file away the world around her. A butcher shop, a wine shop, a dental clinic, a grocery store the size of a postage stamp. Baskets of bright oranges and apples laid out under an awning. The smell of chocolate and butter wafting from a French patisserie, then the scent of coriander and cumin from an Indian café. Petals strewn on the path under a pub's hanging baskets of flowers. Cuts of bologna and sausage suspended in a window. People bustling up from and down to an Underground station, their boots splashing through shallow puddles, their voices a mix of half a dozen different languages.

She paid particular attention to them—older women with exercise gear on underneath their winter coats, a rowdy bunch of football fans wearing Chelsea FC shirts, businessmen rushing along with briefcases held over their heads, tourists wheeling suitcases and squinting at maps on their phones, teenagers laughing together while huddled under transparent umbrellas, some of them still in their school uniforms. Then she turned the corner and watched for the same people to potentially reappear. If she saw the same rushing businessman on a different street in the opposite direction fifteen minutes later, they might be tailing her.

Finally, she ducked into a Caffè Nero shop. There, she picked up a latte for Winter and one for herself, careful to tap a specific credit card to pay. When the Panacea agent assigned to do her drop got the notification on their phone that the card's balance had changed, they would recognize it as Sydney's signal that she was successfully on her way to their rendezvous point.

As she turned toward the exit, she texted Winter.

Eta 20m

He texted back almost immediately. *Hurry. Pining for you.*

She almost laughed out loud at his deadpan, not sure whether to be exasperated or amused.

dsu, she replied.

What?

It stood for *Don't stay up*, but she didn't bother explaining it as she headed out the door and toward the post office. As she went, he texted again.

Have you ever texted in complete words?

Nt, she answered.

This one stood for *No time*, but now she was just messing with him. She imagined his eye roll, smiled a little, then tucked her phone back into her pocket and focused on the street.

Her phone told her it would be a ten-minute walk—enough time for the asset to have checked her availability and dropped what she needed at the location.

This post office's particular mail drops had been her pitch to Sauda for a secure site, too. It was a boring spot, one she'd had checked to ensure no street cams or surveillance was covering, a spot with relatively low traffic in the city, and most importantly, was possible to get to at all hours. If all went well, she would drop Winter's postcard into the mailbox and see a small package secured for her underneath the mailbox, waiting for pickup.

Then she'd use a Necco Wafer—her secret substitute for chalk—from her pocket to mark the bottom of the mailbox to announce a successful retrieval to her asset whenever they checked it out later.

She grinned at the memory of Niall putting a roll of the candy on her desk during her first official training day at Panacea.

"*For you, kid,*" he'd said to Sydney in his trademark grumble. "*Always keep one in your pocket. You never know when you might need it.*"

Sydney had pocketed it immediately. Only then did she realize that no one had ever bought candy for her before. "*Yes, sir,*" she'd answered.

The memory faded. Soon the rain picked up, turning from drizzle into a steady downpour. By the time she arrived at the shuttered post office, a loud symphony was pelting her umbrella. Under the deluge stood a row of cylindrical red mailboxes, dewy under the streetlight, their round sides emblazoned with royal crests.

Right away, she realized something had gone wrong.

The mailbox that they were supposed to use, the last in the line, had no subtle chalk marking on the drop slot. It meant that the asset never arrived. That there was no thin package secured inside the mailbox's slot for her to pick up.

It meant that the drop had been aborted, likely because of someone watching them.

Always assume you're being followed, Sauda told her every chance she got.

So she did assume, and didn't turn back around. She didn't look concerned. Instead, she just headed to the mailbox and unceremoniously dropped in Winter's postcard. As she did, she scanned the streets from the corners of her eyes.

There. She saw what must have tipped off her asset.

A black car on the other side of the street, with a silhouette sitting inside of it, facing her direction.

Sydney didn't look again. But the single glance told her enough. Someone was watching her, after all.

Inwardly, she cursed. Drop aborted. They would have to try again within the next twenty-four hours, before Winter's concert began. But at least this little failed trip told her without a doubt that Eli Morrison was watching her movements. He'd probably have eyes on dozens of people in the city over the next few days.

Her goal was to make herself look as boring as possible. A bodyguard, nothing more.

She turned away from the mailbox without a second look and adjusted the two coffees in her hands. Then she turned to head back to the house.

Only now did the full enormity of their mission settle in. Eli Morrison was no fool. He was a man who indulged in brutality. If they were caught, she knew there was nothing Sauda and Niall would—or could—do to save them. That was part of this gig, after all.

London would be an interesting place to die. Would it happen here?

Sydney had never been afraid of death, simply because she didn't think dead people felt anything. But *dying*? A different matter entirely. She'd experienced that moment many times before, whether during a mission where she'd escaped by a hairsbreadth or when she was still a child trapped in a home she hated. So this was a familiar question to her, something that appeared in her mind at the start of every mission.

Where would she die? Would it be here?

She didn't know the answer, of course—only that when it did happen, she would be alone somewhere, with no one to rescue her but herself. That realization had been with her all her life. Maybe that was why she'd fallen so easily into this line of work. Everyone died alone. Her mother had, after all.

The thought reminded her of her lungs, and as if on cue, a spasm of pain rippled uncomfortably through her chest.

She sucked in her breath instinctively, then let the air out in a slow exercise and quickened her walk. Like hell she was going to die here, her last mission being stuck with an annoying superstar.

And with that thought lodged firmly in her mind, she hurried down the street, not bothering to wonder whether anyone else was watching her.

12

Suspicions

The indoor pool in Winter's house was cool and soothing, the sound of its lapping blending with the patter of rain against the windows and the steady rhythm of nearby voices. Winter lay back in the water and stared at the staircase curling up to the top floor. Several feet away, Leo and Dameon lounged on the couches, picking at a pile of chocolate bars that Claire had dropped off for them.

"We won't see you because there won't be a break," Leo told Winter now as he peeled off the wrapper to a Cadbury Twirl. "Claire said you'll go straight from the concert to the after-party as Penelope's guest of honor."

"Where are you headed?" Winter said to them.

"The clubs," Dameon answered with a shrug. "So don't get into trouble."

"I never get into trouble," Winter protested.

"He means, don't get into trouble *without us*," Leo clarified with a grin.

Now that evening had settled into the corners of the house, the space seemed more sinister than elegant. Winter thought he could see shadows flickering in his peripheral vision, shapes in the silhouettes of trees out in the garden that swayed in the breeze. Now and then came the low rumble of distant thunder. The uneasy electricity in the air suited his mood, and he found himself composing melodies in his head to match the energy, as if trying to distract himself from his real reason for being here.

"Did Claire say if she's allowed inside the party?" Winter asked.

"She's not, either," Dameon replied. "Just you and Ashley."

Winter already knew this, although he also knew they'd expect him to ask. He sat up in the water and leaned his arms against the edge of the pool. "Great," he muttered.

"Don't worry." Dameon smiled, adjusting the large bun of dreadlocks secured high on his head. "You'll feel like Claire's there even if she's not."

As if on cue, Winter's phone pinged against the pool's ledge, and the screen lit up to show a long message from Claire.

Confirmed your car for tomorrow night! It'll be waiting right outside the main entrance, not the side. So brace yourself for a crowd. If you leave in anything other than that car, with anyone I don't know, don't forget to TELL ME, do you understand? No answer means yes!

He wondered what Claire would think of Sydney's three-to-five-letter texts.

"Besides," Leo said. "I think we agreed that you like Ashley's company more than you care to admit."

Dameon glanced around. "Where is she, anyway?"

Remember the house is watching, Winter told himself. "I sent her to deliver some mail for me," he said.

Dameon raised an eyebrow. "You sent your bodyguard away?"

Winter felt the prickles of his friend's suspicions. "I'll be fine," Winter said with a yawn, gesturing around him. "Eli Morrison's got his own guards watching the street, and this house is armed to the teeth with alarms. Besides, she'll be back soon."

Dameon regarded him. "You're worried," he said.

"I'm not," Winter mumbled to the air.

Dameon crossed his arms. "I know when you're lying."

Winter swiveled his gaze away, afraid they would see the truth in his eyes. Bringing the people who knew him best might not have been a good idea.

"Pre-concert nerves," he answered.

"Nothing you haven't handled before," Dameon said. His gaze was penetrating.

"Well, it sounds like a pretty high-profile guest list."

Leo was staring at Winter with a thoughtful expression, too, his usual cheery grin sobering. "Leave him alone," he suddenly said. He nudged Dameon and pulled his legs up into a cross on the couch. "He'll be fine. You remember our first stadium concert, right?"

Dameon's questioning gaze swiveled away. "LA?" he said.

Leo nodded. "We were all terrified. But Winter pulled it off without blinking an eye."

Winter did remember—and Leo wasn't really telling the truth.

It'd happened two years after that fateful fan video of him went viral and he'd been catapulted into stardom. At the time, he could feel the momentum gathering behind that first huge concert, could feel himself pushing at the seams of increasing headlines and sales numbers and records and interviews. The disorienting feeling that he was about to launch so quickly that there would be no ground upon which to steady himself. So ten minutes before showtime, Winter had finally lost his nerve and gone to hide in a closet. Leo had been the one to find him. He could still remember his friend peeking hesitantly through a sliver in the door, then coming inside to sit beside him without a word.

After several long seconds, Winter had whispered shakily, *I can't do this.*

Leo had looked quietly at him, then away. When Winter started stammering out a reason, he shook his head. *You don't have to explain yourself to me,* Leo had said.

His tone was so soft and so easy. Winter had felt too ashamed to confess that all he could think about were the people who wouldn't be out in the audience. His mother. His brother. He knew he was about to step into uncharted waters, and he'd have to do it alone.

They'll all see me, he'd murmured. *What if they don't like what they see?*

Leo studied his face for a moment. He hadn't been the chatty, overly eager, teasing friend then; he'd looked thoughtful and serious, his gaze penetrating. *Hey,* he'd said at last. *Look at me.*

Reluctantly, Winter had lifted his gaze to his friend. He'd hoped the low light in the closet didn't reveal the gloss of tears in his eyes.

Winter, Leo had said, *the people who did come today are all here for you.*

Winter looked skeptically at him.

Leo smiled. *The entire world is about to fall in love with you. I promise.*

A few minutes later, Leo had stood and held a hand down to him. Winter had taken it, letting him pull him up. By the time they headed out to the stage, Leo had returned to his usual self, explaining to a frantic Claire that he'd helped Winter fix a wardrobe malfunction and then giving everyone a slew of advice on helpful hacks for repairing clothes on the fly.

The memory faded, and the lapping of pool water around Winter returned. By the couches, Leo was giving him an encouraging smile, and Winter felt a rush of gratitude.

"Just be yourself," Leo now said. "No big deal."

To Winter's relief, Dameon seemed to drop his suspicion, too, as he reached for another cube of cheese.

Panacea had told him to just be himself, too. So Winter tried to settle into the comfort of that. If he let himself, he could forget that he was here for Panacea at all. That this was just another concert, and just another sleepless night on tour.

The smile on Eli Morrison's face appeared in his thoughts, and the unpleasant churn in his stomach returned.

A faint click came from the other side of the house.

The melodies Winter was quietly composing in the back of his head cut off. He bolted upright, waves splashing against the sides of the pool, at the same time Leo's and Dameon's heads swiveled in sync toward the door.

Sydney's figure materialized from the darkness of the main foyer, her blond hair dampened with rain.

"Hey, Ashley," Leo said with a wave of his hand.

Winter felt some of the tension ebb from his body at the sight of her. Then he took in her expression.

Something had gone wrong.

He was careful not to show it on his face. Instead, he made a show of rubbing water out of his eyes as the boys both called out their greetings to her. Sydney headed over, then stopped near the stairs and put her hands in her pockets, waiting hesitantly.

"Didn't want to bother you guys," she said.

Dameon shot Leo a look, and the two exchanged a subtle nod. Then Dameon stood up, stretching. "We should be calling it a night, anyway," he replied. "We have a pretty early rehearsal."

"Eight A.M.," Leo added. "No rest for the jet-lagged." He stood up and followed in Dameon's wake, nodding once in Winter's direction. "You too. If you show up later than us tomorrow, you have to wear a white leotard to the after-party."

Winter couldn't help cracking a smile. "Deal."

He watched the boys leave. When the front door finally closed behind them, Sydney walked over to sit beside him at the edge of the pool. He was suddenly aware of being nearly naked in front of her.

So what? It was just Sydney. Still, he noticed her gaze hitching for a beat on his chest, then quickly skipping away.

"Hey," he whispered as she leaned her head down toward him. "What happened?"

Sydney's voice was barely perceptible. "We've got a problem," she replied.

What Haunts the Heart

Sydney had the uncanny ability to know when she was dreaming, but not the power to shake herself awake.

Tonight, she was back at the local hospital in Havenville, sitting in her mother's room. She could hear the steady beeping of the heart monitor droning in her ears, smell the tang of phenol cleaner clinging to the air, feel the bed's stiff hospital sheets as she rested her elbows against them. When she looked down at her feet, she saw that she was wearing her ratty old boots from when she was fourteen.

Everything in her wanted to shrink away. She hated, hated, *hated* remembering. Hated that she couldn't stop her brain from going here. Hated that small things on a mission could trigger these dreams. Hated that she couldn't run far enough from them. Hated that she couldn't break out of them.

What had set her off this time? The sudden reminder of her mortality as she did the failed run to the mailbox? The tense conversation she'd had with Winter after she returned, as they figured out what to do next? The planning of a new drop right before she'd gone to bed?

The dream world around her was so visceral that she couldn't shake the possibility that it was real. Sydney could feel her mother shifting in bed, could hear the soft groan escape the woman's lips, could see her mother's face, the wrinkles, the pale, trembling skin, the furrow line between her brows. She'd still been so young, but the sickness had aged her twenty years.

"Ah, Syd," her mother whispered. Sydney's name came out cracked and grated, like salt out of a grinder.

Sydney adjusted her own position, wincing at the stiffness in her body. "Yes, Mama?" she asked. "Do you need me to get you anything?"

Her mother didn't answer right away. When she did, she said, "How long are you planning to stay?"

Sydney had already been on vigil here alone for three straight days and nights. Her soul was tired, and she had homework to make up.

"I don't know," Sydney answered. "But I'm still here for now."

Her mother's eyes cracked open a sliver, and Sydney saw a glimpse of dark blue irises tilted toward her. "No." She shook her head once. "I mean, how long are you planning to stay here? In this town?"

Sydney didn't know how to answer, because she didn't understand the question. "You mean, for how many years?"

Her mother sighed and closed her eyes. "Leave when you can," she whispered. "There's nothing for you in this place."

Sydney wanted to scream at her. How could she leave? Her *mother* was here. Where would she go? If Sydney ever left, it would mean that her mother wasn't around anymore, and that would mean she had died. And Sydney didn't want to think about that.

"What about Dad and Matt?" she asked.

Her mother made a small sound in her throat. "Don't stay for them," she murmured.

Sydney could feel the frustration rising in her tired chest. She didn't understand where this conversation was going. Her father existed mostly on the periphery of her life, true—a man she caught glimpses of whenever he staggered home after a twelve-hour shift, the smell of pigs' blood clinging to every part of his body. The times he did notice her usually involved a drunken rage—once screaming at her for watching *gibberish* and leaving the TV on a foreign-language channel, once lunging at her with a knife for knocking over his beer, once slapping her at dinner when she said she wanted to know what was out there, beyond their town.

Why? He'd leaned against the table and pointed his fork at her. *You're too good for us?*

She'd cradled her stinging cheek. Her brother Matt had snickered.

What a useless mouth to feed you are, her father had said. *Just like your mother.*

Existing in that town sometimes felt to her like being trapped in mud. But sometimes in the summer, when both Dad and Matt were out of the house and her mother came home early from work, she would take Sydney out for ice cream and pick a spot by the river where they could see freight trains crossing the bridge. It was Sydney's favorite memory in the world, those warm days with the sound of insects buzzing around them, mosquito repellent sticky on her skin, and the thought of leaving that behind, of never again sitting by the river with her mother, a chocolate-covered spoon pressed against her tongue, was unbearable to her.

So to hear her mother saying this now—*leave this place, leave Dad and Matt*—felt a little like a rejection of her life. That nothing in this town had ever mattered to Sydney. That her father and brother weren't worth staying for. That her mother was acknowledging something she had never acknowledged before.

Sydney swallowed hard and shifted against the hospital sheets. "Okay, Mama," she said, because it was the only good thing to say.

Her mother nodded idly. Sydney couldn't be sure that she would even remember this conversation, or if the drugs were dragging her into sleep. "That's good," she whispered. "Stay with me a little longer now. I'm cold tonight."

Sydney nodded, her eyelids drooping. God, she was so tired. She knew Dad and Matt wouldn't be coming here anytime soon—Matt was out with friends for the weekend, and Dad had extra shifts. But she couldn't stay any longer without going home.

"I'll just be gone a little while, Mom," she heard herself say. "Then I'll come back. I promise."

Her mother didn't answer. After a while, when it seemed like she'd drifted off, Sydney snuck quietly out.

It was snowing that night, and her boots crunched softly down the white street. The air nipped at her cheeks and stung in her chest. She'd started to feel the occasional spasms in her lungs over the past year, although she never told her mother about them. She never told anybody. Maybe if the secret stayed with her, the potential diagnosis couldn't be real. If she pretended it was all in her head, then maybe it was, maybe she hadn't inherited it.

Sydney had only been home for an hour when she got the call from the hospital. She could feel the floorboards beneath her creak, as if the house were shifting with her in grief.

I'm so deeply sorry to inform you that your mother has passed away . . .

The dream shifted several weeks into the future, after the funeral had passed. It was a cold enough day that school had been canceled, so Sydney went for a walk down the main street several blocks from her house. Her head was tucked like a turtle into the scarf wrapped thickly around her neck. A freak storm had left the world around her bitterly cold, encasing everything in a chrysalis of ice.

She didn't really know where she was going. The wind swirled around her, cutting straight through her jeans and sending spikes of pain down her lungs.

Eventually, she ducked into the pharmacy to get warm. Several homeless people were clustered outside the sliding glass doors, savoring the heat that would momentarily waft over whenever the doors opened. They shifted as Sydney stepped in.

She wandered the aisles for a while, no money in her pocket, not really sure how long she'd be allowed to loiter before they told her to move along. Her heart hung in a low, constant state of grief, and her mind was elsewhere, far from this town. She could feel the pain stretch tight in her chest, her lungs still aching from the cold outside.

Over by the checkout counter, she could hear a family chattering away. Sydney peeked between the aisles and saw a teenage boy standing with his parents. His father placed a hand protectively on the boy's shoulder. His mother leaned down to cup the boy's face in her hands, her smile genuine, her face glowing.

As Sydney watched them, she could feel her anger rising, cresting over her sadness. She wasn't sure why. They'd done nothing wrong. But the fury made the walls close in around her. She could see the pharmacy's aisles narrowing, the cash registers fusing together, everything around her moving inward until she felt like she was being buried alive.

Tears stung her eyes. Maybe the boy had his own hidden pains. But maybe he'd also never known a day when his father waved a knife in his face, had never stood vigil beside his mother's hospital bed. Maybe he already had plans for an entire future laid out before him, while Sydney slowly withered away in this place, cowering every time she heard her father step through the door, hiding from her brother so she wouldn't have to endure his insults.

Leave this place, her mother had whispered to her.

But where could Sydney go? How would she get the money to leave?

And what did other people do to deserve love? A good life?

Was a life still worth anything? Did it still matter to dream big?

Sydney felt the unfairness of it all flood her limbs until her fingers tingled. She glanced again at the family by the checkout counter. Then, through her film of tears, she looked at the goods on the aisle in front of her. Vitamins. Cold medicine. Allergy sprays.

She didn't know exactly why the urge hit her, or why she didn't bother stopping it. Maybe she was just tired of everyone else getting to have what they wanted. Maybe she was tired of grieving, of being left behind, of being trapped.

Maybe this was to balance out the unfairness.

Whatever the reason, she reached out and grabbed one of the bottles of allergy medicine and shoved it into the inner pocket of her coat.

Her hand was there and gone in less than a second.

She could feel the round bottle pressing against her side. It felt amazing. Her heart hammered as she glanced toward the clerks, who didn't even seem to notice she was here.

She snatched a case of aspirin.

Snatched two boxes of nasal spray.

Then she shoved her hands in her pockets and headed back out toward the entrance.

She expected the alarms to go off. But then the glass doors slid open for her. She stepped through, the homeless people shifting on either side of the entrance. No alarm.

She walked stiffly, fear lodged in her throat, waiting for the sound of a clerk yelling at her to stop. Her hands were clammy with cold sweat in her pockets, and her teeth were chattering.

But no one came running after her. She turned the corner, and no one came. She crossed the street and went another block, and no one came.

The crushing anguish that pressed against her heart suddenly gave way to a tide of nauseating euphoria. The stolen medication tucked inside her heavy coat bounced against her side, pills clinking in their bottles.

Goddamn, that felt *so good*.

Her teeth chattered from the rush. She hated herself.

But more than that, she knew she would rather hate herself than bear the pain a second longer.

And she knew she would do everything in her power to steal again.

Sydney shot up in bed, gasping, her body prickling with sweat, her hands still tingling from the rush of her theft. Tears smeared her vision. She looked around wildly, wondering if she'd heard a noise, if the cops were waiting outside for her. If she'd see the rhythmic flash of blue and red lights by the window. But her room stayed empty.

She wasn't back in Havenville. She wasn't reliving her mother's death and the start of her shoplifting. She was just in Kensington, on the night before their mission was supposed to kick into high gear.

But her stomach still churned with sickness, a concoction of grief and anger.

After another long moment, Sydney pulled herself into a sitting position and buried her face in her palms, then wiped her tears away. Moonlight poured across her bed in a diagonal band, outlining her figure and mess of hair in weak blue light. She wished she could call Sauda or Niall, as if their guidance could once again steer her out of the darkness of her own mind.

The sound of a creak in the floorboards snapped her out of her reverie. She turned her head automatically in the direction of the wall. She had heard that sound in her dream right before waking up—the groan of the floor. That must have been what woke her up.

After a moment came the faintest thud of footsteps downstairs. Winter was awake.

Sydney swung her legs over the side of the bed and stood up silently, then moved like a cat across the room to her door, where she pulled it open by the faintest hair. Over the curving stairway, she saw Winter walking around downstairs, barefoot. He was still dressed in his nightclothes, a plain white shirt and gray sleep pants that hung low at his hips, so that when he reached up to run his hand through his mess of hair, he revealed a sliver of his slanting hip bones.

Annoyance and desire flitted through her. She found herself watching him quietly from above. What was he doing awake at this hour, anyway? He stopped to stare out the window for a long time, the moonlight stretching his shadow long behind him. Then he turned away, hands tucked in his pant pockets, and did little sweeps with his feet in half arcs as if he were slow dancing across the floor with himself.

She looked on, hypnotized by the quiet grace of his body. As he moved, he tilted his head up slightly and, with his eyes closed, maneuvered his turns into an effortless pirouette, spinning in silence on one perfectly arched foot, his hands still in his pockets. Her lips parted, and in this moment, she forgot herself. *Ballet training,* she recalled about him. Then his leg dropped again and he stepped smoothly back into a walk.

There was sadness etched into the lines of his body tonight, something she occasionally recognized from his performances. It gave him that secret pull, an aching vulnerability hidden behind the wink and the sidelong smile. As if he both desperately needed the spotlight and yet couldn't bear the attention. There was no one else here, and yet, even now, he looked like a star, like he couldn't help but burn so bright that even the air was drawn to him, that the moon yearned to illuminate him.

Sydney didn't know how long she watched him. And when he finally retreated back up the stairs and she settled into her bed again, she could still see his lonely, mesmerizing dance in her mind, his figure glowing in the darkness.

Maybe his dreams had come to haunt him tonight, too.

Prelude to the Stage

Sydney Cossette had stepped into many roles and worn many outfits. But playing someone who usually ended up in the background meant she tended to don ensembles that made her invisible—an attendant uniform in a parking lot, or a forgettable girl on the subway, or the plain black outfit of a security guard.

Not the bodyguard to a pop star who needed to dress for the equivalent to a costume ball.

Now she stared at herself in the mirror of her room, unsure how to react. Her costume for the night of Winter's concert was a deer, and she looked the part in a two-piece silver Oscar de la Renta lamé outfit, the top half exposing her back down to the small of her spine, the bottom a shimmery pair of pants so billowing that it looked like a long skirt. Her shoes were the same—pointed boots in luxurious dark gray suede, with heels low enough to be practical. Her antlers were elegant, coated in hanging trails of Swarovski crystals, and implanted with surveillance chips. She didn't know whether she felt more annoyed or flattered by them. They were a practical size, and on a band that Winter's stylist had pinned to her hair in such a way that she could pull it off with a single swipe if she needed to—but the headpiece still made her feel awkward, less a secret agent and more a Bambi mannequin.

She looked stunning, though. Definitely the nicest secret agent outfit she'd ever worn. And in spite of herself, she struck a subtle pose, sticking one hip out and tilting her head to see the light shift against the faux skirt.

A light knock sounded on her door, and before she could react, Winter poked his head in. "Our car just arrived," he said. "Claire says she's—"

Then his eyes skipped to her, catching the last bit of her pose, and his words died midsentence. The light changed in his eyes, flickering through a dozen different emotions even as he fought to keep them off his face. His lips parted slightly. He took her in with a single long look, the top and the flowing pants, her pale arms and arched neck, her exposed back.

It certainly wasn't the first time she'd worn something that turned heads—but she also didn't usually care. Not the way she did now, at least, her bared skin prickling pleasantly under the intensity of Winter's stare.

Nor had she expected her own internal reaction to his clothes.

He was wearing just one of half a dozen costume changes he would go through that evening—but it didn't mean he looked anything less than stunning. His inner collar shirt and thin tie were silky black, while the suit itself had a tailored cape fused with the sleeves, the color a shade of deep forest green with silver embroidery at the hems.

His first costume's theme: midnight.

For a second, they just stared at each other.

Then she tore her eyes away from him and met his gaze in the mirror. "Did I say you could come in?" she said.

The hypnotized look vanished from his eyes, and he seemed to snap back into himself as he held his hands up. "Your door was open," he said. "I figured that meant you were okay without a knock." Then a bemused smile appeared on his face. "Or are you just embarrassed to be caught posing?"

Her scowl deepened as she stepped away from the mirror and toward him. "Forget it," she muttered. "We're running late."

Out in the hall, she could still hear his prep team packing up their supplies in the other bedroom-turned-beauty-room. Now that she stood right in front of Winter, she could see the faint dusting of makeup on his features: a subtle foundation, a light darkening of his already dark brows, and the thinnest sheen against his eyelids, as if they'd been painted with moonlight.

He was very obviously trying not to stare too long at her.

"If it helps," he said as they walked together down the hall, leaning down to her so that his breath warmed her ear, "you look beautiful."

Sydney couldn't tell if he was being genuine or making fun of her, but she was glad that he looked away before the flush rose on her cheeks.

"How do you feel?" she asked him as they stepped out of her room and headed toward the stairs.

He shrugged, but she noticed the way his eyes darted around the corridor, afraid to settle. "No more nervous than I do before any concert."

Sydney nodded. She could hear the unspoken words in the air, that this wasn't just any concert. But somehow she knew Winter would pull off his part of the job without a hitch. She, on the other hand, had a Panacea contact she needed to connect with tonight, at a newly approved drop site right outside the concert venue itself. It was a less ideal place, busier and closer to danger, but maybe the chaos of the event would work in her favor.

They reached the top of the stairs. Beside her, Winter offered her his arm. She stared at it dumbly for a second, unsure what to do for once.

"I'm your bodyguard," she said as they stood there.

"Yes. And?"

"Do you help all your bodyguards down the stairs?" She looked skeptically at him.

"This one, I do." Winter smiled a little at her. "Look—you cannot dress like that and not expect me to walk you out to the car. I'm not here to start a public rumor that I'm an asshole."

"If that's your idea of flattery, I'm amazed it's worked out this long for you."

He cast her a withering look. "Just take the arm already, before Claire blows a fuse waiting out there."

Eli Morrison had rented out the Alexandra Palace for his daughter's private birthday concert, a sprawling 196-acre entertainment complex in north London. Under the glory of a spectacular sunset that threw bands of purple and pink across the sky's smattering of rain clouds, even Sydney had to put her cynicism aside and admire the space.

She'd done her requisite research on the palace, of course; it'd been built in 1873, then was burned down and rebuilt twice over the centuries, serving in between as everything from a museum exhibition to World War I refugee center to a news station to a concert venue.

She emerged first from the car in preparation to escort Winter inside. Beside her, Claire stepped out and glanced briefly at the estate before turning her attention to the crowd of fans that had gathered below the palace's lawns. She was dressed in gold and white like a Grecian queen, gold makeup glittering against her dark eyelids.

"How they always find out, I'll never know," she murmured in the direction of the fans. Still, she smiled and nudged Sydney, a satisfied glint in her eyes. "No such thing as bad publicity, right?"

"I'll say," Sydney murmured back as she looked at the scene. There must have been over a thousand people waiting on the lawn directly across from the palace's street entrance, all clustered eagerly together with their signs as police and hired security linked arms before them, struggling to keep the restless crowd from clamoring over the cement barricades. Their cheers rose and fell in rhythm.

A dozen of Morrison's men were already here, lined up in two rows on either side of their cars' doors, ready to escort them along a red carpet that led up the steps to the palace's entrance.

Sydney noted the stream of black sedans lined up behind them, carrying a vast assortment of other celebrities, wealthy elites, and personal invitees. This night would make the news solely based on the importance of its guest list.

A second later, Winter finally emerged from the car, his cape flowing behind him, and waved to his fans. The crowd exploded, surging forward like a tide. The police line undulated as they pushed back.

"You're going to cause a full-on riot out here," Sydney said to him as he offered her his arm.

If the sight of the barely contained mass frightened him at all, he didn't show it on his face. Instead, he winked at Sydney before leading her up the steps toward the entrance's towering portico. "And you're going to be triggering rumors by morning," he replied. "I hope you're ready for it."

As the screams behind them echoed across the night, Leo and Dameon joined their line out of the car as they made their way along the red carpet. Cameras flashed with every step. Sydney kept a straight face through it, her eyes roving the space in apparent protection of Winter. A perfect excuse to note the stream of guests heading inside, along with the palace's interior.

The security check for the event itself began in the inner atrium. As they entered the main hall, Sydney saw a red velvet rope spanning the space, where a line of security staff were checking in the guests against a master list. There was also a metal detector, along with a team of guards scanning purses and bodies.

Sydney's eyes went to the smaller halls that branched off before the security line. A bathroom down the left hall was where she needed to head in order to attempt, once again, to retrieve her Panacea asset's parcel. The postbox would have been a much subtler drop, but at least these milling crowds were full of so many important people that no one's eyes would be fixed on her. She could steal out here, then find her way back inside without stirring up much suspicion.

Besides, Panacea didn't send mediocre assets to deliver things.

Their progress down the red carpet was infuriatingly slow. Eli Morrison had invited half a dozen reporters to the outer atrium, intent on recording just how epic a birthday bash this event would be. Now Winter found himself dodging mics shoved in his direction and being stopped to answer sets of questions.

Finally, they made it inside a quiet hall, then down an elevator to a subterranean series of rooms that must have been meant as private practice and rest areas for performers.

"Ashley, follow Winter to the dressing rooms until he's escorted off backstage," Claire was now telling her as she walked briskly along with them. She nodded at Leo and Dameon. "You boys, too. Behave yourselves. I'm heading back upstairs to take my seat."

"Hope you sit next to a gorgeous heiress," Winter called after her. "And she takes you out on a fancy date."

She turned around long enough to give Winter a playful point of her finger, then disappeared into the stream of people.

In the prep rooms, Dameon and Leo were already running through part of the set when they arrived. Sydney looked on as Winter greeted his friends, laughing at some inside joke while his prep team descended on him.

It took her a second to realize that the team was actually starting to *undress* him, sliding off his cape jacket and unbuttoning his collar shirt as they began transforming him into the first of his stage ensembles.

Undressing.

Sydney quickly averted her eyes, but not before she caught a glimpse of his body. He was built like a dancer, lean and strong, the muscles shifting under the light as he stretched his arms out to either side.

Then one of the designers started undoing his belt, preparing to change his pants. Sydney decided it was time for her to step out to the bathroom.

Two of Morrison's men were at the entrance of the practice room, watching her as she left, but she murmured "bathroom" to them and they seemed to lose interest immediately, their attention shifting to the thousand other little things happening in the chaos around them. Sydney noted this with some satisfaction; Eli's initial suspicions of her had just been grandstanding, after all. Maybe he'd officially dismissed her as nothing more than a bodyguard with benefits.

She made her way down the hall and out beyond the security line toward the bathrooms. Once inside, she noticed with relief the telltale marker left by her Panacea contact—a smudge of red lipstick against the door of the last stall. She wiped the lipstick off with a tissue, locked herself in, then lifted the lid for the toilet's water tank.

The parcel was so slim that anyone who didn't know where to look might never have noticed the gray plastic taped against the inside of the tank. Sydney felt for the groove along its side, then gingerly undid the parcel from the tank and sliced it slowly open along the top with her nail. The packaging gave way without a sound.

Inside were the items from Niall. Winter's earrings identical to the ones he would wear onto the stage. The snake ring. Along with a couple of other things, too—a slim pen with a blinding flash installed on its tip, her hotel crest pin equipped with the hidden needle blade, and new phones installed with Panacea software for tracking and tracing.

Lastly, she saw a tiny symbol scrawled against the inside lining of the package. She paused, then looked closer at it.

It was a scribble of a heart, with a cross drawn through it like a dagger.

She rolled her eyes, a slight smile on her lips. The Panacea asset who'd dropped this parcel off for her was an agent she'd once worked with, someone with whom she'd had a brief fling.

She shook her head. Maybe it was good luck, getting a familiar sign from her past. Maybe this mission would start to go right from now on. She switched out her phone, then opened a small, hidden pocket sewn onto the inside of her pants' waist and dropped the items in. When she clipped it back into place, it seemed to disappear into the billowing fabric, untraceable against the interior's anti-surveillance mesh.

Someone else stepped into the bathroom. Clicking heels echoed against the tiles. Sydney flushed the toilet once and let the noise of it cover the sound of her ripping the parcel into tiny pieces.

Then she stepped out.

And ran right into Penelope Morrison.

More Similar Than Not

Penelope startled by the sinks at the sight of her. The girl was already in costume—a black and white dress that shimmered under the light, along with an elegant silver and gold headpiece that combined the circle of a sun and the crescent of a moon. A jeweled hairpin gleamed beside her ear.

This bathroom was located outside the security area; Sydney had headed here intentionally, prepared to give the excuse to anyone who asked that she was looking for a more private space than the crowded rooms beyond the line.

What was Penelope doing here?

Penelope blinked at her and looked quickly away. Immediately, Sydney could tell that the girl had been sobbing; her eyes were still red, and her makeup had smudged slightly in the corners.

Sydney gave her a reassuring smile and pretended she hadn't noticed anything.

"You're Winter Young's bodyguard, right?" Penelope said after a moment's hesitation, looking at Sydney through the mirror with her wide eyes. "Ashley?"

"Yes, Ms. Morrison," Sydney said as she washed her hands beside the girl.

"You're not going to tell my father's crew I'm in here, are you?"

She shook her head. "I'm Mr. Young's handler, miss, not yours."

At that, Penelope seemed to sag with relief. A little breath escaped her. "Thanks," she said with a rueful laugh, and returned to fixing the corners of her makeup. "I'm just trying to escape them." She paused, then smiled at Ashley's dress. "You look amazing, by the way. I love the antlers."

"Thank you." Sydney was careful to keep her eyes lowered, her posture almost subservient, as she washed her hands. "Just following Mr. Morrison's instructions to have the guards match the theme."

"Actually, it was my instructions." Penelope gave her a sheepish grin. "I didn't want a hundred of my father's men in black suits breaking up the look of my party. They make me nervous. I'm sorry you got caught up in that—I know it sounds obnoxious."

Sydney laughed a little. "You don't need to apologize for giving me an excuse to dress up."

At that, an eager light appeared in her eyes, cutting through her sadness from a moment ago. "Is Winter dressed up already, too?"

"They're prepping him now," Sydney said, giving her a wink. "You must be excited."

Penelope sucked her breath in and lowered her eyes shyly, unable to hold back a smile. "He's the best part of this birthday," she admitted.

Sydney felt a pang of pity for the girl. For the star of the occasion, she didn't seem ecstatic about celebrating. Something about the way Penelope glanced nervously around like a trapped bird reminded Sydney of her own past, of feeling like she was living a life she couldn't escape.

At least Sydney knew the truth of who her father was.

Poor rich people, she told herself wryly. She watched the girl coil an errant strand up onto her head, then glanced at the door.

"You know," Sydney said, "if I run into some of your father's guards, I can tell them you're somewhere else. Give you a little extra time to yourself."

Penelope grabbed a towel to dry her hands. "That's kind of you to offer," she said, casting her a grateful glance.

Sydney shrugged. "I'm used to hiding from fathers, too," she replied.

She had shared this little piece of herself with Penelope as a tactic, part of drawing in the girl's trust. But the way Penelope's wide eyes turned to her in empathy was so genuine that Sydney felt a hint of shame.

Penelope gave her a small, sad smile. "We're the same, then," she said.

They weren't, of course, not really. Penelope's father was a billionaire. Her own father earned seven dollars an hour in a slaughterhouse. But Sydney nodded anyway, taking advantage of the chance to bond.

"More similar than not," she decided to reply.

Penelope shook her head. "Thank you," she said politely, her voice even smaller and shyer than before. "But it's not necessary. I have to give a gift to my dad before the concert starts, anyway—he won't be around afterward. I just . . . needed a moment."

Sydney nodded. So there was still some love underneath the tension between them, however slight. She could hear it in the pauses of Penelope's speech, as if she herself didn't want to admit it.

"I hope you enjoy the rest of your party, Ms. Morrison," she said.

"Please, call me Penelope." She smiled at Sydney. "Only my father's guards say *Ms. Morrison*."

Sydney smiled back. "Penelope, then."

As Penelope turned to leave the bathroom, Sydney noticed a small tattoo on the girl's wrist. At first glance, it looked like an errant line. It took a second for Sydney to recognize it as Italian and translate it in her head.

The heart is wide and deep.

Her mind skimmed over everything she knew about Penelope. Eli was English, through many generations. But her mother was an Italian woman who had been briefly married to Eli and then divorced when Penelope was three. There was so little information about her mother, though, especially after the divorce—word had it that she'd returned to Italy, then passed away years later from an illness.

Sydney couldn't make a judgment one way or the other about the phrase. Maybe it was a phrase that her mother had frequently used. Maybe it was an Italian saying that Sydney wasn't familiar with.

Then Penelope was stepping out the bathroom door, leaving Sydney alone.

Sydney's hand brushed the edge of her waistline, checking for the weight of the parcel's contents in her secret pocket. Then she headed out, too, keeping her head down as she walked back through the security line. The sadness etched on Penelope's face lingered in her mind.

Just how much did Eli Morrison control his daughter's life?

Whatever it was, it was enough for Winter to use. And with any luck, Penelope could be the wedge that cracked her father's illegal empire.

The Superstar and the Tycoon

When the call came for them to head out, Sydney took her place at Winter's side as they ushered him and his dancers down a private corridor toward the theater's backstage door.

He had transformed completely by now into his stage persona, his first performance outfit being one of flowing silver that seemed to shift colors under the light. A light sheen of makeup on his face cast him in a mesmerizing glow. There was a new smoothness to his walk, a fresh confidence in his gait, a mischievous lilt in his voice as he called out a joke to Leo and the boy laughed in return. Sydney couldn't help feeling impressed. It was as if a real person she'd known had disappeared, leaving behind only the idea of one.

They reached the end of the narrow corridor, where an elevator waited for them. Standing in front of the elevator was a line of Eli's guards, who stepped in Sydney's way. She felt herself tense on instinct.

"Our own guards," Leo said enthusiastically. "Look at this royal treatment."

The closest one shook his head at Sydney. "We'll escort them individually from here," he told her. "You may head to your seat in the audience now, Miss Miller."

Sydney cast Winter a brief glance. Already, he, Leo, and Dameon had each been paired with one of Eli's handlers.

Leo glanced skeptically up at his guard. "You coming up onstage to dance with us, too?" he quipped.

The man just stared stony-faced down at him until he looked away uneasily. "I mean, you seem like a people person," he muttered.

Sydney let herself hesitate. This was as far as she could go.

She nodded at the men and took a step away from Winter. He nodded at her. As she looked at him, that stage persona gave way to a glimpse of himself.

I'll be okay, his eyes seemed to say.

She pressed her lips together, then turned back to the guard. "Fine," she said.

Leo entered the tiny elevator first, his handler at his side. He gave them a tense smile. "See you all where the fun is," he said. Then the doors closed on him.

Dameon went next. At last, Winter entered with his new guard. As the doors closed on him, Sydney met his gaze one last time.

He gave her a quick grin. "Enjoy the show," he said.

Then he was gone.

She made her way down to the theater's front entrance, through which now streamed the rest of the invited guests.

She recognized many of them, whether from the news or from general knowledge of the rich and powerful. There were other young people, likely friends and acquaintances of Penelope, trust fund children. Still others were people she knew based on her time at Panacea—people who worked closely with Eli, directors from MI6, diplomats from other European nations. Her skin tingled at her proximity to them all.

There was a scent of danger in the air here.

At the theater hall's entrance, a guard asked for her name and ID, then scanned her card into a reader. The screen flashed green. She was on the guest list.

The space inside was massive, dimly lit by sweeping gradients of spotlights. To her surprise, Winter's stage had not been set up on the original one at the opposite end of the hall, but in the very center of the giant room, on a raised, circular dais. So everyone could see him from all angles.

She looked up. There had been a new system of hooks and swings installed over the dais, along with a series of small black machines placed at regular intervals around the round stage.

Sydney made her way to the front circle of people gathered around the dais, then found her spot. She looked around at the audience.

There was Claire, standing in the front row and talking animatedly with Penelope, who nodded along politely. Sydney noted two other bodyguards of Penelope's that she had recognized when they greeted them at the house.

Then she saw Eli Morrison seated beside them, almost directly in front of her, his figure swathed in shadows. It didn't matter that he blended in, though. He had the sort of presence that triggered the alarms in Sydney's head. It was the way others acted around him, she realized— how two of his associates sitting on his farther side bobbed their heads quickly when he turned to ask them a question, and how their bodies leaned toward him even when he didn't speak, as if afraid to miss a signal. When Eli laughed, it was a warm, generous sound—but the others didn't react like it. They would laugh nervously back, their bodies stiff, as if the sound couldn't reach the rest of them.

As if the man could share a joke with them one moment and then arrange for their disappearance the next. Perhaps they'd even witnessed it before.

Occasionally, she could hear bits and pieces of their murmurs through the noise around them. Dealings on one of Eli's investment funds. Nothing out of the ordinary.

Then she recognized the third person seated almost directly before her. It was Connor Doherty.

Connor Doherty, the young man Niall said handled all of Eli's business finances, who was notoriously absent from almost all of Eli's public meetings. Who was potentially having an affair with Penelope. Who was their ticket to taking Eli down.

Every instinct in Sydney zeroed in on the man, as if she'd just spotted a rare animal. He was unassuming at first glance, lean and slight, his posture slightly wearier than a man in his mid-twenties should be, wearing the plainest costume a person could manage—a standard black suit and tie, with an undecorated black eye mask across his small, narrow face. The kind of person who blended in with a crowd.

Sydney's eyes went to his hands. There she saw the only hints of the expensive taste that Panacea was counting on—a Rolex watch, a thick platinum bracelet, rings set with diamonds. He leaned toward Eli and spoke to him in a low voice that she couldn't make out.

She was in the middle of reading his lips when the space dimmed completely. Fog from the machines around the dais had started to seep through the seats, shrouding her boots, and the first threads of music began to come through the speakers embedded along each row of the arena's seats. When Sydney turned her head up to the ceiling, she could now see a sheet of stars winking into existence.

On the dais, icy blue lights bathed the entire stage, highlighting a silhouette that now rose from beneath the stage, crouched on his knees. The audience let out a burst of cheers as Winter came into view.

He was tied up and gagged, wearing a glittering headpiece of entwined branches and long egret feathers, giving him the illusion of being a bird. His black hair was dusted with silver glitter, and slender rings glinted on his fingers. A white silk scarf blindfolded his eyes, and his arms and legs were bound before him with metal and leather. Around the dais a birdcage of bars rose to surround him.

The music came on, and excitement rippled through the crowd. Nearby, Penelope sucked her breath in sharply and leaned forward, her eyes locked fully on him.

They locked the bird up, locked him deep down low

As the sound of the haunting track filled the room, Winter began his dance. With each heavy beat, he moved to break out of his binds. His wrists twisted and strained against the straps. One of his hands made a flourish of a movement—and inexplicably popped out of the strap, as if it had passed right through the material.

Sydney blinked. At Panacea, she had learned a dozen different ways of breaking out of restraints. She'd taken one look at Winter's binds and known, *really known*, that there was no way he could get out of that on his own. And yet here she was, witnessing him doing exactly that. It looked like his hand was made out of air, the way it just slid soundlessly out of one cuff.

The cuffs and binds must have been made specifically for this performance, she reminded herself. Just a trick of the eye.

Winter arched until the back of his head touched the floor of the dais. He stretched his second bound arm straight up, so all the metal cuffs were clearly visible in the light. As the beat dropped again, he twisted his wrist and—again, Sydney watched in disbelief as he slid right out of the binds. They clattered to the floor. In another smooth gesture, he removed his gag and blindfold. The audience gasped in approval.

They locked me up, but I broke away, broke away

Winter spun to his feet. In time with the music, he spun and arched backward. One leg and ankle slid out of the binds. Then the other. As he did, he pulled his shirt off, exposing for a shocking second his bare upper body before flipping the shirt inside out and sliding it back on in a single move to reveal cobalt blue silk instead. At the same time, his pants unclipped to a layer underneath in the same bold blue hue. Now he looked less like a bird and more like an ocean. The audience rippled with a gasp.

He looked around at the audience, a slight smirk on his lips, his headpiece glittering in the light.

Sydney had watched some of Winter's performances before they began their mission, had studied the way he moved and done her due diligence in researching him. But she'd never seen him perform live before. And in that moment, every dismissive thought she'd ever had about him vanished from her mind.

This wasn't the boy with the sarcastic grin and the quick mouth, the one she couldn't seem to stop bickering with.

This was the superstar.

They tried to catch him, but he turned into the air
Turned into the water, into the sea between you and me

Now the backup dancers arrived, stealing through the aisles in dark figures until they reached the stage. Sydney picked out Dameon and Leo instantly. As the chorus to the track kicked in with a thunderous beat, the dancers slid into a formation around him and then all synced in movement.

In spite of herself, Sydney could feel her heart racing.

They tried to stop me, but I came all this way, all this way

Leo tossed him a bouquet of yellow and white flowers. Winter grabbed it, then hopped off the stage in a fluid move. The audience stirred in delight, parting and drawing forward as he headed toward Penelope. The spotlight followed him.

Came all this way, just to wish you

He stepped right up to her. Under the light, Sydney saw Penelope inhale and give a little laugh.

Just to wish you a happy birthday

The audience burst into a round of laughter and cheers at the tweak in the lyrics that Winter had made for Penelope. He offered her the flowers. She covered her mouth with both hands, trembling, while the friends around her screamed and shoved her in delight. Then she took the bouquet without looking away from him. He smiled sidelong at her and shifted back to the stage as the music changed yet again.

As he turned, his gaze latched on to Sydney.

In spite of herself, Sydney felt her breath hitch at the sear of his attention. He hadn't looked at her like this before—fully entrenched in his stage persona, the light glinting hot in his eyes. For an instant, she felt chained into place.

Then, in a flash, he was back on the dais and joining his dancers in a furious, fast-paced track. The beat shook the floor under Sydney's feet. The lights switched to red, bathing the entire space in scarlet—and then some invisible hook propelled Winter from the stage floor to high up in the air. The audience shrieked.

Sydney let her breath out slowly. What an absolute bastard of a flirt. If Penelope wasn't cheered up after this, then she couldn't be swept off her feet by anything in the world.

A slight movement in the darkness of the audience shook her back into place. She glanced over and across the dais to where Eli Morrison sat. He had risen to his feet along with Connor Doherty and a third man. They exchanged a few more words.

Sydney itched to get closer. But it would be too obvious here if she, Winter's primary bodyguard, left now. She had no doubt Eli's men were watching her from a dozen different spots in the room. So all she could do was let herself steal glances toward Eli and the others.

Then she saw Connor lean toward Eli and, as Winter segued into his final routine, murmur something to the man. She narrowed her eyes, reading his lips enough to decipher the words.

"It has to be tonight, sir."

Eli frowned back at him as the theater shook with the opening bass beats. "No. The meeting is tomorrow." Then came some words she couldn't make out.

"I'm afraid we can't, sir."

Eli was one of the most intimidating men Sydney had crossed paths with, but something in Connor's quiet, pleading gaze seemed to make him think. He didn't answer right away. His eyes followed Winter's movements on the stage, then turned to the silhouette of his daughter.

Sydney counted out the seconds in her head. *Eight, nine, ten, eleven.*

At last, Eli said, "Tonight, then."

There was an urgency in the words, a tension in his body that made Sydney's heart beat a little faster. Something was happening that felt like a ripple in their plans. Her expression never changed, and neither did her gaze, but Eli Morrison's words echoed in her mind, solid and ominous.

Tonight, then.

She had some tailing to do.

Characters on a Stage

Winter Young had been to enough post-concert after-parties to last him a lifetime—but even he was fairly certain he'd never been to one quite like this.

A couple hours after his performance had ended, he found himself walking with Penelope down a flight of stairs curving along the inside of a massive cylinder that descended underground from a private, guarded entrance alongside the Thames River.

"It was called Brunel's Thames Tunnel, actually," Penelope explained to him as they went, one of her hands restlessly tucking her hair behind her ears. Her bejeweled hairpin glittered as her fingers brushed past it. "Some guy named Brunel and his son built the first tunnel to connect underground beneath a major river. Used to be for carriages, and then for trains. My father funded its restoration some years ago into an exhibition space."

Her grip around his arm was tight and nervous, and now and then, he could feel her tremble. Her father wasn't breathing down her neck here, but his presence still loomed in every detail of this party. Even so, it was the most talkative she'd been since they first met.

He cast a quick glance over his shoulder to make sure Sydney was behind him. It felt strange, knowing that none of his friends would be here. Dameon seemed unbothered, content to head into the city to party on his own, but Leo had been unusually quiet after their performance, had watched Winter prepare to leave for the after-party behind the palace without a word.

"Is he feeling okay?" Winter had muttered to Claire as he stood before one of Eli's cars.

"Don't worry about your boys," Claire had told him. "They'll have their own fun." Then she'd given him an encouraging *well done!* look before sending him off.

Now only Sydney was heading down two steps behind him, her silver pants swishing against her legs in a shimmer of fabric with every move she made.

It made his heartbeat speed up. The shine in that outfit had distracted him more than a few times during his performance. Maybe Panacea had gone overboard with her look. When she'd caught him afterward and slipped her hotel crest pin in his pocket, he'd found himself skipping a beat in his answer, his tongue tripping all over itself.

"*For your protection,*" she'd said.

The pin must have been part of Panacea's drop for them, which meant Sydney had collected the parcel successfully.

Then she'd cast him a sidelong smile before falling into step beside him. "*Nice concert,*" she'd added before looking away.

Winter's gaze had darted to her, and then to the glittering sheen of her swaying pants. He'd opened his mouth, realized he had nothing coherent to say, and closed it promptly. She didn't even bother looking at him—which was just as well. Better that she hadn't seen the embarrassment on his face.

Now he forced his attention back to Penelope. "And did Brunel know how to transform his tunnel creation into a party as good as this?" he said.

"Almost," Penelope replied, holding her hand over her mouth to hide a bashful smile. "Apparently it made a better party spot than a transport system. I hear the grand opening had stalls with dancing monkeys and acrobats."

Winter looked down as they made their way along the stairs. Well, the acrobats were definitely still here. Strips of bold yellow silks hung from the shaft's ceiling, and twisted within them were lithe young figures twirling at various heights along either side of the metal stairway. Hanging with them were long, low chandeliers that cast a kaleidoscope of light and shadow against the shaft's walls. The thud of music reverberated throughout the space, and when he looked skyward, he saw that a starry sky's worth of crystal bulbs hung twinkling from the ceiling.

At the bottom of the stairs, they passed a fire-eater blowing out a line of flame through a hoop, eliciting gasps from his little cluster of onlookers. Shops and stalls were set up along the edges of the shaft leading in toward the former train tunnels; there were bar carts and food stations and tables lined with gold gift bags. Servers walked around with silver trays, bearing bite-sized samosas and savory pies, tiny cups of fries and dishes of dumplings drizzled with chili oil.

When he glanced again at Sydney, he noticed that she was doing a sweep of the space, her eyes flitting from one stand to another, a wary scowl on her face. As if she were just a typical bodyguard.

Winter twisted the snake ring idly on his finger. His eyes had been seeking her out constantly the entire evening. As his hand dropped back to his side, it knocked against the tiny vial of toxin sewn into a hidden part of his pocket. The suicide drink, a reminder of their mission. His breath hitched, and he tried to push it from his mind.

They stirred up a commotion as soon as they stepped down onto the shaft's floor. Seconds later, a cluster had gathered around them in a ring, full of eager faces and outstretched hands waiting to be shaken. Cheers of *Happy Birthday!* to Penelope. Winter hung back with her as she smiled graciously to each of their admirers and the circle around them grew larger.

"Winter Young?" one of them exclaimed at him.

Another smiled widely. "I've never seen a performance like that," she breathed, her eyes fixated on him. "You're going to have to teach us some of those moves on the dance floor."

Penelope's grip tightened around Winter's arm as she gave the girl a mock frown. "Get your own superstar," she said.

"Winter! Winter Young!"

His name echoed in a radius around him. Among them walked a few of Eli Morrison's security guards, their massive presence calmly redirecting the growing crowd.

Winter sensed Sydney's presence closer to his side. When he looked at her, she was nearly pressed against him, carefully watching the people approaching. She glared at one young man who got too near for comfort—then stepped between them and pushed the guest steadily back just by walking toward him. The man retreated with a look of confused offense in his eyes.

Winter wanted to laugh a little at the sight. If Sydney hadn't become a secret agent, she really could have found a career in being an effective bodyguard.

They made their way out of the thronging cluster of people, security moving around them in an undulating circle.

"Your bodyguard just pushed away the Prince of Orange-Nassau," Penelope told Winter with a scandalized grin.

"I'll extend my apologies to His Highness later," Winter told her with a lifted eyebrow.

Over her head, he briefly caught Sydney's eye. The two exchanged a knowing look. Still no sign here of the one they needed to see—Connor Doherty. Maybe he didn't attend parties like this. He would have to find a way to bring up the man's name.

They met a couple more of Penelope's friends in quick succession. The music changed, the tempo mellowing into something slow and sultry, and as an open area of the floor filled with other couples, Winter pulled Penelope in for a dance. Here, at last, the crowd around them dispersed a bit, although he could still see people casting them long glances from every part of the room. Nothing he wasn't used to.

Sydney glided off the dance floor to a corner near the wall to give them space. Her eyes still followed their every move. Winter found himself catching her gaze every time they turned.

"So, Miss Morrison," he said as they fell into step with the music, "grade me. On a scale of one to ten, how did I score for your birthday performance?"

Penelope blushed red enough for him to tell even in the low light. "Is ten the highest or the lowest?"

"Ten would be going on the best holiday of your life."

Her smile turned into a giggle. "You get a nine, then."

"A nine!" Winter pushed away with a look of wounded shock on his face. "You don't think I was as good as the best holiday of your life?"

Penelope covered her mouth with one hand as she laughed. Her eyes turned down shyly. "One point deducted only for being too brief."

He put his hand on the small of her back. "Fair enough."

They danced a little longer in pleasant silence. Winter let himself be awed by their surroundings. But instead of looking pleased at his amazement, Penelope seemed to withdraw again, that stiffness returning to her step. He looked back down at her.

"Don't take this the wrong way," he said, leaning closer and lowering his voice. "But would you mind if I offered you a small assessment?"

"What?"

"I noticed something."

"And what's that?"

"You have tension in your dance step." He pulled her back a little and turned with her. "When you move to the side, see? Like you're resisting the move."

She blushed again, embarrassed this time. "Sorry. I'm a little, ah . . . nervous around you."

He could feel her shaking slightly in his arms. "I used to do the same thing early in my career," he reassured her. "That's the only reason why I noticed. My choreographer used to get on my case all the time over it."

At that, she met his gaze fully. "Don't tell me Winter Young was afraid of the stage."

"Oh, terrified. I used to tremble before stepping onstage before a packed stadium. It drove my choreographer nuts. So the first thing I ever learned was to fake a sense of ease. To most people, I looked relaxed. But I knew the stiffness was there." He quieted, then studied her. "Sometimes it takes a nervous person to recognize one."

Her smile took on a rueful tint, and he felt her relax a little toward him, as if grateful for his acknowledgment. "I'm sorry," she started to stammer out, "I don't mean to be—"

"One should never be sorry on her birthday," Winter replied, and she laughed again. Lessons from Sydney and their week of training streamed through Winter's mind. *Always make the people around you trust you.*

"I didn't take you as one who also felt so conscious in the presence of others," she said at last. With the way she phrased it, she didn't mean the crowds around them, but the invisible, all-present hand of one person.

"You're talking about your father, aren't you?" he asked.

She gave him a small smile and turned with him so that he could plainly see Eli's security watching them against the walls. "Don't you feel exhausted, being watched all the time?" she murmured.

Winter cast a meaningful look in Sydney's direction, and found himself momentarily distracted by the way her dress caught the low light. "By that one? Extremely exhausting. But at least I'm in good company."

Penelope regarded him with a new expression in her eyes. Something about their conversation had made her shoulders relax, had helped a bit of ease trickle into her footwork. As if she'd found a kindred spirit.

"Then let's go somewhere with fewer prying eyes." She paused for a moment and took his hand. "Come on."

"Where are we going?"

She tugged him gently along, biting her lip to keep her smile back. "I promise your bodyguard will forgive you."

He glanced instinctively toward Sydney, who watched him go, and turned his head just once, slightly, to tell her to stay put. She nodded in return, understanding immediately. But as he forced his eyes away, he noticed some guy trying to talk to her, a well-dressed man in a white suit and rather garish top hat. He glimpsed Sydney giving him a careful smile and a brief answer before he and Penelope reached the other side of the floor.

She didn't lead him toward the main tables lining the edges of the party, nor the clusters of her guests who waved at them as they passed by. Instead, she took him past the stairs and into a shadowed segment of the space, through a tunnel that had previously been blocked off. The guards stepped aside for them without a second's hesitation.

Winter could feel the warning buzz in his mind at the realization he was leaving Sydney behind completely. He could almost hear Claire in his ear, as if this were the first time he was attending an awards show without her, could feel her upbeat pat on his back.

Be as terrified as you need to be. Just don't you dare show it on camera.

So he kept his muscles relaxed and his smile easy, focusing his attention in curiosity on the tunnel around them.

"There are dozens of abandoned tunnels under the streets of London," Penelope told him as they went. "Not that it means they're unoccupied."

Then she reached the other end of the passageway, where a guard stepped aside and opened the door for them.

A burst of noise and light hit Winter.

Inside, other tables and chairs were laid out, the air hazy with smoke and music. The clientele in here looked a little less like Penelope's friends—the rich young people preening around in the main party space, trying too hard—and more like a crowd that couldn't care less about keeping up with the social scene. Some glanced up, recognizing him, and he heard the usual eager murmurs of his name. But they didn't swarm him, and after a moment, everyone went back to their activities.

Winter saw none of Eli's usual security in here, probably to Penelope's relief—but even though he didn't see the elder Morrison in person, he could feel the danger of the man.

Penelope peered up questioningly at Winter, her eyes twinkling, as if she was eager to show off all the cool corners of her party to him.

Winter saw the man right away. He stood near the edge of a craps table, applauding the current winner of a round. Unlike everyone else in the room, he wore no costume tonight—instead, his vest was proper and plain, his jacket and suit black, his eyes covered with an unembellished black mask. His hair was cut short on both sides and then combed neatly back on top.

The elusive Connor Doherty had finally made an appearance.

Dangerous Games

He was a thin, slight young man, with no unusual features. But just as Sauda had claimed, the little jewelry Connor wore was noticeably expensive. A thin necklace, rings resplendent on his hands, a platinum and gold limited-edition Rolex. He wasn't showy in his attire, but definitely had a penchant for expensive accessories. And now was finally Winter's chance to get close to him.

The hotel crest pin Sydney had slipped him felt heavy in his pocket. Winter noted it, glad to have a hidden weapon with him.

Just be yourself, Sauda had said. And so, because he knew it was what he'd say if he weren't undercover, Winter turned his charisma up, leaned close to Penelope's ear, and whispered, "Who's that?"

Penelope shivered at his breath against her ear. She cast a smile over at the table. "Mr. Doherty is one of my accountants. Why do you ask?"

Identity confirmed, Winter thought. "He has good taste in jewelry," he said honestly.

She grinned, as if pleased that he'd noticed. "Yes," she replied, "I sometimes send him to pick out jewelry for me."

Winter gave her a playful smile. "Can he pick mine out, too?"

Penelope laughed, her cheeks pink. "Never hurts to ask."

He must have noticed them approach, but he didn't look up from where he was watching the action. Instead, as they drew near to the game table, he pushed his glasses higher on his nose and said, "Bored of your birthday already, Miss Morrison?"

"Can't a girl visit the private rooms when she wants?" she said, casting Winter a conspiratorial smile. "We just both wanted a break from the eyes watching us."

Being in here, away from her father's men, seemed to boost Penelope's confidence, as if she were indulging something secret and wholly her own. Winter could sense the straightening of her figure and the fading away of that stiff gait in her walk, the new smugness in her posture at showing this side of herself to him.

Connor offered her an amused smile and a deferential nod. His eyes went to the bejeweled pin in her hair. "Glad you're wearing it," he said.

She lowered her eyes, pleased, and patted it. "It's perfect," she gushed.

Winter watched them closely. He could feel a hint of tension between them, an electricity in the air that didn't exist with usual business associates. But there was also something off about it that he couldn't quite put his finger on. Was Panacea certain they had the whole story about them?

Around them, Winter noticed the other spectators as they each gave Penelope smiles and well wishes.

Connor now said mildly to Penelope. Then he glanced over for the first time, caught sight of Winter, and looked back to the table again with disinterest. His eyes were a pale, watery blue. "You've brought a friend."

So he wasn't much of a fan. Maybe he wasn't a fan of meeting people in general.

Penelope slipped into the spot beside him and shot him a look, something that Winter read as a silent plea to be nice. "This is Winter Young," she said.

"Yes, the *entertainment*," he answered. One of the players threw the dice, and a cheer went up.

"Mr. Young wanted to pay you a compliment," Penelope said.

Winter gave the man a respectful nod. "Sir," he said over the noise.

"Connor Doherty," the man replied, although he didn't extend a hand.

Good, Winter thought. An underestimation. He'd gotten this sort of look before, from people who didn't think there could be much in the brain of a pop star.

"I noticed your worthy collection," Winter said, unfazed, nodding at Connor's jewelry.

Now the man's eyes rose to Winter's own. Sure enough, he looked immediately to the snake ring on Winter's left hand.

For the first time, his eyes widened slightly in interest, then narrowed before he peered closer at it.

"Is that a meteorite?" he said.

So Sauda and Niall had been right to give them this ring. Winter smiled back at Connor and nodded. "This? A genuine stone from the Hierapolis meteorite," he replied. "It made its debut at a Christie's auction recently."

"Yes, I know. I lost the bid on it." Connor made a sound of mock dislike, then looked at Winter with new interest. "Apparently, I lost it to you," he said with a laugh.

Winter acted amused by his words, then said, "Do you want it?"

Connor blinked at him through his glasses. It must have been rare for him to be taken by surprise, because even Penelope seemed to note his expression. "What do you mean?" he said.

"Was custom-made for me from the full meteorite," he said with a wink. "I ordered a bunch of pieces set from it."

Now the man looked genuinely stunned. Then he clapped his hands together and laughed. "Here," he said to the person beside him, handing him his dice. "Finish the game for me. I'm going to have a word."

Winter slid the ring off his finger and handed it to him. Connor took the jewelry in his hand, then held it up to the light to admire the flecks of olivine shining in the rock.

"It takes a man of good taste to set a meteorite as beautiful as this one," he said.

Winter shrugged. "The stone gave me no choice," he said.

Connor smiled at him, then looked at Penelope. "I like this one," he answered.

"He means that," Penelope told Winter, giving Connor a teasing nudge. "I've never seen him this pleased about anything all year."

Winter put his hands into his pockets to hide them, just in case they started trembling. After-party habit. Maybe they didn't suspect him, but it didn't help calm his nerves any. He wondered what Sydney might be thinking out there on the main floor as she watched and waited for him to show up again. Maybe she was silently counting how many minutes he'd been gone and gauging when she might have to come hunt him down. Maybe she approved of how he'd been swept away. Maybe she was eyeing the entrances and exits to the place, working out their best plan should things go wrong.

Maybe she was still chatting with that guy in the damn top hat. Not that he cared, one way or another.

Penelope's hand on his arm shook him out of his thoughts again. Connor had pulled them aside to one of the tables lining the edge of this smaller room, then poured them both a drink. Winter purposely waited a second, looking with admiration around the room until Penelope had taken a sip. It must be safe. He did the same.

Whiskey, a good one.

"You're a fashion connoisseur," Connor said to Winter, pointing his drink at him. He nodded at Winter's outfit. "Are you a connoisseur of astronomy, too, then?"

Winter shook his head. "I just know to appreciate a rare thing," he replied. "And I know that this pallasite meteorite is one of the most precious objects ever to grace our earth."

The answer seemed to please Connor. "And what's so precious about it to you?"

"Because this piece of rock has been around since before anything in our solar system," Winter answered. "It was out there before everything around us, before any civilization, animal, speck of living dirt. And now I get to sport it on my finger." His smile turned sly. "That's a sign we're winning, isn't it?"

It was the kind of answer Winter knew would reflect the personality of whoever he happened to be talking to. It disgusted him nevertheless. Still, Connor smiled again, then eyed him approvingly. "I'll have to show you my personal collection sometime. I think you would appreciate it."

The knot in Winter's stomach twisted. On the surface, he let himself lean forward in interest. "I'd like that."

Connor looked satisfied. Definitely the kind of wealthy man who enjoyed showing another wealthy man his own worth. "We're alike, you know. When he finds something valuable, a wise man either keeps it for himself or sells it to the person who wants it more."

"Wisdom," Winter said with a respectful smile, even as he felt his anger rise. This was a man who worked to buy and sell things that destroyed lives, who blithely wrote down numbers in a ledger as he helped load ships with illegal weapons.

Through the haze and smoke around him, he could almost see Sauda leaning toward him, her eyes solemn. *Have you ever witnessed war?*

And in that moment, he felt the shift inside him. He was no longer just a boy enduring the company of wealthy people, tolerating them in his own ambitions of climbing the world's ladder. He was here for a reason, using the experience of his years in such circles to now take down one of their worst.

A thankless good deed. Sauda's words echoed in his mind. And suddenly, he thought he could understand what had once fueled Artie.

"Now," Connor said with a nod to them both, his eyes returning to the game happening behind him, "if you'd like, I'm happy to invite you into this next round. Be warned, Mr. Young, that we don't always play nicely with others."

"That's a generous offer," Penelope said. Winter could feel her leaning slightly against his arm. "But I think I really am bored with this party." She gave him a smile and a nod. "We can catch up tomorrow?"

Connor gave her an affectionate look of disappointment. "Hard to keep you happy, eh, Miss Morrison?" he said. Then he smiled and held her gaze for a moment. "Don't worry. I won't tell your dad. See you tomorrow."

She nodded, touched his arm, and then turned away with Winter.

As she did, Winter noticed the spark in her eyes fade—and the charming, flirtatious smile she'd given him turning off like a light switch.

Odd. Again, he felt like something was off about the subtle way these two flirted with each other. His mind whirled, trying to pin down what it was—

And then he realized it. It was in the way that spark vanished so abruptly from her eyes.

It was how celebrities acted when they were putting on a show of being in a relationship, for the benefit of drumming up press and getting headlines. It was *an act.*

Winter could spot this kind of false romance every time—he and Claire had a running bet for every time this happened, and he always won. He'd even done it himself before, had been paired up with another popular singer earlier in his career, knew what kind of emotions he was supposed to put on display and how it'd come across to the public. Knew when to turn it off when he sensed no one was paying attention anymore.

Connor and Penelope weren't having an affair. They were *playing* at it.

But why would they do that? To annoy Eli? Was there another reason?

Winter let none of his spiraling thoughts show. All he said to Penelope instead was, "Where to now?"

She smiled hopefully at him, then glanced toward the tunnel leading back to the main floor. "Want to get out of here?"

Winter raised an eyebrow at her. It was hardly the first time he'd ever been propositioned, but somehow being on a mission made him more anxious.

She bit her lip, then seemed to realize exactly what she'd said. She hurriedly looked down. "I don't mean"—she rushed to say—"that is, I'm not trying to insinuate that—" She paused, beet red. "I just meant if you wanted to hang out somewhere more private. That's it."

He smiled at her. "Sure."

She gave him a bashful smile. "Really?"

He looked around the party space. "It might not be obvious," he said, "but I'm an introvert."

She brightened at that. "Me too!" Then she realized her outburst and laughed a little. "My place isn't far from here. I could make us some coffee."

Sydney. Her name was the first thing that popped into Winter's mind. She'd want him to handle this alone, his nerves be damned. Would she follow along? Would she hide out in the bushes outside Penelope's home? He tried to picture how the night would go, how missions usually went for Sydney at this stage.

All roads lead to Penelope, she had said.

So he made himself smile at her. The mission closed in around him like a vise.

"Let's go, then," he replied.

Dead End

Winter and Penelope were gone for a good thirty minutes. Sydney found herself restlessly wandering the party space, checking constantly for messages from Winter, monitoring his location to make sure he was still here. She had to be an attentive bodyguard, after all. Maybe she was starting to believe in her cover so much that her anxiety over his absence was real. She found herself loitering near the tables, picking up a few of the gold spoons and tea light candles out of nervous habit before forcing herself to put them back. Now was not the time to get caught for stealing. Still, she found herself circling back to the tables and, when she was sure no one was watching, finally stashing several spoons in the hidden pocket of her pants. The habit soothed her nerves. Somewhat.

At last she saw them emerge again from the back of the stairs. Sydney caught Winter giving her a single, meaningful glance.

He was leaving the venue alone with Penelope, she gathered as he walked toward her to wave a quick farewell.

"Don't wait up," he told her as Penelope stood behind him.

"Have fun," she replied, drawing close enough to give him a pat on the arm. In one fluid movement, she dropped the pen she'd gotten in the parcel into his pants pocket. "For your protection," she whispered as she brushed past his ear, "since you'll be on your own."

He must have felt the pen drop into his pocket, but he didn't say anything. Instead, he gave her a sidelong wink before turning away. "See you in the morning," he said.

Then he headed back to Penelope and walked to the exit.

Sydney caught sight of his hand and noticed that the snake ring was gone.

Maybe he'd made contact with Connor Doherty already.

Well. He was halfway competent, after all. Surreptitiously, she tapped one of the diamonds on her bracelet and felt her phone buzz in her hidden pocket. The snake ring was recording now.

Winter looked at ease, his head close to Penelope's as they shared a laugh about something on their way up the winding stairs. Sydney watched in approval, then sent Claire a brief message. *HU, Winter leaving party w P. Don't thk I'm invited. He's on his own.*

A reply came back before Sydney was even sure she had sent her message. *Where? For how long?*

dk. They'll b fine.

Claire didn't answer for several seconds. Finally, she responded with *I'll tell his driver. Just make sure he's back by morning.*

Sydney answered with a quick *K*, then headed up the stairs behind them.

Above the tunnel's shaft, the cobblestone streets were slick with rain, their gleaming surfaces reflecting a carousel of color. A car was already waiting out here for Winter and Penelope's emergence. Sydney caught sight of a group of fans loitering some distance away, behind a barricade set up around the shaft's entrance by Morrison's men. Somehow privy, as always, to Winter's location. They screamed and waved as he went by. He gave them a terse nod, then climbed into the sedan behind Penelope.

To the average onlooker, he must have appeared carefree, with a slight smile on his face and the wind blowing wisps of his hair across his face. But Sydney recognized the slight hints of his discomfort. There was a tightening of his jaw, an extra crease in between his brows.

He was headed into the mission alone now, and she wouldn't be there to protect him.

She wanted to frown at herself for worrying. This was what they wanted. What could happen to Winter anyway, when Penelope was with him? Certainly nothing bad, not with Eli's daughter there to witness everything. She had invited him here; he was an international superstar.

Besides. Sydney had another reason to stay behind tonight.

A fresh wind followed a pair of double-decker buses that roared down the street, and she winced against the gust. The smell of rain and the faint tang of the Thames nearby hung heavy on the air, musty and cold and damp, dripping from every balcony and tree branch. The cold air sent an unpleasant twinge through her lungs, but she still relished the crispness of it. She sank herself into the shadows near the entrance until she was entirely unnoticeable, then pulled a folded black jacket out of her purse, throwing it over her silken top. She slipped quickly out of her billowing pants and immediately into a pair of jeans, unclipping the antler band from her head and breaking it into several smaller segments, folding it neatly into her bag. Seconds later, she returned her attention to the sprinkle of guests entering and leaving the venue.

She'd seen Eli and his crew head into the party, but had yet to see them leave. The murmur she'd overheard from Connor Doherty replayed in her mind.

Tonight.

Eli's cargo shipment would be heading out soon. If she could just find a way to get close enough to them, if she could just record evidence in their conversation, she would be set. But Winter hadn't crossed paths with Eli all evening, either.

Another half hour passed after Winter and Penelope left before Sydney finally saw her targets emerge from the entrance.

One of the men was Eli Morrison, and the expression on his face looked stormy. She didn't recognize the other two suited figures with him.

Sydney let herself stay relaxed and slouched against the wall, but every single one of her senses sharpened as she watched the men disappear into a waiting car, which then pulled quietly away from the street.

She turned her phone up and pointed the camera toward the departing car. Then she tapped it on the screen.

A blinking red dot appeared over it.

"Track," she said in a low, clear voice.

The red dot stopped blinking, and the camera swiped away to reveal a dot on her maps.

She pocketed her phone and pushed away from the wall. Her boots turned in the direction of the car.

The sedan paused at the light, then turned left, the same way that Penelope's car had gone. As Sydney reached the intersection and turned with it, the car changed several lanes. Then it veered left into a lane of parked cars and sped up, screeching to a halt at the end and cutting back over into the right lane. It made an abrupt left turn and disappeared around the corner.

A classic maneuver to throw off anyone who might be trying to tail them.

Sydney broke into a sprint. She cut across the traffic, ignoring the honks of complaint from drivers, and burst onto the opposite sidewalk. As she turned the corner, she checked her phone and noted the car making another left, then right. She ran down the street parallel to it, then darted under an archway that led into an alley of mews. At the end of the row, she kicked off against the wall and grabbed the edge of a hanging flower basket for balance, raining petals down as she pulled herself up to clutch the railing of the second floor's balcony. She swung her legs over the side, and jumped up to grab the balcony door's upper ledge. Two more kicks, and she'd grabbed the edge of the roof.

Her lungs squeezed in protest at her sudden burst of activity. She hung there for a second, forcing herself to take in deep, measured breaths, trying to ignore the low waves of pain pulsing through her.

It eased slightly, enough for her to swing herself up onto the roof. She crouched there for a moment, wincing. As she did, she saw the car come back into view, zooming down the street at full speed.

Damn. She couldn't keep chasing it on foot through the city like this. Sauda's gentle scolding came back to her from her recruit days, when she was doing timed laps on the training floor.

Speed it up out there, Cossette! Sauda had called to her.

Sydney had just nodded, swallowed the pain in her lungs, and pushed herself onward.

After, Sauda had made a surprise appearance during dinner, coming to sit beside her as she took a quiet meal by herself in one of the headquarters' dining rooms.

Sydney could still remember straightening up out of respect as the woman approached, and then hunching back down when Sauda gave her a nonchalant wave.

I can run the circuit again tomorrow, Sydney had started to say, in apology for her performance on the track. But Sauda had cut her off with a shake of her head.

Tomorrow, come with me, the woman had replied. *You don't have to run the fastest to beat your opponents.* She'd given Sydney a wry smile. *You just need to be the smartest.*

Now Sydney instinctively fixed her posture and breathed deeply. She ducked low, until her figure was completely hidden behind the chimneys, and then studied the street from her hiding place.

Her gaze settled on a parked motorbike beside a rubbish bin surrounded by black garbage bags.

"Apologies in advance," she muttered, as if the bike's owner could hear her.

As the car drove past her, she darted out from behind the chimneys and swung over the side of the house's roof, dropped down to the balcony, then down further to the street. Once she landed, she ran to the motorbike, pulled out a tiny gadget switch hanging on her keychain, and glanced quickly around. Shuttered row of supermarkets and nurseries, no pedestrians.

She undid the hood of the bike, exposing the tangle of wires underneath. There, she pulled apart the ignition lock and inserted both ends of the wiring into the slots.

Vroom.

Sydney smiled as the engine rewarded her with a satisfying roar. Then she straddled the bike and hit the pedal, skipping with a lurch onto the road.

The wind blew cold against her face, stinging her cheeks. She veered sharply left to follow the car, then slowed down and hung back as the vehicle hit a red light. She turned off the motorcycle's lights. Her outfit blended her into the night.

As they hit a second stop, the car suddenly sped up and made a sharp right when it wasn't its turn to go. The car on the other side of the intersection screeched to a halt. As Sydney sped past it, she could hear its driver shouting something angrily at the disappearing vehicle. She revved her bike. As the intersecting driver started pulling forward, she zoomed past him. The shouts behind her faded away.

Up ahead, the car turned onto a bridge, merging with a rapid stream of other cars. Sydney followed it on. Some distance across the water, she could see the silhouette of Westminster Bridge against the black horizon. Where were they heading?

As soon as the thought crossed her mind, the car made a quick turn halfway on the bridge, its tires bumping hard up the middle divider. Cars behind it swerved, screeching at its abrupt move.

The car skipped over the middle divider and merged onto the lanes going in the opposite direction.

Sydney shifted gears and forced the motorcycle to do a rapid turn several hundred yards down. The bike's wheels slammed against the divider, threatening to flip her, but she hung gamely on to the handles and guided it over. She merged with the opposing lane and revved the engine again.

The car had succeeded in widening the gap between them. But it didn't matter, because when Sydney synced her watch with her phone, the red tracker still showed up on her map. Now it was exiting the bridge and heading south, out of the city center and westward along the Thames.

She kept up her pace. As the end of the bridge appeared, she saw that the street parallel to the bridge was newly jammed with cars, all honking loudly. A second later, she realized that Eli's car had zipped around a street right before it could get stuck behind a garbage truck that had paused to collect the piles of bags at a street corner. Sydney swore under her breath, remembering the neighborhood's late night bin collection schedule.

As the cars ahead of her stalled, she veered sharply off the road and skipped up onto the sidewalk. The bike hurtled straight for a set of stone stairs leading to the top of the short wall running along the riverside.

She gritted her teeth, sped up, and tilted the bike's front wheel off the ground.

She roared up the stairs and launched briefly into the air.

The wheels landed with a thud and a screech on top of the wall. She sped down the riverside.

Moonlight reflected off the rippling black surface of the Thames. The world blurred by her in darkness. Up ahead, she saw the first hints of the car's taillights turning in the evening fog. Then the mist was upon her, and the river disappeared into the gray shroud. All she could see ahead of her were the faint shadows of building silhouettes and the faint scarlet blur of taillights far ahead.

"Display my maps," she called out to her phone.

The screen went bright, and suddenly there appeared a virtual grid of the city before her—the streets and the Thames and the flats lining the other side of the road—all passing her rapidly as she hurtled through the fog.

Up ahead, the car disappeared down another street.

Sydney skipped the motorcycle back down onto the road, then turned with it. They'd gone far outside central London and, according to her maps, had reached a lock on the river in the borough of Richmond. She frowned. If Eli Morrison had business out here, it couldn't be good.

A small pair of footbridges emerged and faded repeatedly in the thickening fog. It was between these footbridges that Sydney saw the red dot on her grid come to a sudden stop.

She stepped on the motorcycle's brakes. The bike sputtered to a halt in the thick of the fog. Sydney opened the hood again and twisted the wiring out of the ignition lock.

The bike's rumbling engine cut off abruptly. Its lights faded, and Sydney found herself shrouded in the night.

The fog muffled the sounds of the water and the distant scream of sirens. Up ahead, she could make out the faint sounds of three voices—none of whom sounded like Eli Morrison—along with their boots tapping on the sidewalk. The roar of a plane overhead covered up any chance of her hearing what they were saying.

As they went, she could hear the footsteps shift from cobblestone to the hollow thud of a pier's gangway. Then one of them changed from walking to being dragged. The boots scraped long lines of noise against the wooden flooring.

Her skin prickled. They either had a prisoner with them, or someone unable or unwilling to walk. Who had Eli brought with them in the car? Who had been held captive in there before they'd climbed in?

She edged silently through the fog toward the sound, and as she drew near, a yacht materialized in the darkness, bobbing easily against the river's gentle current, its lights turned suspiciously down. Against the few lights on inside the boat, she could make out four silhouettes.

Her eyes darted to the name of the boat. *Invictus*. One of the yachts that Eli owned.

Sydney crept closer until she reached the beginning of the pier, then swung her legs over the side of the wall to the grass and dirt along the riverbank. The shadows under the pier stretched long here, and she melted into them, her figure lost in the fog. As the ground sloped into the water, she hopped up into the wooden scaffolding underneath the pier, balancing along the beams until she had reached the end of the pier where the yacht was docked. There, in the safety of the shadows, she stopped at a vantage point where she could glimpse some of the commotion on the deck.

She hit the Record button on her phone and her earring studs activated.

"Wake him up."

A stranger's voice drifted to her through the fog. Sydney picked up the slightest hint of a Corcasian accent, and saw one of the men nodding at the other.

There was a slight shuffle, followed by the sound of a hand slapping a face. Sydney shifted to the other side underneath the pier for a better view. There, she finally caught sight of the prisoner.

It was Eli Morrison.

Every hair stood up on the back of Sydney's neck. He *was* the prisoner.

Eli's head lolled listlessly to one side.

"Can he talk at all?" the first stranger said.

"Not yet," said another, crossing his arms. "Too strong of a shot in the car, I think."

There was some more mumbling, followed by the first stranger's voice again. "How about now?"

Another groan. Then a confused mumble that quickly turned angry.

"Get your goddamn hands off me before I order them cut off."

"I'm afraid you no longer give the orders, sir."

Gone was the charismatic, falsely generous façade she'd met when they first arrived in London. Eli sounded murderous with rage, like the one who could watch a family be tortured, who could order the beheading of an enemy.

Why had he been kidnapped and brought here?

"I had a sample of your shipment brought to us," the first stranger now said. He accepted a small metal cylinder from one of his companions, then walked over to Eli and opened its top.

Sydney craned her neck as he took out the contents.

Then she held her breath. It was a small, translucent object that looked like an ice cube. Even in the darkness, she could tell that it gave off the faintest blue glow. The man held it gingerly—now she saw that he was wearing a heavy set of gloves.

A warning began to buzz in her mind. This had to be a sample of Paramecium, the chemical weapon that Eli Morrison was shipping to South Africa.

The stranger turned it in his palm. "It looks good," he mused in approval. "Your men tell me the ship is fully loaded and ready to be on its way."

"After tonight, I doubt you'll be getting your shipment." Eli's voice had turned low, menacing in its calm.

A sigh. "I'm afraid you're unaware of what's happening here."

Eli's reply sent a chill down Sydney's spine. "No one breaks a contract with me."

"No, Mr. Morrison. I don't think you understand." There was no hint of fear in the other man's voice. "There is nothing to negotiate, because you still owe us."

"What the hell are you talking about?"

"According to our accounts, you are short in your deliveries. We've paid you in full for the past shipment, and yet what we received didn't quite add up to what we ordered."

"You're lying or a fool. Count again and release me."

The man ignored him. Sydney trembled at the realization that some-one could feel so unthreatened by a man like Eli. "We don't appreciate being conned—certainly not by one who thinks we wouldn't notice years of it."

There was no immediate answer this time.

"I have the power to kill you and everyone you love," Eli went on. His voice was still quiet and full of menace, but this time she could hear a note of urgency in it. Of fear. "So think carefully about what you do next."

"And what do you think I can do to your loved ones?" The other man's voice dropped.

The first stranger nodded subtly. His two associates walked over to Eli and restrained him, one of them gripping the man's jaw firmly. As Sydney looked on, the first stranger took the pale blue cube and forced it into Eli's mouth. Before Eli could wrench away, the stranger sealed Eli's mouth completely shut with a wide strip of tape.

Sydney licked her lips and trembled, forcing her breathing to stay calm and measured. They were going to kill him.

I can't let them kill him, she thought immediately. Panacea needed Eli Morrison alive—his death would derail their entire mission, would engulf his network of people, would prevent Panacea from accessing what they needed to access in order to get a warrant for seizing his cargo.

Sydney straightened from her crouch and pulled herself up onto the pier, then stole into the shadows of the ship near the ladder against the hull.

Up on the deck, she heard two of the men arguing in Corcasian. Sydney knew enough of the language to get by, had been beefing up on it right before the mission. Now the words filtered through her ears, and she felt the vast library of languages in her head shift.

"The call's for you," one said.

"Not now," the other growled.

"It's urgent. They want to us to clear out by two and need to know how much longer we'll be."

They. Who were *they*? Or was she misunderstanding the language's pronouns? Sydney listened for clues as they continued muttering to each other in Corcasian, but no one clarified any further.

There was a pause in their argument, broken only by the sound of Eli's muffled grunts as he tried not to bite down on the lethal cube in his mouth. Sydney made her way soundlessly up the ladder until she was almost level with the ship's railing.

From here, she could see the back of Eli's head. She pressed herself as flat against the side of the ship as she could.

"Come with me," the man in charge finally said, waving for his associate to follow him. The other man fell into step without hesitation, leaving the third alone to guard Eli.

Sydney waited until the men's footsteps had faded around the corner of the deck. Then she pulled herself silently over the railing and landed with a soft thud behind the third guard. In the same move, she pulled a knife from her boot and flipped it around in her hand so that she wielded the hilt.

He barely had time to turn before Sydney lashed out at him, slamming the hilt into the back of his knee. His leg buckled—as he stumbled, she struck him viciously in the back of his neck. The man collapsed onto all fours. Sydney moved to hit him again, to knock him unconscious—but to her surprise, he didn't dart toward her. He went for Eli.

She lunged after him. But he ignored her, then reached Eli and swung a fist hard at the man's jaw. It connected with a loud crack.

No!

Sydney had to stifle the scream in her throat. She threw herself forward at the guard, tackling him in the side and sending him toppling to the floor. They both scrambled for an instant before Sydney smashed the hilt of her knife against the man's temple. He finally went limp.

Sydney hopped to her feet and hurried to Eli—

But it was too late.

Eli was foaming at the mouth, bloody bubbles dripping from the edges of the duct tape. Sydney's hand stopped in midair as she thought better of ripping the tape off—Eli suddenly surged up, as if trying to escape the chair he was bound to, his limbs pulling in a desperate attempt to get the shattered Paramecium out. A strangled sob came from his throat.

The sob changed halfway to an uncontrollable cough.

As Sydney looked on in horror, his body contorted backward and his boots scraped frantically against the deck. She took two steps back.

The sound of his muffled grunts changed, turned gurgling. She knew right away that the chemical must be dissolving his throat.

Eli met her eyes once. They were bloodshot and tinged with tears, open so wide that she thought his eyeballs might pop right out. She stared back at him. He recognized her—she could see that in their dying glaze. He looked like he wanted to say something.

Then his gaze clouded over, and he went limp against the chair, foam still dripping down his chin.

Sydney had witnessed plenty of deaths in the two years since she started working for Panacea, had enough nightmares of what she'd seen to last her lifetime. She knew how almost every kind of death sounded—a sigh from a shot, a gasp from a slash to the throat, the thrashing of dying limbs, the crumple of a body slumping.

But this. This was death by a new chemical weapon.

The billionaire tycoon behind one of the biggest trafficking operations in the world. The mogul who owned museums and yachts and sprawling estates. The man that Panacea had focused their attention on for years. The entire reason why Sydney and Winter were here in London.

He was now dead.

"Shit," Sydney whispered to herself. "Shit, *shit!*"

Paramecium. She didn't want to imagine what the chemical had done when it'd broken inside Eli's mouth, didn't want to think about what that little blue cube *could* do once it was loaded back inside its metal cylinder and launched within a city's center by the thousands. There had been a part of her that could believe—until she saw the weapon at work—the shipment was a myth, that maybe it wasn't real at all, that they were just here to find a ledger of numbers.

Well, she'd seen it now.

The cold air swirled against her, and she shivered. Her hand went to her back pocket. When she'd attacked the man, she had managed to swipe his wallet out of his pants and tuck it into her own. She wanted to flip the wallet open now and take a glimpse at who these assailants were, but there was no time. She had to get out of here.

Instead, with a last look at Eli, she hurried to the deck's railing and swung back over the edge. Her hands shook.

Eli Morrison is dead.

And so was their mission.

And in that moment, she froze against the hull's ladder. Cutting through her memory of Eli's dying rasps was the last thing the Corcasian ringleader said.

And what do you think I can do to your loved ones?

Eli's loved ones.

Her thoughts snapped into place.

Penelope. She might be next on their hit list. The realization sent a flood of horror through Sydney's veins.

"Winter," she gasped.

Birds from the Same Cage

Penelope Morrison's entire demeanor changed again the instant she exited the Alexandra Palace and slid into the car that drove them away. She sank into the seat; her muscles relaxed. Winter watched her from the corner of his eye as he pretended to enjoy the passing views of London at night. Up until now, he'd seen the version of her that was an anxious, blushing fan, the rich socialite, the birthday girl.

But the Penelope that now leaned her head back against her headrest with a sigh was a girl that just seemed . . . tired.

"Back to my flat, please," she said to the driver. Even her voice seemed to drop a few notes down to a new normal. The man nodded without a word and pulled away.

"Do you think they'll miss me there?" she said to Winter as they went.

She was clearly hoping for a compliment, so Winter gave it to her. "It's your birthday," he replied, giving her a conspiratorial wink. "Anyone who doesn't should be kicked out immediately."

She laughed and looked out the window. "What should I tell them?"

"That you skipped out with me?" Winter suggested.

Her laugh turned into a giggle. When she glanced out the window a second time, she looked back at him with wide eyes. "I saw a couple of photographers at that street corner!" she gasped. "They snapped us, didn't they?"

His smile turned mischievous. "I apologize in advance, because you're about to get some very salacious tabloid headlines."

She laughed again, shoving him teasingly, and then bit her lip.

Winter shuffled his boots slightly against the floor of the car. He didn't know how far he wanted to take this. And for some reason, he kept imagining Sydney sitting in Penelope's place instead, playing their own little game of teasing each other as they had done back at their house. He imagined Sydney's blue eyes flashing in the darkness of this car, her blond bob whipping around as she smiled at him.

What was Sydney doing right now? Was she somehow following them? Was she waiting back at the house, writing up a report for Sauda with a scowl on her face?

The pen that Sydney had given him sat heavily in his pocket. He didn't dare fiddle with it, but the weight of it there reminded him that he wasn't entirely alone. Sydney was still here, in a way, watching for danger.

After a while, they reached a quiet street in Holland Park, where they pulled up in front of a building draped heavily with ivy.

He made a noise of appreciation. "Nice place."

She sidled out of the car and nodded at him. "Come on in."

They headed inside and toward an elevator at the back of the lobby. When they reached the top floor, they stepped out into a corridor made of glass on either side. Through it, he could see a pretty nightscape of trees silhouetted against rows of chimneyed roofs, all of it outlined beneath the light of a half moon.

"Now, that's a view," he told her.

She smiled at him over her shoulder before unlocking her door and leading them in.

The space didn't look like it belonged to a young heiress. Glass boxes lined the walls, each of them containing what looked like a classic edition of a book, and in the center of the room was an enormous screen surrounded by various gaming consoles and plush couches. It looked less like an heiress's home and more like a studio.

As Penelope removed her sun-and-moon hairpiece with a relieved sigh and unclipped the bejeweled pin from her hair, Winter walked over to one of the books carefully lit from within a glass case. "Is that a Shakespeare First Folio?" he said, glancing at her before returning to admire the book. He let out a whistle. "You have even more expensive taste than your accountant."

Penelope put down her hairpin on the coffee table and smiled in surprise at him. "You actually recognize the first folio?"

He shrugged. "Any good musician ought to have respect for the written word," he said with a smile. "And Shakespeare wasn't bad."

"What's your favorite, then?" she said.

"*The Merchant of Venice,*" he replied automatically.

She must have meant the question as some sort of test, because she looked at him with new awe. "And what's your favorite line?"

He hummed under his breath before answering. "The man that hath no music in himself, nor is not moved with concord of sweet sounds, is fit for treasons, stratagems, and spoils."

She leaned her head against the wall of the kitchen entryway, her smile softer now as she regarded him. "I wouldn't have guessed that," she said.

"That so?" He straightened and gave her a teasing lift of his chin. "What would you have guessed, then?"

"Be not afraid of greatness," she replied, then turned her eyes down shyly.

He laughed. "How much of a narcissist would I have to be to pick that for myself?"

"It's not so bad!" she said before turning back around and heading to the kitchen. "Tea?"

"Sure, thanks. But only if it's herbal. And you don't have to steep it yet. Just give me the tea bag—I'll do it myself."

He heard her laugh from the kitchen. "Particular, are you? No worries."

As she heated up a kettle, Winter sank down onto one of her couches. Her place was quirky but cozy, the kind of space that Claire would approve of. He could see her throwing her head back against the couch and letting herself unwind.

Claire was going to try calling him soon, he was sure of it. He was starting to get used to keeping her out of the loop, and it made him uneasy.

His eyes fell to the hairpin that Penelope had tossed onto the coffee table. *You're wearing it*, Connor had said to her when he'd spotted it in her hair at the party. Maybe it had been a gift from him to her.

Winter stared at it a moment longer. If Sydney were here, he knew she'd swipe it, tuck it smoothly into her pocket and act like nothing had happened.

Not that he was Sydney, or a thief. But his gaze lingered on it, along with his recent realization of the mysterious relationship that Penelope had with her accountant. Maybe the pin was nothing—or maybe it was a useful clue into whatever existed between Connor and Penelope.

And maybe being around Sydney was rubbing off on him in the worst ways. Before Winter could think harder on it, he found himself taking the hairpin and sliding it neatly into his pocket, then leaning back on the couch.

A minute later, Penelope came back to him and handed him a steaming mug. "Hope you don't mind chamomile," she said, nodding to the unopened tea bag she handed him.

"Almost as good as jasmine." Winter ripped the paper and took the bag out, then sank it into the hot water. On the other end of the couch, Penelope cradled her own mug carefully and folded her legs up onto the seat. Her hair was pulled over her shoulder in a fat fishtail of a braid, and as she sat, her free hand came up to idly toy with the end of it.

Maybe Penelope was hoping he'd make some sort of move on her. Maybe she just wanted to talk. Her body was angled toward him, but curled up tightly in a way that shielded her. If Sydney were here, Winter knew she would probably have some kind of analysis on what her posture meant.

If Sydney were here, if Sydney were here—why did she keep entering his thoughts?

"I prefer hanging here," she said after an awkward pause. "I can only stand being at so many of my dad's parties."

Winter removed the tea bag from his mug as the water turned the ideal color and placed it on the small dish Penelope had set on the coffee table. He'd have to be careful how he talked about her father. "This a typical night for you?" he asked.

She shrugged. "Every few nights, at least."

"Exhausting. Why do you go?"

She smiled, eyes downcast. "Because it makes him happy."

For a moment, Winter pitied this girl. If circumstances were different, he could see himself being friends with her, talking about poetry and books and their favorite song lyrics, chatting over tea on her couch. Instead, he was about to implode her life, about to take down the father she worked so hard to please.

"And do you just go through your life making sure your father is happy?" he asked her.

She looked skeptically at him. "Don't judge *me*," she protested. "I saw that video of you partying at four in the morning in Ibiza."

He flashed her a grin. "I didn't know you followed me that closely."

"I think I envy your life a little."

He laughed. "You're the daughter of a billionaire. What about my life makes you even remotely jealous?"

She gave him a meaningful look. "Do you honestly think I could be at a party in Ibiza at four in the morning without several of my father's men watching me from some corner? Reporting back to him about what guy I might be dancing with or which friends I might be around?"

At the mention of her father again, Winter watched her, looking for ways to dig out more information. "What's wrong with a little protection? You're not exactly an average girl."

She hesitated for a moment, her eyes going to the windows that looked out upon the Thames. From their position on the couch, Winter could see the lights of ships lazing up and down the black water.

Finally, she turned back to him. "What was it like for you," she asked, "when you first became famous?"

Her question took him by surprise, and for a moment, he didn't answer. A memory flashed through him of the chaotic weeks after the video of him first went viral, when an avalanche of reporters had clogged his phone. Terrified, he'd hung up on all of them—including Claire, until he saw her same number popping up over and over along with increasingly persuasive text messages.

Please. Just let me have a single conversation with you.

Just learned your full name is Winter Young. Is that true?

Just one convo, Mr. Young. And I promise I'll never bother you again.

He finally relented. And she'd pitched herself so hard that he'd agreed reluctantly to a coffee date.

"It was . . . a little overwhelming," he now said to Penelope with a rueful smile. "I don't know how I would've made it through without a good guide."

She smiled. "You mean your manager, don't you? Claire?"

He nodded. Claire had been a whirlwind, even back then, and she was about the same age that Artie would have been if he were still alive, which he found comforting. There was a nervous optimism about her that reminded him of himself, like something inside her was restless to get out into the world, like she had something to prove. He found himself wanting to be near her because of it, as if some of it might rub off on him if he stuck around long enough.

What I do, Claire had told him during their first in-person meeting, *is discover new talent. And I can tell you that no one I've ever seen has given off the kind of raw potential I saw you give off in that video.*

So? he'd said warily to her. *What's that supposed to mean?*

It means we're going to discover you. She'd smiled gently at him. *Picture who you are when no one else is around. Picture the version of yourself that makes you the happiest. That's who we're going to find.*

The memory faded, and Winter regarded Penelope again. "Why do you ask?"

Penelope looked toward the window as she nursed her mug. "It must be nice," she said after a while, "to remember a time before and a time after. To know you built something, from the ground." She looked quickly at him. "I don't mean to complain about my life. I know I grew up with a silver spoon." Then she floundered a bit, as if trying to find the right words. "But sometimes I wonder . . . what it's like to have lived purposefully, you know? If there's any meaning to me being here. If I—*anyone*—deserve all this, just born to spend my life shuffling from one party to the next."

Meaning. And he understood her, knew that she must have spent her whole life thus far searching for purpose, what the point of everything was if she already had it all, why she deserved to live like this when so many others didn't. Whether she had anything to give in return. They were the same thoughts that haunted him.

"Maybe you just need to do a thankless good deed," he said.

She stared into her mug of cooling tea. "Maybe," she echoed.

Suddenly, it occurred to Winter that she hadn't wanted to bring him back here for a fling or a casual chat. She thought he was a kindred spirit. She needed to talk to him because she felt alone, because she needed to commiserate with someone who she thought might understand her.

A part of him felt annoyed at that. Poor little rich girl and her rich problems. He remembered hating people like this before he hit it big, that the only things that grieved them were things that the rest of the world could only wish they had.

But this wasn't all that grieved her. He could sense there was more, things she wasn't telling him. He weighed for a moment the risk of bringing it up, then leaned slightly toward her. *Gain her trust. Let her believe that her act has you fooled.*

"Is that why you're seeing your accountant behind your father's back?" he asked.

Penelope blinked at him, as if caught like a deer in headlights. "I'm not seeing him," she whispered. "Who told you that?"

Winter laughed and held a hand up. "It's okay. I've kept so many relationship secrets for friends that I don't even register them anymore. So you're safe with me."

She seemed to let out a breath, even though her eyes still looked startled. Then she laughed a little, too, and blushed into her mug. "Are we really that obvious?" she asked him ruefully.

"Like a neon sign," Winter replied with a smile. "I'm kidding—you were subtle. If I wasn't so used to analyzing other celebrity couples, I wouldn't have guessed."

She was silent for a long moment after that. Winter was wondering if he'd said too much when she finally sighed and looked back at him. "It's nothing serious. Just a bit of fun for me. Connor's nice."

Not nice enough, apparently, Winter thought, puzzling over her words. Why was she pretending to carry on an affair with someone she wasn't actually seeing? What was fun about that? "He seems like it," he said aloud instead.

She smiled a little. "My mother would have liked him."

Her mother? Inwardly, Winter perked up. Sauda and Niall had told him that they knew almost nothing about Penelope's mother, and here she was, mentioning the woman. "Would have?" Winter asked.

"She died a while ago," Penelope replied.

The silence settled back in around them. There was real grief in her answer, remnants of what sounded like genuine love.

"I'm sorry," Winter murmured.

She gave him a small smile at that, and Winter felt the trust build between them, the relaxing of Penelope's shoulders that seemed to mean she was relieved to confide in him. The realization sent guilt coursing through him.

"She would have liked to see me keep something that was just mine," Penelope went on.

"I'm sure she would have wanted you to have everything you desire," Winter offered gently.

"Do *you* have everything you desire?" she asked him.

Sydney flashed through his mind again, her dark blue eyes and silvery dress and bare back. The thought of her in this moment surprised him, and the unexpected leap in his heart must have registered on his face, because Penelope tilted her head thoughtfully at him.

"No," he answered honestly.

She looked back down into her mug. Her expression was soft and vulnerable now, and she looked even more fragile than he remembered from their first meeting.

"Then I hope we both get what we really want," she said.

He put down his mug and faced her. "Look, I . . ." he started to say, searching for the right words.

And then, in that moment of hesitation, he noticed her flinch slightly toward the window, as if she'd seen some kind of movement on the street. He glanced with her.

There, he saw a dark figure standing on the other side of the street, crouched behind a stone gate.

What caught his eye was the faintest glint of something metallic pointed in their direction. And suddenly, his mind raced back to the lessons he'd gotten with Sydney at Panacea's training center.

"Get down!"

He flung himself at Penelope right before she could make a sound. Just as he barreled into her, he heard the shot crack through the glass window.

It was the subtlest sound—such a small, quiet *ping* that he thought at first that he'd imagined it.

Penelope didn't make a sound. He immediately scrambled up—for a terrifying second, he thought that maybe the bullet had hit her after all. But then he saw her stir where she lay stricken on the couch, her eyes wide and skin ghost-white. At once, something seemed to come alive in her. She rolled to the floor, hitting the carpet at the same time he did.

His eyes darted to a hole in the couch cushions, inches away from where they'd both been sitting. His gaze swung to the window, where a tiny, perfect circle was in the glass, where it had been drilled right through.

For a moment, all he could do was let the reality sink in. That somebody wanted Penelope dead. That everything could seem to be going right one minute and then spiral completely out of his control the next.

And he had the sense that their mission had just taken a turn out of his hands.

Pivot

Not until Sydney managed to find her way back onto the streets of London did the force of everything hit her—the realization that Eli Morrison, the man they had been sent here to arrest, had just been murdered on board his own yacht.

And even though she hadn't been the one to kill him, she felt like his blood was staining her hands, that she had been the one to compromise their mission. She could still hear the sickening gurgle of his destroyed throat in her mind, see the recognition in his eyes as he stared wide-eyed at her.

Worst of all, the possibility that Winter was in the line of fire right now.

She'd sent him several subtle messages, asking him the time and where he was, when he'd be returning. Natural messages from a bodyguard.

Nothing. No replies.

His tracker had last pinged from Penelope's home. So Sydney had rushed there, staking out a shadowed place in the bushes in the hopes she could make something out. But the apartment was dark now, as if Penelope had gone to bed. Or she wasn't there at all.

She texted him several more times as she raced back to the home she shared with him in Kensington. As she stepped through the front door, she kept one hand lightly on the handle of the gun tucked in her pocket.

The house was dark, the bedrooms empty. Winter hadn't returned here yet, either.

After several attempts, she finally got a signal for his tracker again. It seemed to show he was moving through the streets of London in a car in the direction of the house.

Sydney spent the next half hour pacing carefully through each room in the dark, her gun drawn, checking every door and closet and pantry. Then she made her way upstairs and scoured her bedroom before heading into Winter's.

The space was impeccably tidy, tidier than she would expect the bedroom of a pop star to be. The bed was perfectly made, his clothes put neatly away and folded as if on display at a department store. In the bathroom, his towel was folded over the shower door as if done by an attendant.

On his dresser was a cup of water, a pen, and the notebook that she'd seen him scribbling in on the car ride from the airport. He hadn't taken it with him to the concert and after-party.

Sydney looked away from it and checked every corner of the room. When she was satisfied that no stranger had tampered with his things, she settled again on the notebook. Once again, she felt the urge to steal rise in her chest at the sight of something valuable. Besides, she knew she should check it—the notebook was exactly the kind of thing where someone would leave a tracker or listening device. She'd once discovered a chip half the size of her smallest nail taped to the back of a room service menu in one of her hotel rooms.

Sydney picked up the notebook and opened it. The leather surface was soft with use, opened and closed a million times by his hands. She flipped through the first few pages.

They contained hundreds of lines of text—fragments of sentences, floating words, bars of music she didn't know how to read, and sketches. A branch bursting with leaves, a study of someone's hand, a pretty alleyway drawn out with just a few lines. He wasn't bad.

As she turned to the last page, she stopped on the final lines of some lyrics he had written down.

I look at you and it all fills my head
this swirl of (every) thought
(every) nightmare (every) dread
Do you ever feel scared like I do
Ever hate yourself like I do
Ever destroy yourself for someone else?
Do you ever feel guilty for everyone's mistakes?
Ever wish you could take someone else's place?
Do you ever feel like dying?
Do you ever want to live forever?

And this hurricane goes on and on
Every time I look at you
You are my meditation
Am I ever yours, too?

Winter had written this recently, probably even last night, after she'd seen him dancing alone downstairs. She found herself rereading the words and storing them in her mind, enjoying the way they sounded, wondering idly who had inspired them.

Then she blinked and closed the book. She was getting distracted. Her fingers ran along the inner binding of the notebook, then across the inside and outside of its jacket. No trace of tampering, at least.

She had just put the notebook back when she heard the front door downstairs open and shut.

Every muscle in her froze at the sound of the soft click. Winter? Or was it Eli's men? Or the men who had killed Eli? She moved on silent feet into her bedroom, settling in a corner and facing the door.

There, she cocked her gun at the door and waited. The dark stillness of the apartment threatened to overwhelm her.

At last she heard slow, cautious steps heading up the stairs. Whoever it was moved quietly. The only sound that gave them away was the faint creak of a weak step.

The bedroom door swung slowly open toward her. She hoisted her gun from her corner. The figure emerged.

Winter.

He was wielding an umbrella like a weapon—and at her movement, he swung in her direction. She shifted her weight instinctively to one side. Then his eyes widened as he recognized her. His hand dropped, and he leaned heavily against the door frame.

"Holy hell," he snapped at her, throwing his umbrella down. He looked terrifyingly pale. "I could have killed you."

Relief flooded through her at the sight of him, then embarrassment as tears stung her eyes. She hadn't realized how afraid she was of him getting killed. Of potentially being the one to find him dead. "Not with that thing, you couldn't," she replied instead, sheathing her gun with a flourish. "Are you okay?"

He nodded wearily. There was a gloss of fear in his eyes, and with a start, she realized he'd been afraid for her. "Something happened to you," he said.

She stared at him. "And to you."

He hesitated, then said in a low, hoarse voice, "A sniper tried to kill Penelope. Shot straight through the glass of her apartment window. She's with Connor now, at his place."

Sydney felt her throat constrict at his words. *And what do you think I can do to your loved ones?* The sense of spiraling hit her again, and she fought to keep calm. She reached Winter and immediately started scanning him for any sign of injuries. Her fingers brushed the skin of his arm. "Are you hurt?"

He shook his head. His eyes stayed steadily on hers, searching for the secrets behind her haunted expression. "No. You?"

There was a heavy pause. Then she took a deep breath and said, "Eli Morrison is dead."

For a moment, all they could do was stare at each other.

Their mission was over. Now they were embroiled in something new, something for which they had no plans.

"Sauda and Niall wanted a call as soon as you returned," Sydney whispered in the silence. "Glad you made it."

They locked the door and checked the shades on the window. Then they settled in the middle of the floor. Sydney pulled out a small lens, then snapped it into place on her phone's camera and placed the phone carefully on the carpet between them. She tapped out a few instructions on it.

A muted animation appeared between them, showing a loading circle around a green phone. Seconds later, the animation disappeared to make way for Sauda's bust hovering in midair as a hologram, her brows knotted with worry. Beside her appeared Niall, who scooted forward at the sight of them.

Sauda's eyes found Sydney's immediately. Although she said nothing, Sydney could tell that she was searching for signs of injury. Then the woman said, "What happened?"

Her tone was crisp and cold, a voice that Sydney knew well. "I tailed Eli Morrison and three of his associates down to Teddington Lock tonight," she replied. "They dragged Eli on board one of his yachts. The *Invictus*. I couldn't catch their entire conversation, but what I did catch was spoken in Corcasian." She shook her head. "Here."

She tapped something else on her phone. As Sauda and Niall looked on, a file began to play, filling the air around them with the darkness of a foggy night and lapping water, of angry murmurs overhead. Winter sucked in his breath as the video played out, as the Paramecium cube appeared and Sydney made her move, as the guard then hit Eli and the man died choking on the chemical weapon.

When the recording finished, Niall said quietly, "Send us the file."

"Yes, sir."

As she uploaded the recording, Sydney stared across the hologram at Winter. There was a strange look on his face—horror, clearly, for the kind of scene that he had never witnessed before in his life . . . but also something else. A haunting. Sydney didn't know what else to call it.

She nodded at him. "Tell them what happened to you tonight," she said.

Both Niall's and Sauda's gazes flickered to Winter. He cleared his throat, tapped on his phone, and played for them a recording from his bugged earrings, the entire conversation he'd had with Penelope. It ended with the sound of them dropping frantically to the floor.

"One shot came through the window," Winter said as the video finished. "It left a bullet hole in the window, but no other cracks. Hit one of the couch cushions between us, inches away from her."

Niall rubbed a hand across his face and sighed. Then he looked again at Sydney and asked, "Eli Morrison's time of death?"

"Zero three sixteen," Sydney said automatically.

"Did you ID any of the others present?"

Sydney pulled the wallet out of her pocket that she'd stolen from Eli's killer, then flipped it open for everyone to see. Inside was the faded driver's license of an unsmiling man with dark eyes and a coarsely shaven beard, the ID stuffed into the same slot as a crumpled wad of Corcasian cash.

Recognition sparked in Niall's eyes. "You stole this off of him?" he asked.

Sydney nodded. "All of them spoke Corcasian. The third also spoke English. One had a slight irregularity in his walk, possibly an injury somewhere on his right leg."

"That's Edward Johannsen," Sauda said, nodding at the ID. "One of the buyers we've been tracking."

"What does that mean?" Sydney asked.

"It means the Corcasians are in town with the express permission of their government, and that their prime minister sanctioned Eli Morrison's murder. I wouldn't be surprised if they also sent the sniper after Penelope. They will try a hit on her again soon."

"Why would they want her dead?" Winter asked.

"Doesn't matter," Sauda replied.

"What do you mean, it doesn't matter?" Sydney said.

"It doesn't matter," Niall said, "because your jobs there are done."

Sydney blinked. "What do you mean, done? We need to put together a new mission."

"As in, we're bringing you both home. We're not entangling ourselves in official Corcasian government business without regrouping with the CIA. Everything just got a lot messier."

Sydney narrowed her eyes. "I thought Panacea operated free of all the red tape that the CIA has to deal with."

Niall fixed a stern gaze on her. "Don't be such a child," he grumbled. "We can take certain liberties, but we aren't here to start a bigger war than we want to prevent."

"We haven't solved anything!" Sydney hissed.

"You weren't there to solve anything," Sauda said coolly. "You were there to do a job. And now that job's dead."

"What about all that talk of making the world better? Of saving the lives of half a million people? Of being able to do what's right over what's diplomatic? Or was that just recruitment talk?" Sydney clenched her teeth. "That ship's still bound for Cape Town. We leave now, and half a million people will die."

"Then so be it," Sauda snapped. Sydney quieted instantly. Sauda's temper came rarely, but when it did, it seemed to suck all the air out of the room, leaving Sydney breathless.

"What's the first rule?" the woman said in a low voice.

"Come home alive," Sydney murmured back.

Sauda nodded once. "The ripple effect of Eli's murder has only just begun. We answer to higher powers. We'll do what we can, we'll figure out a new path, but we also know when we must step back. You can't save the world if you're dead. Do I make myself clear?"

"Yes, ma'am," Sydney whispered. She could feel tears of fury welling in her eyes.

"Say it louder."

"*Yes, ma'am.*"

She could see Niall looking at her with those furrowed brows, the expression in his eyes more sympathetic than stern, telling her silently to behave. He opened his mouth for a moment, but then closed it.

"Good." Sauda glanced at Winter, who still sat silently, watching the exchange, his face still haunted. "Apologies for the mess you've been dragged into, Mr. Young."

"What about Winter's appearance at the final party tomorrow?" Sydney demanded. "Penelope has thousands of guests in attendance here, and I suspect she'll push through in order to avoid a scene. She doesn't know about her father yet, either. We pull Winter out now, and it'll look too suspicious."

"Let her figure out her guests and her scene," Sauda said. She glanced at Niall. "Flight ETA?"

Niall looked like he was typing away at something. "Early tomorrow morning, at nine."

Sauda nodded. "Don't say a word to anyone. When Penelope's final party rolls around in seventeen hours, you should both be back here in America. Understood?"

Sydney wanted to scream at them both. She could feel the frustration searing through her bones, stinging the tip of her tongue. Her skin tingled with anger. They had just gotten a breakthrough. And now all of it had been a waste of time.

When she spoke again, though, her voice came out steady and cold. "Yes, ma'am."

"You know there's no other way," Sauda told her, her words solemn.

"You taught me there's always a way," Sydney replied.

"In the training arena, yes. In the real world?" The woman's eyes flickered, and for a moment, Sydney felt as she had when Sauda first discovered her stealing habits, when she'd sat in Sauda's office as Sauda patiently ran her through drill after drill of resisting the temptation to take.

It's impossible, Sydney remembered saying as she failed a drill.

Nothing's impossible, Sauda had replied. *Do it again.*

But now the woman was staring at her with a look of resignation. "In the real world," she went on, "we are pushed by forces greater than ourselves. Survival depends on knowing when to succumb to those forces."

"But—"

"No more questions, Sydney."

Sauda's gaze was so piercing that Sydney finally looked away toward Winter. He said nothing.

"See you both at customs," Niall said.

Then he and Sauda ended the call, and their images vanished.

Sydney let out a long, slow breath. Her shoulders hunched with sudden exhaustion, and she stared down at her open palms curled in her lap. Then she looked up again, locking eyes with Winter on the other side of her silent phone.

"I'm sorry," she said softly.

He shrugged and looked away toward the shaded window. "What for?"

"I know this isn't what you expected."

"Has it ever gone how you expected?"

She shook her head. "More often than not, no," she admitted.

"It never does," he murmured.

The haunted expression still hovered on his face, and in it, she could see a remnant of something in his distant past, memories plaguing his mind. It reminded her of the way he'd looked during the tour of Panacea's headquarters, when she had brought up Artie Young more callously than she should have.

His eyes skipped back to hers, and his grieving look vanished as quickly as it had come. He looked down. "We can't leave like this."

She nodded. "And we won't."

He searched her gaze. She stared calmly back. There was something hypnotically soothing about his presence, something that gave her strength. She wanted to be nearer to him. She wanted to do something about the sudden charge that the air seemed to hold.

"You're suggesting going rogue?" he asked.

"Maybe."

A pause. "Sauda and Niall are going to be so pissed off at you."

She shrugged. "Let me handle Sauda and Niall. This is bigger than any of us now. So if I have to go it alone, I will."

Her phrasing made him scowl. "What do you mean, alone?"

"I mean I'm going to do it, but you shouldn't. You never signed up for this."

The way his gaze now seared into hers sent a jolt through her heart. She frowned at him. "I signed up to be your partner on this mission."

"And I'm telling you to get on that flight tomorrow morning."

"What are you going to do here without my help?"

She cast him a withering look. "I can work faster without you."

He leaned toward her. "Would you have known that the so-called affair happening between Penelope and Connor Doherty is nothing more than an act?"

"It's—what?" she said.

"I've witnessed enough secret relationships in my world to know a fake one when I see it." Winter reached into his pocket and pulled out a bejeweled hairpin. Immediately, Sydney recognized it as the same hairpin that Penelope had worn at the Alexandra Palace. "I took this from her flat," he said as he handed it over.

She gave him a skeptical glance. "You stole it?"

"I think I learned more from you than I should," he answered dryly. "Based on what I heard at the after-party, Connor gifted this to her. I thought it might be a useful clue for us about their relationship."

"Which you said was an act," Sydney said, turning the pin carefully in her hands. The diamonds crusting it glittered.

He nodded. "They aren't seeing each other. They're only pretending. I don't know why."

Sydney's fingers ran across the hairpin. They stopped as she touched something metal underneath the diamonds. She took a closer look.

"This is more than a hairpin," she murmured, holding it up so Winter could see the port installed under it. "It's a mini-drive. There's data on this thing."

They stared at each other for a moment before returning to the hairpin.

"There are things happening under the surface here that we don't understand," Winter finally said in a low voice. "And you are going to need someone to help you if you're going to stay."

She took a deep breath, her eyes still on the hairpin. "You don't need to do this. You don't have to put yourself in this kind of danger. This isn't even your line of work."

"Hey." He held his hands up. "Where you go, I go. Right?"

She felt a tingle down her limbs at his words. *Where you go, I go.*

No one had ever promised her anything like that. Where she went, she went alone.

And yet, she could feel the earnestness in his voice. The nearness of him.

"I'm just not used to people staying," she said.

It took her a moment to realize that she'd said something unguarded to him, that he was now staring at her with a questioning gaze. She let her guard down around people like Niall and Sauda—and even they saw a filtered version of her. But Winter wasn't a secret agent. He was a superstar who somehow happened to be one of the most normal people she'd ever met, and something about that combination made her say things like this to him.

He was still studying her with slender dark eyes. "What now?" he said quietly. "We only have six hours."

"All we have to do is buy ourselves some more time," she said.

He frowned at her. "What do you mean?"

"You want to help me? Then we're about to take advantage of who you are." She gave him a small, dark smile. "We're about to cause an uproar."

The Hunter, the Hunted

22

ATTEMPT ON WINTER YOUNG'S LIFE!
RUMORS ALLEGE GUNFIRE AT WINTER YOUNG IN HEIRESS'S HOME
WINTER YOUNG ATTACKED AFTER PRIVATE PARTY

Leaking rumors about gunfire at the home of Penelope Morrison turned out to be the easiest thing in the world. Within minutes of Sydney posting anonymously about it on one of Winter's fan channels online, people began showing up outside their house. An hour later, a rowdy crowd holding homemade signs had gathered in a shifting mass.

"What the hell is going on out here?" Claire yelled over the phone. Winter had to hold the phone slightly away from his ear as the screams coming from Claire's side of the call clashed against the screams directly outside. He raised an eyebrow at Sydney.

Sydney held up her hands. "Okay," she murmured to him. "I didn't expect this big of a response."

You insult me, he mouthed back.

"*Gunfire?*" Claire's voice rose into a squeak as Winter walked toward one of the curtained windows on their first floor. "You got shot at last night, and the Associated Press knows about it before I do?"

"Penelope Morrison made me promise not to tell," Winter answered. "I don't know how word got out."

"And do you work for Penelope Morrison?" Claire demanded.

"Well, technically, while we're here—yes."

Claire sighed in exasperation. "Never mind. Why the hell doesn't she want this out?"

"Because she doesn't want to talk to the media about how she almost died? We've been down that kind of road before. She wanted the matter privately investigated by the Met. Look—I'm okay. It was a stray bullet. Nothing hit me."

He could almost hear Claire narrowing her eyes on the other side. "You're okay," she said incredulously.

"Yes." He gingerly pushed aside the curtain of the window to see a sea of fans—a thousand, at least—being held back by a flimsy line of desperate police. A hint of worry twisted in him. He hoped no sniper gun was trained on him now—not with all these bystanders in the potential line of fire.

"Whatever you do," Claire said as Winter gave the crowd a single wave of his hand, "don't look out the window and wave at them. You'll cause a riot."

Sure enough, the instant the words were out of Claire's mouth, the crowd burst into louder shrieks at Winter's gesture. The sea of people undulated, and here and there, the police line temporarily broke.

"I just wanted them to know I'm okay," he said over the phone. "We're not trying to encourage rumors here."

Claire groaned. "Forget it. Don't you dare leave that house, Winter Young. We'll come to you and strategize."

She hung up. As she did, Winter saw the stream of texts from Leo and Dameon on his phone.

What the hell is going on?

Did someone really try to shoot you last night?

Everything in him ached to confide in his friends. He shoved his phone back in his pocket and took a deep breath. Was he making a mistake? He could still hardly process what had happened the night before—the party, the shooting, the argument with Panacea. The strange new pact he seemed to have with Sydney, with whom he was now officially playing the agent gone rogue. Loneliness gripped him like a vise.

The bare handful of hours he'd gotten to sleep before morning certainly didn't help, either.

He walked over to where Sydney had taken a seat near the indoor pool, reading a message on her phone. Then he leaned close to her, so that their words wouldn't be picked up, and whispered, "They're on their way over. How's your end?"

She nodded tersely. "It's impossible for us to sneak to the airport in this mess. Sauda's aware of the news leak. Niall has postponed our flight. It should also protect Penelope from anyone attempting a second strike on her." She held up her phone. "And give Panacea time to unlock the data I pulled from Penelope's hairpin."

"We can't read it?" he asked.

She shook her head. "Encrypted. Niall just let me know he received my upload. Whatever it is, it must be important. While they're working, I've got some footage from Doherty's snake ring." The sound of trickling water muted her voice. "Look."

Winter stared down at her phone to see a black-and-white video playing from inside what appeared to be a museum, coming from the point of view of a man with a familiar voice.

"When?" he asked.

"This morning," she whispered back. "This is the Victoria and Albert Museum, in South Kensington."

He recognized the interior now—the shallow pool in the central courtyard, the luminescent Chihuly sculpture hanging low from the main lobby, the rotunda filled with fashion through the centuries. The video swung jerkily as it broadcast from the ring on Connor's finger.

"Looks like the museum's empty," he said.

She nodded. "Hasn't opened yet."

As they looked on, Connor made his way through a set of double doors, then into what seemed like a maze of back corridors.

"Eli donated the newest extension to the museum ten years ago," Sydney explained, "and in return, earned a private wing of his own here that is mostly kept away from the public. Looks like Connor's using a back entrance."

Winter narrowed his eyes. "Well, I'm guessing he's not just enjoying a leisurely day indulging in the arts."

"Not after last night," she mumbled. "If Penelope was the target, he might be moving to secure Eli's holdings from her father's attackers."

At last, Connor reached the end of a new wing where four guards were posted at each corner. He raised his hand in a possible greeting, and the video turned briefly up to show the ceiling of the wing arched up in an elegant dome. No windows were in this space—and even though Winter knew they were two stories up, he had the sudden feeling of stepping into a sepulcher.

As he walked through the small corridor, one of the men nodded in silent greeting to him, then stepped aside. Connor pushed open one of the double doors before him and led them into a room lined with white, elegantly carved pillars.

Winter couldn't help letting out a faint whistle.

It was Connor's personal collection that he'd donated to the museum.

There were jewels of all kinds in here, colorful diamonds and sapphires and rubies, rare jade so pale it looked translucent, blocks of raw quartz, then rows upon rows of jewelry, all protected in individual cases.

"Look," Sydney whispered. She zoomed in on one of the jewelry boxes sitting in a thick receptacle of glass. As she did, she tapped another button on the screen.

The video recording shifted into what looked like an infrared mode.

He saw the outline appear plainly behind the glass cases. He sucked his breath in sharply.

"There's a hidden room in there," he said.

Sydney nodded, although she was frowning. As Winter studied the box further, he noticed the silhouette of a face emerge against the jewelry box's glass surface. He recoiled at the eerie sight.

Connor stopped before the box. For a second, nothing happened. Then there was the faint sound of a click, followed by a door sliding silently open against the wall.

The man stepped inside. And the snake ring's footage cut off.

Sydney cursed. "That room must have fortified walls," she whispered. "The video feed can't transmit from inside."

Minutes crawled by. Just when Winter thought they wouldn't see any more footage, the feed flickered back to life. Connor was already back outside in the small corridor, walking past the four guards again.

Winter's mouth felt dry. His hands clenched and unclenched at his sides. Hadn't Sauda said Eli's ledgers were kept somewhere in central London?

"How do we get in there?" he murmured.

Sydney's brows were furrowed, her eyes stormy with thought. "The code to open that room seems to be made with pattern recognition of the blood vessels under the skin of Connor's face," she said.

Winter frowned. "So, short of dragging his decapitated head in there, we're not getting in? And before you suggest it, I'd really prefer if we didn't decapitate him."

"No one needs to be decapitated. We just needed a good 3D hologram of his face." She reached over to tap his earrings. "Which you got last night at the party."

The touch of her cool skin against his earlobe sent a shiver down his spine. He looked closely at the image again. "Can we tell what's inside?"

She shook her head. "Not until we get in ourselves. But all we need is one piece of evidence. Just one, and it'll be enough to stop that shipment."

His heartbeat quickened. *Just one, and it'll be enough.* But Eli Morrison was dead, and they didn't even know who had done it, nor who was running his empire right now and dealing with the Corcasians in his absence. They were working with zero leads, and they were running out of time.

"What do you need to get in?" he whispered to her instead.

She smiled tightly. "The floor plans to the museum," she answered. "And every blueprint we can get our hands on."

Half an hour later, Claire had managed to be escorted into the house along with Leo, Dameon, and half a dozen other security crew. Even so, her braided bun looked slightly disheveled, and she was sweating slightly despite the cool air outside.

"What's the game plan?" Leo asked as they huddled in the living room, busying himself by setting down glasses of whiskey for them. Claire shot him a disapproving look about the alcohol, but didn't turn the drink down. "I can't remember the last time you caused this much of a ruckus."

"It was when he did the devil skit," Dameon said, picking up one of the glasses. "We had protesters in Orlando—that one guy broke our windshield."

"I'll tell you the game plan." Claire narrowed her eyes at Winter as she sipped at her drink. "We should be rushing you out of London, except now we have a full circus outside and navigating the freeway to the airport will be more dangerous than just keeping you here." She tapped at her phone in annoyance. "Does Eli Morrison ever pick up?"

The mention of his name roiled the unease in Winter's stomach. His mind still whirled from the footage that Sydney had shown him. "Don't worry about me. I'll be fine." He shook his head. "But that doesn't mean the rest of you need to be here."

Leo stared at him in disbelief. "What?"

Dameon scowled. "Wait, you're going to stay here by yourself in this madness?"

"What can you possibly help with?" Winter answered.

"I don't know," he said. "Keeping people from clawing your skin off? Walking with you?"

"You'll make it harder than it needs to be," Winter argued, glancing at Claire. "Send them home."

"Agreed." Claire looked at Leo and Dameon. "I'm flying the two of you out for now. The less I have to keep track of, the easier my job will be."

Leo started to protest, his eyes almost panicked. "You were nearly killed!" he said to Winter. "So what if the freeways are going to be wild? Isn't anything safer than staying here?"

Claire tapped on the table with her phone, disrupting their argument. "We're moving your flight up," she said, eyeing Leo and Dameon. "End of story."

"And you should be flying out, too," Winter said to her. There was an uneasy churning in his gut as he said it, the premonition that things were about to get worse. "No reason for you to stay when you could be safely on board a plane."

That made her turn to him, startled. "Why would I leave?"

His tone turned annoyed. "Does your safety not count for anything?"

"There's more you're not telling me, Winter Young," Claire pressed, lowering her voice. "You think I can't sense that, after all our years together?"

Damn Claire and her intuition, Winter thought. But he just shook his head. "I'm telling you there's not," he said. "Do I have to have a secret in order to be protective?"

"No. But you have one, don't you?"

Winter scowled and looked at Dameon. "Help me."

Dameon shrugged. "You're the boss," he replied.

Winter looked back at Claire. "I'm not asking you. I'm ordering you. Go home now, or you're fired."

Claire flinched as if she'd been slapped. "Excuse me?"

In all their years together, he had never said such a thing to her, threatened her as if she was his subordinate. The hurt in her eyes made him wince. But there were more dangerous players in the game now. He imagined the faceless sniper pointing his crosshairs in Claire's direction. Pulling the trigger.

Panacea had promised to protect his crew, but he couldn't count on that now.

"Please, Claire," he whispered. "Just do this."

Her lips tightened, and she sat back, her posture now stiff and distant. "As you say, Mr. Young," she said, her words barbed.

Winter opened his mouth, trying to form an apology, but no words came out. All he could do was look on as Claire rose from the couch and turned away.

"Claire," he managed to say. "Wait."

She didn't look back.

Dameon fixed his steady eyes on Winter, searching for an answer. But Winter kept his hands in his pockets, tense as Claire called for their security team to prepare for them to leave.

Then Dameon stepped toward him.

"Winter," he murmured in his ear. "Remember when you used to come to me?"

Winter stilled at the reminder of their past.

There will always be a part of me in love with you, Dameon had told him back then, right before the end of their affair.

But not all of you, Winter had added.

Not all of me, Dameon had admitted.

Now Winter met Dameon's eyes as the boy leaned close. "I know you've always kept your secrets close," he whispered. "And I'm not going to start asking about them now. But just take care of yourself, okay? Come home safe."

"Okay," Winter murmured back, swallowing.

Dameon held his gaze a breath longer before looking away.

Then Leo turned to Winter. There was naked fear in his friend's eyes now, and a slight sheen of sweat glimmered on the boy's skin. Winter felt a surge of guilt for putting them all in this position. So much for a thankless good deed. All he'd done was endanger the people he cared about.

"Look, Winter . . ." Leo said, then trailed off, his brows furrowed.

"It's going to be okay," Winter replied, trying to offer him a smile. He glanced at Dameon. "We're all going to be okay."

"Okay," Dameon said in his quiet voice. As Claire motioned for them to prepare to rush out the door, he nodded at Winter. "Watch yourself out here, yeah? We'll see you back in the States."

"See you there," Winter replied. They all exchanged a wordless nod.

His eyes settled on Claire. She still looked distant, her gaze wary, her lips tight. They exchanged a terse nod, too.

"Stay safe," he told her.

"Stay safe," she murmured. Her eyes flickered to Sydney, who stood back by the drinks on the coffee table. "Keep him safe," she called out.

Sydney nodded once.

Then Claire was opening the door, and the thunderous noise from the crowd outside hit them in a wave. Security guards shouted at Claire, and Claire shouted in turn at the boys.

As they hurried out, Leo suddenly wrapped Winter in an embrace. In his ear, Leo whispered fiercely, "Don't touch those drinks."

Winter blinked, confused. Leo released him, his eyes locked on him for a fraction of a second. Then he turned away and disappeared into the throng of police with Claire and Dameon, and the door shut.

Winter stood there for a second, dazed. What? Had he just heard those words? Had he made it up?

Don't touch those drinks.

As if on cue, he heard a slight clink behind him. He looked back. The drinks that Leo had poured out for them were still sitting on the low table. Sydney was there now, her eyes on her phone's footage, her drink already touching her lips. Their eyes met.

Panic surged through him. "Don't—" he started to say.

But it was too late.

A strange, stricken look passed over her face. Immediately, she dropped the glass in her hand—it shattered against the floor. Right as the realization washed over Winter.

Poison.

23

Breaking the Wall

There was no taste of it on the rim of the glass—but all it took was a look at Winter, before he even spoke, for Sydney to know that something was wrong.

Then she felt it. The heat. She hurriedly wiped her lips clean against her sleeve, but the poison was already trickling down her throat, leaving a trail of slow-burning fire in its wake.

It took Sydney another second to realize that Winter had gripped her shoulders and was trying to say something to her—but she wasn't really processing what. She was concentrating too hard on keeping her mind still. Her thoughts fluttered frantically, as if she were struggling to contain them. She could already feel the first hints of fire in her stomach, a pulse that rushed through her veins, turning her to ice. Damn, this one acted fast.

She recognized this feeling. She'd taken toxins before during training, could still remember the pain in her gut as Sauda fed her an antidote and then had medics pump her stomach.

How embarrassing, she thought idly as she felt Winter scoop her up in his arms. Her world spun.

She had never been poisoned before, not for real. Not out in the field.

It was a strange sensation and, somehow, not entirely unpleasant. There was no pain, although she found herself in the grip of an intense heat that consumed every part of her body, could feel the heat emanating from her and the bitter cold of everything else around her in comparison. No sweat, though.

Maybe she had a fever.

Her breathing came in shallow, whistling gasps. Her lungs heaved. She could hear her teeth chattering loudly. The kitchen blurred past her, noon light painting stripes so bright against the floor that they swam blindingly in her vision. The patterns in the marble counter swirled.

"Get me in the pool," she managed to utter through her gasps. She needed to cool down.

Winter didn't hesitate. Sydney leaned heavily against him and saw the shimmering surface of the pool growing nearer in her vision. The waterfall flowing down into it against the glass wall seemed to roar in her ears.

Then there was a splash, and she could feel Winter frantically dragging her into the water and the blessed coolness of it soaking through her clothes.

Winter propped her up, waist deep, against the shallow edge of the pool near the waterfall. "Focus on me," she heard him say. When she struggled to obey, she could make out his face leaning down toward hers. "Focus on me. Focus on me."

His voice sounded so far away. Somehow that seemed funny to her when he was obviously so close, and Sydney fought an urge to laugh. Her mind swam with exhaustion. She could feel herself heaving, her lungs struggling for air. Water lapped against her.

"Upstairs," she finally managed to blurt out, the word tangling on her tongue.

"I can't leave you here."

"Upstairs," she tried to repeat. "My bag."

This time he winced, glancing up at the winding staircase. "Make sure you keep pressed against the pool's edge," he told her. "I'll be right back."

Then he was gone, his warm presence giving way for the cold lapping of water around her. Her skin felt so hot that she swore she must be heating up the pool on her own.

For a moment, she thought he'd left the house entirely, that she was now all alone.

The idea filled her with sudden terror. Her breaths quickened. *Whistle. Whistle.* Strands of her damp hair clung to the sides of her face. What had Sauda told her to do if she couldn't reach her bag of antidotes? God, she felt so tired. It took every bit of her strength just to steady herself against the pool's edge. She could still smell the lingering fumes of the poisoned drink on her clothes, and the scent made her head swim, made her wipe her lips over and over with the pool's water to cleanse it further.

She needed to take the shirt off.

She gritted her teeth as she undid the first few buttons of her wet shirt, then stopped to concentrate on getting oxygen. *Whistle. Whistle.* Her lungs struggled. Where was Winter? Had he left?

She was on her own.

There was nothing new about that—she'd been locked in solitary confinement before on a mission, had to break out of countless places by herself. She'd sent him away, after all. Why did it matter to her that Winter wasn't by her side?

Sydney shivered so violently that she thought she might be having a seizure right here in the pool. Could you be aware of yourself when you were having a seizure? The question floated through her mind and faded.

And suddenly, she saw the memory around her—the small apartment she'd been given near Panacea's headquarters for the duration of her training, and Sauda and Niall standing in the living room, waiting with her as two inspectors searched her place.

I'm going to ask you again, Ms. Cossette, Sauda said to her, the woman's eyes cool and calm. *Have you ever stolen from headquarters?*

Think carefully before you answer, Niall warned her.

Sydney shook her head instinctively. She could feel the pressure in her lungs, the perpetual strain tightening even more with her anxiety. *Never,* she replied.

Sauda narrowed her eyes. At the time, Sydney couldn't tell that Sauda already knew she was lying, that the woman had noted the subtle signs her body gave off.

The inspectors eventually found her stash—a floorboard under her bed that revealed a compartment filled with items she'd stolen from the building throughout the three months she'd been there so far. Salt and pepper shakers. Forks and knives. Training gloves and paperweights, lightbulbs and boxes of paper clips from the utility closet, pens embedded with blades used during her training sessions, copper wiring stripped from gadgets. The list went on and on. They laid it all out before her feet.

Sydney couldn't bear to look up into Niall's face. It didn't matter, anyway. She could tell from the angle of his posture that he had his arms crossed, that his brows were probably furrowed in disappointment.

When Sauda spoke again, her voice was quiet. *I think we both know what this means, Sydney,* she said.

Expulsion, of course. They couldn't have a spy stealing from headquarters. Sydney nodded without a word.

And she had taken it well enough the next day, sitting stone-faced before the two agents as they questioned her extensively about each of the items she'd stolen. After all, she'd expected this. Of course she was unfit for such a classified job, one where people's lives would be placed in her hands. Of course she'd fail out of recruitment training and be sent back to her small, awful life in her hometown.

At last, Sauda turned to Niall. *Verdict?* she asked him.

Sydney braced herself, her eyes still downturned. Whatever it was that Niall answered Sauda with, it must have been a look, because Sydney didn't hear anything.

Sauda cleared her throat. Sydney looked up to see the woman studying her with narrowed eyes, and Sydney tensed, bracing herself for the worst.

Well, Sydney? Sauda asked her. *Do you have anything to say?*

Sydney swallowed hard. Her eyes went momentarily to Niall. The man crossed his arms over his chest and regarded her. Somehow, the disappointment on his face hurt her more than anything her own father had ever said to her. All she could think about was the way the man had confronted her in the hallway of her old school, how he'd offered her the chance at a new life. How she had thrown it away so carelessly.

I'm sorry, she whispered. *I don't deserve to stay.*

Sauda tilted her head. *Deserve is an interesting word,* she said. *It implies worth. And worth is something earned by doing, not by being.*

Sydney looked at her. *Do you mean . . .*

Your compulsion to steal is a symptom of trauma, Sauda went on. *You will study it extensively in your psychology training.* She nodded. *You're the smartest recruit we've had in years. I know you can learn to control the impulse.*

But you need to be honest with us, Sydney, Niall said. *You have to try. We can't help you if we don't know. Understand?*

Sydney searched the man's face and found kindness under his stern gaze. It was such an unfamiliar expression to her that she didn't know how to answer. Didn't understand why he wanted to give her another chance.

So she asked him. *Why do you care if I stay?*

There appeared in the man's eyes a sadness so deep that it seemed to hollow right through him. He grunted and looked down. *Just don't like wasting potential,* he replied with a shrug.

She could feel the tightness in her lungs, the truth of her condition that would one day catch up to her. She could tell them now; she could be honest about everything.

But the sight of her stolen objects lined up on the table killed the words on her tongue.

So she said, quietly, *I understand.*

Niall and Sauda exchanged a look.

Then Niall studied her face with those kind eyes. *You can stay,* he said.

It was the gentle rumble of his voice that did it. Sydney put her face in her hands, felt the dam of her emotions crack, and sobbed like her heart might shatter.

Niall left the room first. After he did, and after she had calmed down, Sauda said to her in a soft voice, "*He has a daughter. They don't talk anymore. That's all you need to know, and I recommend you not ask questions about it.*"

The memory vanished, and Sydney returned to herself, shivering desperately. Her lungs wheezed, a reminder of the secret she still kept from them, that she was still too scared to reveal. Someday, one way or another, it would catch up to her.

Or perhaps she wouldn't ever have to worry about it. Not if she died today.

She knew she needed to stay in the cool water. But it was so, so, so, so hot. She wanted to be bathed in ice.

No one was coming back for her. A familiar fear settled into her stomach. She would die here, by herself.

No one would care that she was gone.

And then, just as she thought this was how she would end, that she would be found drowned in the water—

Winter came rushing back, vaulting into the pool with a loud splash.

She couldn't tell if she was dreaming or not. She thought she might be crying in relief. Or maybe it was just the water. She couldn't tell. She saw him holding a hand out to her and then wrapping his arm around her back, gently urging her to lean forward, to drink something. He looked soaked.

She looked on weakly as he popped the vial's lid, flipped it upside down on a syringe, and loaded it all with one hand, as if he'd been doing it all his life. Another surprise, in what seemed to be an endless string of surprises. So he'd been paying attention during their training after all, even when she'd only demonstrated this to him once, had probably practiced on his own.

He pointed the syringe at her lips. "Drink," he ordered her.

His voice was low and steady. If he was scared, she couldn't tell. She felt his cool fingers gently cradling the back of her neck as she tilted her head enough to take the syringe contents.

She could barely swallow. The pain of it seared down her throat like fire. She winced, coughing and gagging. The antidote stung as it coated her lips.

"You have to finish all of it," he said.

She managed to glare at him, but still forced herself to do as he said.

Almost immediately, she felt the fever inside her break. And then the world around her no longer felt like a tundra, but like a baking desert, as if all the heat suffocating her body had rushed out into the world. She couldn't bear it simmering around her. Her entire body burst into sweat. She couldn't stop. She could feel it pouring down the sides of her face and drenching the collar of her open shirt, dripping down the damp strands of her hair, leaking into the water.

She could feel herself finally able to take a full, gasping breath of air.

"It's okay," Winter said repeatedly. "Can you hear me?"

She nodded numbly. His hair was wet and studded with dew, glistening from the bright light coming in. Beads of water ran down his face. Vaguely, she became aware that his hands were on either side of her face, holding her in a firm, gentle embrace. He was staring at her as if she might disappear at any second.

Maybe she was hallucinating. The water seemed unusually bright, its surface glittering under beams of sunlight. She could feel herself falling asleep, and the realization filled her with dread. She tried to focus on Winter's gaze, as if looking at him could keep her awake.

If she fell asleep, she might not wake up.

"You were right," she finally managed to say. The words slurred from her mouth.

He blinked, as if surprised and relieved by her words. "About the poison?" he asked, the urgency plain in his voice.

"About my lungs," she whispered. They gave a painful spasm as she said it. "You were right—about my lungs—I haven't told them yet."

An understanding rippled across his gaze. He shook his head. "And I won't, either," he replied. "Just stay awake. Okay? Just stay awake."

"Don't go," she tried to say. Her hands gripped feverishly at his sleeves.

"I'm not going anywhere," he replied.

She counted out the seconds. Gradually, gradually, she could feel the world around her gaining some sense of focus, although her head still felt light and fuzzy.

"Winter," she now breathed out his name.

He nodded at her, his eyes still on her, his hands still on the sides of her face. Now she was starting to gain some feeling in her arms again, some strength in her muscles. She could feel the slight warmth of his skin against hers. She could sense the calluses on his palms and the slight stirring of his breath against her face.

One of his hands came up to wipe something wet from her cheeks. She realized she was crying.

"You're okay," he murmured to her in his lovely, melodic voice, and it was the most soothing sound in the world. "You're okay."

"I'm okay," she whispered. Her words sounded more like hers now. "I'm okay."

Now it was Winter's turn to break down. To her surprise, he pulled his hands abruptly away from her and covered his own face with his palms. Then he started weeping. He wept like his heart might give out. She watched in calm fascination at the tears that dripped down his hands and spilled to his chin. Winter Young was famous for being composed in public, for never giving a bad interview or getting caught with his guard down. She didn't think she could imagine him crying like this.

He looked so . . . human. He looked like just a boy, overwhelmed and exhausted.

She reached through the haze in her mind for the memory of Winter's story about his mother, about the day he'd lost his brother, and felt that curious twist of pity in her stomach again. Or maybe it wasn't pity. Maybe whatever she felt for him was the reason why she always seemed to be searching for an excuse to look at him or follow him or check up on him.

Maybe she liked him more than she cared to admit.

Maybe she was falling for him a bit.

He wiped his eyes hurriedly, then held her face again. She realized for the first time that his hands were trembling. "Just rest," he said, his voice hoarse. "We'll contact Sauda, get a check on what exactly got used on you."

Sydney's tears changed to quiet laughter. She couldn't believe the ridiculousness of this moment. She was the secret agent, was supposed to be the one reassuring him—and yet she was propped up in an indoor pool and letting a pop star cradle her head.

He smiled a little at her laughter. She found herself admiring the faint creases forming at the edges of his eyes, noting the spark of relief in his expression. The afternoon light washed over them, outlining him in bright gold.

This was all too ridiculous. Every single one of her inhibitions felt like it'd vanished into thin air. Could poison do that, too? All she wanted to do was stare at this beautiful boy. She felt the tug of him hard in her chest, felt the wall crumbling between them.

"The lyrics in your notebook," she heard herself murmur, without warning.

It took her a second to realize that she hadn't thought the words, but spoken them out loud. Maybe there was still some poisoned drink left in the living room—she could take it and just let herself sink under the water and die of embarrassment.

Winter's eyebrow lifted, but he didn't ask why she'd looked through it. "Which ones?" he said instead.

The words returned through the haze of her mind. "'*You are my meditation*,'" she replied. "Who is it about?"

He was quiet for a moment, and she bit her lip to keep more words from shooting out of her mouth. *God*, what the hell was wrong with her?

"You," he answered.

Sydney stared at him. The world still felt like it was tilting around her. His eyes turned down at her gaze, as if he hadn't meant to admit it.

"I was just playing around," he muttered.

You. You.

She let the word wrap around her, felt the walls of her heart break down.

She didn't know why she did it.

But she leaned toward him, and, as if it were always meant to be this way between them, she pressed her lips to his and kissed him.

24

Meant to Be

t felt like a jolt of electricity shooting through her body.

Winter stiffened in shock at her kiss.

Then he gave way. She felt his hands pull her face to his, her body drifting through the water to press against his. Their kiss deepened. His lips were so soft. The rush of heat through her felt different this time, alive and warm and good and absolutely, wholly overpowering. She wrapped her wet arms around his neck as he pulled her to him. There was desperation in their movement, some urgency born from adrenaline and fear. And maybe something more, too. A faint groan emerged from his throat, a sound of relief and pleasure and deep want. It was the sexiest thing she'd ever heard.

She'd kissed enough boys before for the novelty to have long worn off. But here, somehow, she felt like a novice. She could feel her hands reaching for his soaked shirt, tugging its hem out, then her fingers running under the fabric sticking to his wet stomach. His skin was smooth and slick. As if from a distance, she sensed herself straddling him, her thighs pressed against his torso, knocking him slightly off balance so that he had to prop an arm up behind him to keep from falling backward in the pool.

Well, this is unprofessional. The voice in her head flared to life, but it was drowned out by her desire in this moment. She couldn't care less whether or not they were on a mission or that their lives were in danger. She had been so focused for so long on nothing but survival, on getting the job done, that she'd forgotten entirely about her heart. So she let it free.

All she wanted right now was him. Every bit of him. She wanted to be consumed by his fire and lost to it.

Her mind swam in the fog of the antidote. She broke free long enough to gasp as she felt his hand against the skin of her back, sliding up. His lips were on her neck now, trailing along her collarbone. The buttons of her shirt were still undone from her feverish attempt earlier to take it off. She closed her eyes, waiting for him to touch her anywhere, everywhere. Waiting for him to carry her out of this pool and upstairs to the bedroom and strip the wet clothes off of her, for him to consume her.

Him, this boy who—only a couple of weeks ago—she'd wished would fall off the face of the planet.

Or maybe she'd never really believed that at all.

What is Winter Young like in bed?

The thought sprang to her mind and filled her with fire. She couldn't believe herself. A week ago, she would have shaken her head in disgust at the thought.

Why did she want him?

Why did this feel so right?

Before she could find out, he pulled away. Sydney gasped at his sudden departure and the disappointment of cool air between them.

"Wait," he breathed, his cheeks flushed. The collar of his shirt was disheveled from where she'd tugged at it, the buttons undone halfway down his chest, and she could see his body exposed underneath. He met her gaze, his pupils dilated, his eyes hazy with want. "Wait," he repeated, shaking his head. "Stop. You're—we're, I mean—not in our right mind."

Not in my right mind?

The buzz of heat and desire that had been raging through her cut short as if snipped in two. Vanished in an instant. She stared at him, bewildered for a moment.

"I know what I'm doing," she retorted.

"Do you?" He looked skeptically at her. "You were just poisoned! Do you even remember what happened?"

"Of course!" she snapped, then frowned. Already the memories of what'd just happened were turning fuzzy. How had they gotten here into the pool? Had Winter carried her? Had he given her something? She'd thought she remembered it, but now it felt like a blanket had fallen back over her mind, clouding it in doubt.

At the sight of her confusion, Winter shook his head and pulled himself further away. He gave her a rueful smile. "Sorry," he murmured. "Got carried away."

Sydney knew he was right, but she still felt irritation pouring cold against her emotions. The one time she threw herself at a guy and let her heart go, he decided to be chivalrous?

Why couldn't he just let her make this mistake?

A mistake. Right.

Her feelings had been thrown into a storm with the poison and anti-dote and sheer pressure of their mission, and she had lost her senses with it. A mistake. That was all this was.

Something else cleared a little in her head, and Sydney felt the first hint of her cold logic returning, her shield piecing itself back together. She blinked, suddenly exhausted.

Of course this was a mistake.

"Same," she muttered, pulling herself straighter against the edge of the pool. She looked down and buttoned her shirt. The heat from their kiss still coursed through her, and to her embarrassment, she could still feel it burning against her cheeks.

His hand was still there, a hairsbreadth from hers. Everything in him looked like he wanted to touch her again, but he didn't.

"We can't do this," he finally whispered.

Never had Sydney felt so annoyed with him. But she pushed the feeling down, forcing herself to look like she didn't care that Winter's hands had been on her just seconds ago, that she had been fumbling all over him herself.

"Believe me, I don't want to," she heard herself agree. "Unprofessional."

Winter shook his head. "No, I meant the rest of this mission."

She frowned. The heat rose again, unbidden, in her cheeks, and for a moment, she wanted the poison coursing back through her system so she didn't have the mind to be embarrassed. "And why not?" she said.

"You were just poisoned!"

She gave him an unbothered look. "I once stole the key to a locked cell to break out an informant scheduled for execution at a maximum-security prison while I had a hundred-and-four-degree fever."

He stared wordlessly at her.

"So this will be easy," she clarified.

He blinked, but she didn't feel like explaining further. Instead, she looked back out toward the living room, where shards of glass littered the floor, then at Winter again. Through the lifting fog in her mind, she recalled the panicked look she'd seen on his face right before she'd touched her lips to her glass. The memory of him starting to say something to her. *Don't—!*

"Winter," she said carefully, "you were going to warn me before I sipped from that drink, weren't you?"

Winter stared at her, stricken. Then nodded.

"Why?" she asked. "How did you know?"

He didn't answer. His face turned toward the door. Sydney found her mind revving back up as she studied his body language, the stiffness of his posture, the way he leaned unconsciously in the direction where Claire and his friends had left. She waited patiently for him to look back at her.

When he finally did, his expression seemed haunted. "Leo whispered something to me right before he stepped out."

"And what did he say?"

Winter met her eyes. "Don't touch the drinks."

She was silent for a long moment. Her mind spun. Nothing about Leo had ever turned up in Panacea's research about him—he had never been anything but a loyal friend and colleague to Winter. He had no ties to Eli Morrison.

But this was unmistakable.

"I watched the others drink without any issues," she replied slowly, turning back to him. "Leo prepared all those glasses. He had to have known which to set in front of me. In front of *you*."

Winter's eyes had constricted now. "No."

"He did," she replied gently. She fixed him with a steady gaze. "Winter, Leo tried to poison us."

Friends and Enemies

t made no sense.

Leo had been with him since nearly the beginning of Winter's career. He had been on every tour, had teased and taunted him mercilessly, had attempted to teach him how to cook a dozen times. He had listened quietly whenever Winter was worn down from stress or exhaustion, had comforted him through a dozen heartbreaks, cheered him alongside Dameon as life pushed them higher.

Leo had been there for him for so long. It was impossible.

And yet he found himself staring down at the broken glass on the floor, the whiskey still spilled against the wood.

"This is XC," Sydney said, standing up from where she was running a test on the lip of the glass. "A new nerve agent."

She still looked unsteady, her movements a little slower than they should be, but her speech and thoughts seemed to be back to normal. Better than how she'd been just half an hour earlier, at least, when she was gasping in the pool. When she was kissing him in desperation, and he was doing the same in turn.

Now he found himself looking at her, his mind clouded with uncertainty. What if Claire had been in on it? What about Dameon?

Suddenly, everyone he'd ever known seemed like shadow figures in his head, walking through this city of secrets. He didn't know which direction to turn, whom he could call. There was no one he could think of in this moment that he could talk to.

There was no one he could trust.

He thought of Penelope, of the distant look she got in her eyes when he asked her how she coped whenever she felt lonely.

"There's an explanation for everything," Sydney said in the silence. "You just have to trust your instincts."

There was still a fog in her eyes and, framed by those long brown lashes, it made her look a little lost. But otherwise she seemed alert again, that slight furrow returning to her brow and a faint scowl touching the edges of her lips. She was wearing his oversized sweater, and he couldn't help but notice the way it exposed the creamy skin of her left shoulder. There was a birthmark there, the little dark smudge he'd kissed earlier.

He could still feel a faint tingle on his lips.

She shifted and spoke again. "Leo could have been bribed."

"There isn't enough money in the world to make Leo want to hurt someone," Winter snapped.

"Blackmail, then. I've no doubt he didn't want to do it—no one confesses their crime directly to their victim like that, warns you like that, puts himself at risk, and actually *wants* to hurt you. His hand was forced, one way or the other. Surely there's someone in the world he loves more than you, who could be used against him. Did you notice anything strange about Leo recently?"

Blackmail. Winter thought about Leo's sisters and his parents, his aunts, his house that was always full of festive, loving, laughing relatives.

"He was fine during warm-ups," he said slowly.

But hadn't Leo seemed uncharacteristically quiet when the concert finished? No. That was just because he couldn't come to the after-party. Wasn't it?

"After the concert," he whispered to Sydney. "He didn't say a word."

Sydney looked carefully at him. "And when was he alone, without us all, before that?"

"The elevator," they both said at the same time.

Winter's hands began to tremble. Hadn't he, Leo, and Dameon each taken the tiny elevator up to the backstage area? What if Leo's handler had said something to him then?

Blackmail.

If Morrison's people had threatened Leo's family, Leo would have done as they asked. Winter could feel it in his gut, could sense his instinct pointing him in the right direction, as Sydney had told him it would. And even then, Leo must have been tortured enough about it not to be able to go through with everything, had been afraid enough for Winter to risk putting his family in danger just to warn him about the drinks.

The realization felt like a tide of nausea in his stomach. The room suddenly seemed like it was tilting.

Sydney must have seen the look change on his face, because she nodded. Each minute brought with it more clarity.

"We don't know if any of that is true," he whispered.

"It's possible, though," she said. "Isn't it?"

"That would mean someone knows what we're doing here," Winter replied quietly. "And they'll know soon that Leo failed to deliver on his end of the bargain."

"Leo's going to be on a plane back to America in an hour," she said. "But we have to get *you* out of London."

Winter frowned. "What? You're the one that got poisoned."

"This is my job. Not yours."

"You said where I go, you go."

"Well, that was before someone smeared a bunch of nerve agent on your glass and tried to kill you."

He sighed. "No."

"I'm not asking you, Winter."

"I can't leave you here."

"Can't you?"

"You're not even operating with Panacea's support behind you. You'll be in London alone."

"What did you think an agent's job involved?" A slant of light had begun to creep across Sydney's face, casting her deep blue eyes in gold. "I work better that way."

"What about the massive diversion you needed from me? What about—"

"A diversion was a good idea when I didn't think anyone was hunting you down." She snapped her fingers. "No one needs your big distraction to be you getting killed. I can get into the museum by myself just fine. Better, actually."

"Why are you like this?" he said.

"Like what?" she shot back.

"Why are you always so insistent on suffering alone?"

"Because there's no point in suffering together, not when it's impractical. You've already done the job you've been sent here to do—you got us close enough to Connor Doherty and Penelope Morrison, you've helped us uncover what could be the secret vault where we'll find the evidence that we need. I needed you to be here before. There's no need for you now."

As always, her words stung him in a way he wasn't used to. Or maybe he was too used to it. Unneeded, unwanted. Maybe he deserved it, after how he'd sent the others off. How long had it been since he'd felt this affected by a girl? He'd been so confident swearing off love. Now he found himself staring at Sydney's face and felt the stirring of something very different.

Maybe he didn't need to stay. But he wanted to. The thought of leaving her here . . .

"Please tell me you're not serious," he tried again. "There are probably dozens of dangerous people in this city involved in Morrison's killing—you'll be in the crosshairs of both them and Morrison's loyals. And if the plane takes off this evening with only Penelope and me, how will you escape?"

"Panacea will send another plane eventually."

"Eventually," he said flatly.

"This is no longer your mission, Winter." Suddenly Sydney sounded angry. She glared at him, then pushed his arm away from her. To his relief and dismay, she could stand easily on her own now, the effects of the poison all but gone. "Get away from here and back to the States."

"And then what?"

She threw her hands up at him. "What do you want me to say? And then it's done. We're done. What'd you think would happen at this point? Go back to your life and leave me alone."

He opened his mouth, ready to say more, but she had already turned away from him and was heading toward the stairs. It took but a few more seconds for her to disappear up the steps.

His muscles tensed, ready to dash off in her direction and find another way—any way—to stop her. But he didn't.

Their brief moment of madness, of their hands all over each other, now seemed a million years away.

Why the hell was he arguing with her on this? She was right. He'd done his job, what Panacea had sent him here to do. His part was finished. Now he had become a liability, and Sydney clearly had no interest in letting that hold her back from what she needed to do.

And maybe whatever feelings he thought he had for her were an illusion. That would be a good thing. What kind of future could he have with a girl like Sydney, anyway? This mission was simply a chance collision of their two worlds. He was a performer. His life existed on the stage, under the spotlight. And Sydney? Sydney belonged to a secret world, moving in the spaces where Winter didn't—shouldn't—go. He had already entangled one of his closest friends in the snare of a trap originally set for himself. Maybe he'd affected the others, too, in ways he didn't even know about yet.

He couldn't afford to be in a relationship with Sydney. Not even a friendship. Not if he valued their safety and their lives.

But for now, he was still embroiled in this—and Sydney had taught him to follow his instinct. And something in his instinct told him that, if he left her behind now, if he just walked away from people he had come to care about, he would regret it for the rest of his life.

He was done carrying the weight of regrets on his shoulders.

Winter turned away from the stairs and toward the front door. As he did, he carefully slid his finger against the tiny tracker embedded into the side of his phone and pulled it out. He slid it under a coaster on a side table.

Then he pulled out his phone and dialed a number he'd never dialed before.

It only rang once.

"Hello?" said Penelope. Her voice sounded small and a little startled.

"It's me."

Her voice started trembling. He could hear the threat of tears in them. "Winter? Oh my god, I saw the press—are you still trapped in your house?"

"Don't worry about me. How are *you*?"

"Holding up okay. Winter, look, I have to tell you—"

He glanced over his shoulder as he reached the door. "We need to talk. Can I meet you early at the palace pavilion?"

"Early?" She hesitated a moment. "Sure."

"Thanks. See you soon."

Just Another Job

To Sydney's relief, the train she took toward the Victoria and Albert Museum was crowded, giving her the chance to disappear into the rush of people. Her head had cleared now, along with her reflexes and her memory. And the way she'd had to send Winter away.

Maybe she had overdone it. She'd been so angry, and she wasn't even sure who she was angry at. Him, probably. Herself, more likely. Or whoever had tried to kill them. Maybe she was mad at this whole situation, the way everything had gone so horribly wrong, the way she had let herself go off the rails with him. The reality that someone wanted them dead. The realization that their relationship was so clearly a dead end.

The train arrived at South Kensington, and she stepped off with a purposely nonchalant gait, invisible among the flood of tourists and locals, choosing the tunnel toward the museum's underground entrance instead of the main entrance up on the street. Better to rip the Band-Aid off. She knew the plane that Sauda had sent was probably already at Heathrow, ready and waiting for them. With any luck, Winter would soon be there, too, taking off without her.

With any luck, the way she'd left him would be the last time she ever saw him. And he would be alive because of it.

The pang that shot through her chest was so sharp that she sucked her breath in. His hands cupping her face, pulling her to him. The tears glistening in his eyes. The warmth of his breath against her neck, his lips on her skin.

She forced her mind to pivot and quickened her steps down the tunnel. The sound of her boots was lost among the echoes of voices around her. As she went, she glanced at her phone and checked on Winter's location. His tracker was still pinging from the house. Soon it should show him making his way to the airport.

She closed the tracker and kept going. She'd had to part from plenty of fellow operatives in the past without so much as a backward glance.

And this was just another job.

She had memorized the layout of the Victoria and Albert Museum during her train ride. It was a massive, magnificent old building chock-full of security cameras, sensors attached to every door, security tables at the main entrances, and dozens of staff that walked the grounds at all open hours.

The underground entrance, though, was more lax, especially on a weekday before noon. As she approached the nondescript door, the lone guard lounging in a chair beside it cast her a bored glance and just nodded her in. She gave him a sweet smile in return.

The museum hummed with a moderate crowd. Sydney forced herself to take her time, wandering through the sculpture hall and admiring the Rodin collection like a tourist so that security would forget about her and move on to watching others that entered the space. Then she wandered slowly through the fashion exhibit and past the giant Chihuly chandelier hanging in the main rotunda. A throng of schoolchildren wove around her.

Finally, she made her way upstairs, where each floor's crowd grew progressively sparser, until she was several halls away from Eli Morrison's newly donated wing, where Connor Doherty's collection was housed. As she passed the stairs leading up to it, she noted the velvet rope blocking the way.

INSTALLATION IN PROGRESS, said the sign. As expected.

She entered a hall with no one in it. There, she stood at a corner beside a glass display of ceramics—and tilted her phone up to the nearest blinking fire alarm.

On her screen appeared a grid showing the thousands of fire alarms in the building. She scrolled past them before picking one located at the opposite end of the museum.

She tapped on it.

An electronic screech shattered the silence, echoing throughout the museum's marble halls.

Now Sydney had a time limit. Over the ongoing scream of the alarm, an announcement came on over the speakers.

"Guests and staff, please make your way to the nearest exit. We apologize for the inconvenience."

She smiled slightly. A forced evacuation of all staff.

Sure enough, she saw three security guards make their way down from the roped-off wing holding Connor's personal collection. Sydney waited until they had disappeared down the stairs. Then she ducked under the velvet rope and sprinted up the steps—before slipping behind one of the pillars at the corridor at the top.

Three of the four guards that had been standing at attention up here were now gone—but a lone guard remained near the doors of the private collection, looking annoyed and a little uncertain about whether or not he was supposed to stay.

Sydney scowled at the sight of him and held up her phone again. Then she tapped her screen and waited until she caught the frequency channel of the man's radio.

Moments later, she heard it give a telltale crackle. He looked down at it.

You still there? she typed rapidly on her phone.

A voice, deep and male and full of static, came on his radio. "You still there?" it said, speaking Sydney's typed words.

The man blinked. "Yes?"

"Get your bloody ass down here," it said as Sydney typed, as if someone in charge downstairs was summoning him.

He returned his radio to his belt and muttered something about being pushed around. He glanced once at the doors behind him. Moments later, he went hurrying down the corridor in the wake of his fellow guards. Sydney pressed herself against the pillar as he rushed by.

He'd almost made it past her before a real guard's voice came on his speaker, making him stop in his tracks.

"Faulty trigger, they're saying," the voice said. "You still there?"

He halted. "What, I'm staying now?" he snapped.

"Did I say to leave?" came the reply.

Sydney's chest tightened. *Goddamnit*, she thought. *Plan B, then.* She hated Plan B. So crude.

The man looked around. He turned toward the pillar where she was hiding.

Sydney moved before his gaze could latch onto her. With a single leap, she aimed at his neck and hit him hard in his Adam's apple.

His eyes widened. His hands flew to his throat as he made a low, choking sound.

Sydney struck him hard in the jaw with the edge of her phone. He stumbled, dazed. She hit him again—his limbs went limp. She caught him before he could fall, staggering under his weight, then dragged him awkwardly to the side of the hall so he was partly hidden behind the pillars. Let the other guards look around for him for a few seconds and spare her some more time.

She propped the unconscious man up in the shadows, then darted to the double doors he was guarding. She slid inside without a sound, closing them behind her as if she had never been in the hall at all.

She found herself standing in Connor Doherty's private collection, surrounded by a breathtaking array of precious stones.

The fire alarms were still screeching, but Sydney knew this room must have its own alarm system.

She took out her roll of Necco Wafers, poured a bunch of the candy into her palm, and then used the edge of her phone to crush them into as fine a powder as she could manage with her limited time. When she was finished, she blew it into the air in a cloud of glittering dust. As she did, she saw a faint grid of laser lines show up here and there, momentarily visible from the slightly reflective nature of the candy's artificial additives. She took a quick photo before the grid vanished back into nothing.

Then she carefully made her way through the space, her movements steady as she followed the lines on her phone.

Winter would ace this, she thought as she went. His face sprang unbidden into her mind. She imagined how easily his graceful body might slip through the lines, how quickly he'd be able to move across the room.

Stop getting distracted, she scolded herself. Winter should be halfway to the airport by now. She was operating alone.

She went to the display case located in front of the spot where the infrared display had shown the secret room's outline. Her skin prickled as she moved. No matter how many times she checked a room, she always felt watched, like there was still a camera in here that she hadn't accounted for.

She put her phone on the floor in front of the glass display case, then stepped aside. A perfect hologram of Connor Doherty appeared an instant later, hovering over the phone, as if he were standing right here in the room.

The display case's glass seemed to flicker. She felt the shelf shudder against the back wall of the room. Then the wall slid open, revealing a small, secret space that now lit up with soft blue light.

Sydney's heart jumped into her throat. She was in.

It looked like a panic room. Maybe that was all it was. As she stepped in, though, she saw that what she'd thought was a wall wasn't one at all—but white boxes all stacked on top of one another, floor to ceiling.

She pulled one of them down and opened it.

Notebooks. Written ledgers. There were smaller boxes, too, and when

Sydney opened one of them, it contained digital drives as small and thin as her nail, stacked on top of each other. Even these couldn't be nearly the total amount of transactions done by an organization as large as Eli's empire. This was just the merest fraction, maybe a month's worth of deals. These had to be their latest—anything older would be destroyed, with no reason to keep the files around as incriminating evidence.

She couldn't help grinning. Jackpot.

She had no time to sift through all of these documents and figure out what they needed. Sydney thumbed through the files, noting their organizational pattern. Not by date, nor by letter, but by clients. She recognized the names of a few organizations known to work with Eli Morrison's holdings.

Files. What they needed.

She pulled down another box. Noted the names.

Pulled a third one down.

There was a pattern to them now, sorted by oldest to newest. She shuffled her way to the end of the files, where a final stack of boxes sat. There, she pulled the top box off and opened it.

Schedules. Ship departure times, counts of containers.

Too little time. Sydney scanned the documents with her phone, as many as she could bear.

Too little time, too little time.

Outside, Sydney heard the slight crackle and beeps of security cameras coming online. She scanned a few more documents, then shoved the box back. Somewhere among what she had recorded on her phone must be evidence of Morrison's recent trafficking.

She tapped an image of Sauda on her phone, then started transmitting the first of the files.

It didn't even get a chance to start before she heard a voice behind her.

"Busy?"

Sydney whirled around and came face-to-face with Connor Doherty.

She reacted instantly. Her leg came up—she kicked out at him, aiming for his throat. But he moved shockingly fast. This was no mere account manager. He'd been trained to kill.

He dodged her move and seized her wrist instead. Sydney twisted out of his grasp, but before she could lunge at him again, he stepped back.

No. Sydney darted forward, but the door slid closed in the blink of an eye. Before it shut completely, she caught a glimpse of Connor smiling at her, her phone in his hand.

Then the door sealed, and the blue light went out, trapping her in darkness.

27

Silent Beat

True to her word, Penelope was the first person Winter saw when his car passed through the gates of Kensington Palace and arrived at the pavilion.

Against the backdrop of the palace's Sunken Garden, the serenity of potted winter flowers and glittering red Christmas bulbs on hedges against a long, rectangular pool, she looked resplendent, dressed in a gold-studded leather jacket and a sweeping, pleated blue dress, her dark hair pulled up into an elegant bun. Ready for her birthday reception.

Not that she seemed in the mood for a celebration. He could tell right away that she'd been crying; the corners of her eyes were still pink, the skin under her lids dark from lack of sleep. She looked small and stiff as she kept her arms folded tightly in front of her chest.

Winter felt a twist of guilt in his stomach at what he was about to tell her.

A bodyguard approached his door and opened it. As he stepped out, Penelope hurried over to him, offering him a small smile of greeting before looping her arm through his and leading him along the edge of the Sunken Garden's central pool. They were early, of course, and the rest of the lush surroundings were dotted mostly with staff as they positioned enormous arrangements of Christmas roses in front of the heated pavilion. Birds chirped under the cold morning sun, and a fresh breeze chilled the air, setting the bushes trembling.

The serenity of the space felt less like a peaceful moment and more like the silent beats in a song right before a heavy rhythm kicked in. The kind of quiet that tensed Winter's muscles, warning of something big. He kept his hands in his pockets, his fingers fiddling with the pen from Panacea that he now had tucked against the inside lining. It wasn't a huge weapon, but at least the pen's hidden blade gave him some sense of protection.

"How are you holding up?" Winter asked Penelope in a low voice.

She didn't look at him. The arm she'd looped through his was trembling, and through the fabric of his clothes, he could tell her hand was ice-cold.

"Well enough," she replied. "You?"

"Same."

She looked behind him. "Where's your bodyguard?"

"Watching from a distance," he replied. Then he leaned closer to her. "We need to have a talk."

She took a deep, shuddering breath. "If this is about the shooter, I—"

"This isn't about your shooter." He cleared his throat. "It's about your father."

"My father?" Her eyes darted up to his, hopeful and questioning. "You saw him? I've been trying to reach him since last night."

Winter paused for a moment, wondering if he should be the one to tell her. But anyone who might tell her now would be in Morrison's circles, and someone had tried to kill her. So he leaned closer, posing as if he were just a boy flirting with a girl. A few staffers in the distance looked over at them, their expressions curious.

"I'm deeply sorry to tell you this," he said in a low voice. "But when I do, I need you to not show any emotions."

Fear flickered in her eyes, as if she was bracing herself for news she'd already assumed. She searched his face frantically.

A pause. "Your father was killed last night."

They kept walking.

Penelope managed to keep a straight face, her eyes downcast. But he felt the tremor that shuddered through her body, the sudden stiffness of her posture, the way she clung to his arm as if she might fall. He steadied against her, pulling her arm to his body. The color had drained from her face in the changing light. So, she hadn't heard.

"I'm so sorry," he whispered again.

"That's impossible," she whispered back.

"Believe me, I wish I could tell you something different," he said softly.

"He's just busy," she answered in a firm voice tinged with anger. Her eyes went up now, going to the pavilion and the thick winter roses cascading down its sides. "He's scheduled to show up here in an hour. He's going to lead a toast."

She met his eyes defiantly again. It was all he could do to give her a grave look in return.

She started shaking her head, and he squeezed her hand slightly as it clenched at the crook of his elbow. His gaze darted to the people milling about inside the pavilion.

"I know the weight of what I'm asking from you," he whispered to her, "but try to keep your composure. You aren't safe here."

But Penelope just pulled her arm away. "No, *you* don't understand. He said—he told me—"

"Told you what? When did you last speak to him?"

"When you were performing on the stage." Her eyes darted from the pavilion to him. "When we were at the Alexandra Palace. He told me he'd be here."

He gave her a sad look. "I'm so sorry."

She swallowed hard, and behind her incredulity, he could see her struggling to hold the tears back. Her eyes went back to the ground again. She was good at it, this restraint. He wondered how many times in the past she'd had to do it, and what for.

"How can you possibly know this?" she said hoarsely. "*Why* do you know?"

"I can't tell you everything yet," he replied. "But whoever targeted you last night in your apartment also targeted your father. They succeeded with him. Might mean they'll make another attempt with you."

"He died when we were in my flat?" she whispered.

Winter nodded.

She took his arm again, this time as if for support. He could feel her hand trembling slightly against his elbow, her grip so tight that her knuckles had turned white.

"I need to tell someone," she suddenly said.

"No."

Anger flashed through her gaze. "You don't have the right to tell me that."

The words came out of Winter sharper than he intended. "Maybe not," he replied. "But you have to listen to me. Please. You can't tell anyone else."

"But I—"

Winter stopped their walk for a moment and turned to face her. He leaned down to her ear so that no one else could see his lips moving. "We don't know who did it," he whispered, "and that means everyone close to you is a potential suspect."

When he pulled slightly away, she was glaring at him, eyes glossy with suspicion. "Including you."

"I have absolutely nothing to gain from hurting you."

"Why should I believe that?"

"I can't give you any convincing evidence," he replied, "other than the truth that your life depends on it."

She tightened her lips at him, as if trying to reconcile this with the faith she had in her idol, and then looked back at the party. More guests had arrived now.

"What do you want me to do?" she finally murmured.

"Leave with me."

She blinked at him. "What? When?"

"As soon as you can slip away."

"You mean—now?" She looked around helplessly. "I can't." She swallowed again and pulled back on his arm. "My guests."

Now she truly looked like she might fly into a frantic state. Winter's mind whirled, trying to figure out what to do if she were to have a breakdown here. How would he explain it? How would he get them out of here?

"I know. But we don't have a choice."

"There—there are a thousand dignitaries and elite here from all over the world. Connor will expect to see me the instant he arrives." Her speech quickened, breathless with fear, and suddenly Winter realized she might be in danger from the accountant. "He'll be here any moment. We won't make it halfway to the airport before he realizes I'm gone."

He couldn't let Connor lead Penelope somewhere after her toast.

"It's going to be okay," he said to her. "We'll both make our appearance in front of your cake, so you can say a few words. Just for an hour. Can you do that?"

She nodded numbly.

"Good. Make our appearance, put the crowd's minds at ease, and then leave as everyone mingles. They won't notice you're gone after you've already said your piece."

Penelope stopped walking. There was a lost expression on her face that felt familiar to him, the loneliness of being used to bearing things on her own, and he found himself feeling afraid, wondering if he could really keep her safe, if he and Sydney could pull all of this off.

Then she straightened, forcing herself to lift her chin. He could still see the gloss in her eyes. But when she spoke, her voice stayed steady enough to disguise her emotions.

"Come with me," she said without looking at him. "I need to greet some people."

He nodded and followed in her wake. As he did, he typed out a quick message to Sydney.

She'll leave with us.

He stared at his phone for a few seconds, hoping to see a reply.

Nothing. He put his phone away reluctantly, then went with Penelope to greet her first guest. In the back of his mind, he kept waiting for the reassuring buzz of Sydney's answer. She always responded.

But this time, she didn't.

Bullseye

I t wasn't until the sun had moved overhead and the shadows in the garden disappeared that Winter finally got a response from Sydney.

His phone buzzed right as Penelope cut into her cake, that trained smile still plastered on her face. As the audience around her in the pavilion cheered and flashes went off, Winter took a subtle step back from the crowd and looked at the message that had popped up for him.

Where are you?

Overwhelming relief. That was Winter's first reaction. The message had clearly been sent from Sydney's phone, and he knew she must still be transmitting from inside the museum. Her tracker said as much.

His second reaction was confusion. Sydney should be able to see the tracker he'd left behind, still broadcasting from the living room of the house. She should think he was there.

Also, it was an oddly wordy message from her. Sydney used abbreviations in her messages every chance she got—she didn't type anything out fully if she didn't have to. He would have expected her to write, *Where r u?* Or even just *Wru?* and leave him to figure it out on his own.

Maybe she was concerned about him, and wanted to make sure he understood her on his first read. Maybe she was dictating the words out loud into her phone and it translated her words properly.

The crowd around him laughed in unison at something that Penelope said. He texted back.

Birthday reception.

He braced himself after he sent it, waiting for her reprimand — that instead of being on a plane, he was still here and preparing to help Penelope escape with him.

Her reply came.

Okay.

Winter stopped, frowning down at his phone.

No sarcasm, no annoyance over why he was running around London. No comment on why his tracker was still broadcasting from the house.

But most of all, the word *Okay* spelled perfectly out.

Sydney never wrote out *Okay.* She would have just sent the letter *K.*

Winter felt a shiver crawl down his spine. The image of Sydney faded from his mind like a puff of smoke. Nobody stood on the other side now except darkness. His hands tightened against the sides of his phone, and he tried to keep his breathing even.

What if the person sending him messages wasn't Sydney?

That would only mean one thing.

Something had happened to her.

Around him, people let out a cheer as Penelope popped a bottle of champagne and laughed as she poured it over an elaborate tower of glasses. Still no Connor Doherty present.

Winter had felt the buzz of danger back when Sauda had ushered him into that car after his concert—but this time, the buzz was real. It traveled to his hands and down his spine, sending rivulets of heat through him. Something was unraveling.

Whoever it was on Sydney's phone wanted him to stay.

He needed to get out of here.

There was a storm on the horizon—he could see the edge of dark clouds slicing right behind London's cityscape beyond the garden, spilling darkness across a beautiful afternoon sky, hinting at the down-pour that would come later. The sensation churning in Winter's head now reminded him of the night when he'd heard his mother's broken conversation downstairs, when they'd first learned of Artie's death. His head filled with fog. He had the strange feeling that he wasn't even here.

He didn't care about the failed mission anymore.

All he could think about was Sydney.

She must have gotten caught.

I should have gone with her.

Then, through the blur of his thoughts, he saw Penelope look in his direction. She still looked shaken, but she gestured for him to step forward.

"—to the boy who helped make this celebration one for the history books!" she said now as Winter reached her. "And one who certainly needs no introduction."

The crowd around them screamed their approval. Penelope handed Winter the microphone, and he took it, fighting to contain his compo-sure. Minutes after this, he was supposed to lead Penelope off the main floor and, as the crowd gathered around the cake, take her down the garden's hedge maze and away into a cab heading for the airport.

But something had happened to Sydney.

He forced a smile onto his face. His gaze swept out at the audience, seeing a thousand faces and unable to hang on to any of them. Everyone looked like a suspect.

Then Penelope's eyes flickered to the crowd, just for a second.

He looked in the same direction. As he did, he saw something glint.

There was no time for him to do anything.

The pop was muffled, the sound so muted by the cheers of the audi-ence and the echo of his own voice that Winter didn't hear it.

One instant, he was standing—the next, he was hurtling backward. The shock rocketed his shoulder before the pain hit him.

He hit the ground with a thud. It knocked the breath out of him in a single whoosh.

He heard a rush of confused gasps ripple around him. Then a couple of screams.

Winter gasped for air. Was he lying on the floor? How had he gotten down here? He tried to get up, but pain seared his shoulder and he cried out.

Now there were people rushing toward him—black-suited bodyguards, guests in tuxes screaming for someone to call the police. The tang of something metallic hung in the air.

Blood?

Somewhere far away, he thought he could hear someone calling his name. *Winter. Winter!*

Where had Penelope gone?

There were more people now. Pain pulsed from his upper chest, leaving him frozen. The world began to close around him, funneling his vision down to nothing. He had the vague sensation of being hoisted up in someone's arms, his body being limp. The last thought that flittered across his mind was realization of what had just happened.

He'd just been shot.

29
The Good Daughter

For a while, all he was aware of was the pain.

It washed over him in waves—the agony rippled from his shoulder to his limbs to every part of his body, a throbbing ache that left him short of breath.

His mind swam in what felt like mud. There had been the distant sensation of someone lifting him onto a gurney and wheeling him away, of medics in forest green uniforms, of strangers shouting down at him, asking him if he would be okay.

He thought he could remember the interior of a truck. The screams of a crowd that had flooded outside to see the vehicle drive off with him in it. The shrieks of an ambulance wailing from directly outside. The rumble under the vehicle from the road. A murmur from his lips that came and went.

Sydney. Sydney.

Someone else had been sitting in the truck with him, too. Penelope Morrison.

Even in that state, he'd known that was wrong. Penelope shouldn't have been inside the ambulance with him. She'd looked deadly calm, her voice low as she'd exchanged some words with the driver. The driver had answered her politely and turned as she directed.

Maybe he'd been having a nightmare.

Now the world around him lightened. Darkness receded to the corners of his mind. His surroundings sharpened.

He squinted immediately. Fluorescent lights glared overhead, and around him were rows and rows of shelves, each filled with identical metal canisters secured inside heavy crates.

Some part of his mind recoiled at the sight, recalling the images shown to him in Panacea's headquarters.

Paramecium.

He squeezed his eyes shut again. The glare from the lights danced behind his closed lids. The dreamlike quality of the last few hours—days? He wasn't sure—left him feeling unmoored. A place like this didn't match at all with what had just happened at the party—unless he'd hallucinated that, too.

There *had* been a party, right? He'd hurried into the royal gardens and walked along the pool with Penelope, had spoken to her in a low, urgent voice. She had stared up at him with those wide eyes and braced herself and gone forward anyway into the pavilion, had stood beside him. He'd felt the shock from a bullet rocketing him backward, had hit the grass hard.

That was no dream. He had been shot right there and taken away in an ambulance with the crowd's screams still ringing in his ears.

None of that seemed accurate, though. If he had really been put into an ambulance, why hadn't they taken him to a hospital?

He moaned as pain shot through him again, setting him trembling.

And with that movement, he realized he was tied down.

Suddenly, he sensed the presence of another person beside him. With all the strength he could muster, he turned to his side and looked over to see Penelope Morrison sitting in a chair next to him, her body haloed in light from a door slightly ajar behind her. Half a dozen guards stood spread out around the room. She observed him as he struggled once more against the bonds that held him down.

"I wouldn't move too much, if I were you," Penelope said. "That was a glancing blow, but you've got enough damage in your shoulder muscles to bleed more than you can handle. You might be dead before we even reach open water."

Open water? Were they out at sea?

His mind continued to clear. Now he was aware of the rough cut of rope against his wrists and ankles, and the feeling of a hard table underneath his body. Beyond the slit in the ajar door, he could see a sprawling deck lined with stacks of shipping containers, the metal grid holding them in place rising eight stories against the blue sky. A lone seagull perched high on the edge of the structure. The unmistakable smell of salt and sea wafted inside. Waves crashed in the distance.

"You're on board my cargo ship," Penelope explained, guessing what he wanted to ask her. She glanced back once at the open door, her eyes as wide and innocent as he remembered from their first meeting. The contrast with her words was jarring. "The North Sea is quite choppy at this time of year. Forgive the unsteady ride."

On board a cargo ship. Winter was headed with Morrison's shipments to Cape Town.

"No one will be looking for you here," Penelope added.

He struggled to understand what was happening through his clearing mind. There was nothing on Penelope Morrison. She had a blank slate, a public image so sparse and clean that not even Panacea had suspected her of being anything more than a young heiress unfortunate enough to have a late mother and criminal father.

Wasn't that who she was? Just an unfortunate young heiress? Who was this girl sitting beside him, observing him in his wounded state with a calm face and a cold voice? It made no sense.

He gritted his teeth as the pain washed over him again. "Who—" he managed to ask after the agony ebbed slightly. His voice came out hoarse and broken. He tried again. "Who are you?"

"Penelope Morrison," she answered matter-of-factly.

"You're not the Penelope I knew yesterday."

"I'm exactly the same." She blinked at him, almost shyly, as she did when they first met. "You just didn't notice."

His mind swam at her words. This version of her didn't match her previous self at all. Who had been the girl who'd been such a fan of his that she could barely look him in the eye, who'd quoted Shakespeare with him, who'd curled up on the sofa beside him and confessed her insecurities, who'd fought back tears over her father's death? Was that all an act?

"Wait." He closed his eyes again before opening them. "Last night in your apartment. The bullet."

She gave him a nod. "The bullet through my window was meant for you, Winter, not me."

Of course it was. The entire reason why Penelope must have led him back there was to take him out.

His muscles trembled from the exertion of having been held in place for hours. The pain in his shoulder throbbed. How long had Penelope known about their entire plan? How had she kept everything hidden for so long? He looked at her now and wondered how he could have ever thought she was a shy, excited, blushing fan, someone anxious and naïve. The girl staring back at him had the calm demeanor of a killer.

Of her father.

His gaze went again to the canisters of chemical weapons around them. *Paramecium.* The hackles rose on his neck.

He could still feel the subtle weight of the tiny vial of toxin in his pocket that Panacea had given him. Could now hear the echo of Sauda's voice, telling him he might need it someday. Well, would it be today? If he managed to twist his arm enough, he could pull it out and bite it open, could drink the contents. The possibility made him tremble.

"Why would you want me dead?" he croaked out. "Why are you doing this?"

She turned her eyes down, and for a second, he saw a flash of real grief in her. "Why do you think you were really invited to my birthday celebrations?" she said quietly.

"All I came here to do was to put on a private concert for a fan," he responded.

She gave him a penetrating stare. "Is that so? Because I was under the impression that a covert organization called Panacea sent you and another agent here to take down my father."

Winter stared back at her, frozen in disbelief. Penelope knew everything. She had been aware from the start.

She sighed. "If Panacea were responsible for the death of my father, then *I* wouldn't be, right?"

All along, Penelope Morrison had been the one orchestrating everything behind the scenes—the invitation to her party, the planned execution of her father, the seizing of his shipments. She had known about Panacea's recruitment of him even before he did.

"You let me give the ring to Connor," he said.

She looked evenly at him—and he realized that she'd purposely led him into the private party room with Connor so they could meet, had probably planted false documents in Connor's hidden museum vault. If he and Sydney were silenced now, then Panacea would look responsible for what happened to Eli Morrison, and remain empty-handed in terms of evidence to convict him. Penelope would get away clean again, the good daughter horrified by what happened to her father.

They had thought they were using her as their pawn, when she was using them all along to cover her own plans.

How did she know?

"Why would you want the publicity of my shooting around you?" he said hoarsely.

One of the guards near her handed her a pair of gloves. She took them and started pulling them on. "Maybe a fan crazed with jealousy wanted you dead. Maybe someone couldn't stand the idea of you being close with anyone, being my private guest." She smiled, somehow still wearing a naïve expression on her face. "Whatever the reason for a random person to shoot you from a crowd, your story will generate such a firestorm of interest that any news about my father's death would be reduced to a footnote." At his expression, she shook her head mournfully. "I'm a true fan, if that's what you're wondering," she said. "And I'm sorry it has to be like this. I regret this is how we'll say goodbye."

He had been brought here to be assassinated. He thought of his hazy memories in the ambulance, the way the driver had acquiesced calmly to Penelope's directions. She'd arranged for him to be taken here, when the world probably thought he was at a hospital.

"I know why others would want your father dead," he ventured. "But why do *you*? Why all this effort?"

Penelope stayed silent as she pulled on her second glove.

"You murdered him because of something he did," Winter continued. "Was it something done to you?"

Still no answer.

"To someone you loved?" he pushed.

There was the faintest tremor on her face, and in that tremor, Winter saw some sense of loss, some memory of a broken family, that felt familiar to him. His instincts stirred. "Your mother?" he guessed.

This time, Penelope looked away for a split second before settling back on him. He had hit true.

"I heard she passed away from an illness," Winter said.

At that, anger sparked in her eyes. "My mother didn't die from an illness," she answered coldly. "She died because my father killed her."

Winter felt a chill ripple through him. So this was it.

Penelope turned away from him, walked over to one of the shelves, and gingerly took one of the canisters in her hands.

"She met my father during her side job," she continued in a soft, quiet voice. "Catering one of his parties. I watched him hit her for years. It was my earliest memory. She always told me that he didn't mean it. He isolated her, cut her off from her family, refused to let her speak to them, ignored their pleas. The day he finally killed her in a rage, I was five. I'll have nightmares for the rest of my life of what he did to her." She looked at him, and this time all her innocence was gone, replaced by the expression of someone haunted beyond her years. "I watched his power protect him, how it allowed him to sit there with a team of detectives and police who all quietly understood that they were to erase the evidence. I promised myself then that I would kill him someday."

Her words swam in Winter's mind. So that was the reason behind it all. He pictured the charismatic smile of her father, then his elegant hands stained with the blood of his late wife.

Attending parties to make her father happy. Being the nice girl. She had hidden herself away so well.

"You grieved his death," he said, "even though you ordered it."

For a moment, he saw a glimmer of the softhearted girl he thought he knew. She looked away. Her fingers ran lightly across a phrase in Italian tattooed on her wrist. "He was still my father," she said.

"But you're not going to stop his endeavor," he said, his eyes darting around the room. "This ship's still sailing for Cape Town with its illegal haul."

Penelope opened the top of the canister and reached in. She pulled out a small cube that looked like it was made of glass, its translucent surface a very faint tint of blue.

"Think, Winter Young. What does someone like me have to lose if you and your agency successfully convict my late father of how he built his empire?"

He narrowed his eyes. "Money."

The fragile part of Penelope's heart retreated behind a hard shell. "Do you know what happens to all of my father's wealth if you finally get evidence against him? Frozen. Confiscated." She held the cube carefully as she walked over to him. "And I'll be damned if I see all of that end up with some government instead of me, all the money that should have gone instead to my mother."

"So you took matters into your own hands."

"It was the deal I made with the Corcasians, in exchange for their cooperation in helping me." She shrugged. "It's my inheritance. My right. I want the ghost of my father to know that all the money he'd hoarded so zealously will now go into everything my mother had ever dreamed of. A fund in her name. An estate that belongs to her side of the family."

Penelope's inheritance. It made sense. This wasn't the first time authorities had trained their eyes on Eli Morrison, and even if they couldn't succeed this time, the evidence was steadily mounting against the man. It was only a matter of time before his assets would be seized.

But Penelope was clean. She hid her tracks even better than her father did, and if she got to the money before authorities could, it'd be hers. And somehow, he knew she would get out of all this without a single shred of evidence tying her to any of his criminal doings, to his death, or to Winter's.

Or Sydney's.

"I understand why you're doing this," he said. "Truly. But please don't go through with it. You're giving your mother's family blood money."

"I don't think this is your call to make," she replied coolly.

"This isn't who you want to be," he pleaded. "I know you meant it genuinely when you said you desired meaning in your life."

"This is meaningful to me," she replied.

His gaze fell onto the cube in her hands. A chill rippled through him. "You're going to ship tons of this chemical weapon into the hands of terrorists."

"I'm working with Connor Doherty for a reason," she replied.

He narrowed his eyes. "Then why am I still alive at all? Why am I here?"

"Because you took something from my flat that didn't belong to you." She folded her arms. "And I want it back."

Her bejeweled hairpin. The encrypted data that Sydney had pulled from it and given to Panacea. In a flash, he realized that it must be incriminating evidence of Penelope's involvement in everything.

"I don't have it," he said.

"You know where it is. Or maybe who has it."

The sound of footsteps against the deck made Winter turn. Penelope looked over.

"Finally," she muttered.

A man stepped out from behind the nearest row of shipping containers, walking with a calm, easy gait, dressed as properly as ever, his eyes hidden behind a pair of shades. Connor.

Immediately behind him came two men that Winter recognized as former bodyguards for Eli—except this time, they were dragging between them a slight, slender figure, her short blond hair bobbing weakly with her bent head.

Winter couldn't see the girl's face, but he recognized her instantly. Terror jolted through his body.

Sydney.

30 Trapped

S ydney looked up as they stopped in the room. Paramecium canisters everywhere, secured against the shelves.

Her gaze darted to Penelope, then to the cube she held in her hand. Images flashed through her mind of Eli Morrison's death, the way foam had dripped from his mouth as the chemical destroyed the inside of his body. The Paramecium was everywhere now, all around them, as if death had been manufactured and packaged for the shelves and now waited for a chance to be freed. Her skin crawled, and everything in her wanted to pull away from the cube.

Her gaze darted to Winter.

Shot in the chest, a good few inches shy of his heart, with a bullet slender enough to leave a small wound. She could tell just by the bloodstain dotting the white bandages wrapped around his bare chest. Judging from the way he was breathing, the injury hurt but hadn't pierced his lung cavity—in all likelihood, it had torn into his chest muscle and lodged deep in there.

He'd need attention soon. All that blood loss had made him weak; the coloration of his face was ghostly pale, and a sheen of sweat glistened against his skin. If he went into shock out here, in the middle of the ocean, he'd die even before Penelope's interrogation could really begin.

It took every bit of Sydney's willpower not to scream and lunge right there, to direct all her strength at reaching the young woman. Instead, she sank into the calm of her mind and lowered her head again. Let herself go slack.

No one with a bad hand ever won by revealing it early.

They stopped abruptly before the table. Sydney heard Penelope rise in a smooth motion, then looked up to see her holding out the cube.

"Where's the hairpin?" Penelope asked Sydney now.

"I lost it," Sydney lied, glancing toward Connor.

Penelope glanced at Winter. "Maybe you gave it to him. Shall I ask?"

Winter stayed quiet.

Say something! she screamed at him in her head. *Tell any lie!* By the time Penelope figured it out, Winter could have also worked out a way to escape.

But he didn't speak.

"Be done with him already," Connor said to Penelope with a sigh. "Everyone still thinks he's at the hospital, anyway. Tell them to send out word that he succumbed to his fan's gunshot wound. We can get intel out of the girl instead."

Sydney met Winter's eyes, could see him trembling from the strain of his bonds. How could they have missed the clues about Penelope? How had she hidden her true self so well?

Penelope turned her hardened gaze back on them, then gestured again at her guards.

Sydney felt the two men holding her shove her violently forward. She fell hard to the floor, curling instinctively inward as if to protect herself, and forced her head to stay down.

She heard the restraints on Winter's wrists pull taut above her and knew that he must have seen her fall.

"Let me ask again," Penelope said. Her voice seemed to stay the same, but Sydney could hear the slightest hardening of the words. "Where is it?"

Thoughts raced through Sydney's head. By now, Sauda and Niall would know of their predicament—her brief signal to them should have done that much. She knew Panacea would be doing all they could in order to get them out. But they still had no way of knowing where Winter and Sydney were being kept, especially now that they were on board a moving ship. Their devices had all been stripped from them. They were off the grid, and still on their own.

Their only saving grace was the fact that Winter's body was missing from a hospital. News about his being shot onstage should have hit the newswires already. That meant every fan on the planet was searching desperately for updates on how Winter was doing. If Panacea couldn't find them, then maybe the rest of the world could.

She knew Penelope knew this. Winter would have to die soon. The sound of the waves crashing against the hull of the ship echoed through Sydney's body.

"Still no answer?" Penelope said, and this time Sydney looked up from the ground. The girl looked mournful, as if they were forcing her to be cruel. "Please, Winter. I could have sworn you cared for her more than this."

Sydney's eyes darted to Winter. He was still lying on the table, his head turned toward her as far as he could manage, and his eyes were wide, glossy with fear. Gone was the flirt, the graceful swagger and the mischievous grin. He looked at her as if pleading with her to do something, as if something from her training with Panacea might kick in at any moment to save them.

He looked at her in the way he had when she'd been poisoned.

Before she could say anything, one of the guards seized a fistful of her hair and forced her head up. She winced as he pulled hard enough to bring her momentarily off the ground.

"Hold her mouth open," Penelope said.

Sydney saw the girl approach her, then hold up the cube. Everything in her seemed to narrow into a blade. Her fear funneled her concentration into a needle.

"Stop! Stop!"

Winter's voice, hoarse and anguished, cut through the moment.

Sydney met his eyes and saw resignation there. *No,* she wanted to yell at him. *No, do not let them break you now.*

Winter tore his eyes away from her and back toward Penelope. "I had it. Back at the house. It's in my luggage—I never gave it to her."

Sydney couldn't believe her ears.

The lie slipped from his lips like water, so devoid of hesitation and so crystal clear in its desperation that for an instant she forgot Panacea existed. And here she'd thought Winter was too terrified to know what to do or say. A memory came back to her of Winter from his first performance—the way he'd transformed in a second from a tied-up boy against the floor to a dark-eyed heartbreaker. The way he'd broken free from his bonds.

Only now did she see his hands twisting subtly against the restraints, moving so quietly that it might as well be a magic act. He was working on freeing himself, and no one even noticed.

Sauda would be proud.

Penelope narrowed her eyes at him. The beat of hesitation before she answered told Sydney everything she needed to know. Winter's words had taken the young woman by surprise, and now she was considering the truth of it.

"That's a relief," she said to Winter.

Then she took the cube and shoved it in Winter's mouth.

Winter froze, paralyzed, too afraid to move.

Penelope took a length of duct tape from one of the guards and sealed the cube tightly inside Winter's mouth.

Sydney shivered at the cold efficiency of her movements contrasted with her wide, doe-like eyes.

"Thank you for your help," she said. "I'll have someone check for it."

On the table, Winter closed his eyes and shivered against his gag. His hands continued to work.

Sydney laid her head down on the ground, as if exhausted by the truth coming out—but instead, she used the opportunity to study Winter. *Don't move,* she pleaded silently. *Don't move.*

He stared back at her. The look he gave her now wasn't desperate or pleading—but meaningful. He swallowed behind the gag.

Sydney saw his hands twist again.

And in a flash, she understood.

Her eyes went to the nearest guard, then to the knife at his belt.

Penelope leaned back in her chair and shook her head in disappointment at Winter. "A perfect life," she mused. She looked at Sydney. "And here you are, wasting it all for Panacea."

Sydney tensed, prepared to make her move. Everything in her focused on Winter.

Then he suddenly lunged to one side. In the blink of an eye, his hand slipped through one of the bonds, and his arm came fully free. In the next instant, he'd ripped the tape from his mouth and spat the cube out into his hand.

At the same time, Sydney jumped to her feet. The guard beside her only had time to put his hand on the holster of his gun before she spun toward him and turned her back—her tied hands closed around the knife's handle and yanked it out from his belt.

She sensed more than saw the man swing his gun toward her. She threw her entire weight at him—he lost his balance and toppled backward. As he did, she wedged the knife into the knot of the rope tying her hands and shoved it in as hard as she could. She felt the blade cut into the strands. Just enough.

She pulled against it with all her might.

The rope protested a second, then tugged free.

Then she glanced at Winter. At the same time that he tossed the cube toward her, she threw the knife toward him.

He caught the knife. She caught the cube through the rope.

Sydney could feel the burn of the cube in her hand. She put it on the ground and positioned her boot over it. "No one move," she said.

Penelope stiffened. Two guards stepped forward, their bodies shielding her. Connor froze, eyeing them warily.

She looked at Winter.

There was only one place they could head to right now, their only potential link with the outside world. The bridge.

"Go," she said quietly to Winter.

He met her gaze once, then darted out of the room. Somehow, she could tell that he knew exactly where she wanted him to head.

The bridge was at the opposite end of the ship—and they had a dozen armed men after them. She could feel the coming strain in her lungs already. Knew that she couldn't make that kind of run.

And Winter had been shot in the shoulder.

Sydney shifted so that her back faced the door. Penelope glared at her as she went.

Then her eyes flickered slightly to the corner behind Sydney.

Sydney's eyes followed her stare instinctively.

It only took a second—

And then Connor lunged at her, reaching down for the cube under her foot.

Sydney thought of Eli's horrified expression as the object broke in his mouth.

This was their only chance to survive.

Sydney gritted her teeth. She tugged her shirt up over her nose and mouth.

Then she flipped the cube up onto her boot and kicked it hard at the wall—where it shattered.

Not Over Yet

Pain radiated from the wound in Winter's chest. He winced as he darted between two narrow rows of shipping containers, suspending himself over them by pressing his hands and feet hard against either wall, and melted into the long shadows. The movement sent spasms of agony through him—he grimaced, squeezing his eyes shut. His breaths came in shallow bursts. Cold ocean wind streamed through his hair and stung his cheeks. The sun was starting to set.

Behind him came commotion from the room he had just escaped. Strangled shouts, the sounds of choking. Connor's strangled scream.

Then he saw Sydney sprinting out first, her eyes squeezed shut, her shirt pulled over her mouth.

The Paramecium cube must have shattered.

She caught sight of him and hurried in his direction. He gestured for her to follow him through the shadows.

There were other guards on board the ship. He could see flickers of movement in the distance between the towers of containers, muffled commands being shouted. Maybe Penelope had already alerted the rest of the ship that they were loose.

As Sydney caught up with him, he heard the telltale sound of the slight wheeze at the end of her breaths. It was how he got whenever he pushed himself too hard during tour. Her lungs must be aching.

At his expression, Sydney scowled and shook her head, waving it away. "I'm fine," she snapped, glancing instead in the direction of the setting sun. "Bridge."

Strands of Winter's hair caught against his face as he looked toward the bridge. "We can't go straight," he said, nodding to where he saw multiple guards running. The pain from his chest made him light-headed.

Sydney nodded, scanning the deck. "We need to separate, too," she replied. "Gives us two chances to get there."

The sun had descended halfway into the ocean by now. Their silhouettes, along with the towering outlines of stacks and skeletons of cell grids were lit by brilliant orange and gold. Seeing them moving against this was too easy—although it also meant they could vanish into the long, stretching shadows.

He clutched his chest and looked up the steel pillars of the grids. At least four stories high.

Sydney caught his expression. "I'll go up," she said, nodding at the top of the grid towers. "You go down." She gestured at the hatches leading belowdecks.

"No," he said, shaking his head. "Your breathing."

"You've been shot."

"I can scale it faster," he said through gritted teeth. "I'll be safer up there. It's too high up for them to get a clear shot, so they'll have to follow me up. You'll get there sooner than me."

He could see worry flickering in Sydney's eyes. When she spoke, though, her voice was steady. "Fine," she said, pulling out a gun.

He hadn't even seen her take it off one of the guards. *Thief hands,* he thought admiringly.

"Don't wait for me if you get there first."

She met his gaze solemnly. "Same to you. Just send the call for help."

They lingered near each other for a second, as if reluctant to part. For an instant, Winter realized that this could be the last time they ever saw each other. He found himself taking in the tangle of her hair, the bloody scrape on her cheek. The stormy blue of her eyes.

"See you there," she murmured to him, her eyes upturned to his.

He nodded. "See you there."

She nodded back. Then she sprinted for the hatch, and he tore his stare away to speed toward the nearest steel pillar.

His wound screamed as he began hauling himself up the scaffolding's ladder. *Just like one of your moves during the last tour. Just like rehearsals.* His muscle memory kicked in, and he let it guide him through the pain. The world around him seemed to flash as the pillar blocked part of the setting sun's glare—and if he let himself, he could fall into believing that this was another one of his stage acts, that the whistle of the wind around him was the cheers from the audience, the light blinding him came from the spotlights pointing down at his moving figure. Everything in him trembled. His strength was faltering already.

Down below, he heard the first sounds from arriving guards. Then, the unmistakable ping of a bullet against the steel grid. Up he continued.

He could feel blood leaking from his wound, and when he looked, he could see the bandage underneath his torn shirt turning a deeper crimson.

How had Artie felt when he was shot? Had he been afraid to die, regretted joining these types of missions? Had he felt sadness that he would never see his family again?

Winter looked up, yearning for the top of the grid. Two more stories. His body shook.

Another bullet pinged near him. He heard it in a daze—somehow, the shouts from down below seemed to come from some other timeline, like everything happening around him was merely a movie playing. Maybe nothing that had ever happened to him had been real. His entire life was a stage.

Keep going. He chanced a glimpse down to see two of the men now attempting to follow him, and a third waving in the direction of the crane that loomed between him and the bridge.

His heart sank as he saw a fourth open the hatch below and head down with two more men.

He'd seen how fast Sydney could move. With the halls as narrow as they probably were down there, she at least had a chance of staving them off.

One more story.

He clenched his teeth as his next pull sent pain jolting through him. Sweat drenched his skin and dripped down the sides of his face. His hands trembled, his grip barely steady. He could feel the wind beneath him, could sense how easily he could plummet right now to his death.

Keep going.

At the horizon, the sun was sinking rapidly into the ocean, and the colors of the sky shifted, the oranges more brilliant, the pinks so exaggerated they looked fake.

He thought of the pier, and Artie at his side, and the way he'd laughed as he kicked at one of the wooden support beams. Winter's arms moved numbly, pulling him up. His head swam with nausea and fog. The world around him seemed to tilt.

And then—

The steel pillar stopped abruptly, and he felt his hands land on a flat surface, and he was up, up at the top of the grid, the wind blasting in his face. Somehow, he managed to pull himself over the top, and then crouched there, dizzy with life, one hand pressed against his wound.

Down below, one of the men was halfway up the grid. He would be here soon.

Move.

The command rang in Winter's head, and he turned his gaze in the direction of the bridge. He dragged himself to his feet. And he ran for his life.

The grids were wider than he could have hoped for—even with his unsteady balance and loss of blood, he found himself able to navigate them. Ahead of him, the blinding sun sank further into the ocean, and the colors of the sky shifted yet again, pinks to purples.

He looked over his shoulder to see that the guard chasing him down had now reached the top of the grid and was racing toward him faster than Winter could run.

The pain in his chest now seemed to reach every part of his body, and he felt his head swim from the loss of blood. He tried to force his muscles to move as he'd always been able to, to make the show go on. But he couldn't this time.

I can't do this.

The thought seared through his mind with a dreadful finality. He lay where he was, the bridge still out of reach, the sun finally sinking into the sea. Through his blurring vision, he saw the gunman step up to him and stand over his prone figure.

"Artie," he found himself whispering, the name slipping out as if from somewhere deep in his subconscious. He wondered what his brother's final thoughts were, and whether he'd felt any fear.

Sydney. Sydney would never let him give up like this. But she wasn't here, and he was alone.

So all Winter could do was watch the gunman stand overhead and point the barrel of his gun down directly at him.

All he could do was watch him press against the trigger.

Then his hand brushed against the lining of his pants pocket. Sydney's hotel crest pin. He'd completely forgotten about it.

No time to think. He grabbed it—the blade shot out of the pin, a needle gleaming in the setting sun.

He stabbed upward at the same time the man fired the gun.

The Final Flight

There was something about this flight, her sprint down these narrow, fluorescent-lit halls directly below the freight ship's deck, that reminded Sydney of her hallway back home.

As she went, she kept trying in vain to latch her phone to the ship's signal board. Was Winter still climbing up there? Had he made it yet to the bridge? She heard footsteps echoing behind her and darted down an intersection into a dimly lit portion of the hall. Her own steps clanked loudly, but she had no time to stop in her tracks now. All she knew was that there would be more steps chasing her if Winter had not climbed up the grid.

She wondered if he was still on his way. She wondered if he was still alive.

Several portholes appeared on the side of the wall, and she slowed momentarily to look outside, noting the side of the ship that she could see. She was nearing the bridge now.

Without warning, she turned another corner and ran right into two guards.

They stared at her for a split second. In that moment, Sydney crouched and rammed into the first guard. He grunted, seemingly surprised by her force, and slammed hard into the wall. The second guard pulled out his gun—but she was on him before he could use it, bringing her elbow up to knock him viciously in the jaw. His head hit the wall hard—his body crumpled.

The first guard seized her wrist and twisted it—

Go with the motion, Niall had taught her.

So she did. In the instant the guard tried twisting her wrist, she twisted with it, flipping against the wall before turning her momentum back toward him. In one move, she kicked out at him and connected with his chest.

He flew backward against the wall. She seized the second guard's gun from its holster and whipped it hard against the first guard's face.

His head jerked to one side. The light blinked out in his eyes, and he slumped against the wall.

Sydney pocketed the second gun and kept running, not bothering to look back at the unconscious bodies. Her lungs squeezed in protest, and she felt the familiar ache rippling through her chest. She saw her mother lying on her deathbed, wheezing in a slow rhythm, muttering at Sydney to stay.

It morphed into the memory of her wheezing alone in her room after one of her more intense training sessions, refusing to call Niall or Sauda for help for fear of revealing the truth to them.

Can you go early tomorrow? Niall had texted her that night in regard to a new mission.

Yes, she'd responded immediately.

Are you sure you can do it?

She'd gritted her teeth as she typed, *I can do it.*

She could do anything. She was going to become the best damn agent they ever had, worthy of staying, worthy of doing something meaningful, even if it killed her.

Run, she told herself now. She ignored her lungs and forced herself onward.

At last she saw a ladder at the end of the corridor that led back up to the surface. The bridge should be up ahead—and with any luck, Winter should have arrived there long before she did.

She climbed up the ladder and threw her strength into opening the hatch. Evening light greeted her, along with a rush of cool, breezy air and the sight of the bridge window above a flight of stairs.

Sydney didn't even allow herself a moment to feel relief. She just darted up onto the deck and toward the bridge. Already she could see men sprinting toward her from the other end of the deck. Winter was nowhere to be seen.

The world around her seemed to slow. Her field of vision tunneled. *Winter wasn't here. He didn't make it.*

No. She didn't know that for sure. Stairs first. Her mind lurched back to her task. She was pushing her lungs past their abilities, and she felt them protest, her breaths turning rapid. Still, she hopped up the steps, then slammed herself against the door leading into the bridge and burst into the space.

Penelope Morrison was already here.

She stood with her arms behind her back, watching Sydney with a deadly calm. A few of her men stood around her, their guns pointed at Sydney. And behind Penelope was the bridge's control board, the lights flickering on and off against the lengthening evening.

Stabs of pain shot through her chest, sharp enough to make stars explode across her vision. Sydney could see the phone behind the girl, her signal out to the rest of the world, her chance to alert Panacea to their location and their status.

But the phone's line was already cut.

Her link to the outside world was severed.

"Shoot her," Penelope said simply.

Sydney threw herself to the floor as the first shots fired. She reached into her pocket, found her pen, and shut her eyes. Then she slammed it against the ground.

Light exploded everywhere. Penelope flinched back with her hands up, partly shielded from the blinding glare by the bodies of her men. They cried out, their hands flying instinctively to their faces.

Sydney could see the glare even through the lids of her closed eyes. The world flashed a searing red. She knew it was bright enough to leave spots in her vision for a while.

Memorize every room you ever walk into, Niall had taught her. *You never know when you'll need to escape it blindfolded.*

She didn't have time to wait around for her vision to steady. Now she thought of where each person had stood and where their cries came from. She rushed toward the first guard—before he could blink the glare from his eyes, she hit him hard in the throat. He made a choked sound before crumpling. She rammed into the second, then used the momentum of his body to knock into the third.

He cracked his head on the floor and went limp.

The phone was out. Her mind raced, urging her to stop lest her lungs seize.

If you can't be fast, be smart, she reminded herself.

The ship's signal flares.

She felt the cold barrel of a gun press against her temple.

"Stubborn as me," Penelope grumbled, her firing arm steady.

Where was Winter?

They'd caught him. He was dead.

The thought rushed through Sydney in a blitz of grief. She'd been on missions before where agents had been killed. But Winter—

A burst of rage hit her. Sydney jerked to one side and flung a fist out at the same time. She struck Penelope's arm right as the gun fired.

The blast sounded like an explosion, so close that Sydney felt the heat of it against her skin.

Penelope swung the gun back toward her, but Sydney brought her head back and butted her as hard as she could.

Penelope stumbled backward. Sydney lunged at her, aiming to knock the gun out of the girl's hand—but Penelope had already recovered and turned to one side with surprising speed. She looked dazed, though. The girl wasn't trained for combat, not with that fragile body.

But that didn't mean her guards weren't still ruthless.

Already, Sydney saw the men recovering, two of them dragging themselves onto their feet and the third up and facing her. The spasms in her lungs pulled her breathing tight—once, twice, so acutely that she hunched forward for a second. She couldn't keep fighting so many of them. Sydney turned her eyes toward the bridge's windows.

"It's too bad," Penelope said to her as she circled in an attempt to get closer to an exit. "I think we could have been friends."

"And why's that?" Sydney shot back, her voice thin with pain.

"Because loss drives you, too."

There was no disdain or taunt in her voice. Only genuine empathy. Somehow, Penelope could sense it in Sydney, the wounds that she worked so relentlessly to fill. Their conversation before the concert flashed back to her. Maybe people like them were always drawn to each other.

The first of Penelope's guards lunged at Sydney. This time, when she darted away from his hit, he pivoted with her and caught her on the jaw with a glancing blow.

Stars exploded in her vision, and pain lanced through her jaw. She whirled, knocking against the bridge's console board.

Sydney didn't try to attack him again. She was running out of time and strength. Instead, she scrambled up onto the board—her hand found the sliced phone and she slammed it against the window as hard as she could.

Once. Twice.

The glass shattered. As the guard reached for her leg, she pulled herself through the opening, ignoring how the broken glass slashed her hand as she went.

"I know what you're feeling," she called back at Penelope, her voice straining.

Penelope's jaw tightened, offended. "You don't."

"I do." She met the girl's eyes steadily. "And this isn't going to earn you the peace you want."

"And did you find your peace?" she said.

"I left my nightmares behind me."

Penelope turned her head up at Sydney. She looked sad. "I think you just brought them with you."

Then Sydney was on the outside of the bridge and sliding down to the deck. Cold wind streamed through her hair.

She hit the floor and scrambled up quickly enough to see Penelope turn back inside. The girl must know that Sydney was heading for the signal flares—and sure enough, Penelope burst out of the bridge's door and headed toward its back side, where the signal flares were likely kept in a watertight container.

She was going to destroy them.

Penelope's guards rounded the bridge and charged at her. She struggled up to her feet—but one of them had already gotten hold of her leg. In a single move, she was swept off her feet. Her chin hit the edge of the bridge window, and her vision went blurry for an instant from the impact. She kicked out blindly.

Now the man swung her, sweeping her across the floor. She gasped as she felt her ankle twist the wrong way. Her body went tumbling across the deck. Her lungs pulled taut—she was having real trouble breathing now. Instinctively, she rolled—and felt a bullet ping off the metal of the deck right next to where her face had been. The guard pressed the trigger down at her again—Sydney's hands flew up in vain to her face.

The gun clicked empty this time. Out of bullets.

He snarled and lunged down for her.

Sydney kicked up with her good leg—her boot connected with his groin. The man's eyes bulged; his entire body went stiff. Sydney kicked him again, this time striking him hard across the face. The light blinked out in his eyes, and he crumpled to the deck.

Sydney pulled herself up, gasping for air, her chest pain making her double over with each labored breath. She thought of a past mission where she'd been captured and trapped in a prison cell, where a guard had kicked her so viciously in the stomach that she'd felt like she was drowning. Her eyes swept across the grid towering around her, the silhouettes stark against the lengthening evening and the artificial lights that now flared up. No sign of Winter.

He was dead. The realization of Penelope's earlier words to her now stabbed straight through her chest. The casual tilt of his face, the mischievous, sidelong grin he sometimes gave her.

He was gone. He must be.

Why the hell did she get attached to someone like him? Why did they have to take him away from his perfect life and put him in danger? What would they tell the world? His mother?

Would she care? Would she be relieved?

She never should have let him go. He was wounded. He never should have been climbing—

No time. No time. Sydney forced herself to her feet again, tearing her eyes away from the grid and back in the direction that Penelope had gone. A new, white-hot rage engulfed her. She ignored the agony from her throbbing ankle and started hobbling as fast as she could around the bridge. Her focus narrowed into a bright tunnel. Her breath wheezed loudly. Her lungs screamed for her to stop.

Contact Panacea. Contact the outside world.

Right as she reached the wall where the flares were located, her lungs finally reached their breaking point. They seized—and Sydney collapsed, struggling for air. She was lying in a prison cell again, gasping like a fish.

She felt the other girl's presence more than she saw her. The shadows on the floor flickered, and Sydney looked up through her swimming vision to see Penelope jumping down at her.

Somehow, through her fight to breathe, Sydney managed to roll out of the way—but Penelope saw the movement coming and shifted with her. Then Penelope was on top of her, pinning her down with her legs, and her hands were wrapped tightly around Sydney's neck.

Penelope wasn't nearly as strong as her, but Sydney was too exhausted to fend her off. She fought to suck in enough air—her chest exploded with pain each time—her eyes widened in agony. She was going to drown here. She tried to roll the girl off, but when she glanced to her side, she saw two more of Penelope's guards running toward them. One of them pointed a gun at her.

It was over. Sydney knew her lips must be turning blue now, her mouth opening and closing in gasps. The darkness was closing in, along with the inevitability of her death. So, this was how she was going to go. Alone, on board this ship, after having failed a mission, out of breath. Her partner gone.

Sydney clawed for Penelope's face, but the lack of air had weakened her and thrown her off, and Penelope stayed grimly on. The girl's eyes had gone flat now, but behind it, Sydney could still see the pulse of that strange empathy, as if Penelope were choking herself.

This was how it would end. Tears sprang up in Sydney's eyes as she struggled to breathe. Her head tilted in the direction of the flares.

And only then did she see him.

He looked hunched, and the hand clutching his wounded shoulder was covered in blood, and his black hair was streaked with blood, and his arms were slashed in blood, but Winter was *standing there,* right by the flares, with something clutched in his other fist. Sydney's lips trembled.

Winter.

Blood sprinkled his arms and leaked down his chest. But he was here. *He was still alive.*

And suddenly, she remembered being rescued from the prison cell during her past mission, of Niall's gruff, kind face bending down to her, his hands helping her to her feet. *Time to go, kid,* he'd said.

Winter lifted his good arm and pointed the object high into the air.

A flare.

And right as Penelope noticed where Sydney was looking, Winter fired it.

Worthy

H e didn't wait to see if the flare went high enough, or whether or not it burst. The instant he'd fired it, he just dropped it and sprinted for Sydney. His wound sent spasms of agony through him, but all he could focus on was the sight of her there on the floor, of Penelope's hands around her neck, the tears glossy in her eyes. All he could do was react to the look in her eyes, the blueness of her lips.

As if she was making peace with her own death.

Oh, hell no. Winter's hands clenched into fists as he ran.

As the first guard approached him, he turned sideways and kicked off the wall of the bridge, then twisted so that his boots connected right with the guard's face. The move caught the other man completely by surprise. Winter took the moment to kick straight at the man's armed hand. The gun flew out of his grasp and spun across the deck toward Penelope.

As if in slow motion, he could see Penelope reaching for the spinning gun. He forced himself forward.

His boot hit the gun before she could reach it. It spun sideways. He dropped and rolled with it. Tears seared his vision from the pain. He clenched his jaw and reached for the weapon with the last of his strength.

Then his hand closed around the grip. He twisted against the floor to point it at Penelope. Pinned beneath her, Sydney's movements had stilled.

Penelope stared at him, then gave him a hard smile. Her hands stayed locked around Sydney's neck.

You can't do it, her eyes said. Strangely, in this moment, he saw a spark of something he recognized in her, some wild, deep well of anger that he'd first noticed at her apartment.

Suddenly, he felt someone barrel hard into him. Hands clawed at his face and scrambled for his gun.

In the blur, he recognized his attacker—it was Connor, his face bloody from the Paramecium that had exploded in the storage room, his eyes bloodshot and teary from the chemical burn. His growl rattled harshly in his throat, as if he were dying.

Still, he was strong. Winter fell to the floor at the attack. He fought to hang onto his gun—but Connor seized his wrist, forcing him to drop it. Winter kicked it before the man could grab the handle. The weapon went skidding across the deck.

Somewhere in the distance, Winter thought he heard the sound of helicopter blades.

Connor swung a fist at his face. Winter managed to duck the blow— but a second fist caught him on his jaw. Stars exploded across his vision. He twisted away and rolled, recalling a bit of choreography he'd once learned, then struggled to his feet.

But he was no trained fighter. All he had were tricks and illusions. And he was running out of time.

Connor lunged for the gun that Winter had kicked across the deck. Winter bolted after him. He managed to catch the man's shoes. They both tumbled to the floor.

Connor looked back and twisted his wounded lips at Winter. When he spoke, the words came out in a gurgling rattle. "You'll die with me," he hissed. He kicked at Winter's arms. Winter winced as the man's shoe hit his knuckles. A second kick.

Winter couldn't hang on any longer. He released Connor, and the man pulled free. He reached for the gun.

It was over. Winter looked on helplessly as the man neared the gun, braced himself for when Connor would grab the weapon and swing it around at him. Nearby, Penelope was getting off Sydney.

Again, he thought he heard helicopter blades, but everything seemed slow and far away. They weren't going to make it out of here alive. Sydney moved a little against the floor, her head still turned toward him, but he saw her eyes flutter closed. Her body was contorting in pain as she fought for air.

No. *No.*

It was losing Artie all over again. It was waking up at six A.M. to the sound of his mother's anguished voice from downstairs, her asking in disbelief over and over if they had identified the right body. It was him sitting helplessly at the top of the stairs, knowing he had just let his brother go off to his death without ever saying his proper goodbyes. It was being unable to save a person he loved.

A person he loved.

He could feel himself deteriorating rapidly, the adrenaline that had carried him this entire time finally crashing as his blood loss began catching up to him. His chest felt numb, his limbs tingling. The run he'd done just minutes earlier up on the steel grid seemed impossible now.

Sydney seemed to turn weakly in his direction. For a moment, he thought they exchanged a final look.

Then something made her look up and away from him. He blinked slowly.

How did Artie feel, when he finally died? Was he afraid?

And for a moment, Winter thought he saw his brother crouching beside him, those thoughtful dark eyes turned down at him and a furrow in his brow. He gave Winter a sad smile.

Winter looked up at him, yearning to reach him, knowing even now that he couldn't.

I really thought I had more time with you, he whispered, more to himself than anyone else. *All I ever wanted was to be like you.*

The last thing he saw was Artie reaching down for his hand.

No, it wasn't Artie. It was—

—a soldier in black gear?

And then the beating of helicopter blades became overwhelming, seemed to engulf him. Was he imagining things?

The bullet from Connor's gun never came. Instead, the black-clad soldier was shouting in his face, asking if he could hear him. Winter could only stare back in confusion. He must be hallucinating.

The world around him was fading into nothingness. All he wanted to focus on were the words that seemed to come from somewhere in his past, as if in a dream, words that echoed in his mind right before he slipped entirely into darkness. Words from Artie.

Be like you, Winter.

34 Breathe

The helicopter.

Then, two more.

And then there were agents everywhere. She heard a voice blaring from a megaphone overhead. The wind whipped up by the helicopters sent dust flying and her hair whipping against her face.

Panacea must have found them. They must have seen the flare.

But all Sydney could focus on was the overwhelming pain in her lungs, the feeling of drowning in the air, of being unable to draw her breath. As if in a dream, she saw a team of paramedics rushing to them, dropping from the sky one after another, could vaguely feel the shudder of their boots pounding against the deck. All she could do was struggle to keep Winter in her fading view as their bodies clustered around them, peeking between the jumble of legs to see his still figure even as they checked her pulse and her limbs for wounds.

Their shouts rushed past her with the sound of the wind.

He might not make it.

As if from a distance, she felt an oxygen mask press against her face. Everything in her body surged forward at it, her soul flinging itself at the air in a desperate attempt to breathe it in.

She knew she should be listening for Penelope's arrest, looking on as agents cuffed the girl's arms behind her back, noting the look on her face as she met Sydney's gaze, as if this wouldn't be the last time they'd cross paths.

She should be thinking about what to say when she had to confront Niall and Sauda.

But in this moment, all she could do was fight to breathe in, breathe out. She could hear a paramedic above her, shouting encouragement. *Breathe in, breathe out.*

Even as she felt herself lifted onto a gurney and strapped down, she kept her head turned in Winter's direction, afraid to lose sight of him. The first time she ever saw him, he had walked into Panacea's head-quarters with all the swagger and insecurity of a star, back straight, eyes burning with life, hungry for the chance to prove himself. Desperate for *something.*

Even now, she couldn't look away from him, could feel the aura of him in the air.

She tried to envision the world's grief, should Winter not pull through.

If she were to die, would anyone mourn?

One of the paramedics was shouting something in her face. It took her a moment to recognize the man's furrowed brows. Not a paramedic at all.

It was Niall.

"Cossette!" he shouted down at her, but Sydney could barely hear him over the noise of the helicopters. "Breathe, kid, come on."

The only time Niall ever called Sydney by her last name was when he was afraid for her. Sydney felt a wash of relief at his presence, then a wave of anguish. She knew this would be the end of everything.

"You're such a goddamn pain in the ass," Niall interrupted. "Stop trying to argue with me and just breathe!"

Sydney blinked, embarrassed by the tears that suddenly welled in her eyes. She wanted to tell him that she was sorry. She wanted to ask him what had happened between him and his real daughter. She wanted to know if he could ever forgive her.

She reached out weakly for his hand, as if she were a child, and he grabbed it, as if he were a father. Niall wasn't looking at her now; he was shouting instructions at others. She tried again to speak, but the world was closing rapidly in, and the edges of her vision faded into black. She looked again for Winter, but the darkness had turned opaque.

Breathe in. Breathe out.

Then even that instinct dissipated, and she fell into an endless black.

35

The Family You Find

The first thing Winter Young learned upon waking was that headlines about his shooting had blanketed the world. He could hear the commotion outside the hospital from his suite, a spacious room with a set of double windows that overlooked the building's front courtyard. They were chanting his name down there, and every now and then a ripple of cheers would rise up, and Winter could only guess it was because they had seen some update on his status.

The other news he saw on the screen in his room—and the news he found himself much more interested in—was a headline about the seizure of a cargo ship in the North Sea. In a daze, he watched authorities swarming the ship's deck, their flashlights shining inside opened containers to find thousands of tons of illegal chemical weapons meant to be transported through the Suez Canal.

No news about Sydney.

Aside from the chanting outside, the room felt serene. Sunlight streamed in thick and golden from the windows, illuminating the vases of flowers that lined the far wall in rows. The scent of roses filled the space with their heady sweetness. Was he still in London? The light was so bright and cheery that he couldn't be sure. It reminded him of waking up in the hospital after collapsing onstage two years back—the sense that nothing felt quite real, that he wasn't really here, that this wasn't his body. Even the ache in his chest from his wound felt distant, a dull throbbing that he could tell was being held back by a massive dose of painkillers.

Winter's eyes shifted to the rest of the room. Two of his usual security team were in here, too, seated quietly on either side of his bed.

Their presence brought Winter's reality into focus. He stretched a little, winced as the movement lit up every part of his body with pain, and pulled himself laboriously up into a full sitting position. He rubbed his temples as the fog in his head began to clear and sharper thoughts came through. Sydney must be here, too. Or maybe she'd been discharged already. Or maybe Panacea had come for her and taken her somewhere else. Had she survived? Was she okay? He had no idea, and the not knowing tugged at his chest.

One of the security guards smiled slightly at him. Winter nodded in return.

The man's eyes darted to the doorway, where a pair of figures now arrived at the doorframe. One of them had an unmistakable serenity about him, while the other was wringing his hands nervously.

Leo and Dameon.

They both must have been out in the waiting room for a while—their clothes looked rumpled and slept-in, and dark circles bruised the skin beneath their eyes. Leo's curly hair was a wild tangle, the kind he got whenever he ran his hands through it too much. Dameon studied Winter with his familiar, quiet look.

Leo let out a long breath. "The nurse said you just woke up," he said.

He pushed away from the doorframe, but one of Winter's guards immediately stepped forward, straightening his intimidating frame. He gave Leo a warning glare.

"Easy, boy," he said.

Then Winter saw the tracking device on Leo's ankle. He had definitely been arrested. Guilt flooded Winter's veins.

"It's okay," Winter said to the security guard. The man nodded, settling back against the wall, his eyes still locked on Leo.

Leo held his hands up. "Sorry, sorry," he murmured. "No sudden movements, right. I just . . . Claire said that if Winter woke up today, I could talk to him as long as security was in the room." He turned his eyes toward Winter. "As long as I kept it brief."

Dameon nodded, and Winter was relieved to see the boy put a reassuring hand on Leo's shoulder. At least they were okay. "We won't stay long," Dameon said. "I know you still need to rest."

"Thank you," Winter murmured at them as they came over to the side of his bed. "For being here."

For a moment, the three just stared at each other.

Then Leo whispered, "How are you?"

Winter hesitated, not sure how to respond. "Okay, I guess," he replied. "A little sore." He met his friend's eyes. "I'm more worried about you."

Leo shook his head, closed his eyes, and looked down. A long moment of silence passed before he could speak again.

"I'm sorry. I'm so sorry. God, Winter—I—"

He cut off, not trusting the steadiness of his voice anymore, and started to cry.

It was a low, mournful sound. Winter didn't try to stop him. He just took his friend's hand and pulled him gently forward, then leaned against his shoulder in a quiet embrace. Dameon waited in silence, letting them have their moment.

After a long while, Leo collected himself. His body shuddered as he leaned away enough to speak again. "My flight back to the US is later tonight," he murmured, almost to himself. "But I needed to tell you in person what happened. I have to let you know that I never meant any of it, I never wanted—"

Winter held up a hand at the boy's rising panic. "Hey," he said quietly. "I'm here. You're here. And we're going to be okay." Then he met his friend's eyes steadily. "Take your time."

Leo swallowed hard. His hands fiddled at his sides before tucking back into his pockets.

"They—" he said hoarsely, "they threatened my family—"

He broke off again, and Winter felt a rush of guilt and shame. So it had been blackmail, after all. He pictured Leo's family, all his sisters and aunts, his parents. He pictured Leo terrified.

"Claire said the police are investigating a supposed plot to extort you," Dameon filled in when Leo fell silent to compose himself. "Apparently, the extortion group had installed one of their own among the security guards at the concert."

Leo nodded quietly, and Dameon stopped to let him speak.

"He told me he knew who I was," Leo said in a small voice. "He knew the names of my mom and dad, my older sisters. He knew my home address." He looked stricken. "I don't know. He said it was just going to be a sleep draft, that they were just going to rob the safe at your house and leave you and Ashley unconscious. I didn't know what to do. I—"

"It's okay," Winter said softly.

Leo shook his head rapidly, not listening. "They told me they wouldn't hurt you. They just wanted to steal from your apartment. But that shouldn't have mattered, Winter. I'm sorry. I was just so afraid. How did they know so much? I just—"

Winter reached out and held up a hand. "Hey," he said. "You don't have to explain yourself to me."

Leo cut off midsentence, his eyes swollen from crying. Winter knew he was thinking back on the moment before their first stadium concert, where he'd said the same thing to him in that closet.

Winter had done this to his friend. Had put him in a position where he couldn't help but commit a crime. And now Leo would face the consequences for it. He never should have brought them here, for something that he had only wanted to do by himself. *For* himself. Why couldn't he have refused to let them come along? He could have dealt with Claire's suspicions and spared Leo all this trauma.

He should have gone through this alone.

Beside Leo, Dameon watched Winter with his quiet eyes. When Winter met his gaze, he saw something else there, as if Dameon was asking him a question without saying a word aloud.

Winter tore his gaze away. "I'm sorry," he said. He could hear the emotion in his own voice. "You were both only there because of me. I put you in that position."

"We're all adults," Dameon replied, and this time, Winter saw sympathy in his friend's eyes. "We came here with you because we wanted to."

"I'm just glad you're safe," Leo replied. He looked around the room, a little lost, uncertain of what to do next.

"Hey," Winter said, and his friend turned to him. "You're going to be okay. I promise. Your family will be safe, and so will you."

"And you?" It was a question, and Leo's voice sounded uncharacteristically hesitant.

Dameon's gaze was searching Winter's face, the corners of his lips turned down into a thoughtful frown.

Winter looked back at Leo. "Me too," he said with a nod. "We'll figure everything out together."

Leo seemed desperate to believe it. "Okay," he answered.

Over by the door, Claire cleared her throat, and Leo shifted against Winter's bed to look at her.

"Just a few more minutes, boys," she said. "Leo, I heard from your dad. Give him a call when you're done here, okay?"

As Leo answered her, Dameon suddenly leaned closer to Winter. "Hey," he whispered, his voice calm and warm. Winter blinked at him. "I know there's something going on with you that you can't talk about. Something big."

Winter felt heat rising on the back of his neck. "I don't know what you mean," he said.

Dameon shook his head. "You do," he replied. He gave Winter a small smile. "I haven't been at your side almost every day for five years to not sense when something's up with you."

Winter stared quietly back at him, not knowing how to respond.

When he didn't answer right away, Dameon nodded once. "I know you have your reasons, and you don't have to tell me what they are. Maybe someday you will." He searched Winter's face again. "Just remember who's here for you. You don't have to work alone."

Alone. It was a coincidental statement for Dameon to make—and reminded him of how Sydney had once told him about the loneliness of being an agent. Winter felt himself nodding in return. He thought of all the times when Dameon was able to read his mind, sense his emotions, know when he was exhausted or sad or uncomfortable without ever hearing Winter utter a word about it. His instincts were always impeccable.

Then Leo was turning back to them, and Dameon had leaned slightly away again, the knowing light in his eyes fading to their usual serenity. He nudged Leo. "We should go," he said, glancing at Winter. "Let him rest."

Leo nodded. "Right. Yes." He gave Winter a hesitant smile. "See you back in the States?"

Maybe Winter would take his secrets to his grave. But at least he could still walk through the rest of his life with them. He smiled, then leaned toward Dameon and Leo as if they were huddling before a concert. They leaned instinctively to him in return. He felt their arms around his shoulders, pulling him in. Over their shoulders and by the door, Winter saw Claire rest her head against the doorframe and give him a knowing nod.

"I have news," she said.

The Heart Is Wide and Deep

Claire waited for the boys to leave before entering. For once, she didn't look entirely put together. Her yellow collar shirt had a noticeable coffee stain on its sleeve, and a smudge was clear on her glasses, as if she'd fallen asleep with them pressed against her face and hadn't bothered to wipe them clean yet.

Winter raised an eyebrow at the sight of her coffee cup—a disposable one from the hospital. "You never drink anything that's not cold brew," he said, right before she put the cup down on his dresser and enveloped him in a hug.

"Limited options at the hospital," she said. "But believe me, I've got one of our guys out right now searching for a decent cup of coffee."

"Ouch," he groaned.

"Sorry," she breathed, letting go of him and extending her arms wide. "How are you feeling? I know it's only been a week."

Winter blinked. He didn't know he'd been in here for that long. Already, the memory of Leo and Dameon visiting him earlier felt like a blur. He shrugged, careful of what he could say in front of her. He had just run a dangerous mission for a private agency; he'd been shot and kidnapped and nearly killed. His body felt destroyed in a way that it'd never been even after his most grueling performances. His mind was unsteady, exhausted.

"What have the doctors been saying?" he asked.

Claire reached out to put a hand on his arm. "That you'll make a full recovery," she said, looking him firmly in the eye. "And you'll be back in the studio before you know it. Just give yourself a solid month after we're home, okay? No strenuous activity in the meantime. And then we've got you on some physical therapy for a few weeks. You're going to have to deal with the media a bit, too, because you're the biggest news story anywhere right now. You can't walk down the street without hearing someone talking about it." She took a breath, then gave him a small smile. "Don't worry about a thing. All the media and court stuff, I'll handle. You're going to be okay."

You're going to be okay. He didn't know if that would ever be true again. There was a huge segment of his life that he couldn't share with Claire, and she was here, trying to console him. "I'm sorry," he murmured. "That you had to endure all this. I know that—"

She waved her hand at him. "Don't you dare start apologizing. Just let me be relieved."

You don't even know the half of it, he thought, aching to tell her everything. Instead, he just said, "And Ashley?" He squinted questioningly up at her, heart in his throat. "Is she . . ."

"Last I heard, she left the city to check in with her family." Claire nodded. "She wasn't being treated here. Don't worry, though. She said she'd be back."

Her family. Sydney had most definitely lied to Claire about what had happened—but at least it sounded like she'd made a faster recovery than Winter. He could still see her blue lips, her body writhing in pain.

Panacea might have brought their own doctors for Sydney. She might not even be in the country anymore. But her words relieved some of the building pressure in Winter's chest. At least she'd made it.

What if she'd returned to the States without him? The realization startled him. What if she had to leave without telling him goodbye? What if he never saw her again?

"I'm not worried," he said.

"Oh, I think you're a little worried." Claire smiled briefly at him. "Something happened between you two, and don't think you can keep that from me." She straightened, and her smile wavered. "But she's not why I came in here to see you."

"Why?" Winter looked at her. "What's going on?"

"There's someone in the waiting room who has been here for a while, waiting for you to wake up again."

Winter glanced up at her. She gave him a quiet nod.

"Your mother, Winter."

Oh.

He felt heat flush his cheeks, followed by a wave of terror. Of all the people he'd expected to come visit, he hadn't even considered his mother.

"I promised her I'd let her know the instant you were awake." Claire sounded unsure now. "Do you want to see her?"

I'm not ready. The truth echoed inside him. He was still unsteady from the conversation with Leo, still not quite able to take in everything that had happened.

But he found himself nodding. "Of course." The answer sounded mechanical, his urgency fake. A son was supposed to be happy to see his mother, wasn't he?

Claire nodded at him, doubt still in her eyes, before rising and patting his shoulder once. "I'll be back," she said to him. "We have a lot more to discuss about your next steps." She quieted, and her voice turned somber. "But take your time, understand? Let me handle the rest."

He didn't want Claire to leave the room yet, and his lips parted, wanting to ask her to stay a little longer, but then she was gone, heels clicking. He heard a low murmur of voices outside. The sound of someone that made him sit up more stiffly in bed.

And then a new silhouette was standing in the doorway, her hair as straight and neatly pinned as ever, the white pearls around her neck, the collar tucked behind her sweater ironed and starched.

She hesitated at the doorway as their eyes met. "Baby bear," she said.

"Hi, Mom," he replied, his throat dry.

She stepped in hesitantly, her eyes darting momentarily to the windows as the chants rose and fell again, and then came over to stand awkwardly at the foot of his bed. Her hands folded in front of her, fumbling for a moment before grabbing each other for support.

It took her a few long seconds before she seemed to will herself to bend toward him and give him an awkward hug.

"You look pale," she said in a soft voice, her eyes searching his face.

"I'm doing okay," he replied. He forced his legs to curl up a bit, making room at the foot of the bed, smoothing the bedsheet because he knew she couldn't sit on wrinkles. "Here, Mom. There's plenty of space."

"Meí shì. I don't want you to be uncomfortable," she said, even as she slowly seated herself at the farthest edge, as if the bed was forcing them into close proximity.

The quiet gathered thick between them. It was how Winter always felt in her presence—like a child, no matter how old he got, like he could never quite escape the feeling of being small and hungry for her acceptance. Even now, he could feel his brain revving up, spinning nervously for what he could share with her in the hopes that it might make her proud for a moment.

"Claire called me the instant it happened," his mother finally said. She wrung her hands repeatedly, and Winter watched the skin on her fingers turn light yellow from the pressure. "I couldn't watch the video footage they kept showing on TV. They say there was an extortion scheme."

He nodded. "That's what I hear."

His mother seemed to tremble. "I hope they lock them away for good."

Winter struggled to take in her words, unsure what to say in response. "Me too," he finally managed.

Another beat passed between them.

"I brought you some food," his mother went on. "Pastries. They're still warm, so you should eat them soon. Oh." She frowned, her brows furrowing. "I forgot them in the car." She started getting up from the bed. "Wǒ qù ná. I—"

"No, it's okay," Winter said, and she paused to look at him. "I don't mind them cold. Thank you."

"Of course. The shop was just around the corner from here. I should have gotten something else for you." Her eyes darted around the room, settling on everything except for him. "I realized I don't know what you like for breakfast. You did used to eat lemon bread."

"I meant, thank you for coming all the way here," Winter added. "To see me."

His mother paled at those words. Her eyes widened a little, and in them, he could see the glimmer of hurt. "Why do you say that?"

He blinked. "Say what?"

She lowered herself back onto the bed and folded her arms. "I'm your mother," she said after another silence. She sounded as if she were convincing herself. "A son shouldn't have to thank his mother for visiting him."

Winter let out a breath, guilt clouding his head. He didn't know what to say anymore. "That's not what I meant," he started again. "I'm just glad to see you, Mom."

She shook her head. "It is what you meant," she replied, holding a hand up. "And it's okay. I know I haven't been a good mother to you."

Winter felt his heart quickening. Five minutes in, and he was already screwing up their conversation. "No, Mom, that's not true."

She looked directly at him, and the expression in her eyes made him stop.

"I haven't been a good mother to you, Winter Young," she said again, slower and quieter. "And I haven't been honest about that."

Winter opened his mouth again, but the silence went on, and the chants from outside filled the space between them. They stared at each other.

At last, his mother broke their stare and looked at a spot on the bed. "Before Artie, I had a plan for everything. Good things require a plan, you know?" She glanced up at him, then quickly down again. "But after everything happened, I . . ."

She folded her hands in her lap and studied her pale fingers for a moment. Winter stayed quiet as she trailed off, his heart bleeding, unwilling to break the silence lest this version of his mother retreat back into her shell. For the first time since that night on the balcony, he could see a piece of her heart exposed.

"I'm not as strong as you are, baby bear. I can't bear the weight of it. So I run." She turned quieter. "I run and I run away from you. And I'm so sorry. But I promise I'm trying my best. I want to be here. I want you to know that, okay?"

He noticed she didn't say that she would stop running. She knew she couldn't, and he knew, too.

There was an urge in him to tell her that he wasn't what happened in her past. That he was more than just a reminder of her pain. But the words remained unspoken. It didn't matter how many times his mother left him, how many times she forgot him or neglected him. All that mattered to him in this moment was that she had come to see him today. His whole heart wrapped around this knowledge, this seemingly small gesture that he knew had been so difficult for her.

"I know, Mom," he said gently. He fought to steady his voice as if his life depended on it. "It's okay. You're here."

She searched his face, her jaw tight from holding back unshed tears, and nodded repeatedly in a small, quick motion. A glimmer of a smile appeared on the edges of her lips. "I'm really proud of you, baby bear. You've done so well."

Now he was truly in danger of crying. He pulled himself back and held tight, as if this were all just one of his acts, and swallowed hard.

"Thank you, Mom."

They fell back into their silence. This time, there was peace to it, and Winter caught himself counting the seconds out, relishing each of them and storing them away somewhere safe in his memory. Like the times when they used to ride the bus together, side by side, quiet. Like the times after dinner when they sat across from one another, their food half-eaten on the table, each of them lost for a few minutes in their own, better world.

Maybe it wasn't closeness. Maybe it never would be. But at least, in these moments, he felt nearer to understanding her than he ever had. And he knew that, whenever she needed someone with whom to share her grieving heart, he would come to her side. Whenever she was overwhelmed by the parts of her brain that tragedy had broken, he would care for her. He knew she would never reciprocate it. But he would still be there for the scraps of her love for the rest of his life.

Then he heard his mother sniffle, saw her pull her handkerchief from her pocket and wipe her nose once before pocketing it. She looked at him again and smiled, and he knew her heart had receded again, eager to move on.

"You take your time and get well," she said. "Call me when you need me. And when you head back out on the road, I want you to be careful, okay?"

She was reaching the limit of what she could bear around him. He could feel her aching to get away already, the nearness of him resurfacing all of her demons that she'd spent so many years trying to bury.

"Okay," he said, offering her a smile. But he found himself wishing her goodbye again, knowing she would be gone for a long time, and wishing some peace for her in her endless journey to fill the empty spaces in her mind. Wishing he could help her.

"Okay," she repeated, and the awkwardness between them returned.

She rose to her feet, her hands wringing again, her eyes flitting about. For a moment, she hesitated. Then she stepped toward him, stopped halfway, and reconsidered.

"Take care of yourself, baby bear," she said again. Then she turned around and left the room.

Winter stared at the door long after she stepped out and disappeared. Then his breath released, and he realized his entire body was trembling.

Suddenly, the new aloneness in his room felt overwhelming. He wanted to swing his legs over the side of the bed and go running after her, if only for a bit of company. He felt the loneliness crowd around him, the weight of that ever-present depression pushing against the corners of his mind.

And then, in the middle of that crush—

He saw Claire's head peek over the side of the open door.

She didn't say anything. She didn't have to, at the look on his face. All she did was walk in, sit down on the bed, and take his hand in hers. She squeezed it, and he felt himself relax at the warmth of her palms.

How did she always know when he needed her?

"How are you feeling?" she asked him quietly, the question different this time than when she'd asked just a little while ago.

Winter couldn't answer. All he could do was look down, holding his breath, still counting seconds in his head.

He felt Claire wrap her arms around him, felt himself lean into her embrace in exhaustion.

"Go easy on yourself," she murmured. "It's okay to not be okay."

He nodded against her. And then, finally, he let himself cry.

Loyalty to a Secret

The sun had begun its slow descent when Sydney arrived back at the hospital.

Sauda sat in the car with her. She had been in Sydney's hospital room—a different hospital than Winter's, as a precaution—as they tended to her kaleidoscope of wounds, had remained silent through the doctor's reports under the guise that she was an Elite Securities representative.

When Sydney could breathe well enough again without oxygen therapy, they'd taken a drive together, and there in the safety of the car, Sydney had debriefed her on the rest of the mission.

Now Sauda pulled their car to a stop at the rear of the building, then leaned back in her seat. Sydney looked straight ahead, tensing in the awkward silence between the two.

"You don't need me to stay any longer?" she asked Sauda after she couldn't bear the pause anymore.

Sauda shook her head. "I think you've done enough for one mission," she replied with a raised eyebrow.

Sydney didn't look at her. She was too afraid.

"You said it with such a straight face," Sauda began. "That you understood our orders. And then you went off and deliberately disobeyed every single one."

"I'm sorry."

"I'm not convinced that you are." Sauda gave her a stern, sidelong glare. "You realize Niall and I don't make these calls lightly, right? This all could have gone so much worse."

"But it didn't," Sydney muttered, her voice so small and sullen that she could barely hear it herself.

Sauda frowned at her. "No, it didn't," she replied. Then she sighed. "I suppose it's our fault."

"For training me to think for myself?"

The woman waved a frustrated hand once in the air. "For caring too much."

In her answer, Sydney thought she heard the hint of someone else Sauda once was—someone with a hotter head and quicker temper, who wore her heart on her sleeve. Sydney studied her, but the woman didn't say more.

"And is that my last mission?" Sydney asked quietly after a while.

"Last mission?" Sauda answered.

Sydney hesitated a long moment. Her heart was hammering now. "My lungs," she said. "I didn't tell you. I'm sure Niall knows by now, too."

When Sauda didn't answer, Sydney turned her eyes up at the woman. There, she saw a soft expression.

"Sydney," she said gently. "We know."

Sydney blinked. "You knew about my condition?"

"Why do you think I always taught you that it's better to be smart than fast?" Sauda gave her a smile. "I wove breathing therapy into all of your training."

All this time, Sydney had boxed herself in tighter and tighter, feeling the suffocation of her secrets as surely as she felt the strain in her lungs. Thinking she had somehow managed to keep everything hidden. They knew. They had always known.

"Why did you keep me on?" she murmured.

"This is not some kind of temporary work-for-hire job," Sauda answered. "You are one of us now. That means Niall and I made a joint decision on everything that comes with you, that the parts of you that may challenge us are overshadowed by the parts of you that can benefit this agency." Sauda fixed her gaze on Sydney. "You may operate on your own in the field, but you are never truly alone."

Sydney swallowed hard. She could feel the weight in her throat, the threat of tears building in her eyes.

"The future doesn't have to haunt your present, Sydney," Sauda said. "And neither does your past. I hope that someday you'll be able to embrace this. Understand?"

Sydney cleared her throat, forcing back her tears so that she could answer. "Yes, ma'am," she whispered.

Sauda looked over at her, studied her expression, and gave her a small smile before looking away. "Remind me," she said, "to tell you about all the trouble I got into as a new Panacea agent."

Sydney looked quickly at her. "What do you mean, as a new Panacea agent?"

"I mean, my stories might help you get your footing."

She was talking about the promotion, about Sydney moving from an associate to a full operative, with a permanent, dedicated team and a partner.

Sydney laughed, then hurriedly wiped away her tears. She tried to imagine her mentor as a brash, rebellious young operative, going against her orders and causing mayhem. Somehow, it didn't seem so surprising.

Sauda straightened, a note of formality returning to her voice. "Don't get too excited yet. I still need to run it past headquarters. And at this point, Niall sounds like he'd rather wrap you in bubble packaging than agree."

"Yes, ma'am."

"And don't assume you'll get out of all this with no consequences. When we arrive back in the States, we'll discuss next steps. I can have you on a plane with me in a few hours. All you need to do is stay in the car, and we'll head to the airport right now."

Right now. Without saying another word to Winter. Some of her euphoria wavered, and Sydney felt the sinking disappointment in her stomach. They would leave without warning, disappear from his radar so thoroughly that he would have no way of contacting her again.

Sauda must have sensed her hesitation—or perhaps she caught the way Sydney's eyes shifted in the direction of the hospital. The building's front lawn was still clustered with thousands of fans, all eagerly waiting for updates about Winter even though medical staff had come out several times to ask them to disperse.

"Or you can fly back in the morning," Sauda then added with an understanding nod. "It'll give you some time to wrap up any personal loose ends you have."

Personal loose ends. There was a slight emphasis on the words, and it was how Sydney realized Sauda knew about her growing feelings for Winter.

It was also Sauda's way of telling her that she needed to bid him goodbye.

Of course she should. This happened at the end of every mission—she cut the necessary ties with the people she worked with, and then she went back to her life. She had been trained in how to say farewell a thousand different ways, to a thousand different kinds of people. She was good at it.

So why was she hesitating now?

"I'll come back tonight with you," Sydney finally said, forcing the words out. They came out steadier than she thought they would. Cooler. "Hold a spot on the plane for me."

Sauda studied her. A moment passed in silence before she said, softly, "I'm sorry, Syd."

Sydney stared at the hospital. "For what?"

"You know."

Her unspoken answer filled Sydney's mind.

She waited a moment longer before she finally turned to Sauda. "How do you and Niall do it?" she asked.

"Do what?" Sauda replied.

"Stand staying apart from each other? Never taking the plunge on being together?"

Sauda didn't answer right away. "Because we care about each other," she said. "And when you care about someone, you want them to have a good life. A happy life." Her voice turned quieter. "We can't give each other that."

Sydney nodded. She had always known this was the answer. When they signed up for Panacea, the agency swore them to something above love. Above commitment to another person. Loyalty to a secret above all else. It was a security issue, of course, but most of all, it was an issue of faithfulness. Panacea was the love of their lives. You couldn't dedicate yourself fully if you prioritized someone else. It was her sacrifice in exchange for the privilege of doing important work, the kind that changed people's lives without them ever realizing it, the kind that she felt in her bones.

If Sauda and Niall ever broke that rule, the agency would require them to separate immediately, or fire them. A life together was impossible.

A life with *Winter* was impossible.

"It's the way of things," Sauda added after a while.

"The way of things," Sydney echoed. She took a long breath and felt the slight, ever-present strain of it in her lungs. She thought she saw a glimmer of sadness for her in the woman's eyes.

There was nothing to be sad about, she told herself. She was going to get her promotion. This was all she'd ever wanted.

Nothing else.

Then Sauda nodded at Sydney before leaning back in the car's seat. "Nine o'clock," she said. "I'll have a car sent to wherever you are."

The Sun and the Moon

Sydney entered the back of the hospital alone. A nurse at the check-in desk recognized her, rose from her seat, and motioned an assistant over to escort her upstairs to Winter's suite. Sydney walked in a daze, and for once, she found herself not caring to notice the doctors and nurses passing her by, the number of steps on the stairs, the wan color the fluorescent lights turned people's faces.

The assistant stopped short of Winter's doorway and motioned politely for her to come forward. Then he left, and she stood alone.

When Sydney stepped inside the suite, she saw an empty, rumpled bed. A lean silhouette stood at the window, his hands in his pockets, his sleeves rolled up to his elbows, exposing the trail of geometric lines and serpent tattoo winding around his left forearm. His blue-black hair was as perfectly messy as she remembered from their first meeting. Only the slightest hint of bandages underneath his shirt reminded her of his wound.

In spite of herself, she found herself pausing for a moment to admire him. That spark of his shone through, even now.

Winter looked over his shoulder at her.

"Want to get out of here?" he asked.

She gave him a skeptical look. "With that crowd outside?"

"Claire's already arranged a secret car and a place," he said. The smile on his face was small, wistful. "Let's go."

✦ ✦ ✦

Two hours left until she had to meet Sauda at the airport.

By the time they arrived at the entrance to Kew Gardens, the sun had just set, and the sky was awash in pink and purple.

"Shouldn't this place be closed by now?" Sydney asked as they stepped in to see a vast expanse of grounds devoid of people.

"Sort of," Winter answered. He leaned toward her and nudged her gently with his shoulder. "I called in a favor."

Sydney had to smile a little. "Someday I'll get used to your perks."

He lifted an expectant eyebrow at her, then offered her his elbow as he tucked his hands into his pockets. "Is that your way of telling me we'll have future dates, Miss Cossette?"

She accepted his arm. "Are you calling this a date, Mr. Young?"

He shrugged nonchalantly. "I'm not calling it a business meeting, if that's what you're asking."

She laughed. A light breeze blew around them, and Winter leaned slightly into her as if to shield her from the cool air. She could tell that his gait was still stiff, the pain of his wound slowing him down. Her own steps were awkward, given the way her ankle had been twisted on the cargo ship. But neither of them said a word about it. For a while, they walked in a comfortable silence, taking in the beauty of the gardens around them. The grounds seemed to go on and on, rows of perfectly trimmed hedges and ponds surrounded by quiet walking paths and wooden benches. Some distance away, a massive greenhouse rose in architectural splendor, its glass reflecting the colors of the darkening sky. The trees lining the vast pool across from the structure divided the sky with their slender winter branches, casting long, elegant shadows across the grass.

Sydney closed her eyes and savored the crisp air, taking in the shifting of seasons. All she could think about was the warmth of Winter's body walking beside her, guiding her along the magical paths.

As they passed an elegant temple of classical white columns, Winter cleared his throat. "Where do you go after this?" he asked her in a low voice. "Or is that classified?"

"Classified," Sydney answered automatically, then regretted shutting him down so quickly. *Loyalty first to a secret.* "Probably back to headquarters for a bit, to see out the remainder of this case and answer any questions that might come up after the CIA makes its arrests. It'll go on for a few months yet."

"Anything I should be concerned about?"

She shook her head. "I think you're free to go back to your life now," she said. "Wherever that might take you next."

"I have a few things of my own to sort out with Claire and my team," he said. Then he hesitated for a moment. "Go easy on Leo, will you? Tell Sauda it wasn't his fault. That he was forced into a . . ."

"I know." Sydney nodded. "We'll take care of it. His charges will be dropped."

Winter nodded as if a weight had been lifted from his shoulders.

As he did, Sydney reached into the breast pocket of her jacket and pulled something out for him. It was a business card for the Claremont Hotel, the kind that any patron to the place could probably get—on one side, an embossed image of the hotel's crest in thin gold threading, and on the other, a simple phone number.

"If you're ever in need of help," Sydney said, "call us. Give the operator your name and tell them you'd like to book the London Suite. They'll run your voice through an analyzer and then patch you through to Panacea."

Winter stared at the card, then pocketed it carefully with a nod. "Thank you."

"It's not much. You helped save a lot of people." She gave him a little nudge. "I think you did all right."

At that, something brightened within him. A thankless good deed. He looked away, as if embarrassed, but she could see the glimmer of a smile on his lips. "That's the nicest thing you've ever said to me," he muttered.

Sydney smiled, too, and concentrated on their path. The light dimmed further, and the colors in the garden faded into blues.

"Off on your world tour soon, then?" she asked.

"And on to the next mission for you?" he answered.

She nodded. "On to the next," she echoed.

They were both circling around the conversation that neither one of them wanted to have, the acknowledgment of what they both knew was inevitable.

That this was it. They had completed their mission together, and their futures held paths that led them in opposite directions. Winter would return to the spotlight, where he belonged, where he needed to be. And Sydney would go back to her life in the shadows, the world underneath what everyone knew. A spy and a superstar could never make it work.

So she stopped in her tracks and tried to gather the right words. She was used to goodbyes, but she had never said goodbye before to Winter Young.

"Look, I . . ." she began.

He took her hand in his and pulled her gently to him. His head leaned down toward her.

"Dance with me," he murmured in her ear.

She hesitated, then fell into step with him. Together in the twilight, they turned in a small, slow circle. She leaned her head against his shoulder and felt his breath warm against her hair. A low vibration made her realize that he was humming.

The realization began to sink in that she might never see him again after this. Oh, she would catch him on TV with the rest of the world, might even get to attend his concerts or watch his interviews. But moments like this, whatever this was, would never happen again. And a new feeling splintered in her heart, a pining that felt so sharp and painful that she sucked her breath in, surprised by the suddenness of it.

Winter stirred against her. "Are you okay?" he whispered.

No, she wanted to answer. But she nodded against his shoulder and said, "Fine."

He didn't answer. She wondered if he was splintering just the same, if something about their bond felt different than the ones he must have formed with dozens of others before her, or if she was just the latest in his life's string of love interests. If he had ever danced in a quiet garden like this with anyone else, leaning into her as if it might be their last moments together. He was a performer, after all, a master of illusion. He was the one and only Winter Young. This could all be a part of his act, and maybe he didn't even realize it.

After a while, he pulled away enough to look at her.

"I'm sorry," he said.

"For what?"

"Because . . ." He paused, then frowned, like he had lost what he was trying to say. "Because I can't follow you."

There was something small and lonely in his gaze, the look of a boy who had been left behind before. And Sydney felt her own heart twist in response, the part of her that just wanted to escape everything, the part that could only hold together if she were alone.

She swallowed and studied his face. "I'm sorry, too. For the same."

He gave her a wry smile. "A little like the sun and moon, aren't we? Never in the sky at the same time."

"Technically, the moon can sometimes be seen during the day, so that's not entirely true."

His smile turned withering. "I'm trying to be romantic, and you're the worst."

Romantic. She could feel her face warming and looked down, tucking a hair behind her ear. A small smile twitched at the corner of her lips. "Sorry. Not my strong suit."

He laughed. The sound filled her heart. "I think I just mean . . . that I'm really going to miss you."

"Me too," she whispered.

She could feel the air tightening between them, aching to pull them together. She could see him wanting to lean toward her, wanting *her*, and herself drawing near to close the gap between them. A farewell kiss.

"I . . ." he breathed, golden light on his lashes, "I don't think this is a good idea."

"It's not," she murmured back.

He gave her a sad smile. "I have a feeling we are destined to make bad decisions forever."

She felt her heart crack more. "I sincerely hope so."

He looked down and offered her his hand. She took it, then enclosed it in a handshake.

His smile tilted up at one end. "It's been an honor, Sydney Cossette."

"The honor's mine, Winter Young," she said.

Then he tugged her toward him in their handshake, leaned down, and kissed her.

She closed her eyes, savoring his warm touch, the tingle that rushed through her, the heat that flooded every limb. Savoring the fleeting seconds of this final embrace. Remembering the lyrics she'd once seen in his notebook.

You are my meditation?

Then she thought of the gray day when she had stood in front of Niall and pleaded with him in a low voice to take her away from everything, that in exchange, she was willing to walk away from her old life. She had given up everything at the chance of a blank slate, devoid of emotional attachments, of love and its cousin grief. Of throwing herself entirely into something that mattered to her, that felt significant and important. She had decided that what she wanted was not relationships with people like Winter but taking down people that caused others pain. That every step she took further into Panacea was a step she took away from her old home.

So, reluctantly, she pulled away. The first stars had begun blinking into existence overhead. Sydney could still taste him on her mouth, could feel the unspoken want that lingered between them.

Stay.

But neither of them said it.

At last, Winter nodded back toward the entrance. "I think your car's here," he said.

She nodded. Tore away her heart. Took a step backward.

"Goodbye," she said.

"Goodbye," he said.

As she turned to walk back toward the front of the garden, Sydney allowed herself this small, small break in her blank slate. She allowed herself to think all the words she wanted to say to him.

I will miss you, Winter Young, and your shadow walking beside mine. Don't forget to look for me now and then.

I might just be there in the sky.

Could Have, Should Have

There were a million things Winter could have done instead.

He could have offered to ride to the airport with her.

He could have asked her to stay another hour, found some way to take her to a coffee shop or a private dinner.

He could have offered to fly her home on his own plane, asked her to take a spontaneous trip somewhere with him, just for a day, get to relax for a moment and just see each other as they were instead of what their roles were.

He could have told her the truth.

How, for instance, he'd felt his gaze drawn to her the instant he first saw her, that when she got angry at him, the color of her eyes seemed to darken like a storm. He never told her that, in all the thousands of events he'd ever attended, among all the beautiful and extraordinary people he'd met over the years, he had never met anyone like her. He never confessed to her that she lingered on his mind at every hour, as present as the bits of music that were always coming into being in his thoughts.

That he wished he could kiss her without it being a desperate moment or a farewell.

He should have just let himself be selfish, open his heart and damn the consequences for her, damn the consequences for himself, for those around him, for those he cared about.

He should have told her he was falling in love with her.

But he didn't.

Maybe it was for the best.

Instead, he looked on as she got into the waiting car, waved goodbye to her one last time, and said nothing. Afterward, he stood by himself for a time in the garden, his eyes still turned in the direction in which the car had disappeared. He waited until the night had truly settled.

Then he walked away.

CLAREMONT

MISSION LOG

AGENT A: "So, what now?"

AGENT B: "Now she gets her promotion."

AGENT A: "Of course. Although sending her into the field as a full operative means we'll be calling on her almost immediately after she's recovered from this."

AGENT B: "You're always so worried."

AGENT A: "She's a good investment."

AGENT B: "What about him? He gets a certificate of completion?"

AGENT A: "We don't do certificates."

AGENT B: "I was kidding, god. What I mean is that this is where his involvement with us ends?"

AGENT A: "Yes."

AGENT B: "No more contact. No letters of recommendation. No phone calls. No gift baskets."

AGENT A: "He's a smart boy. He'll understand."

AGENT B: "Are you sure this is permanent, though?"

AGENT A: "When are we going to need a superstar again?"

AGENT B: "He was pretty good, you have to admit."

AGENT A: "Fine, he was. But he nearly died working for us, and we're never even going to thank him for it. Let the boy go back to his spotlight."

AGENT B: "I suppose."

AGENT A: "You don't look convinced."

AGENT B: "███████'s not going to be happy about this."

AGENT A: "She just told me she couldn't be happier."

AGENT B: "████, darling. You can't possibly believe ████████ came out of all that with no affection for the boy. He has enough charm in his little finger to generate electricity for a small town."

AGENT A: "Then it's definitely for the best that they don't see each other again."

AGENT B: "True. But ████████ still needs a regular partner as a full agent, and she could play as his bodyguard whenever we needed, as if she were on his contract. By all objective measures, they made an effective pair."

AGENT A: "They disobeyed orders and blew up a chemical weapon on board a cargo ship. We're still finishing up the paperwork explaining all that to the Director."

AGENT B: "Okay, so they were a handful. But I seem to remember another pair out in the field that were the same."

AGENT A: "We were different. Why are you looking at me like that?"

AGENT B: "No reason. I just like it when your brows do that thing."

AGENT A: "If this is how ████████ and ███████ are going to be, I hope we never pair them for another mission."

AGENT B: "I don't know."

AGENT A: "Why?"

AGENT B: "Sometimes . . . people just fit."

One Year Later

The top headlines tonight were that Winter had shattered the latest world record for highest album sales in a release week. He heard the news as he finished up a final round of rehearsal in the dance studio, right as he picked up the phone and was greeted by Claire's squeakily excited voice.

"Winter," she said. He could practically see her clapping her hands together in anticipation. "*Winter.* This is the best news to start our year on. Do you know I'm already getting bids from cities for your next tour, and we haven't even decided when that will be yet? I love it. I love you."

A small smile emerged on his lips. "Same back to you," he said. From the corner of the studio, he saw Dameon and Leo waving at him, making exaggerated gestures to join him for a late dinner in an hour. He waved back, throwing them a thumbs-up sign.

"Back on your feet in no time." Claire was still talking, somewhat oblivious to Winter's answer. "Now, I have you set up for a string of interviews next week, but do you want some days in between to rest before kicking them off? I can bump a few of them to the following week. I can—"

"Claire," he interrupted, crouching down by his bag. "Take a breath. Let's celebrate for a second before we let the rest of the world in."

"Okay. Okay." Claire let out a loud breath over the phone, the sound filled with her own brand of joy and quavering with sudden emotion. "I'm so proud of you, kid. So proud."

Winter stopped what he was doing and smiled to himself again. "Please don't cry," he said.

Claire made a *shh* sound, and Winter pictured her hand now waving impatiently at him. "I'm not," she protested with a squeak. "Now, stop pandering to me and go have dinner. Enjoy yourself. Don't drink too much. I don't want your publicist to deal with you trending online for some three A.M. mishap."

Then she hung up. Without her bubbly energy, and the easy chaos of his teammates, the studio felt suddenly empty. Winter leaned back on his hands and let himself soak in the silence. His breaths were still rapid from his workout, and he could feel the beat of his heart still going frantically.

Record breaker. He was relieved for the good news. Life had been, well, overwhelming recently. Too much for him to dwell on right now.

Instead, in this moment, he let himself feel that familiar longing, the absence of the other world that he'd been allowed such a tiny taste of.

And the people in it.

This time, the longing brought with it a jab of pain.

His thoughts about Sydney had been daily for the first few weeks after he left London to recuperate fully at home, sometimes so overpowering that he could barely bring himself to get out of bed. But now they had faded to something manageable, the image of her small, fierce face framed with blond hair pushed inevitably aside for the crowd of concerts and parties and banquets and galas and interviews that all came back with regular force once he returned to his work.

Sometimes he forgot entirely, and that strange world felt so distant that he wondered if perhaps he had imagined the whole thing, that it had all been a fever dream.

But sometimes, he would walk past a cobblestone street or a quiet, hedged garden. Sometimes he would see an elegant bridge or a particular frame of airplane. And those thoughts would return to his mind.

She would return.

He laughed and shook his head. The one time a girl managed to work her way into his headspace was the one time he would probably never see her again. It was his lot in life. Sydney was probably halfway around the world right now, slapping some criminal senseless with the butt of a gun. She'd probably forgotten all about him.

The pain stabbed at him again, and he winced at the thought.

He wondered who she might be partnered with now. Was she holed up with him somewhere in some hotel, undercover as man and wife? As business partners?

You've got a real knack for torturing yourself, he thought, and pushed the images away to the back of his mind. For weeks, he'd imagined himself stepping out of his studio after practice and into a car full of Panacea agents again, that maybe Sydney would be in there, offering him some other mission.

But no. The cars that picked him up only ever had chauffeurs in them.

He rubbed his neck with his towel, then threw the rest of his stuff into his bag and slung it over his back. He pushed himself to his feet.

The instant he stood up, he saw her through the full-length mirrors.

She was standing just inside the entrance door, leaning casually against the wall with her hands in her pockets and one leg crossed in front of the other, dressed in ripped black jeans and a slouchy sweater that slid slightly down one shoulder.

Her blond bob was a little shorter, but other than that, Sydney Cossette looked exactly the same.

Winter spun around, half expecting to see no one standing there at all. That he had just hallucinated the image of her in the mirror, the latest manifestation of his mind playing tricks on him.

But there she was, the real-life version, her stance the mirror image of the one in her reflection.

At the expression on his face, she smiled.

"I hope you remember me, Mr. Young," she said.

That same hoarse voice. Winter suddenly felt like he was falling, like the warmth traveling through his veins might melt him. Apparently, none of his feelings had changed.

He broke into a slow grin. "What are you doing here?"

Sydney gave him a bemused smile. "Your autograph?"

He knew right away what she would say next. He knew it by the way his heart leapt, by the way his body lit up at the chance to step back into that strange other world, the world shrouded in shadows and secrecy, the world so different from his own loud, wild, chaotic one. He knew it by the way the air between them seemed to come alive, their old bonds stirred out of hibernation. He knew it by the look in her eyes.

He knew what she would say, and he knew what his own answer would be.

"New mission," Sydney said. "And we thought you'd fit the bill."

"Only if I don't have to work with you again."

She laughed a little. His heart tugged in response. It was the best sound in the world. "I'm afraid you're out of luck there."

"I love bad luck."

She looked sidelong at him. "Want to hear more?"

He smiled. Sometimes the moon and the sun were in the sky at the same time. Then he took a step toward her, back into her world.

"Lead the way."

 X

Acknowledgments

Deepest thanks to my intrepid agent, Kristin Nelson, and the entire NLA team. Thank you for championing this newest story of mine, as you always champion me. I'm forever grateful.

All my gratitude to my wonderful editors and friends, Jen Besser and Kate Meltzer, for your wisdom and kindness, your companionship when it's sunny and your umbrella when it rains. It is the honor of my professional life to build another tale with you both.

Thank you to my tireless, hardworking team at Macmillan Children's and Fierce Reads: Emilia Sowersby, Kathy Wielgosz, Jennifer Healey, Melissa Zar, Teresa Ferraiolo, Leigh Ann Higgins, John Nora, Kelsey Marrujo, and Tatiana Merced-Zarou. A special, huge thank you to Aurora Parlagreco and Jessica Cruickshank for this stunning cover—I don't think I'm ever getting over how beautiful it is. There is so much you all do that may never be publicly acknowledged; this is me publicly acknowledging it. What a joy it is to work with you all.

I'm not a spy (Or am I? Who can say . . .), so I can only write about spyhood from the perspective of an outsider. But several books helped me build Sydney's character—chief among them, a fascinating autobiography by Amaryllis Fox called *Life Undercover: Coming of Age in the CIA*. Thank you for sharing your extraordinary experiences, Ms. Fox. Book research has never been more interesting.

Anyone who knows me knows I belong to the BTS Army. Winter Young is, of course, a fictional superstar—but creativity inspires creativity, and since 2017, watching this talented band of Asian faces and gentle souls win over the world has been a deep source of inspiration and encouragement for me. I can only imagine how hard it was for you all during the pandemic, professionally and personally, but please know that your creations during that time helped pull this writer through, along with countless others. So thank you, Bangtan, for all the joy you've spread. Borahae!

To all the teachers, librarians, and booksellers around the United States—and globally—who continue to fight for diverse books to stay on shelves, thank you, thank you, thank you. Books have been viewed as dangerous since the beginning of time. Thank you for fighting back against that fear, and for your hard work getting books from all perspectives into the hands of readers.

Deepest thanks to my friends and family who have seen this book through many, many iterations with me. All my gratitude to my husband, Primo Gallanosa, for taking extra shifts watching our toddler so that I could work, and to my little boy, for being the absolute light of our lives.

Lastly and most significantly, thank you to *you*, my reader. All my books are written for you, of course, but this one in particular is dedicated to you because my singular goal in writing it was to make you happy. I know we live in turbulent times; I know you've been through a lot. I hope you had fun reading this story and were able to escape for a while with Winter and Sydney. Thank you for giving me the chance to tell you stories. I hope to meet you someday on the road. All my love.